One of a Kind

A Classic Car Romance, Book 2

by

KAT DRENNAN

KC PUBLICATIONS, OJAI, CALIFORNIA

KC Publications
Ojai, CA

DEDICATION

In the final publication days of One of a Kind, the Thomas
Fire burned through every aspect and scene of the settings
described in this book and would end up in a tragic deadly
flood threatening the area that includes the (fictional) Berlin
Compound in Montecito, California.
I am so deeply sorry for the very real, tragic losses of those
affected by the fire and flood.
This book is dedicated to the brave firefighters and local
citizens who worked tirelessly to save life and property,
including my own in Ojai, during this monster of a fire.

Thank you, thank you, thank you.

One of a Kind

Prologue

December, 1995

A loud, arcing boom brings him right out of sleep. Lights flicker and the television screen goes dark.

"Fuck me," he mutters. Just his luck, the night he picks to call on an old friend in his fancy house, the power goes out. It's the first real sleep he's had since getting out of a frickin' cell. Now he's wide awake.

He listens. No sound from upstairs. He isn't surprised. They'd drunk enough scotch this evening to float a battleship. Fine scotch too. Best he's ever had. But that's his host. Always the best of everything.

He slips on his pea coat and goes outside, because, for the first time in six months, he can. The rain has given up for the moment, heavy clouds have lifted just enough to see lights twinkle in the distance. There is no way of telling if the outage has affected any neighbors. There are no neighbors within screaming distance.

He fishes a flashlight out from under the driver's seat of his old mini truck, and thumbs the switch, hopefully. *Hallelujah.* A bright beam makes everything outside its narrow cone disappear.

He exhales, the hairs on the back of his neck raise; a physical sign he's learned to heed.

He whirls around.

Nothing.

Okay.

Okay.

His pupils stretch wide, adjusting to the night.

And then he hears it, a low moan. A cat, maybe, encountering a rival? No. The sound is darker, more primal. Like an animal injured on the road.

Or a human.

He eases forward, stopping just before the curve leading away from the mansion to glance over his shoulder. On the crest of the hill the big house squats like a pale, square face. Its dark portico, a gaping mouth, reminds him of that painting *The Scream.* He squeezes his eyes shut against a visceral memory: viscous rivers of red edging the tiles on their bathroom floor, his mother's eyes staring at the ceiling.

Another moan, louder this time, drags him out of his past, one foot in front of the other, down the long driveway, until his light shines on the source of the noise.

A white Corvette, run up against the light pole across the road, the engine idling out of gear.

Lightning freezes a glimpse of the crash in movie-screen brilliance. His heart slams into his chest. His blood surges.

Jesus. There is a God after all.

Not just any old Corvette.

His.

The victim splayed over the hood in a smear of dark red lifts his head a half an inch. "Help ... me."

Large, heavy raindrops pelt the ground around his feet. He pulls his coat collar up to his ears and moves in for a better look.

There isn't much damage, really, considering the dumbass has thrown himself through the windshield. A bashed in bumper, a chromed side mirror hanging like a half-severed ear.

"Please," comes the voice. The young man wears a fancy coat and tie. His pallor says he's not long for this world. There is probably more blood washing down the hood of the car than left in the poor devil's body.

His fingers twitch around the flashlight shank. He can't believe his good luck. He takes a step closer and listens, turning his head first one way and then the other.

No cars on the road.

No witnesses.

Ignoring the young man's pleas, he opens the driver's door and slides into the seat. The engine continues to idle. He runs his hands around the circumference of the steering wheel he's remembered in dreams, his fingers dipping into indentations slick with rain and blood.

"Can't breathe ..." The injured man's wheeze ends in a bubbling cough.

"Oh for Chrissakes."

He grasps the man's feet, shoeless and limp like a rag doll without any stuffing. He pulls the kid back through the window, cursing when the rear-view mirror on the dash momentarily snags a blood-soaked pocket. Slumped in the passenger seat now, the kid stares at him, eyes hollow and stricken.

"What? You thought I'd call 911?"

The kid blinks one eye and draws in a ragged breath.

"Rich bastards," he says. "Think you have it all figured out. You have no idea what it's like to go without nothing most of your life."

The engine stutters. He revs it until it grumbles to steady life again, shifts into reverse, feels the gears comply.

"Fuck me."

A warm satisfaction courses through his veins, hitting all the empty places and filling him up. With one more glance into the silence on the road, he backs the car slowly away from the pole, across the highway, and up into the seclusion of the estate's curving drive.

❧

He teases the car past the house to a large garden area at the far side of the property, careful to stay on the gravel drive. The doors to the over-sized garage at the edge of the orange grove are still open after the private tour his host had given him earlier. A scotch-driven oversight that plays in his favor.

"What are you doing?" the young man asks, his voice a dry whisper now. His face is nearly white against the car's red leather seat.

"Just stay put, you hear? I'm going to take care of you."

He slides open the door to a shed near the back of the garden. A moment later, he returns with a wheelbarrow, a pick and shovel, and a large canvas tarp.

The kid groans when his head hits the door jamb as he drags him out of the car and onto the tarp. He glances up to the house as he drags the last wet shovel full of dirt out of a shallow trough, his heart pounding in his ears.

The young man is silent, but there's still a slow rise and fall of his chest, and his eyes are on him as he drags the tarp with its burden into the hole. Eyes that look a lot like *hers. Well now, doesn't this just make it all worthwhile?*

"Everything in its time," the old man used to say, and damned if his time hadn't come.

He sits now, catching his breath. "It was mine to begin with, you know. Mine before you were even born."

One more glance at the house. Still dark.

The dying man groans. If he recognizes his tormentor, he gives no sign. His eyes are losing their light, the lids nearly closed.

"This is a bit inconvenient for you, I know. Uncomfortable. And cold, I suspect."

There is no reply. Rivulets of thick, dark red that had pulsed down the young man's face when he first pulled him through the windshield have stopped flowing.

"You probably never had a bad day in your life. Straight A student, best clothes. Off to college in natty sweaters and a classic Corvette." He kicks his chin in the direction of the lights near the ocean. "On your way home for the holiday, I expect. I can't help that, can I? You ran yourself into that pole, after all. You never had a chance."

The rain lets up and the air is suddenly hushed, silent, brooding, as if the orchard of avocado and orange is waiting to see if the kid is dead yet, too.

He pulls a Baby Ruth bar out of his pocket, chomps it down, and waits, sucking peanut chunks out of his teeth, until there is no movement at all.

"Well, okay then," he says on an exhale, mopping his brow in the crook of his arm. "Took you long enough. I knew from the start you weren't going to make it." He drags a hose from the old garage and sprays the rest of the blood and glass off the hood of the car into the hole, folds the canvas over the body and shoulders the shovel.

When he is finished, he edges his work with a few timeworn field stones. He eyes the car possessively as he washes blood off his hands and clothes, the rain has done the rest.

What he wouldn't give to get in and drive it away right now. His fingers tingle at the thought, and the electric desire zips all the way down to his toes. But without a windshield, he'd be stopped by the first CHP that sees him. Add to that the blood all over the seats and he'd find himself back in a jail cell before sunrise. Nope. He's going to have to take the delayed gratification route.

Story of my life.

He gets behind the wheel, slips the car into neutral, then gets out and pushes it through the open garage door, struggling the wheel this way and that until he settles his prize into a place as far into the back of the shop as it will go. It's dark and dank, hulking shapes are draped in dusty, smelly canvas tarps, the kind he hadn't seen since the old man took him camping in his fancy International. A wave of shame clusters in his chest. The old guy was the only person who'd ever shown him a bit of attention. He *wouldna* liked what he'd done. Not at all.

Tears well up and leak down his face.

Fuck that ol' man. Shouldna turned his back on me.

He lifts the bottom of his shirt and wipes away the tears, along with a smudge of sweat and blood.

By the time he drags a tarp off an old Buick, tucks it over the Corvette, and closes the old garage door, the sky to the east has taken on an eerie purple glow and he is too exhausted to take another step. He slumps against the door and slides down, elbows balanced on his knees.

❧

"What are you, nuts?"

The growling voice jars him out of a sweaty nightmare that had him tied up in the backseat of his brother's car, terror clawing at his throat. He lifts his head to see his host standing ten feet away, hands on hips, in a blood red bathrobe cinched tight around an over-sized waist. He carries a highball glass full of ice and deep brown liquid.

"Are the lights on yet?" he asks, ignoring his host's question. He wonders how long the asshole has been watching.

"No. Anything shorted out here?"

"Not that I see, boss," he says, getting to his feet. "I heard a big arcing sound like a transformer blowing and the TV went off and I came out to look around and saw that we left the door open to your shop down here, so I shut it."

"Uh huh."

He pushes off the ground and rubs his hands off on his thighs. "Want me to call it in?"

His host eyes him suspiciously, looking like death, dark shadows under his eyes deepened by the flashlight's beam. With the amount of scotch he'd seen him drink the night before, he was surprised the man had been able to get out of bed at all. Now he glances over his shoulder to where the kid's body lay under a shallow layer of dirt.

"You have got to be the dumbest fuck I have ever run across," says his host. He steadies himself against the open garage door, drains the liquid from his glass, and drops it limp handed into the scruff of weeds along the wall.

"Put the chain and padlock on that door and then get your ass out of here before I call the cops on you myself."

Chapter 1

June, 2015

"What does it feel like, Maddie? Having a baby inside you?" Gina McBain wasn't just making small talk. She really wanted to know.

Maddie led her deeper into the Berlin's dusty old garage, past shiny, chrome beauties in the new addition at the front, to an old section of dismembered relics draped in cobwebs. Maddie liked to call them her steel zombies. Dented fenders, fading paint and missing parts, but with a little TLC, capable, she insisted, of rising from the dead.

She sent Gina a perceptive grin. "Really?"

The tops of Gina's ears burned. "Now, don't go jumping to conclusions. I just, well…" She tilted her head to the garage's cobwebbed ceiling. "The only sense I've had of pregnancy is terror at being late after Luke and I first made love, then relief when it turned out to be a false alarm."

Maddie's eyebrows raised, but she kept quiet, leaving space for Gina to fill in the silence.

Gina lifted a shoulder. "We were just starting college; I was full time caregiver for my mom. There was no room in our lives for marriage back then, let alone a baby. So, yeah. I was relieved."

"And, a little disappointed," Maddie guessed, correctly.

Gina suddenly wished she hadn't brought it up. "Besides, we had just met. He was the son of a Montecito philanthropist and her real estate mogul husband, and I was…nobody."

Maddie leveled a discerning gaze on Gina another long moment before she smoothed her hands over the denim fabric of her overalls and a small belly bump. "And I was raised on a tiny Kentucky tobacco farm…" she said, adding an extra dose of her fading country accent, "…so I *cain't* marry a rich California CEO?"

Gina's embarrassment spread down her neck. "I didn't mean…"

Maddie shot her arm around Gina's waist and pulled her in for a hug. "I know what you meant."

She closed her eyes, lifted her chin and pursed her lips. "It feels like a butterfly kiss right now. Nick says he can feel her move when I'm pressed naked against him. But I think he's just trying to get me naked."

Gina let go a soft laugh, then sighed deeply and sucked in her bottom lip. The shared intimacy was heartwarming, if not too much information.

Maddie had come into all their lives less than a year ago, and since then, Gina felt like she had found a long-lost sister. Maddie'd been through plenty—the loss of her grandfather, a kidnapping, and nearly being shipped overseas in a cargo container. Gina had seen her through all of that. In the space of six months, Maddie and Nick had met, fallen in love, made a baby, and set a date for their wedding. A chain of events that set Gina to thinking about her relationship with Nick's brother, Luke. They'd been together one way or another for seven years. Through college—law school for him and nursing school for her—through his stint at Quantico before opting to devote himself to Santa Barbara. Seven years and they still couldn't keep their hands off each other. Seven years and her heart still did pirouettes when he entered the room, still warmed when he looked in her eyes, still ached when he was away too long. Who needed a marriage contract when you had that kind of love?

But watching Maddie and Nick these days made Gina just a little jealous. There was something more to a relationship than passion and steaming the sheets. And that something was creating a gaping hole in her life.

It was the future she wanted. A future with children and family. The family she had never had.

"You all right?" Maddie asked, giving her an extra squeeze. Her eyes softened with concern.

"Yeah. Sure. I'm just ..." Gina's eyes burned. She pushed hard against the feeling. No tears. She was done with all that. But the waterworks won.

"No." She deflated against a rusty bumper.

Maddie leaned a hip against one of her works in progress. "Aw, honey, you've got it bad, haven't you?"

"What?"

"Flo would say your baby clock is ticking."

Gina huffed out a laugh. "Baby clock. Ha. At this point, I'd be happy just to get a ring on my finger," she said, but she knew Maddie was right. All she'd ever wanted was a family and she'd been willing to wait. Just not so long. "You know, I really thought when he got his promotion to Executive Prosecutor, he'd be willing to stop with the *not now, not yets*. I just—I feel like we're at a dead end.

Maddie threw up her hands and tittered out a laugh. "That man can't breathe without you and you know it." She flipped on a bank of lights near the back of the workspace. "I'm sure it will all work out once Lila's re-election campaign is over."

They took a few more steps into the cobwebbed mess, and Gina kicked at a candy wrapper on the battered cement floor. "Depends on what you mean by working out. With Luke, there's always something. Whenever Lila throws in the towel, he'll run for DA himself, and next, he'll run for governor. All of which takes too much time to worry about making a family."

Maddie gave her an encouraging smile. "All of which will go better for a married man."

"That's what I told him." Gina laughed and puffed herself up, stuffing her fingertips in her tight jean pockets. "It's not that I don't want to get married," she said, imitating his deep voice. "...I just don't have time for it now." They had everything they needed, he'd told her, over and over. *Not everything*, Gina thought as Maddie once again rested her hand on her baby bump.

Maddie giggled softly and turned her Mad Monkey ball cap backward on her head, her short dark hair curling at her ears.

Gina had to smile. Maddie had made her way in a man's world and managed to make it her own. Not even the inborn Berlin 'male gaze' could dampen her spirits.

Gina relaxed a bit, laughing at herself. "He has time to come over at midnight for a little romp in the sheets though."

Maddie wagged her finger at her. "Don't knock the benefits."

She was right. Gina craved those benefits and that was part of the problem. She could never say no to Luke, even if it was for her own good.

"Call me crazy, I assumed benefits would include a future."

"You could always take the woman's prerogative."

"Woman's prerogative?"

"You know. Stop the birth control."

Gina puckered her lips and curved her hand over a chrome side mirror on a rusty old Buick, her ears growing hot again.

"I already did that, but not for the reason you're thinking."

"Oh?"

"I thought maybe if I put my foot down and cut off the freebies, he'd give in, you know? Give me a date, at least. Something to look forward to. I figured going off the pill would keep *me* from giving in. Besides, I hate the way they make me feel."

Maddie raised a brow at her. "*That's* why he's been sleeping at The Compound. How long has this been going on? A week?"

Gina shook her head. If he didn't have the family home in Montecito to go to anytime he wanted would things be different? Probably not.

"Six days," she said, on a soft laugh. "He texted me this morning, with a blue-in-the-face emoticon. Wants to go to Paso Robles Friday, stay at one of those swanky vineyard villas."

"And ..."

"And, tempting as it sounds, I declined. There's a car club thing."

Maddie leaned against the massive trunk of a faded pink Chrysler, and crossed her arms over her pregnancy-plumped breasts. "Give him a taste of his own medicine?"

"That's why I bought the car. Something I've always wanted. Lionel suggested I join their car club. Something for me, you know? In my line of work, I see too many people who let life pass them by, waiting for the right time." She waved the words away with her hand, staving off another threat of tears. Why was she so weepy? It wasn't like her at all. "Anyway," she said with more conviction than she felt, "I'm going on a club drive this weekend with Lionel, his new guy, and the *Krewe of '53*. Let Luke see how it feels to be put on the back burner for a change."

"Good for you, Gee. I'm betting on two weeks, max."

Gina busted out a full-blown laugh. "We'll see." A hint of optimism curled the corners of her mouth upward. Maddie had that effect on her. "So, what's this surprise you have for me?"

"You are going to love it, speaking of the '53." Maddie led Gina past a primered Chevy body to the last bay in the old section of the redesigned garage, Maddie's dog, BéBé, at their heels. "I thought you might like something for your new little car; since I'm parting out the Vette, you might as well have the crown jewel ..."

Gina stopped and cocked her head. "Crown jewel?"

"The steering wheel." Maddie fisted her hands at her waist her eyebrows drawn together, looking as if she'd lost something important.

"What? What is it?"

"Oh, I just thought I'd covered her up the last time I was out here. But ... I guess ... not," she said, waving away her concern like a pesky cobweb. "Look." She opened the door and slid awkwardly into the seat, her stomach collecting a smudge of dirt off the steering wheel. She laughed, brushing it off. "It's a little snugger than the first time I sat here."

BéBé whined and circled the car, her nose to the ground, then jumped over the passenger door into the seat.

"Where do you think you're going, miss priss?" The dog wagged her tail in reply.

Maddie ran both hands over the ivory-colored wheel, large by today's standards. "This is the original '53 Corvette steering wheel. The one on yours is nice, but not accurate for the year. I thought you might like this one. As a gift, for helping us out with the wedding."

Gina leaned in for a closer look. It was beautiful in its simplicity, and unmistakably Corvette with the crossed flag badge prominent at the center. "Wow, you're right. Mine's different, a little fancier, though." She tried to keep the hesitancy out of her voice.

"True. But yours is a later model." Maddie scratched at something caked on the wheel with her fingernail. "When I get it cleaned up it will look really great. And if you ever decide to show it, you won't lose points for having the wrong equipment. We should install it soon, though. Nick's getting nervous about me working out here. Mad Monkey is going on temporary hiatus."

Gina ran her hand over the leather upholstery. "Won't this car be more valuable to you with the original steering wheel?"

"Sure, but I don't plan to restore this one." Maddie slid out of the seat and stood. "It looks great on the outside, but whoever wrecked this thing did a bang-up job, pardon the pun. The frame is tweaked beyond what I want to deal with, and the bottom is rusted out where water pooled up back here before Nick put the new roof over the garage. She's worth more as a parts car. I already sold the trunk and hood badges and some good chrome trim to Lionel and his partner."

A scraping sound caught BéBé's attention. She leapt out of the car and snuffled toward the back of the shop.

"In fact," Maddie went on, "I can't take credit for you needing the correct steering wheel. That was all Lionel's idea."

Gina had to laugh. Her longtime friend and business partner in Helping Hearts looked after her like the brother she'd never had.

"And," Maddie went on, a gleam in her eye. "I've got a guy coming to look at the rear end the week after the wedding."

BéBé yipped, pawed the cement floor and crouched, front end down, backside up in the air.

Gina craned her neck to see over the back of the partially covered Corvette. Goose bumps marched like little soldiers down her arms. "What's got her so upset?"

"BéBé, come here," Maddie ordered. She slipped her fingers under the dog's collar. "Now you stop that."

BéBé reluctantly tried to contain herself.

"I swear, the rats in the avocado orchard here are worse than in my Kentucky tobacco field back home. You'd think those little varmints would prefer fruit to wiring harnesses." She picked up a corner of the tarp. "Help me with this, will you?"

"Sure," Gina said, settling her discomfort.

"Nick's got an exterminator coming out tomorrow morning, so we'll be rid of the little bastards before the wedding." Maddie drew the dusty tarp up over the passenger seats and across the hood of the car. "The whole garage will be tented."

She patted the dust off her hands on her pants and led the way back through the maze of steel zombies, shut down the bank of lights, and headed for the entrance.

Gina scooped up her friend's hand as they walked along. "I really appreciate the steering wheel, Mad. It's good to have something to keep my mind off, *things*."

Maddie squeezed her hand. "Yeah. I'm betting you can outlast him, too."

Gina shook her head. She was thinking in more permanent terms. Seven years was too long to wait to start a life. She should have called things off long ago. She was tired of living day-to-day. Her mind was ready to move on, and she hoped finding something to do besides think about Luke, she could get her heart ready to move on as well. But she didn't want to let on to Maddie yet. Not before the wedding. She and Luke would fulfill their obligation as maid of honor and best man. After that ... Well. There was a big fat zero in her plans for after that.

Chapter 2

Luke stepped out of his slacks and hung them over the hanger he kept in his locker. He pulled the seams straight and even to preserve the press, and did the same with his tie and dress shirt. The silk underwear Gina had given him at Christmas were next, then the socks he'd gotten from her yesterday when he had violated their agreement. What was he supposed to do? Wear his dress slacks to work with loafers and no socks? And no, he hadn't forgotten them on purpose as she'd accused. He'd just fucking forgotten them. The scene replayed in his head and instead of making him angry, it made him horny. Gina in a T-shirt and her pink Sunday panties, wild red hair haloed in the kitchen light was enough to make a man forget his own name, let alone his socks.

"Hey, counselor." The familiar voice startled him back to reality. A morning regular nodded at him, a hand steadying him as he kicked off his shoes. "Haven't seen you here this early in a while."

The Animals, as the early club swimmers were known, swam at 6:30 a.m., rain or shine, every day of the work week.

"Karl," Luke acknowledged. It had been more than six months since he'd worked out regularly with the Animals.

Though swimmers came and went, there were a core group of early birds who would rather die than skip a day in the pool. Karl Rosen, close cut and lean, was CEO of a real estate investment firm, and longtime friend and competitor of his brother's. One of the few professional people in town who knew Luke's history. "Been at my dad's mostly," Luke continued, knowing he didn't have to explain. "Doing laps at home when I can fit them in. Now that he's in full time senior care, I'll be looking to move back to town."

That wasn't exactly the truth, but Rosen didn't really want to know. He was just making small talk, a polite distraction for grown men who got naked behind skinny locker doors and rarely saw one another otherwise. Luke reflexively tightened his abs. Rosen could be a body double for Michael Phelps if he ever needed one. Luke was no slouch, and up until six months ago, he could smoke the guy's ass in the breaststroke any day of the week, but who wouldn't be intimidated by those lats? One good thing about spending less time in bed with Gina, he'd have no excuse not to get himself back in shape. So far, the weight of good things about Gina's ultimatum was extremely light compared to the bad.

"You guys busier now with cruise ships dumping all those tourists on State Street?" Karl asked as he slung a towel over his shoulder.

Luke slipped on a pair of chlorine-scented Speedos, searched for his pull buoy without success, and grabbed his goggles from the hook on his locker door. Busy was an understatement. More cruise ships and the Governor's taxpayer-money-saving plan to release non-violent criminals from State prisons to county systems had his team maxed with misdemeanors and a not few more felonies.

"Tourists and transients," Luke said, reluctant to disclose DA business to an outsider. "A bad combination. So yeah. Busier." He grabbed a towel and a pull buoy from a pile of loaners, and headed out of the locker room.

After a few minutes' dip in the hot tub watching the sky take on the first tinges of pink, he emerged, his body steaming.

He stretched his arms overhead, fingers linked. An early morning soak in the hot tub was a poor trade for shower sex with Gina, but better than nothing at all.

He slid his goggles over his wet hair, and pressed the lenses hard against his eye sockets until he felt the suck on his eyeballs, then curled his toes over the coping.

Who was he kidding? This was insane. Six-frickin'-thirty in the morning? Any self-respecting attorney would still be luxuriating in bed with his woman. Or at least comfortably embedded in a fluffed pillow against his headboard, coffee in one hand and the Wall Street Journal in the other. Or, worst case scenario, a stack of depositions.

He huffed out a breath, bent at the waist to dangle his arms in front of him.

An image of Gina stretched out on her king-sized bed in a skimpy, pale pink pantie and bra set had him suddenly thinking about slipping deep inside his woman instead of fly, back, free. Heat shot straight to his groin just as a pair of gnarly bare feet stepped up to the lane next to him, toes sticking out over the edge of the pool.

"Ready?" Karl asked.

Luke squeezed his eyes shut against the image of Gina's vanilla creme skin. He did not need a Speedo woodie in front of witnesses.

He shook out his hands. "*Arrite,*" he growled. Come on. Get it over with. He crouched, swung his arms in a full arc, and dove into the aqua blue water.

Tepid water exploded against his skull and rushed over his skin, pure, visceral, and usually mind emptying. He pounded through the first twenty-five meters without taking a breath, flipped a near splashless turn against the wall, and thrashed back, drawing up at the start with a healthy gasp of air. Blood raced through his veins with orgasmic intensity, but not enough to get rid of visions of Gina or the ache in his blue fuckin' balls.

He ploughed into the swim again, giving in to his churning thoughts. So many things were going right again. His brother had sublet his condo in Vegas and come home for good, thanks to his soon-to-be wife, Maddie Kerrigan, and their poor excuse for a father who was safely behind the locked doors of a senior care facility in Ojai. If Luke had his way, the old fucker would be locked in a real prison like the criminal he was, a sweeter revenge and a possibility Luke wasn't willing to completely abandon. No matter what happened to his father, Luke would live his life and make his career on the right side of the law, a fact that he hoped his father still had the mental capacity to understand and appreciate. Or choke on, if that's where it went. After three years of catering to the old man's neurotic demands, running back and forth from his duties as Executive Prosecutor in Santa Barbara to the family's Montecito estate, Luke was at last freed to carry on with his career.

He couldn't have done it without Gina. He gulped down a knot of air. She had been right about that, too.

He hit the wall again, lifted his head, and shoved his goggles off his face. The swim coach had left the workout scribbled on a white board propped against a chair at the end of the pool. Luke reviewed it silently, mentally shoving the image of Gina's cherry cola hair spread over the pillow to the back of his mind. Again. A hundred butterfly, and hundred backstroke, a hundred breast—full, soft, pink-tipped breasts—Dammit.

He plunged again, vowing to finish two complete pull downs before getting his first breath and going into his famous breaststroke whip kick. But it wasn't working. The harder he pulled, the tougher it got to get her out of his mind. Getting her back was like a jack rabbit lure, just a few strokes ahead, out of reach. It had been a full week since she'd given him the heave-ho. But it was more than that if he were honest. Things were going right in all corners of his life, but somehow, none of them seemed to come together—not the job, not the election campaign, not family issues—because he couldn't discuss them with his girl.

She couldn't hold out much longer, could she? Would she? He popped through what would be an illegal finish at the far end of the pool and gulped air. Yes. She would, if she thought it would get her what she wanted. Something he just couldn't give right now.

Karl pulled up in the lane next to him, and dragged in a breath. "You still got some gas in the Speedo, man."

If he only knew. "We'll see how much is left when we're done," Luke said. He rubbed water out of his eyes and pushed his goggles back on, some of the anxiety of the week finally melting into the water.

"Hey, guys." Another swimmer dipped into the lane on the other side of him; a long, slender woman with straight hips and the broad back and shoulders of an Olympic medalist. She'd come damn near to beating his times in swim meets in the past. Come on to him a couple of times, too, over the years. Luke had neither the time nor the desire for extracurricular activities of any kind since joining the DA's team. She grinned at him as if she knew his balls hung down to his knees. He glanced at the man on the other side of him. A simple, friendly competition was enough. Had to be.

"Ready?" she asked, sending him a goggle-eyed look.

"Sure, let's go."

They waited another minute while a newcomer slipped into the far lane, then turned their backs to the wall, counted down the last five seconds on the clock. When the big black hand ticked to zero, Luke dipped under the water again, bent his knees and exploded off the wall with everything he had, thrashing out his frustration in a brutal freestyle sprint that left all of them in his wake.

Heart rate ratcheting down to normal, he pulled himself up to the deck, straightened, and ran his hand through his dripping hair to slick it back over his head. Olympic lady popped her lanky body up out of the water, grabbed her towel off the starting block, and nodded at him with thin, unsmiling lips. He'd made sure she'd seen nothing but the bottom of his feet the entire workout.

"Killed it," Karl said, pulling off his goggles. "Have a good day, man."

They slapped a high and low five.

"Yeah. You too." Luke was tired but invigorated. He wiped his face on a towel as he stalked back to the locker rooms. The sky had pinked in the east, casting a rosy glow over the wet pool deck, the clubhouse windows, their bodies.

It would be a good day when he could get back to his regular work without the extra burden of helping his boss run her campaign for her final term as DA. Not that he didn't want Lila to win a third term. He did. She had taught him nearly everything he knew, pulled him along with her. He'd need that extra term to fill out his experience, serve as executive, build a reputation. The next time the position came open, he planned to run for it himself.

Let his dad shove that up his embezzling, murderer's ass.

Truth be told though, it was the campaign that had set Gina off, though he didn't understand why. He'd promised. After the campaign was over, after Nick and Maddie's wedding, after the office settled back down into the regular routine, he'd have time to think about their future.

Boom. Gina had lost it. He came home to her condo drained and exhausted after a sixteen-hour day to find his clothes—suits, ties, pressed slacks and jackets—piled on the porch. Light off, chain lock slotted against him. Sure, she'd locked him out of the bedroom before—and relented the moment she realized she couldn't live without him—but this was different. Felt more permanent.

He went home to the Montecito estate, but couldn't stand the thought of being in that relic of a house. He'd spent the past three days sleeping on the couch in his office in town, showering and changing at the club. His co-workers were beginning to get suspicious. Making remarks. Seeing through it all. If she didn't give in soon, he'd need to get his own apartment in town. And that would feel even more permanent.

He showered off the chlorine, shaved, dressed, and pulled the knot in his tie up close to his shirt collar. If he could wrap things up with the campaign strategy meeting early tonight, he'd give Gina a call, invite her to dinner. A real date. At a decent hour. She'd like that. And maybe, it would be enough.

Chapter 3

Gina angled her Corvette into Lionel's driveway and stopped behind Baby Blue. Next to it was Roland's car, Silver Streak. A little tingle of excitement tripped through her chest. She was doing this. She fist pumped on a decisive "Yes."

A movement near the hedge at the side of the drive caught her eye. A cat, maybe, or some other night varmint, startled at her arrival. It wasn't unusual, because of the recent drought, to find critters that normally drank from running creeks and backwaters scaling walls and slaking their thirst in residential swimming pools and koi ponds. Opossums and raccoons were frequent visitors to the Mesa district, as well as the occasional bobcat and cougar. It hadn't been that long ago someone reported seeing a bear in their backyard up on Foothill road.

Gina hesitated a moment until the hair on the back of her neck settled. Satisfied there was nothing there, she shut down the engine. Okay, she was nervous. That was natural when you did something new, right?

Lionel had been excited to have everyone over, not just to show off his recently renovated home, but to introduce Gina to his new partner. She had heard nothing but "Roland, Roland, Roland" ever since Lionel had joined the *Krewe of '53.*

She was about to finally meet the only young man Lionel had ever invited all the way into his life.

Tonight was a new beginning of sorts for her as well. She had spent a good chunk of her savings on her new car—a cherry red 1953 Corvette. The classic American sports car not only represented her bid at freedom, it fulfilled a childhood fantasy. Lionel had heartily approved of her purchase—a one-of-a-kind classic with a Blue Flame six motor Gina knew nothing about, except that Maddie had assured her she could get it running in no time. Together, they had named her "Little Red."

"You don't want a car you have to haul around on a trailer so it won't get scratched," Maddie had coached her during her search for just the right distraction. "You want a driver. Something you can have fun with."

Something to get her pointed in a different direction. No more weekends spent waiting for Luke Berlin to make time for her between cases. She had always loved to drive, and joining the car club was a natural outgrowth of getting a cutesy classic car. The Krewe promised to keep her date card full, starting with her first official ride in the morning.

She huffed in a deep breath, stepped carefully out of the driver's seat holding a container of homemade meatballs aloft as she closed and locked the door.

A wedge of welcoming yellow light spilled from the front door where a riot of viola, impatiens, and petunias cascaded over a trio of colorful Mexican pots. Lionel's tall frame dominated the doorway in a white linen suit, a pale blue crew neck T, and huarache sandals without socks. He was a prime example of the often-lamented fact that most of the great looking men living up on the Mesa were gay.

"I haven't been here since you redid the entry," Gina said, transferring the tray of meatballs into Lionel's hands. "It's lovely."

Lionel led her inside, swept her past a half wall of blue-green glass etched with a seaweed pattern. In the kitchen, he handed the container off to a lanky blond in tight red pants and an even tighter white T-shirt that showed off his six pack and impressive biceps.

Example number two.

"Compliments go to Roland on that project," Lionel crooned, his tone all admiration. "It's perfect, don't you think?" The smile he beamed at Roland said it all. Gina shook off a sudden surge of loneliness. Was it her imagination or did everyone in her life gush and make goo goo eyes at each other just to remind her she was bordering on single?

"Absolutely," she said, and extended her hand to Roland. "Glad to finally meet you." *Suck it up, Gina. Locking Luke out was your idea, after all.*

"Same here. Lionel says you make the best meatballs on the planet, so I'm looking forward to these." He slid her dish between a platter of luscious looking crab cakes and an iced bowl of caviar, then poured a champagne flute to the brim with Peach Bellini and handed it to her with a flourish. "C'mon, c'mon. Everybody's waiting for our guest of honor."

"Guest of Honor?" Gina shot a confused look at Lionel, who shrugged his shoulders then directed her through to the backyard.

Light from a perfectly oval pool bathed the people standing around it in a soft aqua glow. A dozen revelers gathered around a fire pit, each wearing a weathered bomber jacket emblazoned with the Corvette crossed flags emblem and *Krewe of '53* across the back.

Lionel jangled an Alto wind chime hanging from the patio cover, sending low, melodious notes across the water. "Everyone, I want you to meet our newest Krewe member, Ms. Gina McBain."

Emphasis on *Ms.*

Gina's cheeks heated when the entire lot of them—some singles, some couples, gay and straight—applauded. Lionel handed her a box wrapped in shiny silver paper and tied with a mountain of red zippy ribbon. He raised his hands and shushed the crowd.

"Tell us something about yourself, Gina, and don't go all shy on me."

In the wake of the unexpected attention, she held the wrapped box tight against her chest like a life preserver. Lionel had said nothing about a party, or putting her on the spot for a speech. As far as she knew, she was coming over to meet Roland and pick up her car club jacket for the ride in the morning.

The last time she'd given a speech—and Lionel knew damn well because he'd been in the Communications class with her—she'd ended up giggling uncontrollably until she wet her pants. But as she took in the expectant faces, she knew there was no shrinking out of this one. She wasn't an intern taking classes anymore. She was Lionel's boss, technically, although she depended on him more than he knew. She fortified herself with a sip of the Bellini and cleared her throat.

"Well, this is certainly a surprise."

Lionel stretched a muscled arm possessively behind Roland's back. He lifted a toast to her with a you-can-do-anything smile that reminded her of her mother, momentarily taking her back. The faces in front of her disappeared and she was playing on the floor of her bedroom with the only toy she had wanted for Christmas the year her father left them.

A Barbie Doll in a Corvette.

An ache swelled in her chest, remembering how she had latched on to that car—that fantasy that she would one day be all grown up and have everything she ever wanted and never, ever be sad again.

The memory morphed to that of the woodpecker who routinely slammed its beak against a metal plate on the light pole outside her condo.

Things hadn't exactly turned out all Barbie pink and perfect, but these were to be her new friends in a new adventure. Time to step up and face the music.

She took a deep breath, and forged in. "Since I was a little girl, I wanted a Corvette. I'm sure a lot of you probably had the same fantasy or you wouldn't be here."

Murmurs of agreement purred through the crowd. A willowy woman with dark mocha skin and a close-cut cap of golden hair rolled her eyes and sighed.

"It never occurred to me that the one I'd end up with would be thirty-two years older than me."

More soft laughter and nodding heads. Gina took a sip of Bellini to wet her dry throat. "Little Red needs a lot of TLC, but I'm committed to giving her a new life and looking forward to getting to know all of you at the same time."

"Open the box," someone prompted, and the coaxing echoed around the pool. Gina obliged, knowing exactly what the gift would be. Her very own club jacket, just like theirs with her name embroidered on the front pocket in red to match her car.

Lionel stepped up behind her and helped her into it like the impeccable gentleman he was. He nodded to Roland who hit a remote and Prince's "Little Red Corvette" blasted out of a speaker system on the patio.

Gina let go a laugh and some of her loneliness. "Thank you. Thank you all," she said, relieved to see most of them begin swaying their hips and arms in dance.

She made it through the evening, only thinking a couple of times how excited she was to show the jacket off to Luke. Like the waves of grief she sometimes felt when she thought of her mother, long gone, she let thoughts of Luke roll through. Maybe sometime, down the road, his absence in her life wouldn't feel so fresh and raw. She had given him plenty of chances to make things right and he'd made his choice. Now it was up to her to make good on her resolve.

With promises to meet early in the morning at the departure point near Stearns Wharf, and the sounds of Corvette engines revving and disappearing down the street one-by-one, she stood by her car a moment, then bent to unlock the door. At a momentary loss of footing, she gave a quick yelp. She hadn't had that many Bellini's, had she?

No.

She had mashed something under her boot. She let her keys dangle, stepping back to survey the damage. A pair of burnt birthday candles were stuck to the bottom of her sole. She picked them off gingerly, then glanced to Lionel's porch where he and Roland stood watching.

"It's all good, guys. Thanks again." She slipped the candles into her coat pocket and gave them a quick wave, then got behind the wheel.

She made her way down the winding hill, glad she'd held back on the champagne not only to drive safely, but to be sure of getting a good night's sleep.

Chapter 4

Luke sat in the driver's seat of his new SUV, leaned back against the headrest and stretched, a satisfied smile playing over his face as the power moon roof slid back, revealing the evening sky. It was warm and crystal clear. A high-pressure zone moving up from Mexico had won its battle against June gloom, muscling the usual wall of evening fog out beyond the Channel Islands.

Open spaces between Jacaranda trees arching over the road revealed a light salting of stars and the reddish glow of what must surely be Mars low in the sky.

Good news for Gina's first club ride.

Not that Luke was keeping watch over her. He approved of her expressing herself and her own desires. They were adults, after all. Individuals. She had a mind of her own and he loved that about her.

He tipped his wrist and his watch face lit up. Ten p.m. He'd planned to get here earlier, but the campaign strategy meeting had gotten out of hand, run over time. Nothing he could have done about it.

By now, Gina had probably had dinner, but maybe she'd be interested in a nightcap.

He had broken his promise not to show up at her house unannounced once already. Okay, the missing socks were a lame excuse. He could have, as she'd pointed out, not a little piqued, run into Macy's and bought himself a pair. But tonight, he had a good reason for being here. He was waiting in his car across the street from her condo at ten p.m. because everything had changed. Because nothing ever seemed real until he told her about it, and, fuck yeah, because it had been a full seven days since he'd buried himself inside the only woman that mattered.

He was horny as hell.

She was right, he'd decided after his swim this morning. Right about everything. He didn't have to prosecute every case as if he were the only responsible member of the team and the rest of them were morons. His superior, two-term District Attorney Lila Kasey, had received national recognition for her work in issues involving violence against women. He couldn't ask for a better mentor, or a better advocate. If she had been the DA back when his father had been investigated after the death of Nick's mother, Nick senior might be in jail now instead of in a posh nursing home.

A cold whip of pain curled in his gut at the fleeting memory of his mother's last days, weak and frail and exhausted from her final rounds of chemo. He willed the memory back into its corner, but the sensory discomfort persisted.

Fine hairs frizzed on the back of his neck and arms, his old instincts kicking in. He scanned the darkness in front of him, then studied the street behind him in the side and rearview mirrors.

Nothing.

The whole scene reminded him of his detective days when he'd spent hours alone on stakeout waiting for some deal to go down or some perp to show. Let yourself become tired or complacent and you might miss the one movement or sound that made all the difference.

All was dark and quiet, but his pulse drummed at his temples like something was off. Maybe it was just that his life was on the cusp of something major. Something he hadn't planned, at least not at this stage of the game. That unbalanced feeling set him on edge.

He shifted to settle back in the seat, and stopped midway when a tiny claw dug into his leg way too close to his crotch. The scrawny stray cat that Estevez had fed in the breezeway at the office too many times had been curled in his lap, purring like a wobbly ceiling fan for the entire hour he'd been here.

Now the tiny feline stretched and yawned. Luke picked it up by its nape and placed it gingerly on the seat beside him. It mewled a sleepy protest, then flattened on the towel he'd borrowed from the swim club, and resumed her loud purr.

Luke checked his watch again. Where was Gina? It wasn't like her to be out past eight o'clock. But things had changed. He didn't blame her for not sitting home waiting for him to stagger in after another sixteen-hour day on a case. Which is why he'd spent the afternoon combing the jewelry stores in town for an engagement ring suitable for a Berlin wife. He'd been admiring the deep blue color of a huge sapphire in a nest of high grade diamonds when the call came in.

Lila's words had come over his cell phone matter of factly, but he recognized the edge in her voice. The fear. The finality.

The emergency meeting had changed everything.

Two tiny orbs in his rearview mirror dragged his attention to the present. They grew larger as he watched.

It was about time.

He slouched in the seat as the vintage red Corvette passed by, then pulled into Gina's driveway at the end of the cul-de-sac. It hesitated momentarily as the garage door rolled up, then rolled into the garage next to Gina's Volkswagen Jetta.

Luke drew in a slow breath, and wrapped the sleeping kitty into the towel as the garage door closed. He'd give Gina a few minutes to settle into her pj's before he made his appearance.

The moment her bedroom light went off, he headed for her front door. With his surprise package swaddled behind his back, he raised his hand to knock, but the porch bulb flared on and the door whooshed open before his knuckles hit wood.

Her gaze swept him up and down with her classic *what-the-hell*, amber-eyed glare.

Not a good sign.

He caught his breath, his arm suspended. She wore the soft pink shorts and tank he knew so well, a filmy icing of silk over white skin he loved to touch.

"If you're looking for your pull buoy and kickboard, they're in that plastic bin next to the mailbox at the curb. I put them out for the Purple Heart to pick up in the morning."

He bunched his lips. "So, that's what happened to them. I thought I'd left them at the club." The cat wiggled and squirmed behind his back. He hunched and recovered.

Her eyebrows arched, and her lips pinched in the curious bow he knew so well. You could never put anything over on Gina. She should have been a detective, or a lawyer like himself. But she was a softie. A hopeless empath. Taking everyone else's burdens as her own. A born caregiver. Tonight, he hoped, that would work in his favor.

"What have you got there?" She cocked her head and tried to see what was behind his back.

The varmint shifted. A paw shot out and clawed through the seat of his pants. Then a set of sharp teeth clamped down on his wrist.

"Damn!" He jerked his hand away and the wadded towel tumbled to the doormat. On a feline hiss, the one-eyed gray bounded through the doorway, and scrabble-clawed up the arm of his favorite chair in Gina's living room. Its back arched, every hair of its scrawny, under-fed body standing on end.

"Oh, my *gawd!*" Gina grabbed Luke by the arm and yanked him across the threshold, then shut the door behind him, blocking the chance of the critter's escape. She crept across the wood floor, cautiously.

We have achieved entry.

"It's okay, baby," she cooed, smoothing her hand over the kitten's back. The little bugger's tail went up and hooked over her arm.

Luke pressed his thumb over a bead of blood on the puncture at his wrist. A small price to pay.

"This little guy was left in the alley behind the building and I thought, maybe Milo and Jabba would like to have some company."

"Oh, poor baby, are you okay?" Gina crooned, scooping the feline into her embrace.

"I've been better," Luke said, dryly. She ignored this, as he'd expected. He had blatantly broken the new rules. Again.

Milo bounded from her perch on the cat tree in the corner and trotted up to give the newcomer a sniff. Jabba, who rarely moved from the back of the couch, lifted his head, blinked once, then lay back down. It occurred to Luke he may have just shot himself in the foot. He already had to fight for territory in Gina's bed, a point that, at the moment, was moot.

To his credit, he'd stayed away for three days. No calls, no text. Well, except for the first day, but that was about Lila's election benefit, and Gina was committed to that. Staying away from Gina was a Herculean effort that had left him edgy, cranky, and questioning his masculinity.

A week was too long to go without touching her, watching her do the ordinary things like brushing her thick red fall of hair with her slender fingers.

He drank in the sight of her now, as she gazed love into the good eye of the little cat. He never tired of watching her do what she did best.

Luke's gaze rested on that ivory skin at her nape where he loved to breathe her scent. He shoved his hands deep into his pleated "lawyer pants" as she called them, happy now for the extra room up front.

She cradled the cat in her arms and checked his ears as she headed for the kitchen. "Poor thing. You look like you could use a bath."

"M-m-m-m, a bath would be nice, for starters. You scrub my back and I'll scrub yours." Luke tossed his coat on the back of the sofa, loosened his tie, and followed her.

She ignored him. Again.

Her backside presented a delicious, undulating temptation as she crossed the room. She would probably throw him out any minute now. He would take in every ounce of her until she did.

"It's not going to work, you know." She clipped the words over her shoulder as she turned on the faucet and wet the corner of a dishtowel.

Luke smiled at her back. *We'll see about that.* "Work?"

"If you think bringing me a stray cat will improve your chances of getting into my bedroom tonight, you're wrong."

The wild animal that had only a few seconds before sank its teeth into his skin sat calmly and let her wipe its face, purring like a tiny dirt bike.

"Aw, come on, Geen. You know you miss me." He moved in behind her, close enough to nudge the stray red strands curling at her ear with the tip of his nose. "This has gone on long enough, don't you think? I'm serious."

The cat, already under Gina's spell, pushed its face into her fingers as she wiped sticky spider webs off its whiskers.

"If you were serious, you would have showed up at a decent hour with a dozen roses and little velvet box." She wet the towel again and worked her way down the cat's muddy belly.

Luke cringed. He'd had that velvet box in his hands only a few hours ago. Right before Lila's disturbing call.

Her purse, car keys, and a leather jacket had been dumped haphazardly on the kitchen table. A pair of blue candles fell out of the pocket when he hung it on the back of a chair. He picked them up, fingering the half-burnt spirals.

"Was it somebody's birthday?" he asked as he slumped into the chair.

She angled her head over her shoulder to see what he was doing. "What? Oh. Those. No. They were in Lionel's driveway," she said.

He studied the jacket with a sense of deepening loss. He missed the rhythms of being in her life every day. Watching her brush wild tangles of her soda-pop hair in the morning. Making him a cup of hot chocolate to help him sleep when he got home at midnight, even when he said she didn't have to. The consuming heat of her body spooned against his, urging him into sleep after making love. She was his safe harbor in the unruly storm that was his life. He could face the realities that flooded through his office—people who killed, who raped, who abused, who did nothing but cause mayhem in other people's lives—knowing that coming home to her, no matter how late or tired or beaten down, she would be there in her fuzzy slippers and silky pink underwear; sane, predictable, and welcoming.

He had taken all that for granted. The jacket loomed like an intruder in what had always been exclusively his territory.

She cleared her throat and he glanced up to see her knowing smile. Her warm amber eyes glinted in the kitchen light. "That's my Krewe coat," she said in answer to his unasked question. "For my first ride tomorrow."

He pushed two fingers into the jacket cuff, folded his lips against the urge to curse, then let the sleeve drop. He had to admit, he was disappointed. This was the first weekend he'd had free in what seemed like forever. Wasn't that what she wanted? Him home with her? He wanted to ask her not to go. But he knew better. She'd get over this whole car club thing quicker if he just went along without an argument, so he pushed his urge to complain down hard. Gina was her own person. Always had been.

He settled back in the chair and absorbed the soothing sounds of her voice as she crooned assurances to the cat. She was a born caregiver. This thing with Lila would hit her hard.

He unbuttoned the top button of his white shirt, now stained with muddy paw prints. The night he scooped his clothes off her front porch and the rest of his life out of her condo into a rented U-Haul trailer, it had never occurred to him his banishment would last more than a week. It had happened before, and he'd always worked his way past her resistance, counting on her insatiable desire for him.

The first couple of nights he'd spent on a sofa in Maddie and Nick's guest house on the Berlin's Montecito property. Knowing he and Gina's track record, his brother and his sister-in-law-to-be were more than accommodating. His banishment wouldn't last. But being around the love birds only made him feel lonely, useless, and not a little horny.

Using the long commute as an excuse, he thanked them for their hospitality and moved on to the sofa in his downtown Santa Barbara office. Wouldn't be the first time he'd spent the night there, deep into his caseload.

By the third night there, the building superintendent was threatening to make him pay rent on U-Haul storage in the parking garage, and his team was giving him the fish eye. They knew the workload didn't warrant that much attention.

Nick had suggested he move into the big house. Permanently. After all, his father was no longer there. But the last thing Luke wanted was to slink back to his boyhood room at the Berlin estate. He hadn't slept there since the year his mother died. Neither of the brothers had been comfortable in the cavernous mansion, even though their father had been moved to an elder care facility back in December. Nick and Maddie had moved into the guest house rather than take over the big one, and as far as Luke knew, they had no intention of ever occupying the old Spanish revival relic.

Now, Luke frowned, watching the muscles flex in Gina's arm as she cradled the cat in a brightly colored kitchen towel.

As a meantime compromise, tired of showering at the swim club, he was strongly considering his brother's suggestion to come home. For the short term, he could sleep on the sofa in the mansion library. It was on the ground floor, away from the infamous stairway where Nick's mother had taken her fatal fall. The library had quick passage to the cook's kitchen and the back door. And, their lap pool was infinitely better than the club's where he inevitably ran into—literally—someone who recognized him and felt comfortable poking their nose into county business.

If he were unsuccessful in this latest attempt to win Gina over, he supposed moving home was a reasonable solution. Getting his own apartment would be like admitting defeat.

She had made her point. He got it. It wasn't about where he called home that mattered. It was about who was waiting for him when he got there. And if he wanted it to be Gina, then he'd need to finally pay the price of admission. He was pretty sure it wasn't a scrawny, one-eyed cat, but she had at least gotten him in the door.

He steepled his fingers in front of his nose. *Dammit.* He'd had the ring on his pinky finger not five hours ago.

He zipped off his tie, coiled it into a neat roll on the table, then deflated into the chair like a slashed tire.

When he looked up, Gina was staring at him. Her pursed lips softened for a fraction of a second, and then he saw the shift. Her eyes drilled sharp and deliberately into his. The cat settled into the towel, paws crossed possessively over Gina's arm, claiming her territory; Milo circled her legs. Great. Instead of giving him an advantage, now it was three against one. He should have known.

Gina's toe tapped in her stockinged feet. "You have one minute to tell me what's really going on and then you're going to honor our agreement by leaving."

Luke cleared a clog of uncertainty out of his throat. Hardened criminals and their defense lawyers cringed under his prosecutor's glare, but he shrank under Gina's scrutiny. "What do you mean?"

Gina's eyes narrowed. She massaged behind the cat's ears. "This is not about the cat, is it?"

His eyes went to the jacket.

"Luke?" she clipped.

She was not in a happy place. He cringed, picturing the headline: *Horny Executive Found Strangled after Seeking Sexual Solace from Estranged Girlfriend.*

He tried on a penitent smile. Two pairs of amber eyes glared back at him, one with a perfectly good reason to throw him out, and the other flexing a set of razor sharp claws.

"It's not what you think, Geen."

"And, mister mind reader, what would I be thinking right now?"

"That all I want from you is sex and a place to sleep."

"Gee, I wonder why I would think that?"

He folded in his lips, stretched his legs out straight and shoved his fingers through the long hair at the top of his head. "I deserve that. I know. You're right. About all of it."

Gina shifted her weight to the side, shot a hip, and rolled her hand in a gesture he knew well. "And ..."

"And ..." He knew better than to look at her when he said what he had to say. "I was actually in a jewelry store on upper State when I got the call."

Gina closed her eyes, dropped a shoulder. Disappointment creased the faint fanned lines at the corners of her eyes. The timing sucked. He knew it. But he couldn't change it. Couldn't change what was coming.

"The call," she said, flatly.

Keeping his eyes on the floor, he let the words roll out straightforward. Like a bowling ball tossed too slow down the alley, they would take him straight into the gutter.

"Lila's pulling out of the campaign."

Chapter 5

Gina toed a chair away from the table and sank heavily into it, feeling like all the air had been sucked out of her. This was hard news to hear. She and Lila had become close since Luke moved into the DA's offices downtown. Gina had helped her at home during her last bout with chemo, and they'd celebrated with champagne when the killer cells had been defeated. Lila was the same age her mother would be now. She was without exception the fairest, most empathetic, compassionate person Gina had met within the law enforcement community. A trait that some criticized as weak. Lila believed in community support as a hedge against crime, unlike no-nonsense Luke, a black-and-white, break-the-law-go-to-jail kind of guy.

Lila had been fond of Luke in a motherly sort of way. Familiar with his history, the loss of his own mother, his indomitable spirit, his father's ... reputation. She had hinted at last year's Christmas party that Luke would be an excellent choice to replace her as District Attorney when she was ready to vacate the position.

"His work ethic is impeccable," Lila had told her as she slipped into a seat next to Gina at her otherwise empty table.

Gina had sat alone most of the night, watching Luke work the room, oblivious to the twinkling lights, the pile of gifts under a giant Christmas tree in the corner of the hall, or the fact that she sat alone. No doubt he was hashing out the latest findings in some case where the threads were a tangled mess. Lila's presence took some of the embarrassment out of her obvious abandonment.

"Even when he was just getting started, a public defender with a mountainous caseload and little recognition, I'd never seen anyone more devoted."

True enough. Luke was nothing if not devoted—to the law. According to his brother, Nick, Luke had memorized every rerun of *Law and Order* since he was old enough to turn on the TV by himself. "... Not that I'm ready to quit just yet," Lila had gone on, "but when the day comes ..." She had given Gina a knowing smile, then patted her hand. "What I'm trying to say, dear, is that some things are worth waiting for."

Back then, Gina's heart had swelled with pride even as she tamped down her own frustration. Now Lila's words echoed in Gina's head. Some things are worth waiting for. That weekend she had bought a little silver cup in the expectant mother department at Nordstrom's.

The one that still lay hidden inside a nest of tissue in the back of her lingerie drawer.

Lila had fought off cancer and retirement with equal tenacity, as obsessed with the law as Luke had ever been. Driven. Relentless. In a good way. There was nothing she loved more than serving the residents of Santa Barbara to the best of her ability; conducting the most comprehensive investigation of a crime, nailing the perpetrators, getting justice for the victims. She rarely went on vacation, she had put off having kids until she was far beyond child bearing age, she had divorced one husband and buried another. No wonder she admired Luke. He was just like her.

No sooner had the stinky thoughts crept into Gina's mind than she deeply regretted thinking them. She sank deeper into the chair, as the full meaning of Lila's withdrawal from the race hit her square in the stomach. There was only one reason Lila would call off her bid for re-election.

"A relapse," Gina said, emotion squeezing the words to a hollow whisper. She smoothed the cat's ears down over the back of its head a little too hard, prompting a loud mewling protest.

Luke nodded in the affirmative. "I knew something was off. Unexplained absences, bouts of exhaustion she passed off as not getting enough sleep. She called the meeting early this evening. Admitted the whole thing. When I saw her, I realized I knew what those sunken eyes and that puffy face meant. Seen it before. She'd been struggling to maintain momentum. But it caught up with her, big time."

Gina got up and went to him, rested her hand on his shoulder. It was no secret why he cared so much for Lila; she'd reminded him of his mother, too. They had that in common.

"She should have called me," Gina said, still struggling to put some force behind her words. "We could have set up a game plan, something for now, something for when it gets beyond … You should have told me."

He raised his eyes to hers, his expression wretched and lost. "I am telling you," he said quietly, then sighed like something was dying inside him, and squeezed his eyes shut. "It's already beyond."

"So, she's given up."

He nodded and sent her a look that told her the worst was coming.

"So … what are you going to do?" she prompted, the tiny hairs raising at her nape. She knew the answer, but wanted to hear it from him, not wanting to hear it all at the same time.

"Well …" he huffed out, incredulously. He wiped his hand down his face, his gaze slanting to hers, calculating, measuring. She knew he was weighing what he would say next. "We're not just going to concede to Jocko."

No surprise there. Ellis Greer, former investigator and Assistant DA from Alameda County, was a driven fitness fanatic, attention hound, and known for chaffing under the leadership of the current DA, a woman whom he claimed cared more about the victims of crime than giving people a fair trial.

Gina had heard this rant throughout Lila's last campaign. She would have run unopposed were it not for Jocko. His run gave her a powerful foil against all that she felt was wrong with the system.

No. That wasn't Luke's news. Not what had his shoulders spring loaded. Gina curled the cat tighter in her arms and waited for the other shoe to drop.

Luke got up and paced the room, intensity pushing his stride. "It's early in the game. The team has time to plug in a new candidate." He left the words hanging on the up note, his eyes once again on hers, pleading a case he had yet to verbalize.

Didn't need to.

Luke was the logical person to replace Lila, of course. It was his turn. He'd worked his way through the ranks, put in his time, gotten as much, if not more recognition for his work than Jocko or anyone else in California for that matter. Lila had groomed him for it. And, Gina had to admit, he deserved it.

"You." Gina's heart did a flip-flop that landed with a heavy thud. One part of her wanted to celebrate. But the rest of her knew what it would mean. More work than ever before. Campaigning, dinners, speeches, brown nosing. Whatever time they had would be spent on the campaign trail. Had to be.

He straightened. "We're still inside the announcement window. We haven't lost much time. And, it's what she's always wanted."

"What *you've* always wanted."

Luke stood. "Yes. What I've always wanted."

He paced across the room to the corner brick fireplace, and braced both hands on the mantel. "Where else does the office of Executive Prosecutor lead?" he said, shaking his head.

Away from me.

Gina shook the selfish thought away. But the place inside her that was holding out for what she wanted, what she deserved, ached with the inevitable. Her plan—to make him see that he needed her enough to make time for what she wanted—didn't stand a chance against what was now within his grasp. And no amount of crying, whining, and holding out on him would be enough to turn him from his objective. He would go at it full bore, just like every other goal he'd set for himself. He would be too busy, too stressed, too exhausted for anything else. And when he achieved it and it didn't bring him the illusive release he sought, he'd set another goal and another, and it would never, ever stop.

He'd won. The only way she'd see him would be to enlist in helping him with his campaign. The way she had with Lila. The way she had given up everything important to her to support him for the last three years. The weight of what she had sacrificed sank low in her stomach.

She'd made up her mind. She wanted children. Children needed a father. He said he wanted them, too. Just, not now; not yet. If she heard those four words come out of his mouth one more time, she would ... She would be thirty on her next birthday.

Thirty.

The eggs in her ovaries were already lining up with little day glow signs, marching out in protest. She was running out of time. How did he not see that? And now, here he was, using Lila's illness to get sympathy, bring things back to the status quo.

No.

That wasn't fair. He cared for Lila as much as she did.

He turned away from the mantel, rubbed his hand over his face. "I need your help, Gina. I can't do this without you."

He held his head on an angle, prompting a response the way he sometimes did in the courtroom. She saw that he needed a haircut. That old caregiver instinct was kicking in, along with a deep ache in her belly. A week was too long to go without him in her arms. Without him inside her.

But she had to stay strong. This was no longer about her libido, after all. It was about her future. Their future.

She would help him with his campaign. That was a given. She had helped with each of Lila's and was even now considered one of the team. It had only been one week. Seven days. If she gave in so easily, her own plan—the only way forward that would work for their future—would blow away like sea foam in a windstorm. But oh, how the sight of that tick in his jaw made her ache in all her secret, longing places.

He started to smile, took a step toward her, sending the penalty flags sailing into the air. This was just another in a long string of excuses. If she gave in now, there would be another. And another. She needed to get him out of here. Now. Before she caved.

Her gaze went to the glass cylinder on her mantel, a ragged collection of beach glass and sea shells salvaged on long walks on the sand. Alone. She made up her mind. There would be no more intimacy between them until he got it: he either made the commitment or moved on. It was as simple as that.

Chapter 6

Gina tucked the cat into the corner of the sofa, crossed the room to stand behind him, then took the glass container off the mantel.

She dumped it out on the throw rug near his feet and spread the pieces out in an arch. Milo sauntered over to investigate, her eyes flicking to watch Gina's fingers move over the frosted glass pebbles. She picked through smoothed chunks of beer glass brown, wine bottle green, and half-moons of milky white, sifting the pile back and forth until she found what she was looking for. It was a large chunk of pale green glass from a Coca-Cola bottle. She sat back on her heels and turned it over in her palm.

Luke had been watching with interest. She could see that he didn't know whether to smile or frown. Good. He was off balance. Right where she wanted him.

"You don't see much Coke bottle glass on the beach anymore, especially a nice sized piece like this one," she said, as if none of their earlier conversation had taken place. She tucked her feet under her thighs in a comfortable Yoga pose, and held the frosted glass up to the light. "This is one of my favorites. Do you remember when I got it?"

Luke sighed and lowered himself to sit on the white painted bricks of the hearth. He rested his forearms on his thighs and watched her turn it over and back in her fingers, the lazy grin she loved playing at the corner of his mouth. He shook his head.

"No," she said, before he could answer. "You wouldn't. Because you weren't there."

He gave her a confused look, the smile fading.

"The Acosta case?" she reminded. It had been all over the news. A man's arm had been found in a Dipsy Dumpster behind a Von's grocery store up in Goleta. Further investigation had turned up more body parts at the landfill. It had taken Luke's team weeks to put the evidence together and even longer to create a water-tight case. A woman had shot her husband in the face, then hacked up his body and strewn the pieces in dumpsters all over the city. Luke had slept so many nights at the office, she teased him about having a thing for Detective Estevez.

"We'd made reservations to stay in Cayucos that weekend. I went alone."

He rolled his eyes and let out a long, indulgent sigh. "You know that couldn't be helped, Gina."

She sent him an arched brow in reply. She owed it to those poor little eggs wasting away in her ovaries not to back down.

She let the chunk of glass drop heavily into the pile and sorted through the pieces again, picking out the only piece of deep red. "And this one? This is ruby glass. Popular in the forties. I like to think it came from one of the old Victorian houses that used to be near the Ventura pier, before they built the hotel and condos."

"Gina, look. I know what you're saying, but ..."

She tossed it at him and he caught it by reflex.

"People vs. Anthony Nix," she said, not letting him off the hook. His shoulders bunched. He was getting closer to seeing the picture. The case wasn't his, but he'd become obsessed with it. Nix's wife had been found at the bottom of the Isla Vista cliffs. He'd claimed it was an accident. Luke, driven by his painful past, was intent on proving otherwise. The investigation went on for weeks. Gina had spent her birthday weekend watching the Ventura Beach Classic surf contest. Alone. Nix was never charged.

Luke's hand went to the muscles at the back of his neck and squeezed hard, a move she recognized. He hadn't been getting much sleep. Or exercise.

"Gina," he tried again. His tone bordered on reproachful. "The team was missing the obvious. I had to ..."

She swiped through the pile again, and he fell silent. She picked out several pieces of bottle green glass, arranging them in what would be an infinity sign. "Do you know how long it takes to collect this much beach glass?"

"Gina ..."

"Three years. Since the day you said you wanted us to spend the rest of our lives together. Seven if you count from the beginning. Seven years waiting for the time to be right in your life to make mine whole."

"Honey ..." he started in again.

Honey? It would be so easy to give in. He would need her now more than ever. But if she gave in now, it would be just like it had always been. No. If she was going to make this work, it had to work even if there was an earthquake and a tsunami sucked all the water out of the harbor. Even if he was going to run for District Attorney. She held up her hand.

He slipped down beside her, his shoulder leaning into hers. He picked up a piece of deep blue glass, rubbing his thumb against the smooth surface. The corner of his mouth twitched.

What she really wanted was to press her body against his and relieve the ache that started the moment she'd seen his car parked down the street. But more than that, she wanted a commitment. Seven years should have been enough. No. She didn't know how long even she could hold out. She loved him that much. But she could damn well hold out more than a week. Lila had been right. Some things are worth waiting for.

She unfolded herself from the floor, crossed the room and lifted his jacket off the back of the couch, then tossed it to him.

"Sure you don't want to sleep on it?"

"What? Helping you with your campaign. You know I'll be there. Lila would want that."

"I appreciate that, but you know that's not what I meant." His gaze seared over the bare skin at her chest, touched her breasts and traveled down to her thighs, sending a heat-shot twinge to her sex.

Luke hung the jacket over his shoulder, that confident, lazy grin returning as he sauntered to the door.

"There's no one else in my life, Gina. And there never will be. You know that."

She stalked past him, beating him to the door, shoved it open. "I have an early start in the morning."

Broads. He never cared much for any of 'em ... They think they can just jerk you around and you won't do nothing about it. He sniffs back the first signs of what is probably another rhino virus attack. His throat stings like a big dog, and he considers giving up his vigil to grab some aspirin at the drug store in town. There's only so much pain a guy can take. He chalks his aching head and scratchy throat up to the change in climate from living inside a hot, dry cell to the drafty, damp bench seat of his Datsun mini truck. Better than living in the stairwell of the parking garage at the beachfront, which is where he'd be if he hadn't stashed his truck on a side street in Ojai before his last adventure went south. Sunny California, my ass.

He's been sitting three driveways down from her condo for more than an hour when the fancy SUV pulls up across the street from her driveway. The engine shuts down, but nobody gets out. Damn. He slugs out of a bottle of Coke, the bubbles burning his itchy throat. He'd have to drive right past the asshole to get out of the cul-de-sac. He slumps down in the seat. He can wait. It isn't like he's on a schedule or anything.

In fact, it's kind of a challenge. Who can outwait who. Or is it *whom*?

He knows who it is. Berlin's brother looking to get laid. Who else would be waiting outside her place? Besides himself, of course. From what he'd overheard in the barn, Master Luke will be masturbating until he finds himself a new girlfriend. As far as he is concerned, one broad is as useless at the next. A fuckin' waste of time, considering the physical pay off, something he can achieve in five minutes all by himself.

He pinches himself hard through his pants pocket, easing a sudden pang of arousal. He has to admit, Berlin's redhead has a lot more going for her than that scrawny bitch of his brother's. The tits on Red would make a dead man's dick stand up and march.

A set of headlights appear at the end of the street and his senses go on alert. It's her in that damn Corvette. His pulse quickens. His eyes glide left in their sockets, watching her ease up her driveway and into the garage. He catches a glimpse of her red hair under the garage lights, just before she throws the switch and shuts the rolling door. His fingers twitch on the steering wheel.

Sure enough, the guy gets out of the SUV and stalks across the street. It's him all right. He'd know that arrogant bastard anywhere, the tall frame, the determined shoulders, the dark hair. Add fifty pounds and twenty-five years and he'd be the spittin' image of his asshole father.

He leans forward in his seat to see the front door of her condo open. She lets him in. *Dammit! She let him in.* He punctuates the thought with a prolonged bacon-flavored belch that has Berlin rubbernecking on the porch. He presses himself back into the seat, hiding behind the window post. He chances a peek just as Red grabs Berlin's arm and pulls him inside.

His eyes burn in their sockets as lights come on deeper inside the condo. *Okay. That's okay.* He presses his palm to a dry hot forehead. Better get that aspirin. *Time is on my side, right? Right.* He turns the engine over, pulls away from the curb, and drives into the night.

Chapter 7

Gina awoke to the woodpecker's relentless staccato outside her window, which was probably why her dreams had been tortured by scene after scene of banging her head against irresistible surfaces, mostly surrounding Luke Berlin.

She lay on the bed, the back of her wrist draped over her eyes, trying to ignore the insistent ping of voicemails arriving on her cell phone. No way was she giving in. She had made up her mind. Luke Berlin needed to face the truth. If he wanted her so badly, it was time to take her to church. Or the justice of the peace. Hell, the captain of a harbor dredge would work. Until then, candidate Luke Berlin had run out of credit in her personal life. If he thought he could wait her out, he was mistaken.

She swung her legs over the side of the bed, propped her elbows on her knees, and mashed her palms into her eyes. Except for the promise she'd made to Maddie. And the never-ending events related to it. She and Luke had agreed to be best man and maid of honor for Nick and Maddie back on New Year's Eve.

And, there was the campaign, but she could contract most of that out. If he wanted that faithful woman on his arm for the photo shoots, he'd have to put a ring on her finger.

Seven years was too long to be committed to a man who can't hear your baby mama clock ticking. The thought took her by surprise. Becoming a mother was not something she'd ever planned or focused on. But ever since Maddie had started to show, it was practically all she could think of. *And that's why you're here, Gina.* A pleasant distraction from the routine.

The electronic rooster alarm went off on her cell phone. "All right, all right. The birds win."

She spilled out of bed, rushed through a shower, and rewound her red hair into a topknot, thinking she and that stubborn woodpecker had that in common too. Maybe that was the problem. She fastened it securely with a stout hairpin. Luke's favorite. With one swift move, he would release the pin and watch her hair spill over her shoulders and down her back just the way he liked. Gina liked the way his eyes roamed from her hair to her breasts to the matching red below.

She glared at herself in the mirror. Stop thinking about him. She tucked the ends in around a handful of hair and shoved in a few more pins.

The trip to Pismo Beach had been just what she'd needed. The fog had lifted by some miracle, leaving the coastal cities unshrouded. The sound of the engine and the wind, the Pacific Ocean stretching to the horizon on her left and the rolling hills of the central coast's wine country on her right. She'd felt herself smiling with satisfaction as she took her place in the lineup of '53 Corvettes, occasionally waving to another club member as they meandered up Highway 101. She'd made this trip in her Jetta when it was new, a well-appointed sedan with all the bells and whistles. It practically drove itself. The vintage Corvette was a completely different experience. It demanded her full attention—the feel of the wind in her hair, the road under her wheels, and the excitement in her bones. On this trip, at least, she was in control.

Zipping her new club jacket against the morning chill, she joined the rest of the Krewe of '53 in the parking lot, looking forward to the trip home. Her good friend and fellow RN, Lionel, was right. The best way to get past the pain of ending a relationship was to get busy and stay that way. So far, this trip was exactly what she'd needed. She'd fought the urge to call Luke when she'd arrived safely last night. There was no need for her to check in with anyone. She was free.

The last leg on their journey would take them inland, past Lake Cachuma, and down to Santa Barbara via the back roads.

Gina tossed her overnight bag in the tiny space behind the driver's seat. Lionel had graciously loaned her a vintage hat for Maddie's polo grounds party this afternoon. She dropped it into the leg space in front of the passenger seat, and joined the lineup, tying a vintage silk scarf around her hair. The half hour or so ride over the San Marcos pass would drop her down into the city with enough time to stop in and visit one of her favorite clients and then a quick stop at home to change into her new silk dress before joining the happy couple at the polo field. Not that she was excited about another polo match, but a promise was a promise. Luke's brother had paid an arm and a leg for the tickets as part of a bridal party gift and she couldn't refuse.

Gina's hand dropped unconsciously to her tummy, sending her a warm fuzzy as she thought of Maddie's baby curled in her mother's womb. The trouble was, every time she thought of seeing her own baby one day, he had Luke's blue-sky eyes. Frustrated, she pushed the hold button on baby dreams and concentrated on the road ahead, savoring the lean of the little classic sports car at each turn. The car was no substitute for Luke in her bed, but unlike Luke, it was always there, was a hell of a lot of fun to drive, and she owned it.

She had just chided herself for imagining Luke in the seat next to her begging for a turn at the wheel, when the deer leapt out of a thick cover of Ironwood right in front of her. Gina jammed on the brakes and yanked the steering wheel, barely missing the animal. The little car went into a slide that had the world spinning in slow motion, tires squealing in her ears. Just like they say, her life flashed before her and then, Luke's disgruntled frown took over her senses.

"Turn into the skid!" The words filled her head as though he'd yelled them over her shoulder. She yanked the wheel in the opposite direction of the slide and straightened, then slammed into a berm on the other side of the road and came to a neck wrenching stop.

She gripped the wheel, her heart pounding like a thoroughbred in the home stretch. The deer stopped just beyond the road and blinked at her once, then vanished into the trees when Lionel's baby blue convertible slid to a gravely stop on the road opposite her.

She dropped her forehead hard to the steering wheel and gulped air.

Lionel jogged across the road. "You all right?"

"I ... I think so. That deer. Did you see it? Scared the holy crap out of me. I thought I was going right off the road."

"You almost did, but you corrected out of it like a pro," he said. He whisked off his beret, wiped his forehead in the crook of his arm, and walked around the car. "Everything looks okay. Can you drive?"

She let go of the steering wheel, her hands cramped into claws. She stretched them out slowly and breathed. Her neck was a little stiff, and the front of her head hurt where it had hit the steering wheel when she stopped. She'd probably have a goose egg later, but she was otherwise unhurt. She tried on a smile. "Sure. I think so."

Lionel stooped to retrieve something behind the car. The hat box. "This didn't fare so well." He brushed dirt off the smashed lid and dropped it in her passenger seat.

"Sure you don't want to take it with you? It would probably be safer."

Lionel laughed, and she could see relief in his eyes. "I think it's pretty safe to say you've had your excitement for the day. Besides, you need it for the polo field, right?"

"Right." She let go a little laugh and some relief of her own, then belted the hatbox into the seat for extra measure. Maddie would be disappointed if she showed up to the party without a fancy hat. "Will you follow me for a bit?"

He wiped his hands off on his skinny white jeans, leaving dusty hand prints on his thighs. "Part of our club motto 'no girl left behind,'" he said, securing his hat on his head. She wished she could claim that motto for the rest of her life.

The visit with the McAllisters went as well as expected. Mason was worn out taking care of his wife, but he had refused to put her in a home. Helping Hearts was more of a support to Mason than to his wife. Gina and Lionel had tag teamed on the account, making sure one of them checked in on the McAllisters at least once a day.

Ina was, well, there wasn't much left of the Ina Mason once knew, but he patiently doted on her anyway. The pictures lined up on their sitting room mantel told the story of family and wealth, and sixty years of devotion.

Gina had a soft spot for Mason. She had never known her own father. Her mother had wanted it that way, and because of her grandfather, whose brief time with her had left a loving impression on her soul, the fact that her father was missing in action never mattered much. Mason reminded her of her grandfather. They had the same downturned eyes that took an extra effort to engage in a smile, but when they did, it was magical.

Her service to the McAllisters went far beyond what she did for most clients. She made sure Mason had groceries in the pantry and that the windows in the sitting room were clean, giving a clear view to the gardens outside. And though he insisted he do all the caregiving for his wife, she checked on

Ina, just to say hello, though Ina seldom awoke to respond. Sad to think they had children somewhere in the country who let them continue alone. Gina sent copies of the monthly newsletter she sent to all client families in the hope they would respond at some point. So far, they hadn't.

She chatted with Mason, attending to a cut on his cheekbone. He'd fallen that morning while picking roses for Ina in his garden and nicked it on a trellis as he went down. Two text messages popped up on her phone. The ring tone told her they were from Luke. She ignored them. No doubt he would be making excuses for not showing up at the luncheon.

Two hours later when Gina parked her car next to Maddie's classic Cadillac at the polo field, a cloud of melancholy still hung over her head. Luke's SUV was conspicuously missing. Big surprise.

Not now, not yet. See how he liked those four little words.

As she approached the reserved canopy near the clubhouse, she straightened her borrowed fascinator, a silken, beaded contraption that looked more like a shoe than a hat. A dirty shoe now. She lowered her sunglasses and glared at Maddie's fiancé, Nick. "Told you your brother wouldn't be here."

Nick checked his watch and glanced at Maddie. She stood and rested her hand on Gina's forearm, guiding her to her seat. "He must have been called out on a case."

"He's always called out on a case." Or an investigation, or a hearing, or getting a car wash before driving the DA to lunch. Gina crossed her arms and sat back hard in the white folding chair. "I'm here for you, though. If he can't make it, it's his loss."

"I can cut him a little slack," Nick said. "He's got a lot on his plate."

Gina leaned forward and frowned at Nick. "Your brother can go to hell."

Nick looked like he was about to defend his wayward sibling, until his glance shifted past Gina's shoulder. His eyes narrowed.

Well, what do you know. She sucked in a righteous, and yes, relieved breath, then turned her head just enough to see that it wasn't Luke, but someone she'd never seen before. A perfect stranger in every sense of the word. Dark hair, darker eyes, and chiseled jaw, he could have stalked right out of a Ralph Lauren commercial. His broad shoulders, narrow hips, and confident swagger exuded high maintenance male. Despite the white tights most men wouldn't be caught dead in, his passing turned every female head in his wake.

To Gina's surprise, his dark eyes targeted hers. "The parking attendant said that fifty-five Cadillac out there belongs to someone in this booth."

Maddie stiffened. Nick stood, one hand firmly resting on her shoulder. "Fifty-three, and it belongs to my wife."

Nick's tone was cold, closed, protective of his wife. The way a man should be.

The player in an upcoming match, judging by his team colors, continued his focus on Gina. "Pity, I was hoping to do business with this lovely redhead." His voice, smooth as old scotch, covered a Middle Eastern accent.

Gina's cheeks heated. After what had happened out on the road earlier, she was in no mood to play games with a fool. Taking a cue from Maddie's strained expression, she held her anger in check. "Business?"

Maddie leaned closer to Nick. "The car's not for sale," she said, guardedly.

"Every woman has her price, does she not?" he asked, his eyes still focused on Gina. A shock of mahogany hair sifted over his brow.

Gawd.

Gina squirmed in her seat. The man had swagger, she'd give him that. Part of her wished Luke were there to witness the exchange. The other part was a little flattered. It had been a long time since Luke seared her with a look. Too damn long. Time to wake up and smell the cupcakes.

"Are you staying for the second match?" The player's smile broadened.

"Maybe," she said, drawing a stray wisp of hair behind her ear. He nodded and slipped out of the booth with a grace few men could muster without appearing feminine. He was anything but.

Gina's friend, Angela, whirled into the tented booth with a tray of champagne flutes. A med student working on her LVN, to cover expenses she filled in as a server at the field on weekends. "Oh, my god. Gina! Do you know who that was?"

Gina helped herself to the bubbly. "America's Next Top Hustler?"

Angela rolled her eyes. "Kamal al ... uh ... something." She passed a flute to Maddie. "He's a sheikh's son, here from Dubai. Worth *bill-yuns*," she said, singing the words. She leaned into Gina's ear. "They say what he wants, he gets."

Gina forced her attention back to the field. An erotic image of the two of them riding naked on the back of a polo pony sent a heated charge where it didn't belong. She had just recovered her breath and taken her first sip of the champagne when a familiar presence slipped into the chair next to her and leaned intimately into her shoulder.

Perfect timing.

"Luke. How nice you could make it."

Luke's eyes shot to the dust-smudged hat pinned to the top of her head. "What happened to you?"

Gina glared at him, remembering the woodpecker wearing out her beak against the metal post. "Car accident," she said, deadpanning the truth. It would serve him right to worry a little.

He studied her eyes intensely a moment longer, but instead of worry, what she saw in his eyes made her shiver. His fingers suddenly clenched her elbow in a vice grip, and he whisked her forcefully aside and out from under the canopy.

"Luke," she said unable to mask her confusion. Her heart clanged like an alarm bell. "What is it?"

He lowered her into a chair in the empty booth next to theirs, a hand firmly on her shoulder.

"Tell me about it." His aqua blue eyes narrowed and focused on her as though she were being cross-examined on the witness stand.

She cleared her throat, realizing for the first time he wore the same clothes he'd been wearing the night before: his "Mr. Big" outfit—white shirt, dark tie, pleated gray slacks, the suit jacket hooked over his shoulder by a finger.

"You slept at the office last night." Of course he did. It never occurred to her his absence had anything to do with another woman. The only woman she'd ever had to compete with was Lady Justice.

His expression softened, the intensity in his eyes giving way to fatigue. "Didn't actually sleep at all," he said pointedly.

He sat in the chair next to her, covered his mouth with professionally manicured fingers, and continued to drill her with those eyes. "Tell me what happened to you."

"Okay." She slouched in her seat. "It wasn't that bad, really." She told him how Roland had gotten food poisoning at the dinner the night before, and decided to stay in Pismo, but Lionel insisted he follow her home anyway. She told him about the deer, and the hat flying out of the car, and how Lionel had made sure she was all right, then followed her all the way to the McAllisters' estate. "Then he went back over the pass to stay with Roland."

Luke ran his hand over the top of his head and gripped the back of his neck. "And that was the last time you saw him?"

"Who? Mr. McAllister?" She leaned forward. Her elderly client had seemed a bit tired this afternoon, but not any more than usual. "Has something happened to him?"

Luke clenched his hands between his knees. "No. I'm sure McAllister's fine. I mean Lionel." He cut his eyes away from her.

The pain she saw on his face made her breath catch in her throat. *Lionel?* "I, well, yes ... he waved at me at the McAllister's gate, and turned around ..." Heat drained out of her face. *Lionel.* "Oh, my God. What's happened?" She shot out of the chair and paced to grip the velvet rope across the front of the booth.

Luke stood and put his hands on her shoulders. He took the hat off her head and smoothed a few stray strands behind her ear before he pulled her to his chest. His heart pounded against her ear. "I was on my way back to Montecito to change into some casual clothes for today." His grip intensified. "I heard the call on the scanner—a fatality on the pass. I knew you'd be heading home. I was terrified."

"A fatality!" Gina's legs turned liquid. "I just came from there." Her mind raced in confusion. Fear bit the back of her throat.

"I know. That was my first thought. I tried to get a hold of you, but you didn't answer your goddamned phone. It made me crazy, so I called dispatch and found out the deceased was a male. Gina, I'm so sorry. It was Lionel. He went over a cliff at the summit. I'm afraid he's—gone."

Chapter 8

He flattens himself against a wall outside the convalescent home, like one of those wrangler cutouts he's seen at the barns around the area. One knee up, his heel braced against the stucco, hat slouched down, a cigarette pressed between his lips. The only thing missing is the cowboy hat. And the cigarette, dammit.

The place looks the same as the last time he'd been here, only that was in the Fall and there were no leaves on the sycamore trees. Berlin was a wreck back then. Partly his own doing, but mostly not. How could he know Berlin was such a pansy, losing his mind and all? Maybe he was still that way. Maybe worse. Maybe he wouldn't recognize him.

Weird, thinking about what happens to a person over a lifetime. *Fucking Berlin.* After all he'd done—lied, cheated his partners, stole from them, killed even—he'd never done a lick of jail time. *It's me done that for him. He owes me, that's for sure.*

The screech of air brakes startles him away from the wall. He relaxes as a beverage delivery truck grinds its way to a heavy stop near the back gate. A man bails from the high driver side door and saunters to the back of his truck. He's slim and trim in his khaki uniform with the *Coca-Cola* logo across the pocket of his shirt. The driver punches buttons on a hand-held device and studies the screen.

He pulls back into the shadows. From here he can see the bars of the back gate. He can't help but huff out a chuckle. The old man ended up in jail anyway. Only when they put you in *this* jail, you never get out.

A loud buzz stabs his eardrums, making him jump, sending him back to prison for a moment. He grits his teeth against the knee-jerk reaction to hide, then talks himself down. *It's the old man ended up in this jail, not you.*

The big guys, they get what they need by hulking around and taking what they want. The little guys? It's patience and cunning and stealth. He's good at all three. His jaw relaxes a fraction and he settles back into his vigil.

After a moment, the back door opens. A huge Latino in green scrubs fills the space, his shoulders nearly touching the door jamb on each side. He's like the Chief in *One Flew Over the Cuckoo's Nest*. He opens the service gate to let Coca-Cola Man roll a dolly full of sugar death through the yard.

A moment later the gate clangs open and Coke Man exits for another load. He props the gate open with a rock that could have been left there for that purpose. The attendant swipes a shock of coal black hair behind his ear, then ducks behind the door to help himself to a Coke from the racks in the open machine.

He makes his move, flattens against a shadowed wall behind a heavily trunked bougainvillea vine, his eyes trained on the hulking body of the Chief, who isn't trying to keep people out, he is making sure the "inmates" stay *in*. Right now, his attention is focused on a white-haired man shuffle walking toward the open gate in their direction.

He who hesitates is a dumbass. He steps around the corner of the building.

To his left, a narrow cement path leads behind a block of stucco-walled rooms. He makes for the pathway, glancing over his shoulder only once to see the old man lift his finger and point right at him, but the attendant never looks around, only takes the man's hand and gently turns him away, speaking softly. "You want a soda, Jerry?"

"Is it cold?" he hears the old guy say.

"Sure. Right out of the fridge," answers the attendant.

A cold drink would taste good about now. He'd spent the night in the gully behind the facility without thinking about grabbing at least some fast food before settling in. His mouth is dry and clammy at the same time. It must cost an arm and a leg to be kept in a facility like this one, something he'll never have to worry about. He'd be lucky to end up in some homeless shelter. Jail would be better. The idea spikes a little pang of regret in his gut. He'd done nothing but starve since the day he'd got out.

Pussy. Quit feeling sorry for yourself.

He slips around the back of the building and exhales, eyes darting like bees around a hive. The last time he was here, Berlin had been in a temporary unit. Maybe he would be more settled in now, but it was a place to start.

This side of the block is worse than jail. The windows are so high and small, a person can't slip in or out. He's made his way all the way down the back side of the building to a little alcove with potted plants and benches before he realizes there is a video cam at each end of the walk.

Shit! Is anyone watching? Will they come after him? How stupid can he be? It never occurred to him there would be surveillance cams in this place. Should have. There's camera's every fucking where you go. Smiling into the nearest one, he waves. Maybe whoever's watching will think he's just another of the poor stiffs locked up in this place.

He flexes his shoulders, catches a shuffling sound. A tiny woman with a thin spray of purplish hair fluffing out from her ears pushes an aluminum walker into the space, the back legs poked into bright green tennis balls. She fingers the blooms on the potted plants, smiling and speaking softly to each one as she goes.

A trio of puppies smile at him from her fresh white sweatshirt. Their eager faces tweak a memory deep in his psyche. A shot of warmth hits him, quickly replaced by a cold flood of loathing. An image looms, a woman with a cigarette clenched between red lips. She wears a faded puppy shirt and a menacing grin. All those years ago, all he has endured since, and he still cringes when he thinks of his mother. Nothing. Not the string of foster homes, not even the old man's ultimate betrayal chills his soul like the contempt in her eyes when she looked at him.

His stomach growls. His heart whacks against his ribs, each strike harder than the last.

He staggers, shoots his arm out against the wall. Rough stucco bites his outstretched palm.

The pink haired woman looks up. Her eyes narrow on his.

He freezes. Will she scream? *Shit, shit. Shit.*

But a half-second later, her deeply wrinkled face rearranges itself into a smile. For him.

"Hi sweetie," she says and hobbles the few steps between them. She reaches out to touch his arm.

He lets out his breath. "Um, hullo."

He swallows down the nightmare that invaded his brain, and his stomach clenches again when he hears footsteps hustling from around the corner.

Now what? There's no time to run back the way he came. This was a dumbass idea. But he can't push his fear out of his mind. He's got to talk to Berlin. Get the answer to what's plagued him for twenty years. What's the worst thing could happen? Get arrested for trespassing? He can't stop now. Not until he learns the truth.

On an impulse, he links arms with the woman and pastes on a smile.

Another attendant, a young Hispanic woman in a pink nurse's outfit stops abruptly. "There you are, Miss Harriet," she croons. "I didn't know you had a visitor." She looks askance at him.

He covers his new friend's hand on his arm. "We were just coming back out into the courtyard, weren't we, Harriet?"

The old woman smiles into his eyes as if she were seeing her long-lost child.

Jesus. What has he done?

"Well, bring her around to the table outside. We are getting ready to have a snack."

Snack? His brain reverts to the basics. He is frickin' starving.

Think. Think.

He scans the courtyard. There will be more cameras out in the open, and he isn't here to make a personal appearance on TV. He's lucky the caregiver hasn't already sounded the alarm.

"Actually, I'm here to visit my friend Nicholas." He leans close to the nurse, speaks behind his hand. "Harriet here latched on to me and I didn't want to scare her, so …" He tries to detach the woman's hand from his arm.

The nurse's eyebrows are arched tattoos over deep brown eyes. They furrow now like she's running computer files through her brain. "Nicholas? Oh. You mean Mr. Berlin?"

His heart thumps hard in confirmation. Or panic. He isn't sure which. He looks around again. A few residents are already sitting at tables set up in the shade. A pair of attendants circle slowly, passing out paper cups of fruit. They're hardly more agile than their charges. He could make a run for it right now and get out through the gate before anyone could catch him.

A bad idea. He draws in deep breath through his nose. *You're here now. Just get this done.*

"Yes," he chirps like a twelve-year-old, and clears his throat. "Mr. Berlin," he repeats with conviction.

The nurse slips her arm through Harriet's and gently pulls him out of her grasp, as she glances around the courtyard. "I don't see him out here yet, and if you didn't see him in the dining room, inside, you might check his room. Number twelve, over there," she says, nodding to a bank of rooms on the opposite side of the courtyard.

He breathes a sigh of relief and remembers his manners. "Thank you. That's very helpful."

Harriet smiles sweetly, and gives him a little wave. His stomach knots. He can almost see himself crawling up into her lap and resting his cheek against the soft, sweet puppy faces. She reminds him of his last foster mom. Tender, caring, nothing like any of the rest of them. And then she and the old man betrayed his trust. Took back everything they had given. The memory sends cold fingers around his heart. He shakes himself out of it. *Enough of this shit.*

He sprints across the courtyard to the bank of rooms the caregiver pointed out. There's a deep pain in his hip and he stops to massage it. It has been giving him trouble since the morning he'd spent smashed under a storage cabinet in Berlin's garage while miss pregnant princess Mad Monkey or whatever she called herself these days and her redheaded friend with the giant tits told goo-goo-eyed stories about their boyfriends.

Selling his car for parts? Really? Bitches have a surprise in store, yes they do. His heart revs again just thinking about that morning.

A male attendant emerges from an outside door, pushing past him with a man slumped in a wheelchair drooling onto a white towel safety pinned to the front of his shirt. *There's worse things could happen,* he supposes. *But not much worse.*

He leans against the stucco wall waiting for the pair to clear the doorway. *Hope I die before I get that old.* He rubs the bruise on his hip, his hands already gnarled with arthritis. *Probably will.*

Slipping inside behind them, he glances left, following the arrows indicating room numbers. There's another camera at the end of the hall. He pulls back and leans against a door. A low moan comes from behind it. He sucks in a breath. The image of an old woman's accusing glare fires up his brain like an arc welder's torch. His heart thunks again. *This is a bad idea.* But he's almost in now. Damn if he'd let Berlin go to his death without telling him the truth.

He pushes open the door to Room 12 to find a man sitting in a wheelchair, facing a sliding glass door, his back to the entrance. The chair is well padded, electric, damned expensive. Not the kind they give away free at the senior center. In fact, except for the putty colored walls with holes where some departed occupant's garage-sale prints probably hung, nothing in this room is cheap or ordinary.

An obscenely large armoire of dark wood takes up most of one corner and a large leather chair occupies the other, flanked by a round-topped oak table big enough to seat four. On it is a crisp copy of *The Wall Street Journal* and a glass box holding a dozen or so fat cigars. A matching dresser lines the opposite wall. There is a flat screen TV installed over the dresser. A pair of original paintings of dogs he remembers from Berlin's den overlook a king-sized bed. Next to the armoire is a door to what looks like a private bath. Against the wall adjacent to the leather chair is a bookshelf loaded with books.

Missing is any sign of family—no portraits, personal remembrances, or cherished items, save the cigar box.

Outside, a wrought iron table bathes in the shade of a jacaranda tree; purple blossoms litter the glass table top, and there's large ashtray in the center. He cannot see, but hears the sound of a fountain coming from outside. Someone has gone to a lot of trouble to make the occupant feel at home.

He clears his throat. "Berlin?"

His voice cracks with apprehension. The man doesn't reply.

He takes a step into the room, releases the door to close on its damper. He waits until he hears it snick shut behind him. "Nicholas, you old bastard, is that you?"

The closely cropped grey head turns slightly. "The fuck do you want?" The voice is gravely, and something else. Slurred? Sleepy? Maybe ruined by a stroke? He can't tell.

His gut clinches. This could go really badly. *Coward. What's an old bastard in a wheelchair gonna do to you? Run you down?*

"It's…" He lets his eyes stray to the window and the clearing sky overhead, draws in a quavering breath. "It's Jimmy Ray."

Fingers twitch on the joystick control and the chair slowly turns. The man lifts his eyes and they lock onto his. "You got a lotta nerve coming here."

Berlin's glare tells him that while his body seemed to have failed, most, if not all, of his brain is functioning perfectly well. He isn't the swashbuckling real estate tycoon of twenty years ago who'd had the gall to cheat him out of his share of a Vegas heist gone bad. And not the more subdued rich retiree he'd tied up in his kitchen just before the Cadillac deal went south. But formidable still, the blue eyes piercing and direct, not clouded with drugs or cataracts or the vacant gaze of dementia.

"I heard you went off your nut," Jimmy said. "I wanted to see for myself."

"Some days are better than others." Berlin adjusted a plaid blanket tucked over his lap. "How'd you get in here? I don't have a visitors list."

Jimmy shifts a foot forward; his hip sends a stab of pain down his leg. He eyes the leather chair, but Berlin doesn't offer him a seat, or even blink, for that matter. That fucking intimidating, hateful glare makes his mouth go dry.

He shoves his hands in his pockets and leans against the door. He knows the old man can't touch him, but panic, and the deep-rooted sense he will never have what he wants makes his lips tremble.

"They're taking my car apart."

"*Your* car," Berlin says, hesitantly, as if he doesn't know exactly why Jimmy would pay him a visit. "Ah. The Corvette. How do you figure?"

He slumps further into his fear. The image in his memory hits him, hard. He can almost feel the seething hate well up inside him as his foster father slaps the keys out of his hands. So what if he took it for a joy ride before he got his license? He'd felt wild and free for the first time in his life, his blonde hair flying in the wind, girls giving him the side eye as he pulled up and parked at the Rincon. He'd done every last fucking thing they wanted. Even busted out a couple of Bs on his report card for the first time ever, for *her*. What did she care anymore now that she held in her arms the baby she thought she couldn't have? All the promises and privilege they'd showered on him for showing he was a good citizen after all—all gone out the window in one lucky fuck. *Surprise!* Foster mom and a new baby and Jimmy Ray is a worthless piece of shit.

He straightens, a familiar bitterness gathering at the back of his throat. "Twenty years. That's how long I waited. Did your dirty work and went to jail for it. Struggled to get by while you lived the high life. All the while my car sitting in your garage. Now you're in here." He stabs his gaze around the room, gaining courage, ending on what is obvious about Berlin's condition. "You can't drive. Looks to me like you can't even walk."

Berlin cuts his eyes away, turns his head, and wheels the chair back to face the slider. "And when you show up at the DMV and the run the VIN number and they find out its owner went missing twenty years ago? You going to tell them where to find the body?"

Jimmy flinches at a chill. He hadn't thought that far. "There's ways around that," he says without conviction.

"There's no statute of limitations on murder."

"What. You're going to tell on me *now*? You saw what happened back then." He'd always known deep down Berlin had seen more than he let on. "Why didn't *you* call 911 and save the kid?"

Something to hold over him if the need arose, that was why. And it had worked. "I did every stinking thing you wanted me to do, and more. Even took care of Ross Kerrigan for you. Twenty years, Berlin. I paid my dues. Nobody gives a shit about that kid."

"Tell that to his mother," Berlin said.

Jimmy Ray stood up now, his senses on alert. "She still alive?"

Berlin lifted a shoulder. "How the hell should I know? They never moved though. Just stayed hold up in that great big house."

Jimmy Ray held his breath and watched the old man settle deeper into his chair, shrinking back to the beaten shadow he saw when he first entered the room.

Berlin said, "We all have our own prisons, every one of us."

Jimmy Ray let out his breath slowly, building his nerve. "It should have been mine from the beginning. The old man bought it for *me*, I worked for it, and I'll be goddamned if I'll let those bitches sell it for parts. I'm going to get it out of that garage, and by the looks of you, there's not a fuckin' thing you can do about it."

Jimmy heard a long sigh from the old man, saw his hand white knuckle the chair handle. "Your funeral, Jimmy Ray. That car will be the death of you one way or another."

Chapter 9

Gina's new mantra circled through her head as she drove to the McAllisters'. "Get busy and stay that way." That's what Lionel had told her when she'd whined to him about her dilemma with Luke. In the next breath he'd suggested she buy that Corvette she'd been dreaming of and join his car club. "Life is too short to put off your dreams," he'd said.

She hadn't driven the 'Vette since the day he was killed, nearly a week ago now. Wasn't sure she ever could again.

She had spent the entire week rearranging her schedule to account for his absence, and still, reflexively reached for her phone as she turned off the highway at the base of the McAllisters' Padaro Lane estate, intending to let Lionel know she was stopping in for her daily check. Her heart knew Lionel was gone, but her muscle memory was still stuck in their home health care ballet.

And, he was still right. If she didn't keep herself occupied, she'd cave, and caving was not an option. She owed it to their clients to keep it together. After all, they were the very people she and Lionel had created their practice to serve. The separation—okay, the breakup with Luke—was hard enough to deal with on its own, what with Nick and Maddie's' wedding almost upon them. Her timing to force the issue with Luke had been a little off. As best man and maid of honor in a wedding, they'd be forced together in ways that put emphasis on, well, the problem. Add to that losing her friend and valued employee, Lionel, and she had the makings of a major meltdown.

For the moment, she looked forward to spending a few minutes with Mason. Gina treasured her time with the old man. She admitted she often lingered with him far beyond the time she spent with other clients. They'd talk for hours. He was an avid reader, and had experienced firsthand every major social and political event she could think of. He'd been a conscientious objector in both World War I and II, yet served in France as a chaplain on the battlefield, though he'd later abandoned his faith for a more humanistic point of view. "It was the picture from Apollo 10 that did it," he'd told her. "Made me see how the universe was so much bigger than the early civilizations knew. Time I stopped trying to explain it to others and just started appreciating it for what it is."

There, in the old mansion, it was as if the rest of the world and its problems no longer existed. A green silence enveloped her behind its vine-covered walls, muting the noise of the nearby freeway and crowded shopping area. She understood why Mason refused to leave. Just being there helped her think more clearly and shed some of her grief for the loss of two men in her life. Mason McAllister felt like the grandfather she'd never had, and the sprawling Frank Lloyd Wright style mansion felt like home. She only wished she had more time to spend there.

Helping Hearts would survive, but only if she did some fast footwork to replace Lionel. She hadn't realized what a heavy load he'd carried till he was gone. And that was a shame. Had she ever told him how much she appreciated him? Guilt seeped into her heart.

She needed to add another staff position—a temporary at first—until she found just the right gem to replace him. Like there was such a person. After a week, some of the initial shock of his death had worn off, but disbelief and denial still lingered. She had to keep reminding herself that Lionel was gone.

The wrought iron gate to Mason's drive stood open. Now that was odd. She dropped the phone back into her purse and peered up the concrete road. She arrived at the estate at the same time every morning, unless she called to inform Mason otherwise; still he always waited until she rang the bell at the gate before he buzzed her through.

She turned up the steep drive, gripping the Jetta steering wheel tighter than usual. The sculpted cypress trees took on sinister shapes as she wound her way toward the house. Once the old couple was gone, their daughter's kids would likely sell the family property and net somewhere in the thirty millions. They'd had a son, a couple years younger than their daughter, but never talked of him. At about age twenty, his photographs were conspicuously missing from the family saga that played out in silver frames on the mantel.

Regret stung the empty corners of Gina's heart. This old place was nothing if not for the family that once joyfully lived here in the grace of these two stalwart people, fortune and privilege at their disposal. Gina, raised as an only child by her single mother, would never understand how families could leave their elders alone at their end times. Even the Berlin brothers took care of their father, and there was certainly no love lost between them.

Now, thanks to the financial boost their grandfather had given them, the daughter of the family had married some goldmining mogul and lived in Montreal, while the grandkids had scattered around the globe, leaving their benefactor alone with his failing wife.

Gina did the best she could to help him, often extending her help far beyond the nursing duties she'd been hired to perform. Mason McAllister had closed all but a small sitting room, the kitchen, and two bedrooms at the back of the house. The fourteen thousand square foot mansion had seen better days.

He refused to have anyone except Gina or Lionel care for his wife. Other than a housekeeper who cleaned once a week and shopped for essentials from a small list he provided, and once-a-month gardener whose primary duty was to maintain the rose garden, the caregivers of Helping Hearts were the only other regular visitors to the property.

She had just begun to feel that calming effect that took over whenever she pulled up this driveway when the hair on her nape frizzed. A moment later she saw the reason.

She had turned the corner of the house toward the service entrance near the kitchen. There was Mason slumped on the terra cotta steps, wearing nothing but his thin-strapped undershirt, a pair of white boxer shorts, and bedroom slippers. His head was cradled in arms folded across his spindly white knees which were drawn up to his chest. His thick, white hair, usually slicked straight back like a forties banker, fell stringy over his bare arms.

"Mason!" She grabbed her medical gear and the box of Mason's favorite donuts she'd picked up to share with him, and hurried to his side. "Mason? What are you doing out here? You're shivering."

He lifted his head. His grey-blue eyes uncharacteristically flat and lifeless, barely registered her arrival.

She dropped to his side. "Mason?"

Normally he would greet her at the service entrance, already dressed in a pair of freshly pressed slacks and a casual sweater, a rose from his garden in one hand and a cup of tea in the other. Now, he simply dropped his head into his folded arms again.

"What's happened?"

No response.

The June gloom had finally set in with a vengeance and the steps were wet with heavy beach mist. His arms were bluish and cold. She slipped off her own hoodie and draped it over his shoulders. "Come on. Let's get you inside."

She nearly collapsed under the weight of his lanky six-foot frame. Fixing her arm around his waist, she got him standing, and led him inside to the table in the kitchen nook. She rubbed his ice-cold hands in hers.

"Hold on," she said, and raced to the sitting room where she swiped a knitted throw off the back of the couch, then returned and wrapped it over his shoulders.

The table at the center of the room was strewn with cut roses from the garden, as was the floor around it. It had been his habit to cut fresh flowers for his wife, especially in early summer when the roses were in full bloom. They were usually in a crystal vase at her bedside by the time Gina arrived.

Mason stared at the mess. "Is she awake yet?" he asked in a flattened voice that sounded like it came from a dream.

Gina rubbed her mouth with a shaky hand. What the hell was going on here? The possible answer turned her hands to ice. "I'll just go in and check on her, okay?"

Mason fingered the wilted petals of a yellow rose on the table as if Gina wasn't there.

A few months earlier, Gina had helped Mason refit the maid's quarters next to the kitchen with a hospital bed, and new, frilly curtains over heavy blackouts. Ina hadn't walked on her own for at least a year, and spent most of her time curled in bed, fingers clawed in atrophy, staring out the window or at family photo albums Mason patiently showed her just to get an occasional smile of recognition. More recently, Ina had deteriorated, was prone to rants and sobbing. Today, the room was dark; the blackout curtains not yet opened. From the doorway, Gina could see two bumps under the covers on the end of the bed where Ina's feet would be. As she crept into the room, more of the bed was revealed.

"Ina?" Gina asked, trying to make her voice sound cheerful.

Nothing. That wasn't right. Her morning call usually brought at least a blink or a slight turn of her head on the pillow. The room and the figure on the bed were utterly still in a way that Gina knew well. She shivered. With another step, it was clear why. Where Ina's head should be visible, there was a pale peach satin pillow with a white kitty face embroidered on it, one of a pair that were usually propped neatly in the window seat. On top of that, a heavy silver picture frame, face down.

Gina drew closer. There was no movement. Not the rise and fall of a living person's breath, not the response of waking. Just a profound, final, silence. She recognized the heavy silver picture frame that lay on the pillow, even though it was face down. It was one of the centerpiece family photos of the wide mantel over the fire place in the sitting room. Most likely the wedding photo Mason often took with him when woke his wife in the morning.

Gina swallowed back her reluctance, slipped her hand under the sheet and grasped Ina's skeletal wrist. It was sickeningly cool. No pulse.

Behind Gina, suddenly, a gurgling sound. She turned to see Mason standing in the doorway, tears rolling down his pale, gray cheeks. They knew this day would come. But nothing could prepare them for the actual event. Ina was gone.

Chapter 10

"Mason, I'm so sorry."

He stared at the body on the bed. A man who had done nothing but care for his wife with all his heart and soul—mostly by himself—for the last ten years. A man who had raised two children and loved and cared for three grands.

A man who by the looks of it may have just smothered his wife.

Hot fluid pushed up the back of Gina's throat. She swallowed it down.

"Is she awake yet?" he asked. His voice was reedy thin, powerless, devoid of any emotion at all. He swayed on his feet. Gina scooped an arm under his and helped him sit in a chintz covered chair near the doorway. She leaned against the door jamb, arms crossed, gripping her sides. Helping Hearts provided hospice services to most of its clients, eventually. Assisted in their final moments to make them comfortable. This was the first time anything like this had ever happened. Where was Lionel when you needed him? Where was Luke?

She fingered her phone in her back pocket.

"Mason, do you want to tell me what happened?"

He continued to stare. "Is she awake yet?" he asked again.

Gina gulped air. What on earth had he done? She should call 911. Report the death.

And they'd take Mason away.

Tears welled, the reality sinking in. A man like Mason, ninety-two years old, tired and drained. He wouldn't survive a week in jail. It wasn't fair. Her gaze went back to the bed and the silent figure under the covers. No signs of struggle, the surrounding area was peaceful, serene. If she removed the pillow, what would she see? Maybe nothing. Maybe she was already dead when he put the pillow on her face.

Or maybe it would show traces of blood where fatal pressure had smashed her fragile lips into her teeth.

Her heart sank to a new low at the thought. Mason was old and fragile. He lived for the roses in his garden and the memories that echoed through the halls of his home. His home was his reason for living. Jail would take it all away. She couldn't let that happen.

She lifted the phone out of her pocket, a reflex of the need to tell Lionel. Like a yin to the yang, the responding stab hit. Lionel was gone. She huffed out a sigh for the umpteenth time today. She should call Luke.

She glanced at the window seat where an identical pillow was propped in the corner. What if she simply switched the pillow in the window with the one on the dead woman's face? She could return the picture to the mantel and who would be the wiser? The woman was eighty-eight years old. She was suffering from dementia, congestive heart failure, and recurring pneumonia. Old people die in their sleep every day. Who would question it? Gina could simply report exactly what happened: She had found Mason in mourning when she arrived for her regular visit because his wife had expired overnight.

She took a step toward the window seat and then stopped herself. What was she thinking? No matter how much she cared for Mason, was it up to her to decide his fate? Would he want her to? He was obviously in shock and not thinking clearly. He hadn't actually said he'd smothered his wife.

And then another thought hit with a gut smacking blow. The gate. It had been open before she arrived. What if someone else had been here? Who would do such a thing? Mason wouldn't have opened the gate to someone he wasn't expecting. Someone he didn't know. What if she moved the pillows and destroyed some evidence?

She turned to her old friend and asked "Mason, was someone else here this morning?"

Mason pulled the blanket around his shoulders like an old Indian chief. It took him a full minute to drag his gaze away from the body on the bed. His eyes widened when they landed on Gina as if he'd forgotten she was in the room. His mouth opened for a moment, then closed.

"Someone was here. Last night maybe? And you forgot to close the gate?" she prompted.

His pale grey eyes, once vibrant and alert and full of kindness, strayed to the window. "Someone," he said, flatly. Gina got the sense he was simply repeating her words and lacked awareness of their meaning. Mason was generally sharp for a ninety-two-year-old, so it was disturbing to see him so vacant. Lost. It happened sometimes, when faced with a shock; her clients suffered mild dementia that often reversed when their lives evened out.

"Is she awake yet?" he asked with more animation. He searched Gina's eyes, pleading. When she fisted her hand at her mouth, he nodded gravely, then turned on a pitiable sigh, and ghosted out of the room.

She guided him back to the kitchen and drew water from a large dispenser; the slow glug, glug, glug of bubbles filled the silence in the room as the pot filled, bringing some sense of reality to what had so far been a surreal encounter. She set the pot on the stove and lit the burner.

"It's okay, Mason. You just sit right here. You've had a terrible shock." She said it as much to calm her own racing heartbeat as to reassure him. "Maybe something will come to you."

Lionel would call the police. That's what he would say if she called him. Call the police and get some sweats on the poor guy so he won't be arrested in his boxer shorts.

In a normal situation, acting as a caregiver professional, she would call the police and report the death. She would wait with any family available until the coroner came, made the confirmation, and then take away the body. Done deal. Deaths of older infirmed citizens were rarely investigated.

But this wasn't a normal situation. Mason was acting completely out of character and there was the pillow on the deceased face.

She knew what she had to do. What the law required. Her job had put her in the position of doing it more times than she cared to count. But now, in this soaring house that usually gave her relief from the everyday troubles of the world, she just couldn't bring herself to start the process. Ina would keep a few more minutes.

Her heart was a cold knot in her chest. She had to trust the system to do what was right. No one in their right mind would put the old man in jail at this stage in his life. She slumped into a chair next to Mason and waited for the water to boil.

Mason clutched his gnarled hands together on the table, bluish veins bulging like ancient tree roots over his skin. The man whose prominent property stood as testament to his once powerful role on California's coast, sat withered and broken. Her heart broke for him. Doing nothing was doing him a disservice.

She should call Luke. Run the scenario by him. Get his advice. She took her cell phone out of her pocket and stared at the background photo that popped up when she activated the screen. A selfie of the two of them taken at Christmas time, on a balcony at the Bacara Resort at sunset, heads together, grinning in anticipation of going up to their room.

She clicked the phone off and put it face down on the table, huffing out a laugh at her naiveté. Yeah, right. She knew what his advice would be.

Why would she hesitate? The law was the law.

No.

Luke was the last person she should call. She sucked in a ragged breath. As much as she loved and respected him, she also knew that he could very well be that person who would throw the book at Mason, regardless of his age, or the fact that Ina's death was likely a tender mercy, or that Mason was Gina's client. Luke Berlin was the most unforgiving man she knew when it came to domestic violence of any kind. And as sure as she knew that it was possible Mason could be arrested and the top dog in the DA's office, Luke Berlin, would charge him with murder, she knew that she would defend Mason.

Her lip quivered; she clamped her teeth down hard on it. Did she really have a choice? No. She covered her mouth with fingers that wouldn't stop shaking. The house was quiet except for the hissing and popping of water heating in the pot. *Just calm down and think. Think!* What if someone else had been here? What if they were here still? Was she simply fabricating a fantasy to counter what was obvious?

The teapot screamed; she startled and jumped to her feet, her heart in her throat, jerking her back to her senses. She turned the fire off under the pot, covered it with one of Ina's handmade tea cozies, and brought it to the table.

Mason shifted his vacant gaze to hers.

"It's going to be okay, Mason." She had no idea whether that was a lie or the truth, but she couldn't sit here and offer no comfort at all. "I'm going to call the authorities. We need to report Ina's ... we need to report what's happened."

His gaze slipped back to the window as if she'd just given him the time of day. She had never seen him in such a state.

She selected two cups from the cupboard, opened two packets of Earl Gray tea, and poured them each a cup, eying the white donut bag she'd left on the counter. She dumped the donuts out on a paper towel.

"You should try to eat something." Gina had lost her appetite, but she took a bite of the powdery confection anyway, hoping he would follow her lead. He didn't.

He slumped back in the chair. "Where's Ina?" he asked. His pitiful tone made her want to burst out crying.

"Can I see her?" He started to get up. Gina rested her hand on his skeletal shoulder and gently pushed him back in his seat.

"We'd better not touch anything just yet."

She turned her cell phone over and activated it, her quaking fingers hesitant over the tiny keyboard.

In the end, Gina called Detective Xavier Estevez. The guys at the DA's office called him simply, Harvey. At least she'd be dealing with someone she knew. You could trust a man who would feed a one-eyed stray and try to find it a home, right?

Although she wasn't exactly honest with him.

"Mr. McAllister's wife died during the night," she told him on the phone. "But the front gate was open, which is odd, you know? He never leaves that gate open. So, I was wondering if you could come by before I notify the coroner. Something's ... maybe, not right?" Something was not right all right, and she needed to find out what it was before she made it official.

The tea had barely cooled enough to sip when the dark four-door sedan arrived at the front of the house. Estevez seemed larger than she remembered, the kind of guy you'd want on your side in an argument. But something in the moment set her teeth chattering. This was real now. No switching pillows, no taking it back. Elderly people died every day. Something people in Gina's line of work saw on a regular basis. Nothing to be too alarmed about.

Gina craned her neck to see that Estevez had left his partner in the car. "I told her it was a personal favor," he said at the door. "You took that monster fur ball off my hands and I'm grateful."

He wouldn't be making jokes in a minute. Gina looked at her feet. Estevez reached up and squeezed her shoulder as he came through the kitchen door. "I hear you and One-eyed Peetie are getting along well."

Although relief flooded over her as she followed Estevez through to the kitchen, her hands kept shaking.

He paused just before entering the bedroom. "I'm sorry about your partner, Lionel," Estevez said. "He was a great guy."

"You knew him?"

"Worked with him a couple of times when he worked in the ER in Ventura County. Competent and compassionate, the kind of person you'd hope to be there if you ever ended up in the ER."

Gina nodded, relaxed a bit. Nice of Harvey to acknowledge Lionel's passing. And she was glad she was no longer alone in this situation. But the sense of calm dissolved the moment Estevez saw the figure on the bed with the pillow on her face and the picture frame on top of the pillow. He turned to Gina and lifted his brow.

"You left this part out?"

Gina collapsed in the chintz chair near the window seat. The innocent kitten embroidery that matched the one on the pillow over Ina's face stared back at her, accusing. Whatever happened next, she would have to live with for the rest of her life.

Estevez called his backup on his cell. "I need you to come inside and bring the kit." He folded his arms across his chest and leaned in the doorway, his detective eyes taking in every inch of the room, the floor, and the bed.

A moment later a uniformed officer strode into the bedroom, tall, dark, and female.

"Gina, this is my partner, Rachel Singh."

Rachel, sporting a dark Sandra Bullock ponytail and a sympathetic smile, set the black plastic case on the nightstand next to the bed and offered Gina her hand. "That the old man's wife?" she asked, her eyes wide as she took in the ominous shape on the bed.

Gina stood, took Rachel's hand briefly. "Her name's Ina. The McAllisters are my clients."

Singh nodded back toward the kitchen. "He looks pretty shaken. Are you going to be able to stay with him or should I call a social worker?"

Gina shuddered out a breath. There was no way she was leaving Mason's side if she could help it until she knew exactly what was going to happen. "I'll stay."

Her gaze slid back to the form on the bed. She needed to see what was under that pillow. Harvey cocked his head toward the bedroom door.

"How about staying with Mr. McAllister for now," he said to Rachel. When she was out of earshot he said, "You didn't call Luke." It was a statement, not a question.

Gina laced her fingers in her lap. "No. I--"

She clenched her eyes shut and pinched the bridge of her nose.

He held up his hand. He'd known Luke and Gina long enough not to need an explanation. "Relax. We're going to take this nice and slow."

He snapped a couple of shots with his phone camera, "just for the record," he assured her, and continued to capture images. The body, the area around the bed, the pillow and picture frame.

Gina folded her arms under her breasts and watched in silence as he snapped on latex gloves. He was stepping out of bounds. For her. Something she should not have asked of him. But it was too late now.

Using long-pointed forceps, he lifted the corner of the pillow, careful not to displace the picture frame on top. Exposed to the morning light, the underside of the peach colored pillow case appeared clean.

Gina let out a breath. She could almost see Mason hiding his wife's lifeless face and putting their wedding portrait innocently on top.

He leaned in to get a better look at Ina's face. "There doesn't seem to be any bruising like you might expect if she were smothered. But without a closer look I can't be sure."

Gina couldn't hold down her fears. "Maybe Mason put the picture frame on there after she was gone." That was a big maybe, she knew. She also knew that Ina was extremely weak and frail. It wouldn't have taken much to snuff out her breath for good.

Estevez flicked his gaze to hers. "Maybe." He let the pillow slowly down to rest as he'd found it. "I might be inclined to rule out foul play; but, the pillow places some doubt. It's not my call, Gina. You know that."

She pressed her lips together and nodded. "I should go through regular channels."

He shook his head. "You should have, but I can't *unsee* what I've just seen. Now I'm here, I'm going to have to make the call myself."

"There's the gate," she reminded him, grasping at straws. "Mason would never leave the gate open like that. Maybe someone else was here."

"The open gate will be in my report. I'll stay until the coroner gets here. If he decides to call homicide, then I'll stay for that." He offered his hand and guided her out of the bedroom into the kitchen where Rachel sat with Mason. A little smear of powdered sugar frosted the corner of the detective's mouth.

Gina leaned against the counter, her arms tightly wrapped against a gnawing ache in her stomach. "Will they arrest him, do you think?"

Harvey rubbed his forehead with stiff, tight fingers. It was hard to guess what he was thinking. He always had an air of contemplation about him, as if everything in his life required due consideration before making an answer. And right then, if Gina was any judge, his brain was in full contemplation mode. She could almost hear his synapses humming. His gaze wandered the room, from the old man sitting at the table, to his partner, and back to Gina. "I think you'd better find him some pants."

Chapter 11

He stuffs his drug store binoculars down the front of his shirt and rolls over on his back. The acrid odor of dew-wet Eucalyptus burns the inside of his nose.

The sun is finally out, thank *gawd*. He half froze spending the night in his pickup, what with that broken window and all. It had been a dumb ass plan to lock the keys in it, but hell, maybe it had kept some other asshole from breaking in while he was away. He eyeballs a tiny red mark on his forearm for any sign the TB test he'd gotten that morning was positive. So far, so good. At least the paperwork will guarantee he gets into a shelter for a meal and a bed if he gets back downtown in time. But he can't stand another day without seeing her, maybe sit in her front seat for a few minutes while he formulates a plan.

He creeps further through the orchard, careful to stay low and in the shadows until he can peek out beyond the oleander hedge. He doesn't need the binocs to confirm his fears. The garage is still trussed up tight in orange and white stripes like a big ass circus tent. How long does it take to fumigate for rats anyway? A day? A week?

Disappointment twists through his belly along with an empty growl. The return trip to Ventura will eat up all his gas, but he needs to get back there soon if he wants a meal and a bed. He's already gone through the few packets of aspirin he'd palmed at the shelter. A stop by the ocean front walkway will hopefully yield enough recyclables to buy more.

His gut takes a little dip when he recognizes the hardened rectangle of dirt behind the hedge. Twenty years ago it had been well hidden in the avocado orchard. With the addition of the new garage and the access driveway, trees had been cleared nearly to the spot, separated from open space by only a single hedgerow of oleander bushes. He had expected it would have been overgrown with weeds by now, or at least the line of rocks disarranged. He considers kicking them out of line, but checks himself before he takes the first kick. Better to leave it undisturbed. It's been here this long, no sense drawing attention to it. He can't help but remember Old Berlin's words. *That car will be the death of you.*

It was certainly the death of the kid, and Lionel, too, if he were honest. He bunches his lips in a tight pinch. "Their own damn fault," he mutters, and scoots back away from the hedge. He waits while his heart settles down in his chest, satisfied that no one can see, then makes a hunched sprint out to the property line where he's snipped a sharp-edged slit in the chain link fence behind a gnarly hedge of prickly pear cactus.

The avocados in the grove, all green and bumpy, were hard as rocks. This fruit is a ripe red and irresistible. He picks one from a low hanging paddle, gingerly avoiding clumps of tiny spines. A car engine revs, slows, and he hunkers behind the gnarled cactus. He can't see now, but judging by the low purr of the engine, it's that smooth Jaguar. Once the sound fades, he drops the fruit into his Levi jacket pocket, then bends the chain links back into place. He makes it out just in time. Time is on his side. He can't get to his baby right now because, you know, rat gas. The bright side is—and he always looks for one—nobody else can get to her either.

Chapter 12

Luke slipped into his usual booth at Joe's on downtown State and shrugged out of his jacket. It was their booth, near the front where Gina liked to watch people coming and going on the street. Only Gina wasn't with him. He had promised to leave her alone after the cat incident, and he had made good on that promise. She had agreed to make an exception for business calls related to the campaign, and she'd made good on that promise as well. It felt odd being here without her. He could do it, though. If giving her what she wanted meant leaving her alone for a while, letting her take the lead, then he could do it. For a while.

That didn't mean he liked it. In fact, her absence made him irritable. Familiar noise inside the restaurant—a sudden burst of laughter from the bar, plates and silverware clattering into the bus-person's bin, the woman in the booth behind him talking too loud on her cell phone about a fight she'd had with her ex—conspiring with the hum of old ceiling fans and the six o-clock news on the flat screen over the bar set his teeth on edge, seemed louder than usual, intruded on his space. But he could do this.

Until she came to her senses.

Which she would.

Soon.

Hopefully.

He knew her well enough to know that she needed it sometimes. Though, to his mind, now would be the time she'd need him most. She'd been completely desolated by the news that her partner and longtime friend had been killed not twenty minutes after he'd waved goodbye to her at the McAllisters' front gate. He had hoped, if anything, the loss would break the deadlock. She'd need a shoulder to cry on, if nothing else.

But losing Lionel had only seemed to widen the space between them. Losing her business partner had intensified her need to work harder herself. Maybe it would be for the best, for now. As the new candidate for DA, he'd racked up meetings and public appearances every night for the last week. Tonight was no different. He'd agreed to attend the Chamber of Commerce Mixer, which is why he wanted to fill his stomach on something substantial, like pasta, so he could absorb alcohol without getting bombed.

Gina had arranged his appearance at the mixer, getting his hopes up that the night might end at her place. But she had declined his invitation to join him, and considering what Harvey'd told him about her ordeal this morning at the McAllisters', he hadn't pressed it. That was a whole other can of worms that he wasn't ready to open.

"Hey, counselor." Luke's head popped up at the sound of the familiar voice. The server took obvious note of the empty space across the table from him, giving him a raised brow. Luke refocused on the menu. He was in no mood for explanations. She was the regular server in their section for Tuesday night, was once one of Gina's clients, and had remained a casual acquaintance. "I haven't seen you in here for a while."

"Charline," he said in a short, clipped tone, sending, he hoped, a clear message that he wasn't in the mood for banter. "I'll have whatever's on special." He waved his hand vaguely at the A-frame blackboard at the hostess station behind him.

"Spaghetti with sausage and clams?" she asked. "That's a first."

He sighed. Being a regular had its perks, he rarely had to put in a drink order. But it also had its pitfalls. Gina was good at heading off too much attention. Without her there, he felt vulnerable, exposed.

"Whatever," he said, looking out the window to avoid further conversation. He didn't care what he ate, as long as it filled the empty corners of his stomach sufficiently for the night's activity.

"Ho-kay," she said in a you'll-be-sorry tone, ignoring his attempt to get rid of her. "So, you'll be eating alone?"

Her words hung in the air like a heavy cloud and intensified everything he regretted, number one on that list was choosing to eat where he knew the wait staff, and they knew him. He pushed the extra place setting across the table, checking the urge to grumble. That was all she wanted, he realized after all.

"Yes," he said, as politely as he could muster, dredging up a quick smile. It wasn't her fault Gina wasn't here. She picked up the clean dish and cutlery and hurried away.

He sank deeper into the soft leather of the booth. It was true, after all. They hadn't been here since Christmas time, now that he thought about it. His workload simply hadn't allowed for dinner out. Hadn't allowed for anything. But now it seemed that ever since he'd told Gina he didn't have time for a wedding, he'd found himself alone with absolutely nothing to do. That was all about to change, he told himself. This was the calm before the political tsunami that was coming.

At a movement near the booth, he looked up expecting his server. Instead a scarecrow-thin woman in a black suit with David Bowie shoulder pads cocked her head and posed at the end of his table.

"Mr. Berlin?" she asked. Her lipsticked smile spread over a squarish chin with a dimple in it. "I'm Fiona Blanchard, with *The Bomb*."

Luke had no idea what *The Bomb* was, but he assumed he was about to find out. He stood and shook her outstretched hand, warily. He guessed her at about thirty-five trying to pass for ten years younger.

"Oh, just a second," she said, pulling his arm around her shoulder in a quick, practiced move. She snuggled up under his chin and flashed a selfie before he could pull away. "Nothing like having your picture taken with the next District Attorney." Her voice was husky, like a longtime smoker. She eyed the empty seat across from him. "Mind if we talk a few minutes?"

"If this is about the campaign, you need to make an appointment with my publicist." He hitched up his hip, slipped his wallet out of his pants, and thumbed out a card.

"Calvin Klyne? Really?" Her tone should have crinkled her brow, but nothing moved. Luke had to focus on his hands to keep from staring. She pushed the card back across to his side of the table.

"Really. He's quite capable," he said, pushing the card back. "And you really have to see him."

Silver glitter-tipped nails on long fingers picked it up and dropped it into her small wrist purse. "Lucky for me, this isn't about the campaign. Well, not specifically, anyway."

Something turned in his stomach. Suddenly the thought of spaghetti with sausage and clams felt like a bad idea after all. He caught the eye of his server and gave her the cut throat hand signal. She nodded, and he turned his attention back to the woman sitting across from him. In Gina's spot.

"So, Ms. Blanchard. You have one minute to tell me what this is about because I've decided against dinner."

"Feeling a little edgy tonight? Well, I guess that's understandable," she said, motioning to the same server. "Your first campaign and all, and then your girlfriend walking out on you. How long have you two been together? Three years? Seven? College sweethearts, wasn't it?"

Charline arrived at the table, her expression flush with attitude. "Can I get you something?"

"I'll have a Grey Goose martini, straight up, with a twist."

The server tilted her head to Luke. He shook his head and she left without another word.

Luke sipped a little too much water, the ice cubes bumped his upper lip. "You said this wasn't about the campaign, and my relationships are not for public consumption."

"Oh, but you're wrong," she purred. "See, *The Bomb* is all about relationships, and you just made the short list in the running for our Most Eligible Bachelor of Santa Barbara County."

Jesus. Thank you, Miss Gina, for leaving me open to this. He grabbed his coat and slipped out of the booth. "Don't do me any favors."

She wagged a long finger at him, looking way too much like Michael Jackson in drag. "You never know. This might just be the best thing that ever happened to you."

"It's not going to happen."

Charline served the martini with the bill. Luke dropped a twenty on top of it.

Blanchard took a long sip, leaving a red smear on the lip of the glass. "Ooooh," she said, holding it up in a toast. She snapped another selfie with him. "It already has."

Chapter 13

Gina stood on her bedroom balcony brushing her teeth, her minty green robe tied loosely at her waist. The summer fog had moved in overnight—thick, wet, and brooding. If she were lucky it would burn off by noon and she might get a little sunshine in her day. She could certainly use it.

It had been nearly two weeks since Lionel's accident and nearly one since Ina McAllister's death. The two events tangoed together in her brain, leaving ghostly footprints of pain and guilt. If only she had insisted Lionel stay in Pismo Beach with Roland instead of letting him follow her home. If only she had arrived at the McAllisters' earlier.

It didn't help that she'd lost another of her regular clients this week, even if it was from natural causes and fully expected. The woman had been one of her favorites. Gina had broken her cardinal rule with clients: Don't let yourself get too close. For a hospice nurse, the outcome was always the same. You don't usher a fellow human being through their end times without feeling a loss. But how could you not love someone as canny and vivacious as Lee Meier? A woman who'd done everything humanly possible to live forever. She took every vitamin known to man, was a gluten-free vegan, a Pagan, a self-proclaimed witch who didn't smoke, or drink anything but green tea and kombucha. She had spent the last ten years alone, having outlived everyone in her family, including her two grandchildren. The night she passed away, Gina had been the only one with her. They'd talked long past midnight, sharing dreams, memories, and a rare regret. Gina would never forget Lee's last words, spoken on a sigh with her eyes closed: "I should have eaten the ice cream."

Lee's words came to her now. She was wasting precious moments. Lionel would be the first to agree. It was time to put her life back together, resume her routine, or——-what was coming to her more and more—do something completely different, if she wanted. The point was to get started. Now.

She scuff walked inside, rinsed her mouth and went downstairs to the kitchen where Peetie threaded her scrawny cat body between her legs. Milo, a lanky Maine Coon she'd rescued when a client passed away last year, was already waiting on top of the washer, and Jabba lay on his side near his dish by the slider.

"I suppose you kids want breakfast," Gina crooned. But the cat food bag only yielded two kernels when she dumped it into Milo's bowl. "Good thing I bought a spare," she said, opening the inside door to the garage.

She grabbed the bag of food from the shelf by the door, her eyes falling on the red Corvette.

Come on. Drive me.

She hadn't driven the little car since the day Lionel ... left. Peetie meowed from the doorway. "All right, all right, I'm coming, you little varmint," she said, her eyes still on the car. Getting back into it would be a huge step in the right direction. "That's what he'd want, right, girl?" she asked as she zipped the string off the bag and poured kibble into the waiting bowl. Peetie jumped up on the dryer and rewarded Gina with a few thankful head butts before pushing Milo out of the way to get the first meal.

With one eye permanently sealed shut, and a set of razor sharp claws to make Wolverine jealous, a dainty lady Peetie was not. But once de-flead and shampooed, the cat had become a welcome addition to the family, an integration so seamless it was like the cat had always been there. From the three-story cat tree in the corner of her living room to the catnip mice strewn about the floor of the kitchen, to the fur balls in the hall, Peetie had invaded every square foot of Gina's condo, including Jabba's perch on the back of the couch. She ruffled the fur on the back of the orphan's neck. "You be a good girl now, I'll be back early today."

A half hour later, Gina slipped behind the wheel of the Corvette in a pair of skinny jeans and a white hip-hugging tank instead of her drab green scrubs. She couldn't bring herself to open the closet where she'd hung her club jacket, let alone put it on. Instead, she retrieved a soft, white hoodie from behind the driver's seat and shrugged it on, then tied a silk scarf over her head, a hot pink and gold extravagance she'd purchased before her first ride—before grief and loss had turned her life gray. Wearing it wouldn't cancel out the pain that had taken up residence in her soul, hot pink was hardly the color of mourning. But it did remind her of Lionel.

She rubbed the time-worn brass key between her thumb and forefinger. Her heart rate quickened. Lionel would want that. Lee would too.

Hot pink.

Top down.

Full throttle.

She slipped the key into the ignition, revved the engine into an even purr, and headed for her Friday morning meeting with Angela.

Klatchee was a small neighborhood coffee and tea shop not far from the college and usually bustling with activity. During the school year, the bench across the street served as a shop annex where on weekdays students perched like pigeons, sipping their chai lattes and waiting for the bus to take them on to class. But now, in mid June, students at City College had departed for the summer, leaving the shop and the neighborhood breathing a collective, if not a little lonely, sigh of relief. Today the bench was empty but for one ragged soul. One of the ubiquitous homeless who no doubt had wandered a little too far off State Street.

Gina parked the car across the street from the coffee shop, drawing more than one appreciative glance from passersby. The woman who sat outside with her standard poodle most mornings nodded at Gina in recognition, a welcome gesture of normalcy in her lately off-kilter world.

The barista at the espresso machine tossed a cheery greeting over her shoulder. "The usual, Gina?" she called. The woman prided herself on knowing the names of all her regulars.

Gina's usual was a dark roasted pour-over, black.

All zip, no calories.

She snorted under her breath. The usual would be she and Luke sitting in a quiet booth at the back, reading the paper or checking their respective schedules on their cell phones, in companionable quiet, his toe nudging the back of her calf under the table.

These last two weeks had been anything but usual. Lee's words echoed in her mind. *I should have eaten the ice cream.* The elegant octogenarian was right. Who knew what tomorrow would bring? Gina had made up her mind. Luke or no Luke, she certainly wasn't going to waste time missing out on the ice cream, or the frosting, or whatever else she'd been waiting for. She shifted her purse on her shoulder and pulled out her wallet, giving the colorful chalkboard menu behind the counter some serious consideration for the first time ever.

"I'll have the Graduation special," she said with conviction. If a double shot of espresso piled with whipped cream and a caramel drizzle couldn't shake off the gloom that hung like a pall over her, nothing would. She swiped her ATM card at the counter and turned to find Angela sitting by the window, a tall iced drink in front of her. Gina held up a finger to let her know she'd be right there. "Make that with extra whipped cream, okay?"

The server squirted an obscene mountain of whipped cream in her drink and drizzled caramel over it. "Is there anything else you need?" she asked.

"No," she replied, tamping down the hollow empty feeling Luke's absence had left in her belly. There wasn't enough whipped cream on the planet to fill that void. Her need for Luke twisted in her stomach, a gnawing hunger that seemed to grow with each passing day. She hoped he was feeling the same and that feeling would goad him to action. "On second thought, I'll take some of those chocolate sprinkles," Gina added. That would do her for now, anyway.

"Hey, Angie," she said, scooting into the seat opposite her friend and now her new employee. "Hope you had a good night. I can't tell you what a relief it is to have you helping me out with Mason."

Angela hung a giant leather hobo bag on the back of her chair, tucked her cell phone into the outside pocket, and gave Gina the full attention of a respectful employee reporting to the boss. The fact that they were nearly neighbors, and aside from Maddie, the only other woman Gina considered a close friend, was set aside whenever Angie was on the job. A trait that Gina appreciated. Her livelihood, and the lives of her clients, depended on that kind of serious dedication.

"No problem," Angie said. Her gaze strayed out the window where the bus had stopped across the street. "My weekends are jammed working at the polo field. Night shift at the McAllisters' is the perfect chance to get to my school work uninterrupted."

She fell uncharacteristically silent, fiddling with a napkin collecting condensation under the iced drink in front of her. Gina studied her features. Angie was petite, her hair a shiny dark walnut that just brushed her shoulders, her bottle green eyes large and perceptive. She possessed a natural effervescence that, even when dressed in nurse's scrubs, reminded Gina of root beer floats and teenage sleepovers. But she could be down to earth, too. The girl could get excited over a handsome polo player making eyes at her one minute and go back to studying for a medical school exam the next without skipping a beat. This morning she was pensive, thoughtful.

Gina's trouble antenna went up. Something had happened. At the McAllisters.

She laid her spoon next to her coffee cup, pressed both palms against the table and pushed back a little, feeling a bit guilty that she hadn't mentioned her fears about the open gate. Had Angie heard something? Had Gina put her in a dangerous situation? Did she want to quit? The possibilities crowded in, shifting Gina's fears into overdrive.

"What is it, Ange?" she asked, finally, almost afraid to hear the answer.

Angie straightened in her chair, scraped stray wisps of hair behind both ears. "Nothing, I ..." She sucked half her drink down in one gulp.

Gina narrowed her eyes. "Angie. Did something happen last night?"

Angela slurped the dregs of her mocha noisily, and blotted her lips with her napkin, looking more uncomfortable by the second. "Oh, no. I ..."

"Look, I know it's a hard assignment. If it's too much, we can switch you out with someone else. It's a big house. It can be creepy at night..." Someone could be watching. Gina reached out and covered Angie's hand. "I need you to be straight with me. If something's wrong, I need to hear it. Now."

Angela shrugged, sighed, slumped. "It's...not about Mason. He's fine. Well, as fine as can be expected. It's...it's personal."

"Personal?"

Angie fished into her giant bag and unfolded a newspaper on the table. "I got this out of the newsstand on my way in here. I bought them all, so you wouldn't see them, but. I ..." She slumped, deflated. "I ... think you should see it, after all." She pushed the paper across the table in front of Gina, then sat back and wrung her hands with a "don't-kill-the-messenger" look in her eyes.

Chapter 14

"What in the world ..." Gina drew the paper closer, not sure she was seeing it right.

She was.

Holy shit.

A picture of Luke Berlin, full color, his arm around a woman who looked like Michael Jackson in drag. In *their* restaurant, in *their* booth. She felt like someone had punched the air right out of her. The headline read: CANDIDATE FOR DISTRICT ATTORNEY, LUKE BERLIN, NAMED SANTA BARBARA'S MOST ELIGIBLE BACHELOR. *STORY ON PAGE THREE*. Her hand shook as she fumbled the pages and spread the paper across the table. She caught her breath as she took in the full-page spread. Luke's picture, obviously telephoto, filled the entire insert, Playgirl style, arms lifted to smooth wet hair over his head left nothing to the imagination. Broad shoulders, swimmer's pecs, and plated abs led the eye directly down his flat stomach to the well-filled Speedo.

She flinched at a sudden assault in her ears. It took her a moment to realize the loud hiss was coming from the espresso machine and not inside her skull. "Oh, *gawd.*"

"Gina, I'm so sorry." Angie reached out to her. "I thought it would be better if you saw it now, rather than have someone ask you about it."

Gina didn't know whether to laugh or cry. The paper was dated two nights ago, the night she spent with Lee Meier. The first night Luke hadn't violated their agreement and showed up at her house to try to get past her defenses. And this happens. It was bad enough that he hadn't jumped at the chance to make things right between them the night he brought the cat. God knew the cat thing was getting close. But this? With everything he had at stake? This was downright lunacy.

Angie angled the paper to take another look. "Do you know who she is?"

Gina skimmed the article. There was actually going to be an auction, a date with the competition winner going to the highest bidder, proceeds to The Friendship Shoppe, of course, which seemed a bit disingenuous, since it was run by a church. "Maybe the byline? Fiona Blanchard?"

Gina looked up at Angie in disbelief, the first sizzle of shock fading to a tinge of humor. "I told him he needed a press opportunity, but this isn't exactly what I had in mind."

Angie closed the paper and pushed it back across to Gina. "In his defense, he does have a sort of deer-in-the-headlights look …"

Her gaze flew suddenly past Gina's shoulder to the front door of the café. Her mouth dropped open, then snapped closed. Gina felt a rush of cool air behind her. Angie's expression forced her to turn around.

She scraped the paper into her lap and swallowed on a dry throat. "Luke."

"I was afraid I'd missed you," he said, breathlessly, and scooted next to her on the bench at the bar as if nothing had changed between them. "Hi Angela," he said, nodding at her.

"I ... I need to go," Angie squeaked and gathered her bag and books.

Gina gave her a quick nod. "We'll talk later, Ange."

"Sure," she said, scooping her empty cup off the table.

Gina turned on Luke, seething under a veneer of calm. Dark shadows hollowed his eyes, drawing attention to fine lines at the corners. His white shirt was rumpled under his suit coat.

A part of her felt sorry for him. As much as it had angered her when he'd canceled out on a night on the town or a cozy night at home, she knew he really did throw himself full bore into his work. He was respected as Executive Prosecutor and took the job seriously. He would make an excellent DA, something he'd always dreamed of. It was the kind of a position a woman had to understand.

The other part wanted to stomp his two-timing toes on her way out.

She gathered her things, her cheeks on fire. What on earth did he think he was doing? Torturing her for the fun of it? "You have a lot of nerve showing up here. This is *my* coffee shop."

His arm shot out and caught her by the elbow. "I need to talk to you."

She stopped, giving him her best defiant look, but his eyes shifted to the paper and his jaw dropped. He slipped it away from her, letting go of her arm. Judging by the look on his face, he hadn't seen it yet. But obviously he knew about the pictures, he was the one with the silly ass grin behind the lipstick-smeared martini glass.

"Nice job on the press coverage, counselor. Not what I would have recommended, but it's out there now. Can't take it back."

Luke sent her an apologetic look. "You don't think this was my idea?"

"Well it certainly wasn't mine."

Gina snatched the paper out of his hands and dumped it in the trash bin beside the front door. Luke reached for her sleeve, missed. "Don't even," she said on her way out.

The woman with the dog met her eyes for a fraction of a second and then looked down into her own coffee mug. Gina pushed out into the street as fast as she could make her feet move.

Luke followed her. "Come on, Gee. She came in to Joe's. I'm running for DA. People know who I am. It was like an ambush."

Gina kept moving. "I no longer have an interest in your personal affairs."

"I don't have any personal affairs."

She whirled around, and he nearly ran into her. "Most eligible bachelor in Santa Barbara? You'll be back in the saddle in no time."

He reached around her waist and pulled her close. "Come on, Gee, you know you're the only saddle I want to be in."

She reached her car and dumped her hoodie and bag in the passenger seat. "And then what? We go back to our separate lives in between? There when you need me and otherwise, on my own? I told you I'm done with that and I mean it."

Luke stood his ground, his tie flapping on a sudden gust of breeze. "Look. Forget about that for now. Okay. I can explain. I need to talk to you about ... something else."

He was right. The Most Eligible Bachelor thing was laughable. Not the end of the world. It was simply the latest in a chain of events that had piled up to leave her feeling crushed, useless, insignificant. It was the something else that had her running away. It had been two days since his office had put Mason on house arrest. They were either going to have to charge him with something, or let him go. He was here to give her the bad news.

"So send me a subpoena." She opened her car door and slid in behind the wheel. The image of Ina McAllister's frail body being zipped into a long plastic bag played through in her mind. Her lips quivered. Why hadn't she just grabbed that pillow off the poor woman's face and called the coroner? Chances were no one would have been the wiser. When had any authority ever questioned her about a death that happened during a hospice service? But she knew why. It was the right thing to do. The problem was, Luke had a history of following the letter of the law. Spousal abuse was his personal pet peeve, drilled into his psyche by an abusive father. If Mason had in fact smothered his wife under Luke's watch, he would be indicted, and tried for murder, regardless of his age or the fact that it could only have been a mercy killing.

The idea of Mason going to jail was too much to bear. She dropped her forehead against the wheel. She would not cry in front of him. No here. Not now.

"C'mon, Geen. Let's get out of here." He punched the old-school thumb button on the handle and swung open the door. His velvet soft voice stroked raw empty places inside her, something she'd longed for since that awful morning when she'd discovered Ina's lifeless body. It peeled away her resistance. She had missed him terribly. Wanted to talk to him. Needed to.

Luke slid in behind the steering wheel, forcing her to raise a hip and scoot across the console. "Let's go down to the pier."

Chapter 15

Luke eased the Corvette over the bumpy wooden planks of the wharf and found a space at the end of the parking lot. The first of many launches from the massive cruise ship anchored off shore was making its way across the glassy water to the pier. The overcast had moved off except for a few raggedy gray clouds on the horizon, sending warm hints of the day in store.

Gina angled slightly away from him in the passenger seat, her elbow on the armrest and her chin propped on her knuckles. Her hoodie rested loosely over her head, legs tucked up under her. She made no move to look at him or get out of the car. A section of her hair the color of cherry cola lifted slightly in the breeze.

He wanted nothing more than to touch the silky softness of it, twirl it around his finger, and tease her to turn and look at him. But he knew better. He needed to let her take the lead. He'd been on her shit list before. More times than he cared to admit. His banishment had always ended after a day or two with passionate make-up sex. This time was different. They were coming up on two weeks.

Losing Lionel had been a terrible blow to her, both emotionally and professionally. Luke had half expected Gina would abandon her crusade if for no other reason than to have his willing shoulder to cry on. The incident with Ina McAllister put the kybosh on all of that. She had discovered a crime scene. She was a witness. He was Executive Prosecutor. Lila's illness and medical leave had not only put him in the running for DA, it put him in charge. His close association with a witness to a crime could make that tricky. Gina knew that. Knew what that meant. And that was why she'd called Detective Estevez instead of him when she'd made her discovery.

He let his gaze wander over what he could see of her profile, the curve of her forehead, her refined nose, the full lips that curled up a little when she smiled.

Only this morning, she wasn't smiling. A deep cleft cut between her brows.

He leaned against the seat, draping his arm over the back of it, giving her the space her posture demanded. For the moment.

A group of excited tourists disgorged from the launch and meandered down the pier. Gina followed them with her gaze, eventually bringing her head around to face him. He gave her a concerned smile. She blinked as if startled out of a dream.

"Want to walk out to the end of the pier?" he asked.

She nodded and unfolded her legs. He came around to the passenger door and opened it, offered his hand to help her out of the low-slung doorway. She accepted, her hand cold in his. They advanced through a flock of gulls that scattered and resettled as they went.

"I should have covered the car seats," Gina said, absently, making no attempt to turn back.

He led her by the hand to a spot they often came to watch surfers when the swell came in at just the right angle for the pier break to go off. Earlier that year, it had gone off big enough to blast through the pier and take out a couple of windows in Moby Dick's. Today the Santa Barbara channel was a light azure green, calm and glassy. Relaxed.

Luke leaned against the railing and took her other hand. For the moment at least, she was pliant, willing, though she hadn't yet looked him in the eye.

He waded in cautiously, unsure how far he would get. "I'm really sorry about Ina. It must have been a terrible blow, especially after what happened to Lionel. To have to report it and all."

Gina looked out over the water, lifted her hands away from his. "I ... almost ... didn't."

He cocked his head at her, letting the silence hang between them for a couple of beats. He turned into the railing, rested on his forearms, sucked in a breath. "That wasn't in the police report."

"No. I guess I have Harvey to thank for that." Gina looked at him for the first time, russet halo around her pupils widening to nearly overtake the amber.

Luke deflated, the picture coming clear. He knew her well. She couldn't stand to see anyone suffer. "You ... thought about altering the scene."

She scooped the hoodie off her head and scraped her hair to one side to clear her face. "He's an old man, Luke. He loved his wife. He wouldn't do anything to hurt her."

"Alzheimer's is a devastating disease," Luke said, shifting his feet. "You of all people know it's often worse for the caregiver than the patient."

"Mason is the gentlest, caring, attentive husband a person could be, Luke. It was devastating to him to see her that way."

Luke stared out to the horizon. There was no way to make this conversation easy. "Doesn't justify murder." He tried to make his voice soft, non-threatening, without sugar coating the situation.

A pelican landed on the post a few feet away, settling its awkward wings and beak until it looked like a sculpture.

Gina eyed the creature, then leaned away, giving it some space. "So, you're going to charge him. Send him to jail."

He didn't miss the tremor in her voice. "It's not up to me, Gina."

"Not up to you? You're the Executive Prosecutor and the acting DA. If it's not up to you, then who?"

"I'll send it to the grand jury." Mason had been under house arrest for two days. He was out of time. And he couldn't let his relationship—or lack of it—cloud his decision.

She straightened her shoulders defensively. "Mason wasn't like your father, Luke."

The accusation struck him like dry lightning, setting him on a slow burn. "What's that got to do with anything?"

She pushed closer. Close enough for him to feel the fire in her soul. "Tell me it doesn't have everything to do with it. You could drop the charges right now. He loved his wife. If he did end her life, and I don't think he did, I have no doubt he thought he was releasing her from a body that betrayed her. Betrayed them both. He didn't want her to suffer."

A pair of gulls swooped down and fought over a cluster of mussels someone had left on a fish cleaning sink next to Luke. He batted them away, his jaw tightening.

"He put a pillow over her face and crushed the breath out of her, and you think she didn't suffer?"

Gina cringed. "It didn't look like ..."

"He committed murder, Gina. Planned it out in advance. Did it when he knew you would be there to find it."

"It's not that black and white," she hissed. "Not everyone is vicious or criminally insane."

"Like my father, you mean."

"The man was under a huge a mountain of stress. Stretched to his limits. But he's not a killer. He's no danger to anyone and you know it."

"That's not the point."

"It's exactly the point! He's ninety-two years old. He'll die if you send him to prison. He doesn't care what happens anymore. Besides, he hasn't spoken a lucid word since the night it happened."

"What do you mean?"

"From the time I saw him on the front steps, he's done nothing but ask when he can see his wife. He doesn't remember anything. You read the report. What about the open gate? Someone else might have been in the house that morning. It's not a foregone conclusion."

Luke slapped a hand on the railing, frustrated. "That would be up to a jury to decide."

"You read Estevez's report, right?"

"Gina, I'm not going to gloss it over for you. Everything in that report points to Mason killing his wife. I've already left it longer than I should. His indictment is inevitable."

"You can't consider just for a moment the possibility that someone else …"

"Got through the gate, broke into the house, smothered an eighty-eight-year-old woman with a family portrait and a pillow, and left without disturbing anything else?"

"But there must be fingerprints or something."

Another boatload of cruisers landed at the pier, voices in different languages pitched with excitement to spend the day in town. Luke watched them—young families, senior citizens, singles, people on holiday, enjoying their lives. Anger built in his gut. He waited until the last one of them was out of earshot, letting some of that anger dissipate.

"I can't disclose any details about the investigation."

"Since when do you not share with me?" She blurted out the words, hurt clearly etched in the fine lines around her mouth.

"Since your client decided to kill his wife."

Chapter 16

Gina drew back; the stark reality of his statement hit her in the chest like a fist. "Are you willing to bet our future on that?"

Luke recoiled. "It's my job, Gina. Now that I've picked up the banner for Lila, I'm under more scrutiny than ever. Everything's got to be by the book from here on, you know that."

She rested her elbows on the railing. "Then, you should know that my fingerprints are all over those picture frames from the mantel."

"What?"

"It's my job," she mimicked. "I tell myself not to get too close, but the McAllisters? They were like family to me. Those photographs told their history." Mason's gallery of love. "I've handled all of those pictures at least a half dozen times. Ina liked to see them, to touch them, to hold them. So, I brought them to her. I told Harvey about it."

Luke pushed away from the railing and scrubbed a hand over his chin where his overnight stubble hadn't been shaved.

"You put Estevez on the spot, asking him to come there ahead of the police."

"I was upset. I wanted to talk to someone I knew. Someone I trusted to do the … right thing." The words were out of her mouth before she could stop them.

"And I wouldn't have?" There was an edge to his voice she rarely heard. Her words had cut him deep, but she wasn't taking them back. She stared out at the water, letting the question hang between them.

"The important thing is …" he said at last, undaunted, "... you didn't touch anything, *afterward*."

She gripped the railing hard. Against all the law required of its keepers, Luke had already made up his mind. *If you expect people to change, you'll always be disappointed*, her mother used to say.

Gina turned, pushed away from the railing.

"Gina," he said, softly, hooking her by the arm to bring her back into his space.

His eyes softened. He was dangerously irresistible, stunning in his gray suit, white shirt, and the gemstone blue tie loosened at his neck. He stood now, firm in his convictions, devoted to justice, and yes, dammit, exactly the man she had envisioned he would be when they first met, all those years ago. *It will take strength to hold on to yourself with a man like that*—also her mother's words. As usual, she'd been right.

Gina lifted her chin. She would lay it on the line, and if he didn't like it, then ... it would drive the wedge deeper between them. In this case, the right thing depended on your point of view.

"Luke, you know I admire your strength, your passion for the law. And, I love you for that."

He cocked his head and shoved a hand into his slacks.

"And ..." he said, suspiciously.

"And ... Most of the time you get it right. It's why Lila has faith in you. Why the citizens of this county will probably give their votes to you. But this time, counselor, where Mason is concerned, you are dead wrong."

His eyebrow tweaked up. She pointed a stiff finger in his face, something she hadn't done since the day they'd met.

"You need to consider the possibility that Mason and Ina are victims. Maybe, just maybe, there's something else going on here. If you try Mason and put him in jail, you will be responsible for what happens to him and for whatever else happens because you let someone else run free. Right now, you are in a position to save a man's life. What are you going to do about it?"

"You know I can't play favorites just because he is your client."

"Favorites? The people closest to you can't have the full protection of the law because it might be seen as playing favorites? And what if Mason did do it? What do you think your constituents will say when they find out you charged an old man with murder who did nothing but release his wife from an agonizing death by starvation or pneumonia? Is that what Lila would do?"

"Lila's father wasn't responsible for her mother's death."

Gina's mouth clamped shut. She couldn't believe he'd actually said it. "And Mason McAllister wasn't responsible for yours."

"Is that what this is about? You don't think I can be objective?"

"I think you see everything through that old lens."

"What do you mean?"

"Come on, Luke. You wouldn't be in law enforcement at all today if it wasn't for your obsession with the idea that your father was responsible for your mother's illness. This time, that obsession may just put the wrong person behind bars."

He took a step back, staring at her in disbelief, hurt deepening in his eyes. After a moment, he let out a defeated sigh. He straightened his tie and pushed it up to his collar.

"Mason's still at home now, isn't he?"

"Yes," she said, reluctantly. House arrest was better than hauling him off to jail. "Thank you for that, at least."

"I'll have a security detail assigned to the property until we resolve the issue."

৵

Luke stared at her for a long moment, weighing his next move carefully. Her cheeks still bloomed a bright crimson under the heat of their conversation. She had dug in her heels good on this one, and she wouldn't be budging. If the evidence warranted, and Mason ever went to trial, he could easily see questioning Gina on the witness stand. He hoped it wouldn't come to that. The distance between them was already wider than he could live with.

He reached across the abyss and drew two fingers down the side of her cheek. "I could use some breakfast," he said, testing the waters. "We haven't been to Dawn Patrol in a while." The DP was a local favorite restaurant they could easily walk to from the pier.

"I shouldn't be consorting with the enemy," she said, halfheartedly.

"I just punched out on my official DA time clock."

She sent him a doubtful glance. "Are you trying to bribe me?"

He draped an arm around her shoulders, pulled her close like they had just been talking about the weather.

"No, I'm just hungry for custom hash, is all." He walked her to her car, slipped the keys out of his pocket and held them up. "What are you hungry for?"

Her eyes slid to the flat wedge of his bottom lip. She was weighing her options. His heart revved like the engine under the hood. He was hungry, but not for hash, custom or otherwise.

It must have shown in his eyes, because in the next second, she snatched the keys out of his hand, opened the driver side door, and slid in behind the wheel. "You are despicable."

She started the engine. "If you hurry, you'll make it back to Chapala Street in time for Estevez's morning donut delivery."

Luke stepped gingerly out of the way and watched as she bumped over the wooden planks to follow the line of tourists making their way off the pier.

Chapter 17

Antonia Guadalupe Salazar draped her arm dramatically over Little Red's passenger door. She straightened her shoulders, and twisted the bill of a Roxy ball cap to the front to shade her eyes. "I'm changing my name to Rizzo."

Gina rounded the driveway past the grove house and lower garage, and turned onto the Berlin property's main drive leading off the property. They were on their way for the final fitting of the bridal dresses for Maddie's wedding.

Antonia sent Gina a provocative smile. Gina had to admire the girl's fearless audacity, even if it was hard to manage at times. Unhappy that her father had left her at her aunt's when he took the grounds manager job for the Berlins, Antonia had hitchhiked from the remote California mountain town of Bishop to the sprawling Berlin Estate at the central coast community of Montecito—by herself. Gina and Maddie had ganged up on Salazar and Nick to let her stay. Sending her back where she didn't want to be would only be courting trouble.

Since Maddie had gotten pregnant, the role of watching over the rebellious teen fell primarily to Gina, a responsibility that proved more taxing than she expected, but that she thoroughly enjoyed. She'd done her best to set a good example. Now she questioned whether it was doing any good.

"Rizzo?" Gina sucked in her breath. This is what her influence produced? "I know we talked about a nickname. Like Toni, or Lupe, but Rizzo?"

Antonia smacked her gum defiantly and tossed her head. "You know. The bad girl. From *Grease*."

In the wake of losing two people close to her, the possibility of one going to jail, and seeing the photos of Luke in the gossip rag, Gina had given up ever smiling again. But she supposed that's why she volunteered to take Antonia for the fitting. The young girl's energy and precocity could be challenging, and that's what Gina needed. A challenge. To get her mind off ... everything.

She eyed the young woman in her passenger seat, only then noticing her mass of dark walnut hair was not stuffed up under her ball cap, but had been cut off short. It now curled just at the base of her neck, bangs brushing her brows, adding five years to what already was way too mature a profile for a girl who had just celebrated her Quinceañera.

"Or maybe, Rosie, like Rosie Perez," the girl proposed, sliding her shoulders back and forth, "So I can keep the Mexican part."

"Rosie Perez is Puerto Rican."

"So? She's an actress and that's what I want to be." She pulled a tube of red lipstick out of her pocket and smeared it on in the visor mirror.

Gina cringed. Grateful that they were almost off the property so Mr. Salazar wouldn't see his daughter in this state, Gina accelerated onto the 101 Freeway heading toward Santa Barbara. On their left, the blue green ocean hugged the shoreline, occasionally hidden by lush trees that sheltered pricey homes under their boughs.

The kid had grown up on a scrubby ranch in New Mexico where she and her younger sister had rarely worn shoes, let alone been to the movies or watched TV. The six months she'd lived on the Montecito compound had changed her profoundly, in good ways, but also in ways that worried her father. With that short haircut and bright red lipstick, she did look a little like Rosie Perez, and that worried Gina a lot. "When did you see Rosie?" she asked nonchalantly, hoping to draw the precocious teen out.

"Nick got us cable. And a new computer." She turned suddenly in her seat and faced Gina. "Oh my Gaw! I forgot to tell you."

She rummaged through the rhinestone-studded backpack Maddie had given her when she started school.

"What did you forget to tell me?" Gina asked, hoping her tone didn't sound as overwhelmed as she felt. The last time Antonia forgot to tell her something, she ended up speeding through traffic in three counties at peak hour to pick up the girl's father up from LAX.

Antonia unrolled a sheave of papers. "It says here that James Dean's Porsche, The Little Bastard, got stripped down after he died in it, and everyone who got a part died in a car crash."

Gina made a lane change, concentrating on the road. "And this is relevant to ..."

"Lionel. Maddie used some pieces from that old car in the garage, right? And he got in a crash."

Gina glanced at her briefly and tightened her grip on the wheel. Antonia's eyes were wide with concern.

Gina shook her head. "That old car in the garage is a Corvette, my dear, not a Porsche. All that is just Hollywood myth, designed to get you to go out and watch all the old James Dean movies."

Antonia sighed and fiddled with the ragged fringe of her denim shorts. "I did. You know, I think Nick looks just like him."

"Who? James Dean?"

"Yawh." She sent Gina an incredulous frown. "Even Maddie thinks so. But, don't change the subject."

She seemed more upset than the situation warranted. Gina had learned to let the girl have her funks. She'd been through a lot, losing her mother and all.

Her frown deepened. "You have the steering wheel from it," she said, her voice quavering.

Gina reached across the console and patted the girl's arm. "Lionel's death was a shock, and I'll miss him forever," she said, feeling the now familiar sting at the back of her throat. "It was a terrible accident, honey. That's all."

Antonia squeezed her eyes shut and looked away, reminding Gina she was still a child. She remained quiet, aloof, until they turned into the driveway of the exclusive bridal shop where their dresses, and hopefully happier thoughts, awaited.

♉

Gina traced her fingertips over the pearl beaded bodice of a silk wedding dress the color of pale champagne. The tiny gems warmed quickly to her touch. If she could choose a wedding dress today, this would be the one.

It was silly. She was too old to go all *gaga* about a wedding dress. What would be the point, anyway? If Luke ever got around to asking her to marry him, she would drag him straight to the county courthouse before he changed his mind. He'd be in his dove gray lawyer pants and she'd be wearing scrubs.

She let the dress slip back into place among the others on the rack.

Someone touched her shoulder, making her jump.

"You should try it on," Antonia said, her enthusiasm restored. She pulled the dress out again. "That one would look awesome on your curves."

Gina shook her head. How the girl knew so much about wedding dresses, she hadn't a clue. "Today is about Maddie, honey. Not me."

"I can hear you out there, you know," Maddie crooned from inside the bride's dressing room. She opened the door and stepped out in front of a three-way mirror, her cheeks radiant under the soft lighting. Her off the shoulder mermaid dress was slightly big on her and she held the bodice up with her arm. They had all agreed to fit Maddie's dress to show off her lovely baby bump rather than hide it. The result was stunning.

"Antonia is right. You should try it on if you love it. I don't think Santa Barbara's Most Eligible Bachelor can hold out much longer."

Gina harrumphed out a laugh. "Maid of honor at your wedding is the closest I'm going to get."

Maddie grinned at her in the mirror. The seamstress helped her up onto a rotating platform and began pinning the back of her gown, adjusting the size to fit her still slender backside, but leave room to accommodate her expanding rib cage and baby bump. "That strapless plunging bodice would look incredible on you. You have the boobs for it."

A sleek-haired woman in a fitted business suit appeared behind Gina. "No harm trying," she said in a faint Russian accent.

Antonia leapt up from a pleated satin stool and clapped her hands. "Yeah. Come on Gina," she pleaded, jumping up and down. Gina had to laugh at the spectacle. It was a welcome respite from the gloomy atmosphere she'd lived in for the past few weeks.

She shook her head no, but the sales woman pulled her up by her hands and twisted her this way and that. "Let's see, what are you? A four? Six maybe, with those breasts. We can adjust, no?"

"No, I ... I really don't ..."

The woman raised a sculptured brow. "You never know what life brings, eh?" She was good at her job. Gina peeked at the price tag. She had to be. Not outrageous considering what it was, but definitely out of her price range.

Antonio gave Gina a mischievous grin. Oh no. "Do it, *Titi* Gina," she called, playing up her Spanish accent. "We have time, right? Nothing else to do?"

Aunt Gina. The endearment caught her off guard. Antonia was laying it on thick. Gina checked her watch.

Antonia's dress was completed and hanging in its plastic bag on the outside of the dressing room door. A modest neckline over a silky cloud of aquamarine fluff that ended inches above her knees. Gina's maid of honor dress was a sexier version, lower cut but equally high in the hemline. Thanks to Taylor Swift and Katy Perry, everyone wanted to look like a rock stars, even at their wedding.

"Oh, all right." What the hell. It couldn't hurt. "A six should work." Maddie was the petite girl, Gina had curves.

She wound her hair into a knot on the top of her head and pinned it there with a pencil she found in the dressing room. She stared into the mirror. The woman who stared back at her wore one of Luke's favorite outfits: a tailored chambray shirt over a pair of white chinos. She could almost feel his hands slipping the shirt off, letting it fall. She shifted her hip in frustration, then straightened at the knock on the dressing room door. A moment later she was stepping into a mountain of champagne-colored tulle, topped with a pearl-studded bodice. Antonia zipped her in; the saleswoman added a couple of clips to bring it to a perfect fit.

Maddie had been right. The strapless bodice, with its plunging neckline caressed her breasts, and set off a glow in her cheeks she didn't know she had. For a moment she imagined herself standing at the altar, her hands gently resting in Luke's, his eyes dipping to that place where her breasts slipped below the line of pearls. Her cheeks heated from bliss to embarrassment.

"Gina, get out here so we can see you," Maddie commanded.

Gina turned her back to the mirror and looked over her shoulder. The teardrop keyhole left her bare almost to her tailbone.

"Go out to big mirrors," the woman added, turning her around. "That is your dress, my dear. No doubt."

Gina strode out to the main salon, drawing looks from other patrons in the shop. She turned before the angled mirrors, bathed in peach-colored light specially designed to flatter the skin.

Maddie was back in her baby bump tunic and leggings.

Gina stepped up on the platform, holding her breath.

"Oh my god!" Antonia gasped. "You look so hot! I mean ... pretty. Really pretty, *Titi.*"

Maddie pursed her lips, and gave Gina an Anna Wintour nod. "Stunning. You should put it on hold."

Gina laughed. "Hold? And just how long do you think the store is willing to hold it? Till after the elections? Or, no. Wait. Maybe when Luke runs for Governor in two years? You think? Besides, it's out of my price range."

"You can put it on layaway," the saleswoman suggested. "Pay a little at a time."

Gina scrutinized her image from every angle, the way she looked at her life. Layaway implied hope.

The crazed woodpecker pounded the inside her skull, slowly at first, just to get her attention, but the more comfortable she got inside the dress, the harder it pecked.

Layaway? She could hear the little bugger now, cackling out his woodpecker laugh.

She twisted an arm behind her and twiddled her fingers, unable to grab hold of the clips, then jammed her hands on her hips, glaring at the trio of women—Maddie, Antonia, and the overzealous saleslady. "Will somebody please get this thing off me?"

<h1 style="text-align:center">Chapter 18</h1>

The trip back to Montecito was quiet. Antonia's dress was tucked carefully into the Corvette's tiny trunk. Instead of beaming with excitement, the youngster frowned and stared into the traffic ahead, her ears tightly sealed off from the outside world by a pair of skull-shaped earbuds.

It was just as well. Gina didn't feel like talking. She had come so close to giving in and putting that dress on layaway ...

"Gina!" Antonia shouted. Gina jammed on the brakes, dipping the nose of the car to avoid a collision.

The young girl glared at her, earbuds dangling around her neck. "Maybe you should let me drive if you're going to go off into Never Never Land."

Gina huffed out a sigh. The girl was right. She *had* been daydreaming.

"You were thinking about Luke," she accused. "Why are you mad at him? I think he's nice."

"I'm not mad at him. And he is nice."

"But he says he can't come over any more."

"He says?" Since when did an adult male discuss his love life with a fifteen-year-old? "And when did he bestow this information on you, young lady?"

"Yesterday."

"He told you we had a fight?" She still couldn't believe it.

Antonia sucked in her bottom lip. Gina pretended not to notice.

"Well, he didn't exactly tell me."

"Tell you what?"

"Things. He and Nick were talking and …"

"You eavesdropped," Gina guessed, with some relief.

Antonia clucked her tongue. "I didn't mean to, it just happened, and it wasn't really about you, it was just …" Her expression dissolved from petulant to apologetic. She turned her face to the window and wiped at her cheek. "I shouldn't have said anything," she whispered.

The traffic moved and Gina eased forward. "Antonia Guadalupe Salazar, what's going on?"

"I thought we agreed on Toni?"

"Tell me what you heard and I'll think about it."

"Now you're trying to bribe me."

"Toni," Gina relented, running out of patience. They needed to talk before she took the girl home and she knew right where to go to do it. She cranked up the radio to cut off any further conversation, passed their usual exit and took Padaro Lane instead.

She punched in the code at the McAllister entrance and waited while the gate rolled open.

Toni craned her neck to look around. "What are we doing?"

"I want you to meet a friend of mine."

Gina circled the driveway and stopped the car near the kitchen entrance, then wagged her finger when the girl reflexively grabbed her cell phone and ear plugs. "You won't be needing those."

"But what if Kristen calls me? She's going to have a slumber party and …"

"She can leave a message. Come on."

Angela greeted them at the kitchen door, her dark, glossy hair swept back in a tight bun, a heavy notebook on her hip.

Angela asked, "Is ... there a problem?"

Gina smiled and gave her a reassuring squeeze of the hand. "No. Of course not. I just wanted to stop by and say hello to Mason. How is he?"

Angie's expression relaxed. "He had a good morning; his vitals are good considering all that's happened. He's napping right now."

"Good to know." Better than sitting in a jail cell. "Everything else all right?" Gina was thinking about the open gate on the morning Ina died. She hadn't wanted to alarm Angie, but she couldn't get the image out of her mind. Unlike the Berlin property, which was on the east side of the freeway and surrounded by fencing, Mason's Padaro Lane estate bordered the shoreline. It wouldn't be easy access, but if someone was determined, they could get to the house.

"Sure. Fine," Angie said, putting down her notebook. Her eyes went to Antonia."

"This is ..." She cut her eyes to Antonia a moment. "Toni. The young lady whose dad works for the Berlins."

Angela extended her hand. "Toni, I've heard a lot about you."

Toni beamed at Gina before she took Angela's hand. "This place is cool. Is it all right if I go outside?"

Gina nodded. That was exactly why she'd come. She gestured for Toni to precede them through the French doors.

"We had the final fitting on our wedding dresses. Miss Toni will make a pretty bridesmaid."

"And what about you?"

"Me? Oh ..." Gina had confided in Angie so she knew how hard it was to be involved in this wedding. "It will be over soon, thankfully. Things will get back to normal."

Toni found the wisteria-covered arbor that framed an impressive view of the Pacific, swung inside, and sat.

"I really brought her here for a break. Something's bothering her and this place has a way of calming a person down. I thought we'd just hang out awhile. Maybe she'll open up."

Angie glanced out to the view. "I know what you mean. I'll leave you to it." She gathered her books and her iPad from the patio table. "I was about to make a snack for when Mr. McAllister wakes up, and then it's back to studying."

"Thanks, Ange. You're the best."

"It's pretty here," Toni said. She hooked her fingers through a tangle of vines on the arbor where green leaves were just beginning to fill in around the riot of purple blooms. "Not like the ranch. I mean, it's pretty there too, but this is right on the beach and all."

Gina sat next to her on the bench and studied the girl's profile. Toni was the typical teen, easily excited, easily bruised. Gina thought of herself when she was not much older than Toni. Her mother had been diagnosed with stage IV cervical cancer. A death sentence. It hadn't been easy facing that truth as a teen. Harder still to lose her mother while she was in medical school. Toni had led a Cinderella life since coming to live with her father. Prior to that, he'd worked on a ranch in New Mexico until she lost her own mother. Something they had in common. Maybe that's why Gina took such a personal interest in her.

"You miss your mom," she said on a hunch.

Toni turned, her expression all denial at first. Then her shoulders slumped. "She would have loved to see me be a bridesmaid. She didn't get to see my *Quinceañera* either."

The *Quinceañera* was a traditional Mexican celebration of a young girl turning fifteen.

"You've had to grow up pretty fast, losing your mom so young."

Toni drew in a ragged breath. "It's okay," she said, and huffed it out heavily.

Gina, of all people, knew better. She circled the girl's shoulders with an arm, pulled her in close. "It's not okay, and you have a right to feel sad about it sometimes."

Toni leaned her head on Gina's shoulder. "I don't want to feel sad. I want to forget about it. Not her, you know. But the sadness of losing her."

"I still miss my mother. It's been five years. I think of her almost every day. But I know she wouldn't want me to mope around and be sad. She was a happy person, despite what life dealt her."

"Mama was sad. I know she loved us, but there was always something missing, something she never shared. She was sad, and sad, and sad, and then one day, she was just …" she raised her shoulders in a shrug, "… gone."

Toni straightened, regaining her composure. Her wide brown gaze drifted out to sea. "My dad lights candles under her picture every night, like she's dead. But I never saw her dead. He never took my sister and me to see her."

Gone. Gina understood using the word gone instead of dead. She had used it with her mother. She used it now with Lionel. And Ina. Too many people she loved. Gone.

"Sometimes adults don't tell the whole story. It's too painful."

Toni sniffed. "Like I said, I just want to forget about it, but he's got that shrine lit up every night." Some of her earlier feistiness resurfaced. "He tells her he's coming to be with her soon. In heaven. Does that mean he's going to die too?"

"Oh, honey. It only means he wants it to be true. That someday they'll be together again. That he loves her and isn't thinking of anyone else."

Toni turned suddenly, her dark eyes searching Gina's. "Do you miss Lionel?"

"Of course I do. But—I know it sounds silly—sometimes it feels like he never left. Like he's sitting right here." She patted the top of her shoulder. "Yap, yap, yap," she puppeted with her hand. "He tells me what to do. You know, things he always used to say. It feels like he's still saying them."

Toni glanced away again and rolled her lips in as if she were holding back a flood.

Gina pulled her arm from behind the girl's shoulder, gave her some space on the bench. "You want to tell me what's really bothering you?"

Toni squeezed her eyes shut. "No. Not really. Luke told me not to say anything until he ..."

Gina's mouth dropped open.

When Toni saw her shocked expression, she pressed her fingers tight into her eye sockets, wiped at welling tears. Then she shot out of her seat, fisting her hands beside her head. "Darn it, I can't keep it inside anymore. And it's not right. Lionel was your friend."

"I'm listening," Gina said, the hair standing up on her forearms. It was all she could do not to get up and shake the girl. If Luke were here she would shake him for putting her in this position.

Toni's eyes welled again. "Lionel's happy now, I think."

Gina stared at her, her heart beat pounding. "Because ..."

"Because Roland is with him."

Chapter 19

"Toni, what on earth are you saying?" Toni's expression added to the fear building in Gina's chest.

She swiped at her eyes and went on. "They didn't mean for me to know. It just—" She shrugged. Her gaze slid away from Gina's as though searching for a better place to start. Gina allowed her the time to pull herself together.

"They took me surfing. Nick and his boys, and Luke showed up. He's never come before but he was down there, yesterday, in his gray suit. The guys made a joke about it being a funny wet suit. Nick had a worried look on his face and told us to keep ... getting ... ready and he climbed back up the rocks to talk to Luke." She pushed out the words in spurts.

Gina bit her lip.

"I started to get my board ready, but then I realized I left my wax in the van, so I climbed up and I heard ..." She choked back tears, pacing the ground in front of the arbor. "I heard Luke say 'Roland' and 'off the cliff' and I slipped and they saw me and ..." She covered her mouth, wrapped an arm around her middle, bent over and sobbed.

Gina could hardly breathe. "Roland is with Lionel? You mean, he's ... gone?"

Toni nodded, her face pinched tight. She sank onto the seat next to Gina, leaned into her.

"Luke told me not to tell you or Maddie."

"But why?" That was a cruel thing to load onto a child, even if she was fifteen.

"He said, you would be upset. That you two weren't seeing much of each other and he needed to find the right time to tell you."

Gina rubbed her temples. Typical Luke. There was never a right time for anything and so everything was put off. She was going to let him have it. But right now, she had to impress an important lesson on Toni. One her mother hadn't had the time or the foresight to teach her. She pushed down the shock of hearing about Roland and straightened her shoulders.

"Listen, Toni. We need to get something straight."

Toni wiped her face on her sleeve then gave Gina her full attention; a small sign of relief was visible in her deep brown eyes.

Gina sniffed back tears, cleared her throat. "Luke and Nick are good men. So is your father. We're lucky to have them in our lives." *Someday you'll know how lucky.* "When they hold back the truth, or tell little white lies, they believe it's for our own good. To protect us. To keep us from feeling sad. It's not their fault, it's just the way they're wired."

Toni frowned, nodded.

"But we women?" Gina said, lifting her chin for emphasis. "We need to stick together. A man tells you not to tell your mother, your aunt, your sister, your friend? That's your first clue he's holding back something important. Something that would likely get him—or someone else—in trouble." Or in Luke's case, something to make him accountable. "That's your cue to come and talk to me or Maddie, or even Angie. Women who've got your back. No matter what. Do you understand?"

Toni stared at her with widening eyes. She swallowed. "*Sí.* Yes. Of course," she said, then looked away. "*Pero.* But—"

Gina touched her knee to bring her attention back. "But what?"

Toni laced her fingers tightly in her lap. "Luke said he wasn't allowed to come to your house at night anymore. Did you guys break up?"

If Gina's jaw dropped any lower, it would be sitting in her lap. She snapped it shut with an audible click. Damn him.

"Honey, you shouldn't be worrying about that stuff."

"But he loves you. I know it."

"Sometimes a woman has to stand her ground, Toni. Hold out for what's best for her," she said, defensively. "Now I want you to promise me, short of giving away a birthday surprise or some silly thing like that—and I'm sure you're smart enough to know the difference—you need to see yourself as aligned with the women of this family."

Toni wiped her eyes with the backs of her hands, avoiding Gina's gaze. Gina said "What? There's more?"

"I'm sorry, Geen. I just—I ... scared is all."

Gina grabbed her shoulders, turned her to face her then lifted her chin with two fingers. "Toni, look at me."

Brown eyes, red brimmed and sober, wandered their way to Gina's. "I'm fine, see? Your told me about Roland and I didn't fall apart, didn't explode, didn't dissolve into a puddle on the ground. Right?" That would come later.

Toni nodded. "Right."

"I'm sick about it," Gina went on. "If it's true, it's a terrible thing, and we'll all be touched by it in a very sad way, but there's nothing to be afraid of now."

Toni frowned at her, pulling back. "I'm not afraid for me, I'm afraid for *you.*"

"Me?"

Toni straightened. "Roland had a piece of that car, too. Some chrome stuff." Gina shook her head in denial, but Toni went on, "... and now *you* have the steering wheel."

Kat Drennan

Chapter 20

Luke popped a pod into his office coffeemaker and paced the floor while the machine gurgled out his third cup of Kona Blend. He stopped and gazed out the window, hands on hips. Somewhere out there Gina was with the rest of her girls getting fitted for Maddie's wedding party dresses. It was hard not to resent his brother at the moment. The guy was living in Nirvana while unknowingly creating the opposite for Luke. If Maddie wasn't so darned cute with her baby bulge and happy smile busting out everywhere she went, Gina would probably be perfectly happy to let him cuddle up next to her without any strings attached. But that wasn't fair, and he knew it. Knew it right down to his bones.

The machine stopped gurgling and he pulled out the steaming cup, savoring the rich aroma before taking the first sip. It was a small pleasure in what was surely to be another day in exile.

He sat in his chair and propped his feet up on his desk, something he did only on Sunday and only if he was there by himself. A week ago he would have gone to the pool and thrashed out his frustration. This week was another story. His mental equilibrium was off, something that disturbed him beyond the possibility of any physical release.

Maybe Gina had it right. Things didn't add up the way he wanted. Maybe he should open his mind a little and look at how they did add up instead.

Roland's accident, for one thing, had set his brain spinning out possibilities he wasn't willing to accept. The two men's deaths in such close proximity both in time and place *could* be incredibly grotesque and painful coincidence, but Luke hadn't worked his way up through the law enforcement community believing coincidence. Accepting the premise that these two accidents were not accidents at all wedged someone he loved— the only one who really mattered—right in the middle of it.

Ignoring the possibility, even if it was farfetched, wasn't going to keep her safe.

He sipped his coffee and rubbed the bit of stubble on his unshaven chin. The same was true about what had happened at the McAllisters. What if Mason didn't off his wife? What if Gina was on to something about that gate being open when she arrived? Luke puffed his cheeks, then released a slow breath. He was screwed either way on that one. If he was right, he'd send her aging client to jail, something she'd fight against tooth and nail, in court if she had to, and his personal relationship with her would be in the crapper. Forever. If she was right, it put her squarely in the middle of a nasty, unsolved crime.

He pulled his legs down off the desk, and checked his watch. It was ten forty-five. He put in a call to Estevez, knowing he wouldn't answer. Estevez would call back at eleven, or one minute after the time it took to drop his mother off after attending mass with her at Our Lady of Sorrows church with a kiss on the forehead and a promise to come back for dinner later.

He sat back and waited, fingers stapled over his chest. He had to admire his lieutenant for the way he took care of his mother since his father had died. Wished he had the willpower to say no to the job when it counted.

Not that he wouldn't have preferred to take the day off today, even without the expectation of being with Gina. He was that tired. He hadn't had a moment's sleep since news of Roland's accident reached him. He'd driven straight to the scene, his heart in his throat. He simply could not unsee that silver Corvette wedged between a pair of eucalyptus trees halfway down the embankment, its tail lights eerily lit through wisps of fog. He couldn't banish the persistent fear it was Gina's body they'd find. Of course, the fear was irrational. Gina's Corvette was red, for one thing, and he knew she'd been home when the accident happened because he'd driven by her house and seen her bedroom light on the way he had every night since he'd scooped his belongings off her front porch.

Roland's Corvette had sailed off highway 150 somewhere around midnight, Friday, pitching its driver a hundred feet beyond the wreckage into the boulder-strewn ravine where he was pronounced dead at the scene. He wondered if Roland had any second thoughts in those last micro moments of his life. The thought made him shiver, despite the hot coffee mug he gripped in his hands.

The phone jangled on the desk. He checked his watch. Eleven oh one. Estevez. Right on time.

He picked up the receiver on the third ring. "How was the mass, Lieutenant?"

Luke could hear the gears of Estevez's Porsche grinding down, probably coming off Foothill Road away from his mother's home. "We both know you didn't leave an urgent message on my phone to find out about mass."

Luke let out a tight laugh. If there could be anyone more serious about serving the citizens of Santa Barbara County than himself, it was Lieutenant Xavier Estevez. "No. I've got a job for you. Well, you, or someone I know you can find to do the job."

"I'm all ears," Estevez said, the sound of his engine winding out.

"I hope you're going hands free, Lieutenant."

"You know me. Safety first, counselor."

"Doesn't sound like it. I don't relish the idea of scraping another body off the side of a mountain anytime soon. Especially the body of a friend."

He heard the motor wind out and then shut down. Estevez let out a breath. "Duly noted. *Que paso*, boss?"

"I want you to contact the wrecking company and have both Lionel's and Roland's vehicles taken in to the police evidence yard before some overzealous parts dealer has his way with them." He sipped his coffee, waiting for his lieutenant to question his motive. When none was forthcoming, he went on. "I want them gone over with that fine-tooth comb you guys brag about. Steering, brake systems. Anything that could have been tampered with."

Estevez grunted. "I was wondering when you were going to put that together."

"Yeah?"

"Yeah. Seemed a bit too much for me, too. Those two accidentally wrecking their favorite pieces of machinery? Not likely. I heard Lionel kept his Vette under a velvet blanket in the garage. I didn't say anything because—Gina."

"Um. Speaking of. Where are we on the lab work on the McAllister case?"

"Still in the doghouse, Lawyerpants?"

If it had been anyone else, save his brother maybe, Luke would have come unhinged. Because it was Estevez, he kept his head.

"I hear you're up for a review in a few weeks. Is that right?"

Luke pictured Estevez's eye roll. "Backlog's pretty deep," he said, all sarcasm gone. "I pushed their buttons already and they pushed back. Seems we have a few months' worth of mayhem they think might be more important than the death of an old lady in her bed, but I'll check on it first thing in the morning."

"You might mention that the acting DA would be grateful."

Luke tabled his coffee and frowned, his gaze sliding back to the window. There wasn't one more productive thing he could think of to do to justify being here, short of gleaning through the cold case files and he was damn well not going to go there. He wondered what Gina was doing right then, nixed the idea of breaking the rules and calling her just to hear her voice.

His gaze fell on the Sunday paper. A set of diamond studded earrings sparkled from the top page of the slick advertisement section that wrapped the otherwise anemic weekend newspaper.

Gina's words echoed in his ears. "If you were serious, you'd have been here with a dozen roses and a little velvet box."

She was right. And he was serious. This time, if he didn't get it right, he had the clear sense there would be no going back.

He shoved his keys and wallet in his pants and shot his arms through his jacket sleeves. Why hadn't he thought of it sooner? Today was the perfect day to get the job done.

He plucked his cell phone out of its charger and nearly dropped it when it went off in his hand. The ringtone was the generic jangle that on a Sunday usually meant he'd been selected for a free four-day vacation in the Florida Keys. *I live in Santa Barbara, for chrissakes*, he's said the last time it happened, and the caller hung up.

But since assuming the role of acting DA when Lila had dropped her news, he'd made it policy to take all calls, even on his private line. One never knew what tragedy might have befallen a person in his district. He certainly didn't want to be that guy who lost a chance to catch a criminal because they sent an important call to voicemail. He swiped the screen to answer the call and stuck the phone to his ear.

"Berlin," he said, trying to sound civil.

"Luke. I hope I'm not interrupting anything," a female purred suggestively.

There was something familiar about the voice, but he couldn't quite place it. "Who is this?"

"It's Fiona, pussycat.

Pussycat?

Fiona Blanchard. The gossip rag queen from hell. Damn. Could his day get any worse? "This is my private number. How did you—"

"Uh uh," she said, like a finger waving in his face. "I never reveal my sources. Which brings me to the topic of discussion."

"What discussion?" He wedged the phone between his ear and shoulder, and loaded his laptop into his briefcase.

"It seems a friend of yours saw my little article and decided to share some interesting information with me. Of course, I always keep things confidential, you know, until I need them. But I was thinking, I wonder how far *Candidate* Luke Berlin would go to keep certain information out of the public eye."

"A friend of mine?" The name Ellis Greer, the prosecutor who ran against Lila in the last election came to mind. Greer was an asshole, but he was too smart for outright blackmail.

He should hang up on her right now and put an end to this nonsense. But there was just enough of an edge in her voice to give him a chill. What the hell was she up to?

"What kind of information?"

"Oh, pussycat, you'll have to meet me in person to get the whole story."

Luke heaved out a sigh. "I was just on my way out to do some shopping." The last person he wanted around when he picked out Gina's ring was Fiona Blanchard. "Call Cal in the morning. I have no idea what my calendar looks like at this point, so he's the man to talk to, not me."

"Cal?"

"You know. The card I gave you? It's Sunday, and I make a habit of not working on Sundays."

"Interesting that you answered your office phone then, isn't it?"

Jesus. "I don't have time for this, Ms. Blanchard, so …"

"My source hinted that a serious crime may have happened on your property."

Luke's hand froze on the briefcase cover. It wasn't the first time he'd wondered what his father had been up to all those years he was there alone. He wouldn't put much past the old buzzard. But this woman was fishing, of course. Desperate to keep her gossip rag afloat.

"I'm sure you are aware there are serious consequences for attempting to bribe an officer of the law."

"Of course I'm aware, darling. I wouldn't think of using that kind of information for any personal gain. But I did get the call, nonetheless, and I'm not a little disturbed about it."

Luke snapped the briefcase closed. No way was he going to let Fiona Blanchard screw up his plans. "So, you want to make an official report?" he asked, calling her bluff.

Silence stretched between them. "No, I just—"

"Like I said. Make an appointment with Cal in the morning."

He ended the call and stormed out the door in a way that would have raised the eyebrows of his coworkers if there had been anyone else in the office.

He stood at the jewelry counter at Macy's, studying three sets of rings without a clue which one to choose. The one with the large sapphire stone in the center was something she'd love, not being a fan of pretense or excess or "big ass" diamonds, but it looked too much like a Princess Diana knockoff. The other was all pretense, something his father might bestow on his bride as a sign of his own wealth. The third was a large but conservative design, a cabochon ruby, flanked by a pair of excellent quality diamonds. He could imagine it on her finger when she brushed them through her hair.

The sales clerk was eyeing her watch. "You could put all of them on hold and then your fiancée could make the final selection herself," she suggested.

Luke considered. No, that wouldn't work. He shoved his hands in his pockets, studying the rings on the black velvet display tray the clerk had carried from case to case as he made his selections.

This was ridiculous. Gina wasn't the kind of person to complain. She would love any ring that he picked.

No. Maybe the clerk was right. Gina would want to pick out her own ring. He should wait.

No. He should have a ring in his pocket the next time he saw her. She could exchange it later if she hated it.

He rubbed the back of his neck. *It's not life or death, here, idiot.* But then again, maybe it was.

"You're not that desperate to get out of our bargain, are you?"

He nearly jumped out of his skin at the sound of the voice behind him. His eyes rolled to the ceiling.

"What? Are you stalking me now?" he asked, turning. What he saw squelched his frustration like throwing sand on a fire.

Fiona sent him a sheepish smile, appearing a lot less sure of herself than the last time he'd seen her. In fact, she didn't look anything like the night she'd tracked him down at Joe's. Her blue-black Michael Jackson hair hung limp and flat against her skull, her lips were missing that glossy red lipstick and the fake eyelashes were gone, too, replaced only by dark black eyeliner that did not flatter her pale grey eyes. She wore a black turtleneck shirt over a skirt that made her fit in with the many not-so-young-anymore women who should have gotten off the Goth train years ago, but chose to haunt State street instead.

"Okay," she said, deflated. "I was waiting outside your office when I called. Followed you here. I really need to talk to you before this thing goes too far."

"What, you're afraid you'll lose your story because I'm no longer an 'eligible' bachelor?"

She crossed her arms over her chest and rolled her bare lips in a moment before she went on. "Oh, there's a story here, but not exactly the one I wanted." She slumped against the counter. The clerk sent her a withering look that made her step away from the glass. "Could we go someplace and talk?" She looked over her shoulder as if she were afraid to be seen with him.

The clerk frowned, tapping acrylic nails on the glass countertop.

Luke shot her an indulgent glance. "Could you please put those on hold for me like we talked about?" He thumbed a business card out of his wallet and tossed it on the velvet palette.

Mistake.

Big one.

But he had to get this Blanchard woman off his case. Now.

The clerk's eyebrows raised when she read the card. "Yes, sir, Mr. Berlin." She lifted the velvet tray like a drive-in waitress and let herself into the refuge behind the counter.

He gripped Fiona by her elbow and steered her to the courtyard outside. "You've got ten minutes. This better be good."

She sat on the Spanish-tiled wall surrounding a large fountain. "I liked the one with the ruby."

"You're eating into your time."

"Okay! Okay." She slumped, let her purse drop to rest between her feet. "The week after my story came out on the newsstands, I get this call. The guy says there was a juicy story for me about District Attorney Luke Berlin. Says he'll make it exclusive."

"Why would he call *you?*"

She glared at him for a moment, indignant, then threw up her hands. "How should I know? It's not like I work for the *LA Times* or *Rolling Stone*, you know?" She dug in her purse. "Do you mind if I smoke?"

Her hands were shaking. Luke shrugged, nodded at a NO SMOKING sign not six feet away, and slipped the cigarette out of her fingers. "It's bad for my health," he said, and sat next to her.

She fixed him with an annoyed look, rummaged a moment longer, finally coming up with a battered pack of gum.

"Want one?" The half-wrapped stick she offered looked like it had been dug up from an Egyptian tomb.

"No, thanks." He shook his head and waited while she unwrapped the gum and popped it into her mouth. "What did you tell him?"

"What? Oh. I told him just what I told you. I'm not that kind of journalist, right? And then I just hung up. I'm busy, you know? We're covering that charity Speedo contest and I'm helping the church set up the advertising for it."

Luke rolled his eyes. He was hoping the Speedo contest was something she'd just made up. Apparently it wasn't. All the more reason to get a ring on Gina's finger.

"So." She swallowed and took a deep breath. "A couple of days later he calls back. Tells me it's about a body. Says there's money in it for me if I print the story. Wants me to meet him in person." She scooped her purse into her lap and held it close like a kid with a teddy bear on a stormy night. She started rocking, sent him the fish eye. "I could use the money," she said. "My gig at *The Bomb* is only part time, and I get paid for the advertising, not the story."

Luke nodded. She was right about that. This whole thing smacked of a gossip rag tango and he wasn't going to let her drag him out on that dance floor again. "So what do you want from me?"

She hugged her purse tighter, her shoulders bony and sharp under the thin fabric of her shirt. He wondered briefly what she did when she wasn't stringing for *The Bomb*. Decided he didn't want to know.

"I don't want anything. Really. I'm just—" she glanced over her shoulder toward the steps leading to the underground parking garage. "I'm scared. If there's a body out there, then somebody killed somebody and I don't want the next somebody to be me."

Luke checked his watch. He was due to help Nick with a building project at the Compound. "Tell me why this person would come after you?"

"'Cause I didn't do what he said." Her voice was growing shrill. She rubbed at both temples now, her hands shaking. "I'm really scared, Mr. Berlin. I know I came on strong the other day. Chalk it up to being a hack, just like you said. But this is real. I can feel it. Is there a body on your property?"

Luke laughed. "My family has lived on that property for more than forty years. There's nothing more sinister there than a bunch of rusty old cars and an orchard. And my sister-in-law-to-be has a dog with a nose like a bloodhound. If there was a dead body out there somewhere, we'd all know about it. I think someone is pulling your leg."

Fiona hunched and sent him a worried look. "I don't know," she said in a miserable whine.

"What about a pissed off client? Someone you rubbed the wrong way?"

She lifted a shoulder. "It happens. But no one has ever come after me like that."

Luke raised a brow, and stood, straightening his pants. Considering his personal experience with her, he wasn't so sure about that. "I think you need to relax. Take a step back. You don't know who he is. He doesn't know where you live."

"Cha! Anybody can find out where a person lives. Last night? I thought I heard someone creeping around on my balcony."

"Did you see someone? A car? Anything?"

She shook her head. "No, but, uh ..." her desperation was turning to panic.

He felt sorry for her now. A slightly overripe woman trying to scratch out a living in what was one of the most expensive towns in the Western Hemisphere.

"Okay. I'm listening. But I need something I can work with. A name. A vehicle. A description. You sure you don't have any idea who this is? You're not trying to protect a source?"

"No. This guy is for real. You should hear his voice. It's too creepy. Can't you assign me police protection or something?"

"I think you've been watching too much crime TV. No crime's been committed, so far, there's nothing to be protected from." Unless it was Luke, who'd had about enough of this nonsense and was thinking about throttling her himself. His cell phone jangled. He pulled it out.

The text was from Nick:

Where are you?

Dammit, if it wasn't one thing it was another.

I'll be there in twenty minutes.

So much for not letting Fiona Blanchard pull him off track. He shoved the phone into his pocket.

"Do you have a friend or someone you can spend a few nights with so you won't be alone?"

"No, uh, well, yeah. I suppose I can—"

"Okay then. Let me know if you get any more calls. Try to talk to the guy, play along a little. See if you can get any more of the story. Something for us to go on."

Fiona stood slowly, hung her bag over her arm. "That's it? Go stay with a friend?"

"That and keep up the good work," he said giving her a sound pat on her bony back. "I'm proud of you for not printing a story without any proof."

Chapter 21

Riding on a tide of anger and a full head of steam, Gina's momentum carried her across the parking lot to Luke's offices. She should have confronted him yesterday afternoon when she'd dropped Toni off at the compound. His SUV had been there in the turnabout, but she had talked herself out of it. It was Sunday night. He'd be home and he'd call her.

But he hadn't. And banished or no, that simply wasn't acceptable.

She blew past his assistant's protest and through his office door, ending with both hands splayed flat on his desk. "When were you planning on telling me about Roland?"

Luke blinked at her a moment, then got up and shut his office door, and leaned against it. "When did you find out?"

She folded her arms over her chest, willing her heartbeat to slow from full-speed fury to righteously pissed off. How could he stand there and look so calm?

"Yesterday, from a devastated fifteen-year-old torn up because you dumped it on her then told her not to tell."

"That's not exactly the way it happened," he said, his voice infuriatingly calm. He was holding something back and he wasn't getting away with it. Not this time.

He pushed away from the door and went to his credenza. She followed him with her eyes, holding her position. He picked a coffee pod out a basket and inserted it into the machine, the sight of which made her bristle. She'd given the coffee maker to him for his new private office when he was promoted from investigator to Assistant Prosecutor. It had been a celebration of his promotion, after which, he promised, he would have more time for her.

Not.

She'd been determined to take a step back from him, let herself cool off. Vent alone until she could behave like a reasonable person. But putting it off had only made it worse. Endless circles of frustration, fear, and dread had trudged through her mind in heavy boots, keeping her awake most of the night. Now she could barely hold her anger at bay.

"You should sit down." He gestured to the leather sofa against the wall.

"I'm fine!"

He fixed her with his gaze, his slash eyebrows bunched into an uncharacteristic frown. "Could have fooled me."

He tabled his cup, shoved his hands deep into his pockets, and leaned his tall, swimmer's frame against the credenza.

Her arms prickled with remnants of adrenaline left over from her power walk across the parking lot. "You tell a young girl about a terrible accident, tell her not to tell me, and expect me to make small talk with you?"

He crossed his legs near the ankles and braced his hands next to his hips. "It's not what you think."

His voice was low, wary.

"You are lucky you can't read my mind right now." She didn't try to hide the reprimand in her tone, although it was she who was the lucky one, because besides thinking she'd like to wring his neck, she couldn't banish the thought of hooking her arms around that same neck and—

"Just ... sit down," he said, his voice smooth as caramel. "Please."

"I said, I'm fine."

"Look. She called my cell last night. Worried about you. She tried to get me to go to your house. Patch things up."

Realization dawned. "Wait, *she* called *you?*"

"Apparently my brother thought it necessary to get her a cell phone since all of her girlfriends have them."

Now Gina dropped onto the sofa, her gaze cutting to the window. "She left that part out."

Luke moved closer, sat on the edge of his desk. "Welcome to Teenage land."

Gina wrapped her arms around her middle. They were only a few feet from one another and she felt a million miles away.

She sank deeper into the sofa as she relayed Toni's story. Luke listened with pursed lips.

"Well, part of the story's true, anyway. She did overhear about," he glanced away a moment, "about Roland." He let the name trail out on an exhale.

Gina's adrenaline rush had slowed, replaced by sudden fatigue. She closed her eyes, breathed in deep. "The coffee smells really good." As did the familiar smell of Luke's spicy aftershave.

He rose and went to the machine, slipped a blood red mug under the spigot, and hit the button. His attorney gaze swept down her body, a regretful smile quirked the corner of his mouth as the machine gurgled and steamed.

"She doesn't understand the complexities of adult relationships," Gina said.

"Neither do I, apparently. I told her that you and I were okay, just needed some time to sort things out. More than I probably should have said, but I didn't want to shut her down. It wasn't like I was sharing our intimate secrets. She was truly concerned about you. About us."

"Well I'm concerned about us, too."

Luke sent her a sheepish frown. "Bill and Melinda Gates dated for seven years before they—"

"Really? You are comparing yourself to Bill Gates now?"

He smiled. "Sorry, I was trying to lighten the mood."

The coffee stopped gurgling. He handed Gina the mug, his fingers brushing hers as he let it go.

She gripped the cup with both hands.

"I value my time, as well, Luke. And I didn't come here to make jokes."

She pushed some of her frustration out on a shaky exhale. Sipped the coffee. It helped to soothe the stinging ache at the back of her throat. She sipped again.

"I'm a simple guy. You know that. The timing is off, and having that marriage license doesn't matter to me. I already have everything I want."

Exactly why she banished him from her bed. His words swirled in her head. He had a way of making it all seem logical.

She squeezed her eyes shut. "I don't want to rehash your excuses."

"Then what do you want from me, Gina? To let you go? I can't do that. I don't want to do that."

She stared at him a long moment, wishing she could just let it go. She was that tired of resisting. Tired of the fight. "I want you to tell me about Roland."

Luke blew out a breath. His shoulders relaxed. He moved to the arm of the sofa and sat, his gaze growing darker, visibly slipping into his cop mode.

"His car went off the road on the 154, night before last. He was thrown out. Died instantly."

"Oh." Gina clamped her hand over her mouth, set her mug down on the low table in front of her. "My God."

Luke leveled his gaze at her. "The same spot where Lionel went off."

Gina searched his eyes, shaking her head, until the significance sunk in. "That just doesn't make any sense."

Luke lifted a shoulder. "I should have called you, I know. It was just so soon after Ina, I—"

Gina's lips were suddenly cold. She was lumping it all together. It wasn't fair to blame Luke or Toni. It was just a shock all around. "I didn't know Roland that well. I only met him because Lionel ..." She sucked in a ragged breath; her throat closed and she couldn't finish. "Lionel ..." she tried again, but tears flooded her eyes and spilled down her cheeks. She buried her face in her hands and let go, sobbing for all of them.

Luke tabled his cup, slipped down and sat beside her, circled her shoulder with an arm and pulled her close. "I know, Gina. I'm so sorry."

Oh hell. She leaned unabashedly into his body, accepting the support. She pressed her face into the hardness of his chest and breathed there until the warmth of him spread through her, calmed her. At last she said, "Lionel wasn't just a co-worker. We went through nursing school together, graduated together. At one time, starting out—you remember—we even lived together for a while."

He stroked down the back of her head, a comforting, familiar pressure that made her ache with longing.

"There was no evidence of any other cars at the site. He went off without so much as a skid mark." With her ear pressed hard against his chest, the sound of his voice rolled deep and strong, and resonant.

"But they're safe drivers. I rode with them."

"Safe, maybe. But maybe he didn't care."

"Why would you say that?"

Luke pulled away enough to look into her eyes. "His mother said he was inconsolable after Lionel's death."

"You think it was ... you think he did it on purpose?"

"It's a possibility."

"Makes more sense than Toni's theory."

"Toni?"

"Antonia. It's a long story."

"Toni has a theory," he prompted.

"He was in the '53?"

"Yes. Why?"

She shuddered. It was ridiculous. Crazy. But now she couldn't get the idea out of her head. She told him Toni's story about James Dean's Little Bastard. Luke raised his eyebrows and leaned back in thought, his arm still draped across her shoulders. "Hollywood myths abound."

"Yeah. That's what I told her. But you've got to admit, my spinout, Lionel, and now Roland. All from the same car club?"

"I've been in the cop business too long to believe in coincidence, but it is a dangerous road. There's a wreck up there nearly every weekend."

"I suppose it's a bit farfetched. I mean, who could plan a deer jumping in front of me?"

"That would be pretty tricky to pull off."

Gina thought a minute, something nagged at the back of her mind. "But, don't you find it odd that it happened in the '53s?"

"How so?"

"Well, the Cadillac last December, and now all three Corvettes with pieces from that wreck in Maddie's garage."

"I'm not seeing a connection."

"I'm just saying, it's not the first time someone's gone after one of the Berlin vehicles."

"You mean Jimmy Ray. He's behind bars."

"You sure?"

"Last time I checked."

Gina sat up, all her senses on alert. "You checked?"

She hadn't really been serious. She knew Jimmy Ray Monteplier had been arrested at the *Concours d'Elegance* in Monterey the year before. He was never convicted of Maddie's kidnapping because, despite Maddie's story, the other two crooks had confessed and sworn he'd had nothing to do with it. And the diamond he'd stolen from Maddie's Cadillac proved to be worthless, so there wasn't much to hold him on there. He had been convicted of nothing worse than breaking and entering and assault on a police officer when he tried to get away, which was a felony and had put him in jail for a long time.

"Maddie was very upset," Luke went on. "Nick was worried about her. She had a nightmare about someone breaking into the garage at the compound. Couldn't get it out of her mind. Nick asked me to have Estevez check it out. After what she'd been through, I was happy to do it. That's when he had the extra security cameras added to the building."

Gina sighed. She massaged her fingers into her forehead, then extracted herself from his embrace, breathed a couple of beats.

"I'm sorry. I didn't mean to sound accusing. It's just, I can understand with me. That spin was inconsequential and pretty random. But Lionel, then Ina, now Roland. I've never had so many people—friends—go, like, all at once. It's hard not to think there's more to it. Something we're not seeing."

He cocked his head, absently running his fingers over hers. "Ina died in her own bed, Geen."

"I know." She threw a helpless gaze to the ceiling. "I know," she said again, with more conviction. She took solace in his closeness. His willingness to listen. For all her stubborn, selfish demands he had remained her rock. He was driven and stubborn too. And she loved him that way. She ran a hand over the top of his hair, still a bit ragged around the edges.

He pushed into her caress like little one-eyed Peetie. "I'm sorry, too," he said. "I should have told you about Roland as soon as I heard." He scrubbed his fingers across his lips as if rethinking his approach and picked up his coffee cup. "It's crazy around here right now. I was going to stop by last night, but—"

"Never mind. I don't want to hear it." She had asked him not to. It was she, after all who had rung the finish bell on their relationship, not him. A bell she couldn't un-ring. Besides, she had nearly called him, too. She could feel the heat of him against her thigh even now. She needed to change the subject or they'd be making apologies naked on the sofa. She straightened a little, cleared her throat. "So, you don't foresee an investigation or anything?"

He lifted his shoulders. "You mean into Roland's death? Can you give me something other than a Hollywood legend to go on?"

And an elderly lady who was ready to go anyway. "They were safe drivers. They stressed it in their meetings."

"Of course they did in the meetings. But the Krewe of '53 does have a rebel bent. If they bear any resemblance to Dean, that would be it. They do plenty of 'show' rides, wine crawls, and Highway 1 runs. They're not the only car club whose members race over that pass after midnight. Regularly. Roland was cited two years ago for drifting up on that road."

"Drifting?"

"Going through the curve with the car sideways while keeping the throttle floored."

Gina stared an unseeing moment. Crazy skid marks on deserted roads around the county suddenly made sense.

"But Roland went right off the cliff. No skid marks."

Luke sighed, took another sip of his coffee. "You're right. He wouldn't have drifted in the Vette. It's not set up for it."

Gina scrubbed her face with both hands and let go a sigh. "He wanted to be with Lionel," she whispered.

"What?"

She blew out a resolved breath, picked at cat hair on her scrub pants. "Something Toni said."

His hands slid up over her shoulders, gently eased her back into his arms. She was helpless to resist. This was where she belonged. Where she longed to be. The rest was unbearable, and would continue to be without this. She lay in his embrace until their breathing slowed and synced. At last he loosened his grip, gathered her hair near the base of her neck and brought her face close to his. Close enough to feel his breath on her lips. Her hand slid up the length of his tie, circled the silk knot and pulled him closer. The soft wedge of his lower lip begged to be kissed and she obliged, knowing full well that she couldn't stop there, but she did it anyway because she was helpless to do otherwise.

She nipped it gently, and he answered by covering her mouth with his own, a searing, needy kiss that she felt all the way to her toes. She circled his neck and pulled him tighter into her arms. God, how she'd missed him.

The phone went off in her pocket. He drove his tongue deep as if in defiance, his arms tightening around her in a longing embrace; but she pushed gently away, leaving them both breathless.

"I'd ... better get that." She said it with some relief. The last thing they needed was his assistant bursting through the door and finding them entangled on the couch.

Luke reluctantly loosened his grip, but his eyes were still dark with desire.

She puzzled at a phone number she didn't recognize. It had been forwarded from her business account. If Lionel were around she could let it go and it would transfer to his work number. She would need to change that when she got home to her computer.

"Gina McBain," she said cautiously, still a little out of breath. She smoothed her scrub top over her breasts and pulled it straight into place as she listened. Luke watched her like the trained detective he was. The call was from Melanie, the mocha-skinned Secretary of the Krewe of '53. Gina vaguely remembered meeting her at the party the night she got her jacket.

"Hi Melanie. How are you?" She switched the phone to the other hand so she could brush a stray tendril behind her ear.

"I'm doing all right," Melanie said, her voice solemn. "How are you holding up? It must be hard working without Lionel and all. I hope you're not alone."

She flicked a glance at Luke, sent him a weak smile. "I'm ... getting by."

"Good," Melanie went on. "I'm calling all of the Krewe to let them know Roland's parents and Lionel's mom have decided to combine their memorial services. We're organizing a Krewe procession to the graveside service. I'll be calling you soon to confirm the details. You'll join us, won't you?"

A fresh shot of cold spiked through her. She lifted her gaze to Luke. He slid the knot tight on his tie, his eyes thoughtful, brooding.

"Thanks for the heads up, Melanie. I appreciate you organizing it. I'll … let you know."

She ended the call and let her arm drop to her side.

"What is it?"

She sucked air in through her nose, a cry choking off her throat. When she exhaled, she told him about the call.

He sat on the arm of the couch. "So why the hesitation? Sounds like a good way to help both families cope."

Gina pressed her lips hard together, nodded, eyes shut a moment. "No. I mean, yes. I agree. Combining the memorials is best. It's the Krewe drive that bothers me." She stared at her feet. It was silly, but she couldn't push the worry out of her head. "I … don't know if I'll ever drive my car again after all that's happened."

He studied her, leaving a patch of silence the way he did when he had someone on the witness stand. When she didn't respond, he said, "I'll take the day off. Drive you if you want."

Gina studied the deep blue of his eyes, moved by the compassion, the love she saw there. Longing welled up inside her. She bunched her fingers at her mouth. What if Toni's theory had a grain of truth to it? She knew it was irrational, but she couldn't shake off the fear. Was it safe to drive her car? For either of them?

"I'll let you know in the morning. I'm taking the graveyard shift at Mason's tonight." She wished she hadn't traded shifts with Angela. Wished she could trash her ridiculous plan and take him home right now and prove how sorry she was. "I just can't think right now."

"No worries," he said, his eyes betraying his own reluctance to let her go. He gave her one last, longing look, then rose from the sofa, drew her to him by the hand, and kissed her softly on the forehead. "Call me when you decide.

Chapter 22

Luke's thoughts backpedaled as he drove down the Pacific Coast Highway. What he wanted was to haul his pitiful ass to Gina's and show her why they were both being idiots. He gripped the wheel tighter. That would only piss her off and he knew it. But damn, his family compound in Montecito was the last place he wanted to go.

His brother had good reason to shy away from the mansion on the hill, choosing instead to settle in the more intimate Craftsman bungalow nearer the entrance gate. He'd been seven when his mother broke her neck in a fall down the marble staircase in the mansion's gaudy foyer. Authorities concluded it was a tragic accident. Nick knew better. He'd been wide awake that night, hidden under his bed during his parents' terrible fight. He had no idea then what his mother meant when she accused Nick Senior of cheating. Cards? Gambling? Then he'd heard the sickening thud, his father's low laughter. He'd locked the memory deep until the night Luke's mother died. Cancer might have taken her out in the end, but it was Berlin Senior who wore her down, killed her fight. In a way they were no different. They hated the old man, but lacked the strength to run away.

His heart ached every time he walked into that old relic of a house. Not that they hadn't had great times together, growing up. With acres of orchards and chaparral to play on, all the fruit and avocados they could eat, and horses to ride, their father had given them a life of privilege. But it had cost them. Years of their father's verbal abuse took a brutal emotional toll.

Luke's mother had met Berlin Senior at a fundraiser in Montecito. She was the only girl in a family of boys whose parents owned one of the oldest wineries in Santa Inez. Berlin was handsome back in the day, and considered a good catch since he owned a large amount of property, even though he was new money and therefore somewhat of an outsider. "It was his eyes that first drew me in …" his mother had confessed to Luke once when he'd asked her why she married him. "Blue as the deep ocean and just as mysterious, they grabbed you and pulled you in; and your brother, so sweet and charming. Any hesitation I had just melted."

Big mistake, Luke had thought, but saying so would only add insult to her injury.

They married and Luke was born a year later. Her reputation as a philanthropist lent Nicholas a degree of respectability. But it didn't take long for the mystery to wear thin. Berlin had no time for children or women who cared for them. She picked up where Nick's mother had left off, braving her husband's abuse to provide a shelter for the boys.

Nick graduated from Pepperdine University and moved out, on the path to building his own real estate investment firm. Luke left home the day he turned twenty-one, and headed into law enforcement.

His mother died the following year.

After Senior's manic breakdown, it had been Gina who convinced the boys their father belonged in a home. She had been the second caregiver they'd hired to manage the old man, the first having fled after one day with the bastard. Gina managed his rudeness in stride, refusing to put up with his nonsense. Now Nicholas Sr. was locked away in twenty-four-hour care, suffering brain damage from a stroke that left him wheelchair bound; needing assistance to eat, bathe, and pee.

Luke grit his teeth at the thought. His father's steep decline should have satisfied him, but it didn't. Spousal abuse and family violence were at the top of his *lock-'em-up-and-throw-away-the-key* list for a reason. The asshole belonged in jail.

&

Luke was surprised to see lights on in the mansion when he turned up the drive. He had stayed much longer at the office than he'd planned, and half expected to let himself in by the service entrance at the back of the house. Instead, the oversized front door to the hulking Spanish revival home stood wide open, the soaring crescendo of a U2 anthem exploded into the driveway.

Luke shut down his engine, grabbed his briefcase and shaving kit, and headed for the porch.

He froze in the doorway, lowered the briefcase slowly to the marble floor. Nick stood with his back to him at the bottom of the sweeping stairs, a sledge hammer poised over his shoulder in one hand, and a half empty bottle of tequila in the other.

The anthem faded. Luke said, "Doing some remodeling?"

Nick turned, his gaze hard and feral, tinged with tequila-fed bravado. His features softened when he recognized his brother. "Ah. Luke. Isn't it a little early for you to come out of your lair?" His words formed somewhere between slur and sarcasm.

"I know. Nine o'clock, right? What's gotten into me?" The truth was, he'd been sitting at his desk staring at a stack of depositions since Gina had left, his mind unable to focus on anything but the way she had smelled, the way her lips had yielded to his, the way he'd let her walk out. It was a fuck up. A big one. He should have followed her home, right then and there. Would have, except for the call from his brother.

Nick squinted at him, swayed a little. "Lukey boy," he crooned, levering the sledge on his shoulder. "There's a mattocks for you on the service porch."

"A mattocks?" Luke huffed out a laugh. "I haven't swung a mattocks since Dad made me tear down the fort you built in the orchard."

"You should have told on me."

Luke shrugged. "He'd a done more to you than make you knock it down."

Nick's grip tightened on the sledge. "Fuck him."

"Yeah. But I'm not sure the ladies would appreciate us tearing up these stairs right now." Luke had made a good call coming here instead of going after Gina. If he didn't turn this thing around, both their asses would be in a sling.

He chanced a step forward. "Aren't Maddie's people supposed to use the upstairs during their stay?"

Nick stared at him as if he were trying to remember who he was. He swayed a moment, took a faltering step, then lifted his head and surveyed the marble stairway. He threw his head back and let out a frustrated growl as if someone had punched him in the gut.

"Yeah," he said, on a defeated sigh, and lowered the sledge, but his fingers still white knuckled the handle. "What are you doing here, anyway?"

"Uh, you ... called me? About an hour ago? Said you needed some help getting things ready for the wedding." It had been a call for help. He saw that now. *Don't let me do this.*

Luke understood the feeling. Nick blamed himself for his mother's death, the way Luke blamed himself for not being there when his own mother got sick. The last time they'd been together in this room, Nicholas Senior had his final meltdown.

Since then, Nick's world had come full circle. He was going to be a father. Luke was in awe of his excitement about that event. It was a bit of a disappointment to see him this way now.

The girls had thought sending Nick up to sleep in the mansion the week before the wedding would be romantic.

They'd been living together in the Craftsman for six months. The brief separation would make their coming back together a turning point, like starting new. Or so they reasoned.

Now, Nick stared at the staircase, his hand flexing on the sledge handle. Tension charged the air around him, sharp and cold.

Damn. If Luke couldn't talk him down, he'd have to call Maddie up to the house. He did not want to do that.

"Nick," he said, quiet, but firm.

Nothing.

"Nick," he said again, stepping closer.

At last, Nick's shoulders slumped, his fingers loose on the hammer. "Fuck it."

Luke stepped in and carefully prized the heavy hammer out of his brother's grip.

Nick stared at the tequila bottle in his other hand like he'd forgotten it was there. "Want some?" he asked, lifting as in a toast.

Luke took the bottle, set it on the piano. "How about we save it for your bachelor party?"

Nick sent him a slow blink, then slumped onto the bench. "It just doesn't seem right, you know? That bastard spending his days in a fancy home, being pampered and catered to. Living in the lap of luxury."

Luke scooted in next to his brother, relieved that he had agreed to put the bottle down. "It's not exactly *La Vida Loca*. No tequila, no women. Sometimes I wonder if he's faking it, just to escape from what might eventually put him in jail."

"Still trying to nail his ass, little brother?"

Luke did a quick assessment of Nick's condition. Maybe he'd taken things to the extreme, but was his own obsession any different? Luke may not have tried to take a sledge hammer to the stairs, but hadn't he done nearly the same to his life? Obsessing over every case, like Gina said.

He exhaled long and slow, released some of his own shit. "He's not worth the trouble."

Nick gave him a sleepy stare. Luke answered with a friendly slap on the thigh and got up. "Look, I'm beat. Let's get some sleep. We'll have breakfast down at Esau's in the morning, okay, dude?"

"Not too early, though, right?"

"Right. Not too early."

Nick leaned heavily into Luke as they made their way up the stairs. Luke said, "After the wedding, let's gut this place, rebuild it the way it should be."

"Sounds good to me. As long as I get to take out the stairs."

Another piece of crap stuck in Luke's craw melted away on the thought. "That's the only way it would count, brother." And the only way he'd ever move back to the property for good.

Chapter 23

Gina pulled her car to the side at the McAllisters' entrance to make room for a police unit as it lumbered out through the gate. A uniformed officer she didn't recognize signaled her to stop as the sliding gate closed, preventing her entry. She rolled down her window. "What is it? What's happened?" Her lips prickled with cold.

"Evening, ma'am." He folded his arms over his badged chest. "Just a routine investigation. Can I help you?"

"Help me? I'm Gina McBain. Mason McAllister is my client. I'm relieving the caregiver here."

The officer sent her a stern look, leaned away from his black and white vehicle, and craned his neck to peer into the backseat of her car. Apparently satisfied that she wasn't smuggling in some abomination, he stepped back. "Hold on a minute."

He produced a clipboard from the seat of his car, perused it for what seemed ridiculously long considering that, aside from Angela, the groundskeeper who came once a week, and Lionel, who was dead, she was likely the only other person who visited the place. "Can I see some ID?"

Gina pushed away her annoyance as she dug her wallet out of her purse and showed him her license.

The officer smiled at her and handed her a printed sheet. "We changed the gate code. You can go on in."

She punched in the new code and waited as the ornate wrought iron gate swept away. Apparently, Luke had taken her seriously and ordered police security for the mansion property. A step in the right direction. Her heart squeezed as she progressed up the familiar drive, one that once gave her peace and solace.

Not anymore.

The overcast had surrendered to sundowner winds, bathing the air in a warm yellow light, but she couldn't escape the dark cloud parked over her head. Three people very close to her—people woven into the fabric of her life—had died under curious circumstances in a matter of a few days. Mason had barely uttered a word since. Was it coincidence? Or was there a connection they just couldn't see?

She pushed open the kitchen door. The medical binder she required her caregivers to keep on their patients was open on the kitchen table, but no Angie in sight.

"Angela?"

"I'm in here," Angie called from the sitting room. Gina found her on her cell phone, her fingers trailing the photos on the mantel the way Gina did nearly every time she came into the room.

"I have to go now," Angie whispered into the phone, a warm glow on her cheeks. She ended the call with an apologetic grin. "Sorry. New guy."

Gina laughed softly as she piled her purse and client notebooks on the massive console table behind Mason's oversized sofa.

"No problem. It don't expect you to sit here and stare at Mason's bedroom door while he sleeps."

"I know. And thank you so much," she said, gathering her books and papers in her arms. "I really appreciate you trading shifts with me today, especially after what happened to Roland."

Gina forced down a surge of annoyance. It seemed everyone knew about Roland but her. "How did you hear that?"

Angie's brows went up? "Oh, the guard. At the gate. He told me, that's why they were here. Something about the investigators doing a thorough sweep?"

"Hum."

"It's not a problem, is it? Because I—"

Gina waved her question away. "No. Of course not." It was a good thing. Seeing Luke earlier had nearly destroyed her resolve. One more night away would give her perspective. Something she desperately needed. "I'm happy to be here, in fact."

Angela grinned and let out a breath. "Good. I haven't been on a date in ... gosh, I can't remember when."

"Nursing school has a way of doing that to you." Gina stepped to the mantel. "How's Mason doing, by the way?"

"He's been agitated. Pacing, asking for Ina. Got himself all worked up. I gave him some Ativan. He's sleeping now."

"You noted that in the log, I assume."

"Yes. I'm in here because there was so much activity going on in that back room."

"I'm sorry it upset you. That's probably what upset Mason, now that I think about it."

Angie looped her purse over her arm. "Yeah. They stripped that maid's quarters down to the floor. Hauled out three giant bags of stuff."

Gina's skin prickled on her forearms. "Bags?"

"You know, evidence bags."

"Oh. Yes. Of course." Gina ran her fingers along the mantel where the McAllisters' life was chronicled in pictures, starting with the wedding portrait, then progressing through Christmases, birthdays, graduations. She took down the framed wedding picture like she had done a dozen times before. The happy couple stared out at her in their formal attire. She studied the remaining frames on the mantel. Something was off.

"You say they took all the evidence?"

"Yeah. There's nothing left in that room but the hospice bed and those chintz-covered chairs."

Gina cocked the silver frame at Angela. "But they brought this back in here?"

Angie blew out a breath. "Not that I saw. And I've been sitting in here the whole time. There's virtually nothing left in that room, not even the pillows in the window seat."

A pang of doubt floated in Gina's brain like a dust mote caught in a shaft of light.

Angie sent her a frown, a question in her eyes. "What?"

"Oh, nothing. I just assumed the picture I saw that morning was this one. It was one of the only things that made her smile."

"So …"

"So, judging by the empty space on the mantel, it must have been the picture of Mason's son."

Angie let her purse slip off her shoulder and rest on the table at the back of the sofa. "You mean that handsome hunk in the tight jeans and crew neck sweater? I always thought that kid was his grandson, by the age, you know. And there's no other pictures of him. But then, the clothes would be wrong, right?"

Gina couldn't remember what the young man had been wearing, only that he leaned against the front of a white sports car.

"I always had the feeling I'd seen him before," Angie went on. "His son would be a lot older, don't you think?"

"I suppose." Threads of doubt twisted into a tight knot in Gina's stomach.

"Anyway," Angie went on. "I just assumed he was younger. In fact, in that picture, he reminded me of a friend of my brother's. Older than me, of course. I was just a kid, maybe seven or eight, when they hung out together. I remember him because sometimes when he came over to the house, he'd bring his little sister and a silly game like Pic Up Stix for us to play. I guess he had to babysit her sometimes. She was a late baby, like me."

The knot tightened in Gina's stomach. Mason never, ever, talked about his son. And, there were no other pictures of him on the mantel after the one with the car.

"So, this kid you remember, he'd be, what about forty now?"

"Give or take," Angela said, lifting a shoulder.

"I wonder why there aren't any other pictures of him?"

"Estranged, maybe. You know how families are."

"It just seems odd." Gina's eyes wandered the room. "What's not to love? These kids had the best of everything. Mansion on the ocean. Cars. Horses. Makes you wonder what could have happened to compel a son to stay away and a daughter to move out of the country."

Angie sighed. "Spoiled maybe. My dad struggled to keep his construction business going, my mom worked as a school teacher to take up the slack. We're about as close as it gets and still live on our own. My sister and I see each other every week, and my two brothers live up in Portland now, but they're close with each other. We talk on the phone a lot, and get together at least once in the summer, and then, there's the holidays."

Gina slipped into the leather chair next to the hearth, and tucked her feet under her. So much had happened in the last couple of weeks, she'd almost forgotten what it was like to have a normal conversation. The knot eased in her stomach.

"Nick and Luke turned their backs on their father's money."

"Yes, but wasn't he an asshole?"

Gina smiled. "He was a client, but. Yeah." Asshole was letting him off easy, but Angie didn't need to hear it.

"My mom and I were on our own since she had me. Her parents, devout Catholics, shoved her out the door when she got pregnant. She left and never looked back."

"What about your dad?"

Gina's chest caved in a little. She rarely thought of him, but when she did, it was always with a pang of sadness. "Never in the picture. Mom said he had some idea he was meant to be famous, and her pregnancy got in his way. Turned out he was just another man who needed someone to blame for his failures. He married someone else, eventually had three kids with her. I was never part of his other family. Mom said we weren't special enough for him. He paid child support until he left them, too, and disappeared. Poof! No more child support for either family."

"Guess they weren't special enough, either."

That made Gina laugh out loud. "Guess not. Mom and I did just fine on our own." Except for missing the family she always wanted. He eyes went to the mantel, the pictures, Mason and Ina. "The McAllisters were the closest thing to a family I've had since my mother died."

That wasn't exactly true. She had counted Luke as family for longer than she wanted to admit, and Lionel.

Angie sent her a sympathetic smile. "It's natural to adopt the people around you as family when you don't have any of your own."

Gina let herself share a soft laugh. "Right. Maddie's already talking to her baby bump about her 'Aunt Gina'."

Gina fought an intrusive sense of melancholy. Time for a change of subject.

"So," she said, her tone a couple of notches brighter than she felt. "Who's the new guy?"

Angie's face lit up. "You will not be-*lieve*." She swirled to the center of the room. "Remember that handsome tall dark at the field?"

"The polo player?" Gina didn't know that much about polo, but the sheikh's son who'd asked about Maddie's car could give that Ralph Lauren model a run for his money.

"The very one."

Gina bit her lip. "I ... thought he was a bit ... forward."

Angie shrugged. "I know. He seemed like a jerk that day to me, too, but we talked later, in the restaurant? He's really sweet, in a hunky, GQ sort of way. His father is very, very wealthy, and also very ill. Kamal's here doing some business for him. He hopes to finish it up before the old guy passes."

Angie rattled her story off excitedly. Gina took it with a degree of skepticism. She hadn't liked the man's attitude, though she had to admire his style.

"Anyway, he's off to San Diego this week for a match. That's why the dinner date was so last minute. He wanted to get together before he left."

Gina let go her discomfort. Who was she to object? Angie was a grown up, in charge of her own life. "No worries. Have fun tonight. I got a call that Lionel and Roland's memorial is in the morning. But I've called in one of our other caregivers, so you'll have the afternoon shift tomorrow."

Angie frowned. "That's going to be tough. The memorial, I mean."

"Yes. And I've been debating whether to join in a Krewe drive to the site. Luke volunteered to drive me."

Angela leaned over the chair and gave Gina's shoulder a squeeze on her way to the door. "So, you should let him."

Chapter 24

He leans in deep shadow against a marble wall between the Doric columns of the entrance to a white stone pyramid mausoleum, his shoulders hunched against the soggy marine air. The mausoleum dominates an island of grass that would be overlooking the Santa Barbara Channel except for the friggin' fog. A hundred yards away, give or take, there is a temporary shelter erected near twin mounds covered with cheesy fake grass. From this vantage point, he will be able to watch memorial attendees unobserved—coming, going, and during. His position is a good choice, except that he can't get over the sense he can smell the dead people inside the structure. He's heard of corpses exploding inside some of these stone monuments. Serves them right. Who do they think they are? Pharaohs or something?

Faggots. The older one, the one he got first, was the one with all the dough, his mother dripping old Santa Barbara money. Only way to get your ass buried in this place. Rich, entitled bitch.

His Goodwill dress jacket isn't warm enough to keep out the damp air. The friggin' pockets are sewn shut. Who sews pockets shut?

It's cold but better than having those faggots get cremated and buried at sea. At least from here he can watch the circus. He slides his hands inside opposing sleeves, pulls them taut like a Chinese finger puzzle, and hunkers down to wait for the show to start. Death surrounds him in a heavy cloak and he can't banish image of the last time he saw his mother. Her flat eyes staring at nothing, her neck twisted at an impossible angle, her bottle blond hair floating on blood pooling around her head, his brother gloating. He'd been seven years old. Two weeks later, with his brother finally in juvenile detention, he was swept into a system that he had to admit was better than living with a single alcoholic mom and a tyrannical, sociopath of a brother. On his third round of foster parents, he'd hit pay dirt. A wealthy couple who had so far been unable to have children of their own. They'd been determined to provide him "opportunities" they said would turn his life around. Right.

Sometimes he thinks he would have been better off not knowing how the privileged people lived. Never having anything at all would have been better than having it all taken away.

The cold damp air is making his nose drip. He wipes it on the fabric of his jacket.

He is so creeped out about the odor coming from the tomb, he considers moving to a nearby bench presided over by a winged, lichen-covered statue, and then he hears them coming. The fog-dampened sound is muted but unmistakable—rumbling vintage fifties engines. The first cars materialize from the fog like zombies in a horror film, slow and lumbering, windows blurred by condensation. A pair of vintage Cadillac hearses followed by, one, two, three—he counts as they slowly round the corner and line up between the day glow stanchions at the curb nearest the freshly dug holes. Thirteen 1953 Corvettes, draped in black crepe. A pearl-white late model Cadillac glides into the prime spot closest to the site.

He stands, straightens his tie. He hasn't worn one since his foster mother made him go to Sunday School. He buttons the oversized coat, and gets ready to blend into the back of the crowd. This is probably a dumb idea, but he can't help himself. What will they say? What do they know? What do they imagine?

And then he sees her, that cherry red Corvette, the one with the steering wheel they stole from his car.

He clamps a hand over his mouth to keep from cursing out loud. His spine tingles with excitement, and he no longer feels the cold.

Chapter 25

Luke had arrived ten minutes after her call. She had been struggling with the zipper of her modest black sheath when the knock came at her front door. The sight of him made her catch her breath. Not that she'd never seen him in the dove grey, three-button suit that emphasized his broad shoulders and narrow hips; this suit, or one like it, was his uniform of the day. A uniform that never failed to tease her with the image of the tall frame, tight muscle, and generous endowment that lay beneath. She had been crazy to believe she could hold out for a ring. Oh, she was still going to make him work for it; but seeing him at her door, looking like that, there was no doubt in her mind she would be the one to cave.

The sight of him made her catch her breath along with a crisp note of anxiety. He wore the Santa-Barbara's Most-Eligible-Bachelor moniker well. *You did that*, she thought, stepping aside to let him in. It was time she got over herself and un-did it before he slipped out of her life and into someone else's.

"That was quick," she said, recovering her breath. She worked her fingers at her zipper closure, suddenly aware of his gaze on her breasts pushing against her dress fabric.

He'd turned her gently, zipped her up with all the familiarity of long time intimates. His hand lingered at the back of her neck a moment before he turned her to face him.

"Nick and I had breakfast at Esau's this morning, then rode into town together, so I was … in the neighborhood."

"And, I appreciate it," she said, truthfully. His smile warmed her insides. He was there for her, and on her terms, just like he'd promised. Just enough to let her know what she was missing. The spark was there, just below the surface, waiting for the chance to catch fire. God, she missed his skin against hers. And she was sure it was written all over her face.

He trailed his knuckles over her shoulder, and slipped his hand down to gently caress her fingers. If he swept her into the bedroom right then, she would not say no. Their eyes caught and held. He knew exactly what she was thinking, but instead of pushing to the next level, he gave her the knowing nod of a long-time partner, and it crushed her harder, deeper, than any searing kiss.

"You ready?" He gave her fingers another squeeze.

Ready? Oh hell, yes. If there was ever a time she needed the comfort of his arms, his heat, this was it. If it was anything other than Lionel's memorial service, she'd drag him to her bed in a heartbeat, to hell with getting that ring. But she couldn't, and he knew it, too.

"Not really. But there's no avoiding it."

He cupped her face in his hands and pressed a light kiss to her forehead. His eyes darkened, his gaze reaching deep inside her like a caress. She swallowed hard. Maybe Lionel would understand, cheer her on. But his mother was the one she would be hurting if she showed up late, or not at all.

Sensing her discomfort, Luke broke the spell, giving her arms a brisk rub. "It's cold out there. You should grab a coat; especially if you want to drive with the top down like the rest of the Krewe."

When she returned from her room with her dress coat and bag, he was leaning thoughtfully against the kitchen door to the garage. Milo circled his legs, marking him as her own with loving swipes of her face against his pants. Peetie mewled next to her empty dish on top of the dryer.

"She'll get fur all over you."

Luke knelt and lifted the lanky coon cat to eye level, her body loose as a rag doll. "You hear that, cat? These are my lawyer pants."

Gina slipped the cat out of his hands and replaced it with her coat. "I'd better feed them before we go. They might be here alone for a while, and Peetie eats more than the other two put together." She reached into the cupboard for the kibble. It was a mundane chore, something to help her pretend today wasn't one of the saddest of her life. At the sound of kernels plinking in the dish, Jabba sauntered into the room and plopped onto his side.

"How's Nick holding up in his temporary living arrangement?" Gina asked, scooping a few stray kibbles into the open bag. "According to Maddie, he wasn't too excited about being banished to the big house for a week."

Luke knelt to give Jabba's belly a scratch, his swimmer's shoulders strained under the smooth fabric of his suit. Gina bit her bottom lip and shook off the mental image of those shoulders clutched against her own.

"He's anxious to get on with the wedding, and get ready for the baby." Those shoulders slumped like he'd just remembered a broken promise. Sensed there was more to the story.

"And ..."

He stood, brushed cat fur off his pants. "There's a lot of bad blood in that house, Geen. The walls are steeped in the stink of it. Being there is a strain on him. On both of us." His hands fisted tight, and his chin hardened into that fixed jawline that marked the two men as brothers.

"When I got there last night, he was aiming at the bottom of those stairs with a big ass sledge hammer, ready to smash them to pieces."

"Oh my god, Luke."

"Yeah. If I'd stayed another hour at the office, Nick would be sleeping in the dog house on his honeymoon."

Gina stowed the cat food back in the cupboard. He'd tried to make a light of it for her sake, but Nick going off the rails was no joke right now. She massaged Peetie's shoulders, getting a loud purr as reward.

"Does Maddie know?"

"About the sledge hammer? No. And, I think it's best to keep it between the two of us for now."

"I agree. It's the last thing Maddie needs to worry about right before her wedding."

He sent her a thoughtful look that had her worried about his own state of mind. Luke had done his share of suffering under his father's abuse. But in true Luke form, he straightened, squared his shoulders, and shook it off.

He held her coat aloft and help her slip into it. "I convinced him the timing was off for remodeling, the wedding coming and all. But we did discuss the idea of making some changes to the place. Something I've thought about recently myself."

"Changes? It's almost an historical monument."

"True. But if neither of us can stomach setting foot in the place …"

She had been the caregiver for Nick Senior long enough to know he could send the brothers into a tailspin with a look. The house, indeed, the whole property, though beautiful with its majestic trees and ocean views, could gave off a sinister vibe. She'd felt it the day Nick Sr. had his breakdown. The paramedics had hauled him off to the care facility under heavy sedation, but even after he was gone the ominous threat hung in the air.

Laced over it all was the lingering sadness around the deaths of the two women who had once lived there: First Nick's mother in a fall down those very stairs, and then Luke's from cancer.

Gina shook off a chill. She couldn't lose the idea that a common thread ran through the tragedies of past and present. Now wasn't the time to talk about it.

As if sensing her ambivalence, Luke sent her a sympathetic smile and opened the back door. "We really should get going."

He was right. She'd put it off as long as she could.

"A light remodel sounds like a good project for you two," she said, redirecting the conversation. She slipped her purse over her shoulder, and ducked under his arm into the garage.

∼

Gina stepped out of the car and followed the ushers toward the burial site. She was grateful for the steadying pressure of Luke's hand at the small of her back. Someone had placed an elaborate wreath between the two excavations, red and white racing flags crisscrossed on a white background, a romantic reproduction of the Corvette emblem.

At graveside they joined a line to express their condolences to the parents. Her breath hitched when Luke pulled her arm through his and pressed his hand over hers. Fighting for control, she squeezed back tears and forced herself to look around.

She wasn't surprised at the growing number of people making their way across the Sunset bluff section of the Santa Barbara Cemetery. Lionel was known and loved in many circles, his family tree deeply rooted in Santa Barbara's philanthropic community.

"Thank you for coming," Lionel's mother said when Gina pulled her into a hug. She wore her age well, her chin high, her shoulders straight, despite the circumstances. Not being Catholic, Gina hadn't attended the vigil or the funeral mass the night before.

"I'm so sorry," Gina said, squeezing the woman's hands. "He was such an inspiration and cheerleader for me. I miss him terribly."

Lucille raised her hands to frame Gina's face, a black beaded rosary spilled between her fingers. "You were always a loyal friend to him, Gina."

Gina's heart stuttered. A brief image of her mother and Lionel's sitting together at their graduation ceremony flitted through her mind. Two weeks later Lionel was there for her when her mother died. "He was a good friend to me, too."

Luke shook hands with Roland's mother and father, offered his and Gina's condolences. Gina quietly scanned the mourners. The people invited by Lionel's mother were the Who's Who of Santa Barbara society. Krewe members were easy to spot, most of them sporting their Krewe of '53 jackets, but she honestly hadn't spent enough time in the club to get to know many of them by sight. Most of these had met at the matching hearses to be pallbearers; the rest filed out of their Corvettes and made their way to the canopy.

One man, his suit rumpled and ill-fitting, stood apart from the crowd, as if he thought he had the wrong group. He took a step under the canopy, then turned away quickly when their eyes met.

A brief chill swept over her. "You cold?" He gave her hand a squeeze as he led her to their seats.

"Not really," she told him, rubbing the goosebumps away. "Nervous, I guess. Funerals aren't my thing."

"Are they anybody's?"

"No. I guess not." Though she had heard of funeral crashers. Maybe that guy was one. Luke put his arm around her shoulders, his presence the only warmth in an otherwise dreary day. A moment later, the chill again. She had a sense someone watched her, and turned.

Lieutenant Estevez stood near the back of the crowd, his partner nearby, as well as two other detectives. His eyes met hers and sent her a solemn nod.

A sense of foreboding settled heavy on her shoulders. "What are they doing here?"

Luke squeezed her against his side. "Relax, baby."

His whisper was warm against her ear. *Relax?* With half the detective squad standing in the shadows behind the crowd?

The priest, obviously well fed, and maintaining a look of pleasant respect, lumbered across the grass to join the assembly at the site. He worked his way through the first row, speaking briefly to Lionel's mother and Roland's parents, a thoughtful distraction as the pallbearers moved the twin caskets into position above the mechanical vaults.

Gina stared wide-eyed at the surreal scene, until the knot in her chest made her look away.

She focused instead on the string of Corvettes parked along the winding road adjacent to the site. Lionel's Baby Blue should have been there, and Roland's Silver Streak. Instead they had been hauled to a wrecking yard, hopelessly twisted and silenced forever.

As the priest droned off a final prayer, she closed her eyes and said her own goodbyes. When she opened them, the man she had seen earlier stood next to Little Red. His gaze roamed the interior like a secret admirer, then he leaned in, reaching for the dash. She straightened. A wedge of cold sliced through her. "Luke!" she hissed, grabbing his wrist.

His eyes instantly met hers. "What is it?" he asked, keeping his voice low.

She turned to point they guy out, but there was no one there. Just a row of cars, the street, and beyond that, an empty marble bench with a stone angel presiding over it.

Chapter 26

Luke steadied her by the elbow as they made their way to her car.

"There was someone there," Gina insisted.

He opened the passenger door and gave her a steady hand as she lowered her backside into the low-slung seat and swung in her legs.

"I don't doubt you, babe. These cars are like magnets. Any guy would want a closer look, especially this one."

"At a funeral?" she asked, fastening her seatbelt.

He let go a laugh. "Anywhere."

She sighed, pressed those luscious lips together, her eyes fixed on a monument across the street.

"You gonna be okay?" he asked. She had been fine during the service. Better than he'd expected. The last one she'd attended had been her mother's. Grief had a way of piling on, the more people you lost, the heavier it got. But Gina had held on to the rosy pink bloom on her cheeks as they listened to family and friends extol the virtues of the two men they'd lost. Now the pink was gone, replaced by a disturbing shade of pale.

"I'm fine." Her slow shoulder roll said otherwise.

"You want something to eat?"

The look she gave him made him regret asking, then her gaze shot to a place just over his shoulder. Luke turned to see Estevez heading their way.

"Gina," the Lieutenant greeted, somberly.

"Lieutenant." She gave him a polite smile, then continued sweeping the area with her eyes like she expected an attack. His girl was headed for a meltdown.

Luke shoved a hand in his pocket, found the smooth Corvette key and rubbed his thumb against it. "Can this wait?" he asked the lieutenant.

Estevez flicked a glance at Gina. "You said let you know immediately if we found something."

"I know what I said."

Gina's eyes shot to Estevez. "What did you find?"

Luke cut her off with what he hoped was a reassuring glance. "Not now, babe. You've had enough for one day."

She straightened, crossed her arms over her breasts and sent him a chin jab he could almost feel. "I'll decide if I've had enough. I'd like to hear what the Lieutenant has to say."

Luke studied her face. Her cheeks had a little more color, but she still looked pale. "My guess is you haven't eaten. Let me take you to breakfast. We can call the Lieutenant when we're finished."

She tipped her ear to her shoulder and pursed her lips before she said: "How about we get a cinnamon roll at the Inn and the Lieutenant can meet us there?"

Estevez shrugged, took a step back. "Works for me."

"Objection overruled," Luke mumbled to himself, striding around the back of the car to the driver's seat.

They waited while the Krewe caravanned past, the sounds of their engines fading as they disappeared into the fog.

She relaxed in the seat, put her hand on his thigh. The small cockpit had its advantages. "Sorry I snapped, Luke. Really. I appreciate you driving me. It was a good call. My emotions have been in overdrive. Now this part's over, I'll be fine. And you're right. I didn't eat this morning, or last night."

She rolled her eyes up to the gray sky. "I think I could get down a cinnamon roll."

The light press of her hand on his thigh gave him second thoughts about taking her anywhere but home. It was probably a good thing Estevez was waiting for them or he'd take a shot at breaking her rules. Again. He covered her hand a moment, then lifted it, kissed it, and pressed it into her lap. Her face flushed with color as she cut her eyes away.

An iconic hotel on the Santa Barbara harbor, the Fess Parker Inn sprawled across the street from volleyball courts that would be empty until the overcast skies cleared. Luke scanned the lobby for a quiet corner where they could talk without being recognized.

The political season was heating up and he had been approached more than once about the article in *The Bomb*, and the Speedo contest it promised. He had yet to broach that subject with Gina.

Luke made sure she was comfortable in a high-backed upholstered chair, then headed for the coffee bar for her favorite latte and a cinnamon roll. He returned to find Gina and Estevez leaning close, a sight that set up an uncomfortable dissonance in his head. Estevez was his co-worker and his friend, but when the handsome Latino gave her a gentle hug, something tightened in Luke's gut.

He knew damn well why Gina called Harv when she discovered Ina's body, and it had nothing to do with romance. She was afraid of Luke's reaction, and with good reason because he proved her right. Now the two of them had their heads together like old friends. So yeah. Gut punched would describe how he felt when he joined them.

"Sorry Harv, I only got something for our girl."

Estevez sat back, his arms open wide across the sofa back. "No problem. Took my nephews out for donuts before their soccer practice this morning. I've had my limit of caffeine and sugar for the day."

Luke passed Gina the coffee and roll and took the seat closest to her. His gut relaxed a bit. He had to admire his bachelor friend. With no kids of his own, he played a major role in his widowed sister's life. He'd make a good dad one day, something Luke admired.

"So, what have you got?"

Estevez leaned forward, addressing Gina. "You were right about the possibility someone else was at Mason's the morning Ina was found."

Gina sucked in a breath. "I *knew* it." She ripped off a piece of cinnamon roll and poked it into her mouth.

The news took Luke by surprise. His intent had been to give Gina a reality check. Eliminate the possibilities.

"Go on."

Estevez cleared his throat. "We can't be sure exactly when it happened, but someone has recently jimmied the locks on two of the downstairs windows. One of them was the maid's quarters where Mrs. McAllister slept. There were gouges in the wood casings and they looked fresh, not weathered. We found a large screwdriver in the bushes outside the kitchen terrace."

Luke loosened his tie. The soaring room felt suddenly close, cloying.

"Does any of that sound familiar to you, Gina?"

"You think I tried to break into the McAllister house with a big screwdriver and then left it in the bushes?" She held the other half of the cinnamon roll aloft. "I have a key, and so do my employees."

Estevez leaned back again. "We're not accusing you or your employees, Gina. We just need to eliminate the possibility. Maybe someone got locked out or something? Didn't tell you about it?"

Luke studied her face. The red blotches that flared on her cheeks earlier had drained away, leaving them pale again. She looked vulnerable, tired. It was all he could do not to scoop her up in his arms and run her out of there.

"No," she said, defensively. "We've got to be able to help someone who is distraught or maybe ill and can't answer the door. That's why my employees have spare keys to any residences they serve. Unrestricted access is part of my contract; part of the job. We have to let ourselves in to a client's home more often than you might think."

She laced her fingers in her lap. "Every one of them is bonded and background checked." She leveled a narrow-eyed gaze on Luke. "I told you someone was there. I *felt* it."

He blinked at her, started to shake his head.

"What? You don't believe me?"

He recognized defiance in her tone. It wouldn't do them any good to have her back up. "I've got nothing against intuition. But I'm more interested in facts. Let's just talk through it, okay? Give us a chance."

He shifted his gaze to Estevez. "Can you give me a scenario that puts someone else inside that house besides Mason when Ina died?"

Estevez leaned back, cleared his throat nervously, his gaze shifted to Gina for a second before it landed back on Luke. "All right. Say someone tries to get in, makes too much noise. Mason hears, goes outside. Perp drops down into the bushes, loses the screwdriver."

Luke studied Gina's profile as she listened to the detective. She was all ears, straining for any tidbit that might help her client.

"He would have to be pretty small to hide in those bushes," she said, finally, meeting Luke's gaze. "It's tight-trimmed boxwood. And that doesn't put him inside the house."

"No," Estevez said. "But it gets the door open. Maybe the old man walks around the other side of the house, our intruder sees his chance, slips in before Mason comes back."

Luke stood, paced a few steps away, ran his hand over the back of his neck. *And could have been there when Gina arrived.* The idea that Gina could have been hurt, or worse, send a hot stab of anger through him. "I need more. I can't present a mystery man to the grand jury."

Chapter 27

Mystery man. The notion took Gina back to the memorial. She squeezed her eyes shut, recalling the image.

Small guy.

Standing by her car.

Not in the crowd, not by someone else's car; by *her* car.

Holy shit. She gathered stray hair away from her face and wound it into the messy bun at the back of her head.

"What if he was at the memorial, too?" She tore another hunk off her cinnamon roll and tucked it into her mouth.

Estevez and Luke looked at her like she'd just dropped in from another planet. "Who?" they asked, voices overlapping.

"Mystery Man," she said around a mouthful of frosting and sweetness.

Luke's eyes narrowed on hers. "The guy you *thought* you saw by your car."

Thought she saw? Gina didn't appreciate his doubt. "You don't get to shut me down because you're the big lawyerpants and I'm just a lowly nurse."

"What's that supposed to mean?"

"Just because it isn't batting you over the head, doesn't mean there's not a connection."

"What connection?" Luke asked, his words edged close to a growl.

Damn, she wanted to wring his neck. The closer he got to admitting she might be right, the more stubborn he grew. She stood her ground. "Consider for a moment that Mason didn't smother his wife. If the person who did was also at the memorial, what would that mean?"

Estevez interrupted. "You saw someone strange at the memorial?"

She shifted her eyes to him. "He was at the back of the canopy before it started. Right next to you, come to think of it," she said, pointing with the last hunk of roll. "I wouldn't have thought much of it, except, the guy looked lost. But then, for a fraction of a second, he looked right at me."

She shivered at the memory of the man's eyes meeting hers. "Then later, he was standing by my car."

"Honey," Luke protested. "I didn't see anyone."

"*Honey*," she said, dripping with it. "I'm not a cop, and I don't have your training, but I know what I saw. You didn't see anyone at Mason's either, but darned if Estevez's guys didn't find something."

Estevez snorted, shifting his eyes to Luke. "She has a point."

Luke shrugged it off, his expression pained. "There were lots of people standing around those cars."

"No. Not lots of people. Not during the ceremony. There was one person."

"What did this person look like?" Estevez asked.

She hooked her hands on her hips, closed her eyes. "Small…" She rolled her hand in the air, "… *ish*."

"How small is *ish*?"

Gina bristled. "Seriously?"

"Harv has a point, Geen," Luke argued, backing his man. "We need specifics. If you saw someone—"

"If?" she demanded, shooting out of her seat.

"Why don't we all sit back down," Estevez offered, lowering himself to the sofa. Luke stood his ground.

Gina huffed out a sigh and followed Estevez's example.

He resumed his professional tone. "Both of you. Just humor me a minute, okay? Gina, close your eyes and relax. What's the first thing you remember about him? His size, color of clothes, hair?—any details will help."

She pressed her fingers against her forehead and squeezed her eyes shut. Fine hair raised on her forearms as the image developed slowly like an old Polaroid.

"Rumpled …" She wet her lips. "And *ish* is lot shorter than you, detective," she said, her voice steadying. "Maybe five-seven, five-eight?"

She looked at Luke who was still standing. "And thinner than you. Less fit." She closed her eyes again. "His jacket hung off him like it was too big. Borrowed, or secondhand, maybe. He definitely did not belong in that crowd."

She rolled her lips in a moment as another memory edged in to the front of her thought. Her teeth dug into her bottom lip. "I've seen him before."

"Before today? When? Where?" Luke sat on the arm of her chair and leaned in.

She lifted her eyes to his. She had finally gotten his attention. "Remember the day we met at the coffee shop? Angie and I were there, and you came in?"

"The day of *The Bomb*," he replied. She could hear the regret in his voice.

"Yeah. *That* day." She pushed down pinch of irritation. "Anyway, before you got there, there was a guy sitting on the bus bench across the street."

"When did you first notice him?" Estevez asked.

She rolled her eyes to the ceiling, and ticked off the events from memory. "Um, I parked Little Red and came inside. I ordered coffee and sat near the front window. I got that feeling you get when someone's watching you. So, I glanced out. He was sitting on top of the backrest like a lot of the kids do, and a second before the bus pulled up, our eyes met." *Just like today.* "I remember thinking he was too old for a college kid, and besides, the semester was over. When the bus pulled away, he was gone."

Estevez sat up, straightened his jacket sleeves. "And you think it's the same guy?"

"I don't know. He was skinny, baggy clothes like the guy at the memorial."

"What does your gut say?" Luke prompted.

Gina compared the images in her mind, nodded her head with conviction. "Yeah. It was him."

Luke shook his head like a man who'd been sucker punched. "Why didn't you tell me about this before?"

"I didn't put it together till now. I mean, a bum on a bus bench off State Street? What's special about that?"

Luke shot a glance at Estevez. "What do you think, Harv?"

Estevez rubbed his bottom lip with his thumb, clucked his tongue. "There could be something to it."

"How so?"

"I'm no profiler," Estevez went on. "But it wouldn't be the first time a perp showed up at a victim's funeral."

"Victims?" Luke grunted. "Lionel and Roland? How do you get that?"

"It's a stretch, but if you're trying to make a connection between someone who might have been at Mason's that night and the memorial, maybe, the common thread is Gina."

"What?" Gina shot forward in her chair.

Luke put a calming hand on her knee, his eyes on Estevez. "Give me a scenario," he said, his tone going serious.

Estevez coughed into his fist, a clear attempt to break the growing tension. "Okay. He's stalking her."

Gina huffed out disbelief. "Stalking me?"

Estevez held up a finger to stop her protest. "He knows you work at McAllisters'. Plan A, he breaks in to get to you. The old lady sees him, screams. He hushes her up. Kills her. Plan A blown. So now, he's on to Plan B, whatever that is."

Gina let out the breath she'd been holding. "But that's absurd. I don't even know this guy. Why would he be stalking me?"

"Luke wanted a scenario; that's my best shot. Find out why and we get our Mystery Man."

"And Mason is off the hook." Her voice sounded more confident than she felt. It was easier to focus on Mason's dilemma than get her head around the idea of having a stalker.

Luke gave Estevez an approving nod. "The possibility would be enough to delay an indictment on McAllister until we learn more."

Gina perked up at this.

"I assume you have prints?" Luke asked Estevez.

"On the screwdriver, and on the windowsill, too. They're smeared, but if we have something on record they could be enough to eliminate Mason." Estevez's eyes went to Gina. "You said the guy at the memorial touched your steering wheel?"

"No, I—he …" She closed her eyes and tried to recall the scene. "He was admiring it, he leaned in, I looked away to tell Luke, so I didn't actually see if he touched it."

Luke frowned at her. "We could have it dusted, though I probably already smeared anything useful."

Estevez nodded. "I'll set it up."

Luke's gaze wandered the room before he spoke. "One more thing. I'll take Mason off house arrest, but I want to keep him under protective custody."

Gina asked, "How soon can you get the bracelet off his ankle? It upsets him."

"Harv?"

"You have a caregiver there with him now?"

She checked her watch. "There's a temporary there now, and Angela should be coming on shift shortly."

"Okay. I'll take a caseworker over there as soon as someone is available."

Gina drew a finger through the last gooey smudge of frosting on her plate. The cinnamon tasted bitter sweet on her tongue. "Thank you, Harvey. It means a lot to me." She rose and gave him a generous hug.

The detective returned the hug gingerly, his eyes on Luke. "Don't thank me yet. If you have a stalker, this could get ugly."

Gina couldn't help but scan the room for a short, rumpled man. What she saw instead were two six-foot-plus, broad shouldered lawmen who were on her side.

She straightened her spine. "One thing is for sure, if he was at the memorial, or is skulking round here now, he knows the company I keep."

"Damn straight." Estevez pulled his jacket closed and buttoned it, basking in the compliment. "I'll let you two be on your way. I've got to go write that report."

"Thanks, Lieutenant. I appreciate you coming out today," Luke said.

"No problem," he replied with a casual two-finger salute, then headed for the lobby doors.

Luke eyed Gina's empty plate. "Looks like you got your appetite back."

She hesitated, watching a couple in matching Hawaiian shirts and thick-soled walking shoes drag their roller bags across the marble floor to the registration desk, their footsteps echoing under the soaring hall. She waited until they were out of earshot, then stepped close to Luke. His instant response pressed against her stomach through his sharp-pressed lawyer pants. A buttery heat replaced the cold, empty feeling of loss that had filled her during the memorial.

"It was touch-and-go there for a while," she said, shifting her thigh between his. "But my appetite is returning a bit."

He smiled into her eyes. She could see the man she loved behind it. He gripped her elbows gently and pushed her to a safe distance. "Let's get you home, then."

Chapter 28

Luke crossed his arms over his chest, leaned against the wall, and watched Gina put her Corvette to bed, tucking steel curves under a soft blanket. Her backside brushed against him as she scooted by.

"You could help me, you know. If you're not doing anything."

He angled behind her, cupped his hands over her ass. "Does this help?"

She fisted her hands at her hips. "That's not doing anything."

"It's doing something to me." He pressed the evidence against the small of her back.

With a hand over her stomach, he spread his fingers, and drew her closer, nuzzling into her neck, taking in the scent of her. God how he'd missed it. "You know what I was thinking?"

"I don't see how you could be thinking at all, right now," she accused, but didn't pull away.

He traced the shell of her ear with the tip of his tongue, and couldn't suppress a needy groan. "Oh, there's still a couple of thoughts in there."

"You thought going with me today and maybe cutting Mason a break would get you back in my good graces?"

That was probably true. He nudged a knee between her thighs. "Try again."

"Um, you're horny and desperate, and memorial services turn you on?"

"Such talk from a lady."

She turned in his arms, quickly slid her knee nearly to his groin and sent him a warning look. He took a step away. "All right. I'm horny. And maybe seeing a couple of good men get lowered into their graves makes me feel a little desperate. Who knows what will happen tomorrow? Today might be my last chance."

The intense light in her rusty amber eyes burned with a mixture of lust and defiance. "So, you're ready to concede defeat?"

"Concede? You were about to climb my bones just now and you know it." He reached out to pull her to him again, but she spun out of his hands. "I guess the memorial got me feeling a little desperate, too."

He started to move on her but she stopped him with a hand on his chest. "However, we made an agreement."

He shoved his hands in his pockets. "I never really agreed to it. Besides, what if Estevez is right about a stalker? You need me here for your protection." He was only partially joking.

"Don't push your luck." She ducked under his arm in a swift move that caught him off guard. "I'm perfectly capable of taking care of myself."

She scooted behind the cars and pushed open the back door to the house.

Undaunted, he hung by his fingertips from the kitchen doorframe a moment, followed her progress with his gaze. "You wearing your pink silk panties under that slinky dress?"

She hooked her purse on the back of a kitchen chair. "Such talk from the Executive Prosecutor."

"My mistake," he said, appraisingly. "You'd be wearing the black under that dress, right?"

She tossed her keys on the table and sent him a frown. "This isn't going to get you anywhere."

"Really? Tell me you're not already wet." He grinned at her confidently because he knew he was right. She had nearly melted against him behind the car.

"In your dreams, pal."

"C'mon. You know you miss me."

She slumped against the counter. Her kitchen clock tick tocked, a black cat with rhinestone eyes. The cat-paw minute hand clicked toward three p.m. His chances of getting laid dwindled with each swish of the cat's tail.

The memorial had taken up most of the day. He would need to get into the office at some point. They had just enough time to call a truce and set a real date for the consummation of same.

He had just opened his mouth to make her an offer she couldn't refuse when kitty door flip-flopped on its hinge and the real cat popped in. Peetie gave Luke a one-eyed once over, then sauntered across the throw rug and rubbed against his leg. He bent and picked her up, to which she responded with a satisfied purr. "I have the same effect on all the girls," he drawled.

Gina let go a sigh. "You little hussy," she said, giving the cat's ears a rub. She grinned at him and sat at her table. "So you like your most eligible bachelor status, then?"

"Actually, no."

"Okay then. I concede defeat."

Luke let out a full-on belly laugh. "You do?"

They stared at each other over the table, the cat's purr loud and comforting between them.

Gina slid her hand across the smooth surface and gripped his fingertips. "I'm sorry, Luke. I've been selfish. Petty. I want to get married. Have kids. And I'm over thirty. Watching Maddie's baby bump grow in front of me has been a constant reminder of that fact. But, you and I? We're different than Nick and Maddie. I know that. I'm not selfish enough to make demands on you that might stand in the way of your career. Maybe having children isn't in the cards for me—"

"Whoa, whoa, whoa." He set the cat down and took her other hand. Where's all this coming from? What happened to my fighter?"

She stared at him, her cocky smile going soft and pliant. "I guess I just realized today at the memorial life is too short to waste time fighting."

"You're right about that." He wanted like hell to scoop her up and haul her to the bedroom, but as he teased her fingertips with his, he sensed a hesitancy, a resistance in her gaze. She was softening, but she wasn't there yet.

She released his fingers, got up and leaned her side into the kitchen counter, swiped at imaginary crumbs. "I just want you, Luke. Married, shacking up. What difference does it make?" She shrugged. "Honestly, I don't know what got into me. I could have cared less about having kids until Maddie started to show. Then somehow, I felt left out. It's a hormone thing, I'm sure. It will pass."

He caught the quick shine of tears in her eyes before she turned to look out the kitchen window.

He got up and stood behind her, cupped her shoulders and rested his chin on the top of her head.

"No, Gina. You have every right to want children. Want to be a mother. It's built in with you. Like breathing. You're a born caregiver." He kneaded her shoulders gently the way he knew she loved. "I've been selfish, too. Making every excuse in the book. I didn't think about how my actions affected you."

He turned her into a bear hug, ran his hands over her back in a caress meant to soothe.

Her muscles relaxed as she leaned into him. Heat rose between them, familiar and welcome, sliding down his body and into his soul. She flattened her palms on his chest and smiled up into his eyes, the russet centers overtaking the yellow amber that drove him crazy.

It was a now or never moment. He drew in a deep breath and let it out slow. "I love you, Gina. I don't say it often enough. It's like you're a part of me and it goes without saying. I've taken that for granted."

She started to respond, but he put a finger to her lips. "Let me finish before I lose my nerve."

She rolled in her lips and nodded. He could feel her body tremble with expectation.

God, don't screw this up.

"Truth is," he said, pursing his lips a moment. "I'm a bit of a coward."

She laced her fingers behind his back and leaned away to watch his face. "You know, I've called you a lot of things over the years we've been together, but coward wasn't one of them."

"It's true." He brushed a tiny wisp of cherry cola hair off her forehead and trailed his finger down the side of her cheek. "I like things the way they are because it's comfortable. Taking the next step feels like messing with a good thing. I gotta admit. I'm terrified."

"Terrified?" She let out an amused laugh. "Have I suddenly grown warts and a crooked nose?"

"No. I'm serious. What if—" Words failed him. He'd never voiced his fear to a soul.

"What if, what?" she asked, tapping her fingers on his chest.

"You put a lot of stock in having children. Like they will make our love more perfect than it already is. What if I can't give you what you want?" He blurted the words on a heavy sigh.

She laughed softly. "You mean you're sterile?"

"No, I'm not sterile." He shoved his fingers through his hair. This was so much harder than he thought it would be.

Her hands slid up his sides, his muscles bunched tight under her touch. "You want me, I want you. There's never been a question about that. The rest will take care of itself, don't you think?"

He stared at her a moment, swallowed hard. "It's the rest I'm worried about."

Peetie wound around his feet again. He bent to scoop her up, rubbed her ears gently until her purr filled the quiet that had fallen between them. "What if … I'm like … *him?*"

Gina cocked her head at him. "Him who?"

"My father. There was a rage inside him. We tiptoed around the house to keep from drawing his attention, as if we had any control over the beast. We didn't. It was like a dark cloud hanging over the household, lightning threatening to strike at any moment."

"You're not like that, Luke."

"How do we know? What if having kids is the change that makes it happen?"

"You give him too much power over you. You're not that defenseless little kid anymore."

"I've got his genes."

"Yes, you do. And there's nothing you can do about that. But you also have a huge dose of your mother's genes. She raised two gorgeous boys to be strong, successful men despite their father. She was a shining example of parenting, wouldn't you say? Where's her weight on the scale of Luke's worthiness quotient?"

"Not sure love trumps rage in this equation."

Gina raised a brow. "No, but courage does. That was her strength." She cupped his face between her palms, those discerning eyes burned into his. "I know you, Luke. Maybe better than you know yourself. Sure, you're the tough prosecutor, the FBI-trained cop in fancy lawyer pants. But you're also tender and gentle and kind; strong and fair when you need to be. You're exactly the kind of person that makes a good father."

He rubbed the small of her back. Loved the way she fit herself against him. "That's just it. You see what you want to see in me. What if I'm not *all that?*"

Peetie head-butted him under the chin, insisting on being the center of his attention. He dug his fingers into her fur.

"Did you have any pets when you were a kid?" Gina asked.

"What?"

"You ever see your dad cuddle a cat?"

He massaged Peetie into a loud, sawing purr. They'd never been allowed to have a cat. Or a dog either, for that matter. "I don't see what that's got to do with anything."

She let go a soft laugh. "You wouldn't. But that's okay."

She turned his face to hers with a finger on the side of his cheek. "You think I'm not scared? There's plenty of ways things could go wrong in a family. Jeez, look at mine. There *was* no father, physically or figuratively. Not to mention the fact that I'm the one who actually has to grow a kid inside me and push it out of an orifice that, quite frankly, doesn't seem big enough."

Luke let go a relieved sigh. "I'm afraid I hadn't thought much past putting the kid into you."

She cocked her hips against him. "Yeah. Well, I have. And I've discovered lately that I have some fears of my own."

She went up on tiptoe, threaded her fingers into his hair, her breasts spread soft against him and her breath warmed his lips.

He started to speak, but she stopped him with the tip of a finger. "I'm afraid of a future without you in it." Her eyes shown with threatening tears, her voice faltered. "You deserve the life you want as much as I do. Where is it written that I get to have my way or all bets are off?"

Luke set Peetie aside and cradled her face in his hands, smoothed his thumbs over her brows. The intensity of her gaze melted his heart.

"No. You were right to call me out. Make me see your side. I was the one being selfish." He kissed her ear gently. "And I was leaving out another huge part of the equation."

"Oh?"

"You. You have enough love and care inside you to make up for any missing pieces on my part."

"You're too hard on yourself."

"Are you willing to bet your future on it?"

"Does this mean I win?"

"Wait, didn't you just concede?"

"I don't remember."

"Hum," he said and bent to kiss the soft pillow of her lips. "I do and you did, but more importantly, I surrender. I haven't slept, eaten, done a goddamned thing without questioning the point of doing it without you there."

"So, you missed me?" Her voice was husky with desire.

He reached behind her head and pulled out the big pin holding the massive knot of hair in place. Her eyes glittered bright as dark, red strands spilled over her shoulders. The pleasure he saw there took his breath away. "I miss everything about you."

"Luke." His name on her lips was all he wanted to hear. She stretched her arms up around his neck, gave him the full length of her body. Everything he wanted in this world was here in his arms. "I just want you to be sure," she said softly. "I don't want you to give in now, because I put on the pressure, and be sorry later."

He kissed her softly, touching the tip of her tongue with his before he pulled away and locked on to those her eyes. "I'll never be sorry."

"Not even when there are six kids jumping on the bed on Sunday morning?"

"Wait, six?" He couldn't hold back a snort. He had only just admitted to taking chance on one, right?

"No," she said, dropping her cheek to his chest with a laugh. "New rules."

"New rules? I just figured out how to break the old ones." Her heart beat fast and steady into his chest, making him feel like a new person. He didn't care what the rules were, as long as they included this.

She lifted her gaze back to his. "I declare the new rules to be *no* rules. I love you, Luke Berlin. There's never going to be anyone else for me. Kids, no kids. It doesn't matter anymore. Like you said. Let the rest take care of itself."

He laced his fingers in her hair, tipped her face close and feathered his lips softly against hers. "*You* said that."

"Oh, yeah."

"But I agree. And I promise you, I will take care of the rest and everything that comes with it."

Then he lifted her, spread her legs to wrap around his hips at just the right level to press against his erection. "Give me one good reason not to start taking care of it right now."

"I ... can't think of any," she whispered breathlessly, then she kissed him deeply, her tongue sliding against his, urgent and hungry.

Chapter 29

He carried her to the bedroom and lowered her to her knees on the bed. She pinned him with the rusty-eyed gaze that set his pulse racing. The past few weeks had been sheer torture without her by his side, in his arms, or hot and wet wrapped around him.

Now she peeled her black dress over her head, revealing soft, round breasts cupped in slivers of black silk and a come-get-me smile that made him break out in a sweat. He lost his fucking mind on a rush of pure lust, every inch of him straining to get to her. He ran his hands up her sides, savoring the feel of her luscious, creamy skin under his fingers, thanking the lucky star that had seen fit to bring her back in his life.

She reached behind her back and snapped open her bra, dangled it tantalizingly from her fingertips before she let it fall to the silky duvet covering her bed.

He buried his face between the soft orbs of her breasts and kissed her there, drinking the taste of her. He wouldn't stop until he tasted every inch.

She arched against him, hungry, needy the way he liked; her long, thick hair swirling around them like a cherry cola dream that took him back to the first time he'd had her.

God, his life had never been the same.

Thoughts of the campaign, his father, the caseload from hell all melted away in the heat of her body and the solid connection between them. He kissed her deeply, his tongue craving the sweetness he had missed, lust turning to passion that drove him on.

She answered with all the intensity he had grown to love. His wild, insatiable Gina was back.

She yelped in delighted surprise when he grabbed her around the waist and pulled her roughly against him. His fingers traced down her firm backside, his mouth closed over the soft peak of her breast. She arched against him, every movement driving him further out of his mind.

His blood surged through his heart without bothering to beat. "My god, Gina."

She slipped her hands inside his jacket and pushed it off over his shoulders. Fisting the fabric of his shirt, she pulled him tighter against her.

She took his mouth possessively with hers, slid her tongue deep inside, circling, diving, driving him wild. Then she began unbuttoning his shirt, following each release with a slow, wet kiss against his skin. His erection grew harder as she worked her way toward his zipper, until he could hardly breathe.

"Are you sure you want to go through with this?" she teased. "It will put your Most Eligible Bachelor status in serious jeopardy."

"What a shame," he said as she began to slowly pull his zipper down. He let go a low, throaty moan. "I was so looking forward to that Speedo competition."

"Me, too." She slid her hands inside his pants and pulled them down over his hips. "I'd settle for a private showing."

He yanked off his shirt and boxers, tossed them on the chair in the corner. A moment later he straddled her, his thick, heavy erection pressed hot between them.

"Luke," she cried. She gripped his ass hard, guiding him toward her heat.

"Uh uh, baby, not yet." He cupped the soft cola red thatch between her legs and nuzzled his face into her belly. "I've been waiting for this too long to have it over with so quickly."

He kissed his way down, laved her hot, wet folds, and drew her into his mouth, savoring her sweetness, luxuriating in the sound of her cries of pleasure, her hands in his hair, her growing heat, until his erection had swollen to the point of pain.

He shifted his weight, spread her legs to slip between them and pressed his fingers into the silky hot wetness of her. She strained into him, meeting his probing fingers with her need. So sweet, so willing and so, so hot. He slipped both hands behind her ass and lifted her to meet him.

And then she froze, sucked in a breath.

His hands froze on her ass. "What?" He said breathlessly against her neck, putting on the brakes. He had pressed himself to her slick, wet well, poised to surge into her in one, swift move, but that one push back held him in check.

"Just so you know, this doesn't mean you're moving back into my place."

He stared at her a moment, then kissed her tenderly. "Of course not. Wouldn't dream of it."

He'd be packing his clothes tonight.

"And, I still want that ring on my finger."

"Goes without saying." He kissed behind her ear, worked his way over her shoulder.

"And a date. Soon," she purred.

"You strike a hard bargain." He dipped his head to her breast and feasted there until she moaned and opened herself to him.

"Oh, this is no bargain, Berlin. This is going to cost you, big time."

He poised himself between her legs and teased her there. "Promise?"

She rose to meet him. "Promise."

❧

Luke stood quietly in the bedroom doorway, his gaze roaming over Gina's relaxed body. Late afternoon light slanted across her pillow, highlighting the gold in her silky red hair. The sight of a creamy smooth orb where the sheet slipped away had his mojo rising again.

He could stay the rest of the day. Call Cal and have him juggle his schedule. Even as the thought crossed his mind, he knew he had to go.

Makeup sex is always the best. It was a phrase he used too often. A copout he vowed never to use again. He knew what he had to do. If he got it wrong, there would be no going back.

He looped his tie into a knot, let it hang loose over the front of his shirt.

Gina stirred. He waited until she settled, the longing for her returned, a soul-deep hunger for more than physical release. His days away from her had left him unexpectedly adrift. He didn't deserve someone like Gina—empathetic, serene, idealistic.

She was right about him, of course. In his heart of hearts, he knew he wasn't as cruel and selfish his father had been. To Nick Sr., no woman was worth compromising his will to be in control, on top. Luke could compromise, couldn't he?

A cold hit of doubt flooded his veins. He stood, hands on hips, knowing Gina was wrong about one thing. There was one thing he and his father had in common. Ambition. His father used it to control people around him, use them for his own ends. Luke used it to control his destiny. Raw and calculating, his ambition burned like a fire in his belly. It had compelled him through law school, fired him up as a public defender, and pushed him over the border into prosecution. He welcomed the title of Executive Prosecutor when the DA had appointed him, knowing full well the job would take number one priority over his life. Election to the office of District Attorney was within his grasp. Justice and ambition. It was a heady combination. Both held power. Both were blind.

"Luke?"

He whirled at the sound of her moving on the bed. She sat up suddenly, like an alarm had gone off.

"Huh?"

"What on earth are you thinking about?"

His heart beat like angry fists against his chest.

He willed himself to settle before he stepped to the bedside and sat. "Ah … I was thinking maybe we could go for another round." He toyed with a piece of her hair.

She rose to one elbow and wrapped her fingers around his tie. "Liar."

Her *don't-fuck-with-me* gaze nailed him. "What?"

"Your eyes were on fire, and not in a *good* way."

He stretched out beside her, propped his head on his elbow, and trailed his fingers over her shoulder. She knew him too well. "I have some things to sort out is all."

She circled her arms around his neck and pulled him in for a lazy kiss that drove his senses beyond reason. "Maybe I can help," she murmured, then rolled on top of his outstretched body, her hair spilling over his chest.

He needed to get to the office. He needed to meet with Lila about next week's dinner with the chief of police.

She cocked her hips against his and he lost his mind. What he needed was to sink himself inside her and never come up for air.

Chapter 30

Gina clutched the giftwrap and ribbon bouquet stiffly in front of her, trying to match her steps to the cadence of the recorded wedding march. Where was Luke? Her body hummed with anticipation, the memory of his lips searing down her body still visceral and raw.

The night of the memorial had been the best makeup sex they'd ever had. It had taken every ounce of her restraint to hold her line in the sand for the last few days. Last night had been the worst. She'd caught herself standing in her garage with her keys in her hand, ready to make a midnight run to the compound.

Now, in the light of day, it was easier to remember why she'd put on the brakes in the first place. Here they were, rehearsing for the biggest day in his brother's life, and Luke was a no-show. He had some earthshaking excuse, no doubt, but that was beside the point.

Gina straightened her shoulders, steeling herself against the urge to throw down her ribbon bouquet and stomp out. She would, except that this wedding was everything to her friend, Maddie, and she was going to stick it out, even if she had to grab Senior Salazar as a stand-in for Luke.

The day was still a bit cool, the June gloom still fighting the sun. The fact that her feet were soaking wet didn't help. She would need to remind Salazar to shut off the sprinkler system before next Saturday. The wedding party could do without soggy shoes during the ceremony and the reception after. That's what rehearsals were for, right? Working out the kinks.

Speaking of kinks, he should be here by now. The fact that he wasn't made her uncomfortable as her thoughts strayed back to the last time she'd seen him, standing stark naked in her doorway, slick with the steamy sheen of "makeup" sex.

The image sent a shot of heat to her cheeks and had her knees going to Jell-O.

The chaplain looked up suddenly and caught her eye as if he could feel the heat. Her cheeks flamed even hotter. She buried her face in the flowers.

Stay in the moment, Gina.

Her gaze went to the horizon where the first tinges of sunset pink were beginning to gather.

Who wouldn't love getting married on a private mountaintop hidden in the center of a Mediterranean forest on the Central California coast? Gina would, that was for sure. Magical thinking, she knew. At this point, she wasn't even sure she would be an official bridesmaid, let alone a bride.

Luke's brother, Nick, had taken his position where he belonged next to the chaplain. His hair slicked back from a recent shower, he wore faded jeans and a funky T-shirt with a snarling hog on the front. The rest of the party, except Luke, of course, waited in front of a white pergola that hadn't been there only the week before. Someone had laid out two large squares of black and yellow tape to represent guest seating areas on either side of a long aisle leading up to a flagstone dais. *At least Luke had been telling the truth about where he'd been the last few afternoons.* The boys had transformed the property to a wedding venue fit for a movie star. They had promised to handle the big stuff while Maddie and Gina took care of the food, flowers, and frills and they'd done it beyond her expectations.

Miss Antonia hadn't disappointed either, showing up right on time. Toni flounced just ahead in the flowered skinny jeans Gina had forbidden her to wear. She had accessorized with a tutu of lime tulle low on her hips, and pair of black "Troopa" boots laced almost to her knees. At the end of the aisle she paired with a gawky blonde surfer Gina recognized from one of Nick's Saturday surf camps.

Toni grinned over her shoulder at Gina the moment she and surfer dude linked arms. Gina hoped Salazar was somewhere out in the avocado groves where he couldn't see that grin.

Eyes forward, Gina started down the aisle toward the mark where each couple would split and take their places on either side of the altar.

She was one millisecond away from calling a halt to the practice when she felt a heated presence next to her side.

Luke grinned at her and leaned close enough she could feel his breath against her ear. "You're white knuckling those ribbons." He straightened, and losing the grin, mimicked her stiff pose, eyes forward, chin high.

"You're supposed to be standing up there next to your brother," she said out the corner of her mouth, her pulse ramping up.

He hip-bumped her. "How do you like the new pergola?"

"It's beautiful," Gina conceded, taking in the tall white columns and wide stage-like space. "And I suppose the crime scene tape was your idea, too?"

Luke sniffed. "Ah, that wasn't exactly planned, but I had it in the back of my car, so …"

Gina rolled her eyes. "Hopefully we can leave that part out next week?"

"I don't know, I thought it was a nice touch."

Gina couldn't help but smile. "You and Nick could quit your jobs and go into wedding planning."

He squeezed her hand. "Wait till you see our *big* surprise."

Oh god? What had they done? The music went on and those already in the lineup fidgeted. Gina sent an impatient glare to the chaplain's assistant who blinked his eyes a moment before he realized it was time to change the music to the traditional bride's march.

Luke and his brother exchanged questioning glances as the silence stretched out.

At last, the music changed up, queuing Maddie to start her walk down the aisle. Gina nudged Luke to his spot flanking Nick and took her place on the other side. The two of them searched overhead.

"What are you looking at?" Gina stage whispered, trying to follow their gaze.

At that moment, a stick of a man with a thin, blonde comb-over wearing Bermuda shorts and a Hawaiian shirt danced his way through the guest block holding a joystick controller.

His eyes scanned the air over their heads. "All right, everybody hold, hold, and … smile."

A sound like a giant electric fan came from behind her. She turned to see a whirring contraption zooming right for them. She ducked to avoid being hit. The drone hovered a moment, swept the pergola, then rose and circled the seating area once before it buzzed in on a startled Maddie who was just beginning her glide down the aisle.

"Where the hell did that come from?" Gina arrowed a sharp frown at Luke. Seeing the satisfied look on his face, she knew. *The big surprise.* She had to admit, it wasn't a bad idea, if the guy kept it under control. At last the damned thing circled off to another part of the property, *thank gawd.*

The rest of the rehearsal went off without a hitch. Gina surveyed the new pergola, revising her plans for the flower arrangements. The area where the wedding would take place was now twice as big, thanks to the Brother's Wedding Planning service. They could hide the bare columns with some potted Wisteria, fill in behind the chaplain with a couple of extra palms. By the time she had discussed the possibilities with

Maddie, the sun had dipped behind a dusty gray horizon and the two of them had slipped on their sweaters.

An elegant Italian dinner, a gift from an old friend in Nick's investment firm, had been set up under the trees at the opposite end of the lawn, complete with linen tablecloths, twinkle lights, and a dessert table fit for the wedding itself. Maddie had placed Luke at the far end of the table, operating on old information.

Undaunted, he picked up his place card, plate, and silverware and moved to sit next to Gina.

Maddie studied them. "You two look cozy," she said, raising a curious brow.

"For now," Gina said, sending Luke a serious nod. "How are you doing, Mad? I've been so caught up in trying to get things back on track after Lionel …"

Maddie gave her shoulders a squeeze. "I know, honey. I'm good." She covered Gina's hand with her own. "I was really sorry to hear about Roland, too," Maddie said, "I liked him."

Gina put down her fork. "I know. It was a shock. Lionel barely talked of anything else after Roland had moved in with him. I'd only met him the night before Lionel … this … all started to happen. How did you know him?"

"I met him here, with Lionel, just a few days before the run. Gave him some trim and a badge from that funky old Corvette in the garage. Put them on his car right there." Maddie nodded to the fancy garage only a few yards away from the dessert table.

"Oh. That's right." Roland's car had since been dragged up from the bottom of a ravine and now sat in the police impound lot. Gina shivered at the thought.

"He was so sweet," Maddie went on. "He sent me some chocolates the next day as a thank you." She sighed, and rested her hand on her tummy. "God, his parents must be devastated."

Luke pulled Gina against his side, lending the warmth of his body to the chilling conversation. "Gut wrenching. We met them at the memorial."

"Hey, Luke!" Nick was shouting at them from the other side of the pergola, motioning to get his brother's attention. "I need you here, now."

Luke gave Gina a quick peck on the cheek. "Gotta go." He scooped a pile of lasagna into his mouth, and dropped his fork unceremoniously. "I'll be back," he mimicked, with a salute, and set off to meet Nick under the pergola.

Gina let go a soft laugh. "I've been trying to get the guy to the altar for seven years and he's always too busy, but let his brother get married, and he's all in." She couldn't help smiling as she watched him jog across the grassy lawn.

"So, you two kissed and made up?" Maddie asked with an approving smile. "He looks happier than I've seen him in weeks."

Gina's cheeks heated again. "A little more than kissed," she admitted, the tops of her ears turning hot.

"But, I don't see a ring on that finger."

"I know." Gina dragged out the words on a sigh. "I had a revealing moment at the memorial. And so did Luke. Life is short, you know? Too short for petty arguments." She let her gaze drift away to where Toni and her new friend were exploring along the edge of the avocado grove, eyes welling at the memory of Lionel's casket being lowered into the ground.

She dropped her gaze to her plate. The last thing she wanted was to dampen it with echoes of yesterday. It was supposed to be fun. A celebration. "Did I tell you Angie is working for me now?"

"Angie? From the Polo Field?"

"Yeah. She's finishing her LVN and I thought it would be good experience for her."

"That's nice of you, Geen. She's—"

A flurry of sound like a horde of hummingbirds covered their conversation as the dreaded drone reappeared and hovered over the table. It swooped so close, the air turbulence blew their napkins across the grass.

Gina raised her placemat, warding it off. "Would you mind getting that damned thing out of my face."

Hawaiian shirt guy wiggled his thumbs on the joystick controls and the unit whirred to a soft landing on the end of the table.

"Sorry. Just checking some shots, angles, light. I want it to be just right on the day of the wedding."

Gina glared at him. "Well, we don't need aerial shots of me eating lasagna," Gina said with a wave of her hand. "And I certainly don't want that little beast flying around during the ceremony next week. I don't care what Luke Berlin hired you to do, you're okay to shoot before and after, but not during. Got it?"

"Sure. Of course. I'm just following orders. Sorry for disturbing your meal," he said, inclining his head toward the garages. He took an exaggerated bow. He made a quick adjustment to the contraption, tucked it under his arm and stalked off in the direction of the avocado orchard.

Gina let out a giggle. "Do you think he moonlights as a birthday clown when he's not filming weddings?"

Maddie rolled her eyes. "God save us from that."

She forced herself to relax into the moment, enjoying the energy she saw between her man and his brother as they made their way across the lawn and took their seats again.

Luke tinked his water glass with a fork, his eyes lit with admiration for his brother. "I wanted to say a couple of words while it's just the few of us here. Maddie, I want you to know that Nick is going to make you a wonderful husband and father. I only wish my mother—our mothers—could be here to see this."

Maddie squeezed Nick's hand and smiled into his eyes. Gina's heart thumped against her breastbone. Nick and Maddie made the most beautiful couple. Who would have guessed six months ago that these two opposites would be tying the knot and having a baby.

"Thank you, Luke. I feel like they're here in spirit," Maddie said. The two of them pulled closer, lost in their own world, just as the Chaplain slipped into his seat at the table.

"Nice of you to invite me to dinner."

Luke clapped him on the back. "You're our guest of honor tonight."

He reached into his coat pocket, slipped out a crisp envelope and passed it to the chaplain.

The man's cheeks reddened. He held up his hands. "Oh, no. Nick already paid me."

Luke leaned in and closed the man's hand over the envelope. "Just a little something extra," he said, sending the man a wink. The chaplain looked confused, but wasted no time tucking the envelope into his pocket.

Gina sent him an arch look. "What was that all about?"

He parried with poker-faced grin. "Just some extras, for next week. Nick and I have everything under control. You don't have to worry about a thing."

Gina eyed the hazard tape, and the noisy drone buzzing overhead. What other extras might they have in store? Dare she ask? "At least you're here. I was beginning to think you had reverted to the old Luke."

He raised a brow then crisscrossed an X over his heart with a finger. "Trust me, babe. I'm reformed." He leaned into her neck and planted a kiss hot enough to melt sugar.

Heat pulsed between her legs. "Keep that up and I might take you home with me tonight."

He worked another kiss up her neck. His warm breath tickled the shell of her ear, and sent a shiver up the entire length of her spine. "Promise?"

She sucked in slow breath as he worked his way back to where he started, ending at her collar bone. She would have been embarrassed except a glance in Maddie's direction caught the prospective bride and groom doing the same thing.

A moment later she straightened out of her love-struck stupor. Toni and her new friend surged around the corner of the barn, laughing, their flushed faces only inches apart. Weddings had a way of casting a spell over the guests, and apparently, this one would be no exception.

She nudged Luke away with a smile. "Toni. You need to come over and have your dinner. We girls are due in the kitchen soon to make some important decisions." She pulled Luke in close, ostensibly for another kiss. "And *we* need to keep a better eye on those two."

֍

"Wait. Stop. Can you rewind that?" Luke leaned forward in his chair, hairs prickling at the back of his neck. *What the fuck?* He had let himself relax a moment in the chair in the library of the big house. The rehearsal had gone well, the pergola he and his brother built had turned out fabulous, and the rest of his plans were coming together with a little help from Maddie. A belly full of lasagna had lulled his senses into a satisfied haze. One glance around the room told him Nick and the photographer were feeling the same after the outrageous meal they'd eaten.

It had been a stressful week all around. Nick and Maddie were focused on their big day, only a week away. But for Luke it had been a major turning point in his career. One that promised to take him all the way to his goal, if he played his cards right. With his boss, Lila, dropping out of the running for District Attorney, and Gina back in his corner, he had already drawn into an inside straight. The slim possibility that the issue with Mason might be cleared with evidence from their last-minute investigation dealt another card in his favor. All he needed was his brother's wedding—and their surprise ending—to go his way, and he could see his way clear to the win.

The image on the video slammed him out of his peaceful place.

Butch, the skinny photographer and long-time surf pal of Nick's, pushed his glasses up on his nose. "What, you don't like that long shot? I can—"

"No," Luke said, impatiently waving his hands. "I thought I saw something. Just ease it back a few frames."

The photographer complied.

Nick was at the window where he'd been admiring his handiwork on the pergola. "What? What are you looking at?"

"The bushes. On the edge of the shot," Luke said.

"Hum," Nick mused, rolling is lips. "Think I should get Salazar out there? Trim back the hedges?"

"No. You've got to see the whole thing. Butch, can you start it over from just after your shot of the dinner?"

"Sure. Hold on a sec," Butch replied.

Nick relaxed against the window frame; Luke downed half his beer, the pleasant sense of ease he'd felt only a moment before disintegrating by the second. They watched it back several times. Finally, he waved a hand dismissively in the air.

"Sorry guys. I could have sworn I saw somebody in the bushes there, but I must be hallucinating. Talk of murder and stalkers and running for DA have addled my brain."

Nick leaned away from the window. "Wait. There is something." He narrowed his gaze on the screen. "Have you ever seen that before?"

"What?"

"Roll it back again, Butch," Nick said. When the image cleared, Nick sucked in a breath. In a clearing, just beyond the oldest part of the oleander hedge, a rectangular shape outlined in field stone, stood out against the spring green grasses.

Luke nearly choked on his beer. "Holy shit. What the fuck is that?"

<h1 style="text-align:center">Chapter 31</h1>

Jimmy Ray Monteplier steps gingerly through the hole in the chain-link fence, twists it closed as best he can without tools.

"I don't think the Berlins would appreciate you trespassing on their property."

He straightens like a shot at the sound of the voice. His head smacks a big-ass cactus paddle, embedding a thousand hair-thin barbs in his scalp.

"Dammit," he swears out loud.

Across the road a handsome dickhead smiles at him from the driver's seat of a red Maserati, his perfectly aligned teeth pearl white against a deep olive complexion and eyes Kryptonite green.

"Trespassing?" Jimmy says, feeling a little sheepish. He picks at the clump of cactus needles in his scalp only to transfer the pinprick pain to his fingertips. "No way. I wouldn't do that. I saw these prickly pears and thought I'd get me one, is all," he lies. To add credibility, he lifts a piece of cactus fruit off the ground and drops it into his shirt pocket.

His truck is parked down the street, but he doesn't look in that direction. Instead, he brushes dirt off the front of his flannel shirt, damp from laying on his belly half the day. All he'd wanted was to get into that garage and get a look at his baby. That damned caretaker had been working in the yard all morning and by midafternoon, the place was crawling with people.

He had waited and watched through some kind of wedding practice he hoped would be over soon. But no such luck. After the mincing and *frou frou* music, they had set up an outdoor feast and settled in for the evening.

His stomach growls, reminding him he hasn't eaten anything since the Snickers bar he filched from a sleeping guy's backpack down by the C-Street parking garage. He needs to get back to Ventura if he was to get a meal and a place to sleep for the night.

He eyes the Maserati with derision. He never liked foreign steel. He's heavy American metal all the way.

He sniffs, sizing up the driver. Probably just some snoopy neighbor, rousting anybody he doesn't recognize. *Fuck him. He doesn't know shit.*

He shoves his hands in his pockets, flinching at pain in his fingertips.

"Well, see ya later," he says, casual and cool like he stops by and helps himself to prickly pears every day, and just for good measure, he starts off in the opposite direction of his truck. He'll loop back as soon as the guy leaves.

But the red car throws a U-turn and drives up behind him instead.

"Monteplier, isn't it?"

The man cruises the middle of the street matching the car's speed to Jimmy's slow saunter.

His stomach clinches, sends a sour taste up the back of his throat. He stops, pulls his shirt pocket away from his chest where the cactus barbs have latched onto his nipple.

"Do I know you?"

The man looks him up and down. "You look like you could use a good meal. Why don't you come with me and we can have a little chat over something to eat?"

A little chat? Jimmy's stomach growls, but he keeps walking, considering his options. A guy who knows who he is doesn't drop out of the blue and offer to buy a meal without wanting something in return. If it's to do with the Berlins, it's gotta be worth a hell of a lot more than dinner.

He casts a slant-eyed look at the red car. "Dinner and a thousand bucks," he throws over his shoulder, aiming high. *Why not?*

The Maserati leaps forward on a low purr, then stops a few feet ahead of him, cranking an angle toward the shoulder. The man reaches across the passenger seat and pops open the door. "Five hundred," he says.

Jimmy grits his teeth as his eyes lock on the driver's. *Well shit. Five hundred is better than nothing.* He fishes the prickly fruit out of his pocket, chucks it over his shoulder, and gets in the car.

A half hour later he's mopping enchilada sauce off his chin with a flour tortilla, his stomach bursting with pleasure. Washing the last bite down with a gulp of premium Mexican beer, he wipes his mouth with the back of his hand and looks up from his cleaned plate to find Maserati Man studying him thoughtfully. He rotates a shot glass of Patron tequila between his thumb and forefinger.

The handsome man could pass for a Mexican himself with his dark olive complexion and wavy hair, but his accent gives him away. Pure Middle Eastern.

"You want to tell me what's so interesting on Berlin's property that you'd cut a hole in the fence to get in?"

Jimmy eyes him, thinking about the five hundred dollars. The money will make his life easier until he can get something else going. But he doesn't like the way this guy looks at him. He is no two-bit thief, that's for sure. He's flashy and slick, and drives a Maserati, for fuck sake. Just the kind of criminal never ends up in prison.

"What's it to you?" Jimmy asks, too stubborn not to push his luck.

Maserati sips his tequila, washing it down with swig of Corona. The T-bone steak on his plate lies barely touched. He lifts a shoulder. "I would think an ex-con would be more careful about trespassing. What if someone recognized you, turned you in?"

Jimmy hunches down in the booth. Since the moment the server set the huge plate of enchiladas, rice and beans in front of him, he's thought of nothing but the glorious flavors rolling down his gullet. He had nearly cleaned his plate before he recognized the threat for what it was. The reminder he's more likely to end up somewhere south of Heaven in the end goes down hard. Now all he can think about is how he will get away from this guy in one piece.

He puts down his fork. "I ain't tellin' you nothing until you tell me how you know me and what *you* were doing lurking outside the Berlin property."

The conceited fuck sends him a confident smile. "So I guess that means you don't want any flan for dessert." He raises his hand and motions for the server to bring the check.

Jimmy hates flan, a runny excuse for pudding if he ever tasted one. But he needs more time to figure this thing out. "Flan is good. Yeah. Sure. I'll take some of that."

Maserati man smiles bigger now. "Flan it is, then; that is, if you are willing to fulfill your part of the bargain."

"Bargain?" Jimmy feels the weight of his food in his stomach. A beer belch escapes his gullet as the server heads to their table. "I ain't seen your money yet," he says, his voice low.

"Bring a flan for the gentleman, will you?" Maserati man asks. "And then we'll have the bill."

The trim woman in the embroidered blouse smiles at Maserati man, then shoots Jimmy a derisive look. He supposes she wonders how the two of them ended up at the same table. He wonders that himself as an old crime show warning circles in his head: *Never let a kidnapper get you to the second location.*

The man finishes off his shooter and sends him an arch look like he can read his mind.

Jimmy sniffs, looks around. *Oh, jeez.* How had he missed it? The restaurant is empty. Once the server got her tip he doubted anyone would notice if he were forced to leave under duress.

He's had enough. "Look, I appreciate the meal, but you haven't really told me what you want."

The man picks at his teeth with a toothpick from a dispenser on the table. "It's more important that you know who my father is."

"Your father?"

"You had a deal with him once. In the matter of a big yellow Cadillac. A 1953 Eldorado, I believe."

Holy shit, the sheikh he'd crossed when he failed to deliver the cars from Berlin's garage.

Jimmy's stomach lurches as the server slides the dessert in front of him. The flattening mound of pudding swimming in a pool of runny caramel doesn't make him feel any better. He dips his finger in the syrup and touches it to his tongue.

"I'm … sorry, I'm afraid I don't know what you're talking about." His voice is wobbly and weak, like a kid lying about his homework.

"Oh, I'm pretty sure you do." The man clicks on his cell phone and scrolls through a range of photos until he finds the one he wants. He puts the phone down and slides it across the table. The photo shows the Cadillac being unloaded from a Matson freight container onto a police tow truck, the lights of the Gerald Desmond Bridge over Long Beach Harbor glowing in the background. "Does that jog your memory?"

Jimmy licks his lips. "Now, see. There was nothing I could do about that. My partners? They were just too careless. Got us ID'd and followed." He shakes his head. *Shit, this guy is going to rip me a new asshole.* He holds up his hands in supplication. "It was a fluke I didn't go to prison."

Kamal puts down the toothpick and folds his hands in front of him like a man ready to make his last offer. "You see, my father's got his mind set on having all of his favorite Motorama Classics under one roof before he dies. When you let him down, I tried to win the Cadillac when it went up for auction, but Junior bought it back for his wife. Now they say it's not for sale."

He's leaning forward now and he pounds his fist hard enough on the table to make the silverware bounce.

Jimmy bites his bottom lip hard. It's cold in the restaurant, but sweat trickles down his backbone.

He chooses his words carefully. "I don't understand what you want from me."

"I already told you. I want to know what's so interesting in that garage. How many '53s has she got stashed in there? A Chevy? An Olds? What?"

"You want me to take, like, inventory?" Jimmy's heart pounds in his gut. He can do that. How hard could it be? Except, no way is he going to include the Corvette. That's *his* car.

"Yes. Inventory. How many, what shape."

Jimmy clamps his jaw again. "They're all wrecks," he says. "I already cherry picked the best when I went after them the first time."

"What do you mean, *wrecks?*" Kamal demands.

"Rusty wrecks. You know. Junk. She restores 'em." *Or parts them out.*

"But that Cadillac is in perfect condition."

"Yeah. That's right. She done that herself before she brought the car out West. She's knocked up good, now. Not working on anything." Jimmy shoves his hands in his pockets.

Kamal drums his fingers on the table; his eyes drill into Jimmy's. On the road outside the Berlin's property, he seemed all smooth and under control. Now he's disintegrating, like he could come unhinged. What if the cars aren't what Kamal's father wants? What if he can't even get into the garage to find out? Last thing he needs is some rich Arab out for his hide.

He fingers a pair of birthday candles collecting sand and lint in the bottom of his pocket.

"Look, man." He straightens in his seat. "I could use the money, but I'm not sure I can get what you want. Thanks for dinner. I'll get my own ride back to my car." He drops his napkin on his plate and starts to get up.

Kamal shoots an arm across the table, quick as a rattler, and grabs his wrist hard. "No!" he says, then he lets go like he didn't realize he'd done it. "No. No, I get it. It won't be easy."

He digs his wallet out of his pants, glances quickly around the room. It's just the two of them in the restaurant now. He thumbs out five crisp one hundred dollar bills. Then he adds his business card to the top of the stack and rests his hands on it. "I don't care if the cars are rusted. I don't care if they have rats in the upholstery. I want to know what's in there. And I think you're just the guy to find out for me."

Jimmy stares at him for a long moment. "An inventory."

"Yeah. With VIN numbers."

"And you don't want me to steal nothing."

"No. I'm looking for genuine Motorama classics. And anything else of interest in there," he says with an arch look. "If the VIN numbers check out, there's more money in it for you."

Jimmy perks up a this. *How much more?* He considers pressing him for five figures. But something about those Kryptonite eyes makes him think he might be better off palming the hundreds and getting himself the hell out of there while the getting is good.

He nods and lays his hand over the pile, then scrapes it off the table. "Okay. I … don't know when I can do it, they've got this wedding thing going on, so—"

"I'll be at the polo field till the end of the week. I need to hear from you by then."

Jimmy stuffs the cash into the pocket as he slips out of the booth. The hell with the Ventura shelter. He's staying in a hotel tonight.

"Yeah. Okay. I'm your man," he says, snapping in half one of the candles in his pocket. Things go south, he knows how to fix it. But the money makes him think again. Maybe he's found himself a new partner after all. *Best not to be too hasty.*

Chapter 32

Luke swam up from sleep, caught in the familiar, terrifying dream he would not make it to the surface before his lungs burst. His mouth popped open in a gasp, and his heart flapped under his ribs like a fish out of water.

He hadn't had the drowning dream in years. In fact, now that he thought about it, probably not since the last time he slept in his old room in the mansion the night he decided to leave home for good.

Which is why he'd chosen to sleep in the big leather chair in his father's library. The computer where he'd played the video over and over long after Butch had left and Nick had dragged himself off to bed had slid to one side, the screen dark with a dead battery.

The underbellies of high clouds had just lit with a hint of pink when he set the computer on the coffee table. He went to the tall windows overlooking the east end of the estate, anxiety building in his chest. He'd watched the video over and over and never seen the image that had set him off, yet he couldn't shake the feeling someone had watched the wedding rehearsal most of yesterday afternoon. Maybe he'd simply been reacting to Estevez's stalker scenario. Why on earth would anyone but family and friends be interested in a Berlin wedding?

Fiona Blanchard, maybe? Ambitious and hungry. Her better days had passed her by and she'd grab at anything that might put her back in the spotlight. He'd hoped that his unwillingness to play along with her drama would have slowed her down. On the other hand, would she go to such lengths for that ridiculous smut rag? Maybe. But it didn't make sense someone like Fiona would risk getting caught trespassing for the rehearsal. No. Fiona would show up for the real thing.

He rubbed the back of his neck, working at the kink with his fingertips, unable to get past the nagging thought that he'd missed something important.

What if, even if it seems remote, Gina was right and there was a connection between the boys' accidents and Ina McAllister's death? He fisted his hands at his hips and stared out at the clouds which were quickly turning from pink to a bruised yellow.

"You're up early."

Luke flinched, then turned at the sound of his brother's voice. Nick stood in the library doorway holding a steaming coffee mug in one hand and a stack of folded clothes in the other. He wore a pair of faded jeans and a tattered tee-shirt, completely out of character.

Luke looked at him thoughtfully, returning his fingers to probe the pinch in his neck. "I never went to bed."

Nick dropped the clothes on the coffee table. "Put these on."

Luke held them up, recognizing a pair of work pants and plaid shirt his father had worn to inspect the property. "What's this for?"

"I thought we'd go check out that gravesite in the orchard."

"Gravesite?"

"You know, that weird rock pile we saw on the video. Gave me nightmares."

Luke's gut tightened. He'd been so caught up with the idea of a trespasser, he'd forgotten all about the rocks.

They had agreed last night neither of them remembered seeing it before. He couldn't argue it was an ominous shape.

Between playing Star Wars and real-life Dungeons and Dragons, and harvesting oranges and avocados with their mother, they'd covered every square inch of the groves from the time they were kids until each of them left home. The site reminded him of the old Knott's Berry Farm graveyard. They would have remembered that.

It had to have showed up between the time they'd left home to begin their own lives and the time their dad imploded. Something had happened out there. Something weeds and rocks and time could not erase. A cold tingle pinched the bottom of his spine. What had Fiona said? A body on the property?

Nick pushed the coffee mug into Luke's hand. "I think we should go out and take a look." He sank into one of the leather chairs, nodded at the clothes, and stretched his long legs out.

The tingle spread up Luke's spine and broke out all over his back. Dammit, he didn't want to deal with this right now.

But by the determined expression on his brother's face, he had no choice. He slipped a leg into the trousers, which were too big around the middle, but better than messing up his *Lawyer pants*. He slipped on the shirt, buttoned it. "What about the girls?"

Nick sent him a thoughtful look. "Maddie has an early fitting this morning. Something about her seamstress heading off on a Hawaiian vacation so it was her last chance before the wedding. She'll probably take Antonia with her."

He smiled, sipped, then put down his mug. "I told her she should put elastic around the top of that dress and be done with it." He checked his watch. "They'll be heading out any minute, and I promised to meet her later this afternoon to shop for baby furniture."

Luke had to admire is older brother. "You're a better man than me," he said, shaking his head.

Luke sipped at his coffee, scowled at his shiny leather shoes. They wouldn't fare well in the orchard, but his sneakers were in his office, and by the look of determination on his brother's face, he didn't have time to get them.

"Gina's on duty at McAllister's this morning until Angela takes her shift. They usually overlap a bit on Sundays, planning their week, so she should be occupied most of the morning." He took another sip of brew.

Nick grinned at him. "For a guy in the doghouse you've got a pretty good line on what Gina's up to."

Luke lifted a shoulder. "Things are looking up in that department."

"Good makeup sex?"

"Yeah." The kind he wanted to have for the rest of his life.

Nick clamped his arm around Luke in a man hug, as if he could read his mind. "Next Sunday is going to be awesome."

"Yeah." Luke stared at the pattern in the deep red area rug on the floor. He and Nick used to play with their Hot Wheels on the swirls and colors there when their father wasn't home. When he was, they wouldn't dare bring toys into this room. The thought sent a shudder through his bones.

It was time they rid this place of old ghosts. "No sense putting this off any longer. Let's get started."

Nick clapped his hands together and rubbed them vigorously. "Okay. Most of the tools are out in Salazar's shed, but we can stop by the greenhouse on the way out to the orchard and grab a couple of shovels."

Luke studied his hands. *Soft-as-a-baby's-butt lawyer's hands*, Gina always said. "I thought you just wanted to take a look."

"I don't know about you, but my X-ray vision hasn't been active since I was about ten years old." He clicked out a text and shoved his phone in his back pocket, then bored his eyes into Luke's.

Luke's heart raced on strong coffee and a hint of dread. There were times he wanted to wash his hands of the entire Berlin estate and run like hell. The last time he'd done it, he'd lost his mother. His father's legacy had a way of coming back to bite him, but if his older brother was ready to make a stand, then he supposed he would have to stand with him.

"Okay. Let's do this."

Luke stalked across the lawn with Nick at his side; the aroma of fresh-mowed grass filled his nostrils; his shiny Italian leather shoes were already soaked in the morning's dew.

With shovels balanced on their shoulders, they made their way to the south end of the avocado grove toward the rough area just beyond the oleander hedge.

Salazar emerged from the opposite direction, rumbling expertly through the orchard on the mini backhoe Nick had bought him only a few weeks before.

"What's he doing here?" Luke asked.

"I texted him to meet us."

"I'd rather no one else knew about this yet."

"Why use shovels when you got a backhoe?" Nick reasoned. "Besides, Salazar is in this whether we like it or not. He knows this property better than I do, now. I don't think we could hide anything from him if we wanted to."

Luke pinched the bridge of his nose. He had to agree. Nick paid Salazar a good salary as well as Toni's tuition in private school. Maddie had rescued the man on a trip through the Nevada desert, helped him get himself and his two young daughters safely to his sister's home in Bishop. She'd offered him a job on the Berlin estate when he insisted on paying her back. Now he and his oldest daughter lived in the grove house on the property and he had made himself indispensable to the family.

He directed Salazar to the spot. From the high shot in the video, it was difficult to estimate the size of the odd formation, but standing next to it, it didn't take much imagination to see they hadn't been far off the mark. It was a three by six-foot rectangular mound in the undeveloped rough. It had been there long enough to allow a scanty overgrowth of weeds, but not enough to block out the distinct shape. Indeed, it looked very much like a burial plot in an old Western movie. The only thing missing was a rickety wooden cross.

Nick put down his shovel and rubbed his unshaven chin. They stared at the ground and then at each other. Salazar deftly pushed and pulled at levers and knobs to set the backhoe outriggers and lower the shovel, then waited for Luke to give the word.

Luke jabbed his shovel at the side of the rectangle, ready to take the first chunk of dirt. Nick cleared his throat and let his shovel drop heavily to the ground.

"What?" Luke asked, sharply.

"Maybe … we should call in some official witnesses? You know, like somebody from your team?"

"Why? You think there's a body? I know what it looks like, but …"

"I don't know. That's the thing. You're the one concerned about your career here, right? Always holding me back?"

"This is our property; we can dig if we want. What if we're just adding a few shrubs and we come across some bones or something?"

"What if we come across a crime scene and we mess it up? Compromise evidence? I can't believe I'm telling you, the big shot running for DA."

Luke glared at his brother for a long moment before he heaved his weight into the blade and chunked out the first shovel full of dirt.

"We're not going to find anything." He said it as much to reassure himself as Nick. Besides, they didn't have time to fool around worrying about what somebody would think. They had to do this before the girls got home.

"*¡Oye!*" Salazar climbed down from the backhoe. He pushed Luke away from the edge of the plot. "Senior Luke. Let me dig here with the backhoe. Something I would do anyway, not the boss. Then we see what we see, no?" He kicked at something with the pointy toe of his boot. "*Que es esto?*" he asked, impatiently.

Luke knelt in the dirt for a closer look. A piece of canvas, dirt brown and stiff, protruded from the edge of the formation. A grommet in the corner was rusted and caked in dried mud.

He pulled at the fabric; a chunk of pale green automotive glass tumbled out, but other than that, it didn't budge. The skin on the back of his neck drew together and prickled down his spine.

"Call your office," Nick said.

Drawing a breath through his teeth, Luke stood. "Yeah. Okay." He slid his phone out of his pocket and dialed Estevez's number.

Two hours later they stood under a canopy, staring gap-mouthed at a mostly deteriorated cadaver while the Medical Examiner and his team worked the scene. The canvas wrapping had preserved some of the flesh and clothing, but the damp, clay dirt had done its job well. The bones could be loosely identifiable as human, but that was all.

Estevez examined a wallet that had been excised from the tatters of what must have once been the pants of the deceased. He handed it to Luke.

Luke flipped it open and felt the heat drain out of his face. "Jesus H. Christ."

Chapter 33

Gina was running late for her morning appointment with Angela.

The girlie cake tasting after the rehearsal dinner had progressed to girlie wine tasting, and then Maddie had insisted Gina go for another round of lasagna to soak up the alcohol. By the time she headed home, it was nearly midnight.

Buzzing with the excitement of the evening and too many carbs, her mind ticked through a repeating litany of unresolved issues as she lay awake in her bed. Would the evidence found at Mason's be enough to clear him? Would Luke forgive her for playing the "now or never" card when he faced the biggest challenge of his career? And finally, was she nuts to think there was a connection between the recent loss of her friends?

"God, could I please just go to sleep?" she moaned. And then it hit her. As clear and distinct as if she were holding it in her hands, she could see the picture of Mason's son on the mantel in his sitting room. The handsome young man leaned against the front of a Corvette that looked an awful lot like hers, right down to the wire mesh covers over the headlights. Was that right? Lionel, Roland, herself, and Mason's son all owned a '53? Was that the connection? But how? Mason had lost his son twenty years ago.

Gina's stomach churned. She wanted to talk to Luke.

Her eyes rolled to the clock. It was three a.m. He would not be happy with her if she woke him for something so trivial.

Instead, she got up, went to the kitchen and downed a whole glass of milk, sharing a little with Milo when he showed up at her feet. When she returned to her bed, Peetie leapt to her pillow and curled up next to her shoulder, her comforting purr finally lulling her to sleep.

It felt as if she had only dozed when her alarm went off at six a.m. No way was she dragging herself out of bed yet.

She could forego washing her hair for a few more minutes of sleep. She hit the snooze button.

Three hours later she awoke to the sound of her phone ringing over the incessant beep of the alarm.

"Oh my god, Angie, I'm so sorry."

Angie's soft laugh was reassuring. "Don't worry about it. Everything's fine here. That must have been some rehearsal dinner last night."

"It was way too much fun." A stinging headache was a cruel reminder that a little bit of red wine and chocolate went a long way. "I'll be there shortly."

By the time she made it to the McAllisters' for her regular meeting with Angie, the June gloom had burned off to a warm seventy-five degrees and the dining room French doors had been thrown open to let the balmy day inside.

The two women made fruitless attempts to get Mason to eat a little arugula salad and fingers of his favorite trimmed cucumber sandwiches. They ended up putting him to bed instead.

"It's funny," Angela said, clearing Mason's plate from the table. "A little earlier, he brought me these figs." She set a plate of sliced figs in the center of the table, the jeweled centers of the fruit a delicious pale pink. "Then he went out in the rose garden with his cutting shears. He seemed contented."

Gina finished off one of the sandwiches. "Maybe the roses reminded him of what happened to Ina."

"Yet he still asks about her as if she were just down for a nap. Do you think he'll eventually remember she's gone?"

"Hard to say. Dr. Steinmetz believes he suffered a stroke recently and that could be the cause of his memory failure. It could be temporary, but there's no guarantees."

Angie stared at her a long moment, then frowned. "Makes sense. Even if he had a stroke *after* he found his wife, he might not remember what happened in the minutes leading up to it."

"I'd rather believe *that* than think he's faking memory loss to hide his guilt."

"Is that what Luke thinks?"

"He's got some … *history*. I'm afraid it colors his vision—and his purpose." Gina sighed. "Now that there's some new evidence to consider, he's relaxed a bit, but it's no guarantee he won't go after an indictment again if the evidence falls apart. I was hoping Steinmetz could help provide a defense if it comes to it. Let's hope it doesn't."

Angie rinsed the dish at the sink, and inverted it on the drain board. "What about Mason's daughter? Seems like she would want to be here to help him through this."

"His daughter is planning to come, but one of her kid's college graduation is coming up, so it will be a while yet." Her eyes strayed to the stairs. It was awful to think of the old man up in his room alone. "I wish I could do more for him."

Angie pressed a hand over Gina's shoulder as she returned to sit at the table. "You already have, Gina. He might be in jail right now if it wasn't for you."

"Or worse." She tasted a fresh fig, savoring the texture of fruity seeds on her tongue.

"By the way, Gina. You've been holding out on me."

Gina raised a brow. "As in …"

"As in that hot detective. The one who came by when they took off Mason's ankle monitor."

"You mean Lieutenant Estevez?"

"Lieutenant Estevez," Angie said on a sigh. "Sounds like a heartthrob character from a CSI episode."

Gina laughed. "He is good to look at, I'll give him that. But, just so you know, he's all business. Never saw a man more dedicated to his job." *Unless it was Luke, of course.* "You're seeing someone now, right? I forgot to ask about that date you had the other night."

"The Sheik's son? Hard to resist a guy that looks like he belongs on the cover of GQ. And that Maserati? Oh. My. *Gawd.*" Angie fanned herself with a napkin. "I was in love the moment I buckled in. With the car, that is." She held out her hand. "Check this out. He gave it to me when we were at dinner." A string of sterling charms and jeweled beads danced around her wrist. "He wouldn't take no for an answer."

Gina fingered a bead in the shape of a jaguar head with two ruby eyes. "Why would you say no?"

Angie tilted her head and pursed her lips in thought. "I don't know. Something about him. So confident, so …"

"Pushy?" Gina's memory was a little fuzzy about that day, having first spun out her car, then learned of Lionel's accident, but that much she remembered.

Angie scrunched her lips a moment, considering. "Entitled. To tell the truth he was more interested in Maddie's Cadillac than me. The Cadillac and whatever's in that garage of hers. It was almost like the bracelet was payment in advance." She picked up her pen, and clicked it open and shut a few times. "Anyway, a little bit of that uber-handsome, exotic bravado goes a long way. He wanted to fly me to Belize next weekend. Do you believe it? I told him I was committed to work for the next month."

Gina let go a soft laugh. "That was probably a good idea." She used the last sandwich to push the remains of her salad onto her fork.

"Here, let me get that," Angie offered, and walked Gina's plate to the sink.

"Thanks, Ange." She let go a purging breath, pleased that her head had stopped stinging.

"Anyway, after meeting that detective," Angie went on, rinsing Gina's plate. "I'm keeping my options open."

"Listen, girlfriend. Be warned, it's not wise to date a cop who's in love with his job." Gina pushed away from the table and stood. "And that's from a person who should know."

She heard Angie's soft laugh at her back as she headed for the sitting room, the picture of Mason's son in her mind. At the mantel, she stopped short, resting her fingers in the empty space where it should have been.

"Angie, could you come in here a minute?"

Angie joined her, drying her hands on a kitchen towel.

"Do you know what happened to the photo of Mason's son?"

Angie glanced at the mantel. "I … suppose they took it in the evidence bags when they went through Ina's room."

"Evidence bags?"

"Yeah. They got the last of them this morning."

Gina's chest hollowed. "Huh."

She moved down the mantel and picked up the wedding photo in its heavy silver frame. "I assumed the picture on the pillow was this one. Mason often took it with him when he sat with Ina."

Angie shrugged. "I guess it must have been the picture of the son then, if that's the one that's missing."

Gina clamped her hand over her mouth and reality hit. She stepped away from the mantel, stunned. Why hadn't she thought of it before?

She raced to the kitchen, tossed her wallet and other items out of her purse until she got her hands on her cell phone and punched in Luke's number. The call went straight to voicemail.

"Luke, please call me when you get this."

"What is it, Gina?" Angie stood in the kitchen doorway, her eyes wide.

"Could we finish up later?" Gina scrolled through her phone calendar. "I've got Hannah Kemp scheduled to spell you at four. I'll try to get back to you before then."

Angie shrugged. "Works for me, but—"

Gina closed the door before she heard the rest of Angie's objection. Her heart played a staccato against her ribs as she slid behind the wheel of her Jetta. But before she could start the engine, her phone chimed Maddie's ringtone.

She purposely calmed herself before answering. "Hey, little momma."

"Hey! There you are." She sounded relieved. "I hadn't heard from you this morning, so I got a little worried."

"I'm fine. Just slow getting started today is all."

Maddie let go a soft laugh. "One advantage of being preggers. No alcohol for me. Anyway, I'm here at Longboards with Toni. I need you to do us a favor, if you're up to it, that is."

"I …" She dug her fingers into her hair. "Of course." She was crazy to talk to Luke, but she had committed to have Maddie's back all week as her maid of honor. Besides, now that she thought about it, Maddie could answer her question better than anyone. "I'm at Mason's so give me a half hour?"

"Is there something wrong, Gina?" Maddie asked. "You sound upset."

"No! No. It's just … I'll fill you in when I get there." *Or, maybe not.* If what she suspected was true, the news could upset Maddie at a time when she was most vulnerable. The last thing they needed was a big honking police investigation on the property with the wedding only a week away. The image of Luke's hazard tape ribbon came to mind.

Chapter 34

Luke handed the wallet to his brother, wiped his forehead on his shirtsleeve, and waited for his reaction. A second later, the color drained out of Nick's face, too. "You're shittin' me. Aiden McAllister? After all this time?"

Luke kicked at loose dirt at the edge of the excavation. A sick feeling gnawed the pit of his stomach. Finding the body only confirmed what he'd known on some level all along. Something horrible had happened on the Berlin estate and there was no doubt in his mind his father had something to do with it.

Estevez was on the phone ordering black and whites to block the driveway. The last thing they needed was the press to get through. Anyone who'd been around twenty years ago would have already heard enough on the police scanners to put two and two together and come looking for blood.

He waited for Estevez to end the call then passed the ID to the lieutenant. Estevez nodded without batting an eye. "Looks like we found our missing link."

"Ya think?" Luke gripped the back of his neck, pinched hard. The irony was he'd been staring at his cold case files just the other morning. A quick look might have given him a clue.

"I need you here, Harv. But I want you to get Rachel on the cold case files for the missing McAllister boy. There's a reason this is all coming up now and I want to find out what that is before someone else ends up in the morgue."

Nick lowered himself to a rock near the excavation. "I'd better call Maddie and tell her to go shopping without me. I don't want the girls back here until this thing—the body—is off the premises."

Luke paced, nodded. "Yeah. I need to call Gina, too. My ass will already be in the deep fryer for letting her last two calls go to voicemail."

Nick hauled himself up looking uncharacteristically bewildered. After the recent incident with the sledge hammer, Luke had been worried about his brother. He almost wished Maddie were here to help Nick deal with the turmoil he could see brewing on his face; but Luke agreed, this was no place for the girls right now. He pulled out his phone, hit Gina's number. The voicemail recording greeted him.

Again.

He left her a message he hoped would satisfy her without losing the ground he'd gained getting back into her good graces. Then, like a *déjà vu* nightmare, the phone went off in his hand.

He swiped the screen and put it to his ear.

"Somebody's following me." The desperate voice was a gravely stage whisper.

"Fiona? I can't talk just now, we're right in the middle of—"

"It's him. I know it is." She was breathing hard into the phone. "I saw him. Short guy. Raggedy skinny. Walks with a limp."

"Look. I've got a situation here. I need you to work with Cal." Luke paced the length of the canopy as a team of latex-gloved investigators in sterile masks descended on the scene.

"You said get a description, I got you one."

"That could be half the homeless guys on State street," her replied, keeping his voice low.

The team unfurled a heavy plastic tarp and laid it next to the body. There wasn't a lot he could do here for the moment. God he didn't have time for—and then it hit him. He swayed under the weight of it. Someone had told Fiona about a body. And damned if one didn't show up.

"Where are you?" he asked.

"I'm driving, now." Her voice notched up in pitch. "But I was in The Village when I first noticed him. I stopped for cigarettes. I can't afford to buy anything else in Montecito Village. Anyway, I got the cigs and did a little window shopping, going from shop to shop, like you do, and I kept seeing this same guy. He didn't look like he belonged there any more than I did, so he stood out. Then, when I pulled onto Olive Mill Road, there he was in my rearview mirror. I made a bunch of turns through the neighborhood. I think I lost him, so I got back on Channel Drive and headed for the pier. I figure, go where there's people, right?"

There was a manic edge in her voice. He was either dealing with a crazy woman or they'd caught a break. He wasn't sure which but he couldn't take any chances. "Right. Go on. What's he driving?"

"A small, light gray pickup. It's old. Piece a junk."

"So where exactly are you?"

"I'm in front of the Fess Parker Inn."

"Just, keep it together, Fiona. It's probably nothing, but better to play it safe. I want you to pull into the hotel lot and park as close to the entrance as you can. What are you driving?"

"A blue Subaru Outback. The driver-side fender is smashed in. Last year, I had a little accident and my deductible is high so I—"

Estevez strolled up beside him and started to turn away when he saw Luke was on the phone. Luke held up a finger to keep him there.

"Fiona. Just park. Lock your doors. Wait for me to get there, all right? I won't be long." He ended the call before she could argue.

Estevez raised a brow.

"You got everything under control here?" Luke asked.

Estevez nodded. "Nick doesn't look very well, though."

Luke glanced across the site, saw his brother sitting on the park bench outside the garage doors. Salazar stood next to him and handed him a tall, cold drink.

"Looks like he's in good hands," Luke said, stuffing his phone in his pocket. "I need to run a quick errand. Let Nick know, would you? And for chrissakes, call me if you find anything else."

Estevez gave him his two-fingered salute.

Ten minutes later, Luke cruised into the parking lot at the Fess Parker Inn. A blue Subaru with a bashed in fender was parked in a handicapped space near the main entrance.

The driver's side door was ajar.

Fiona was nowhere in sight.

"Dammit." Luke smacked his steering wheel with both hands. He should have known she wouldn't do as he asked. He shut down his engine, went to the hotel lobby, and scanned the interior. No sign of her. He waited outside the ladies' room a couple minutes before asking a woman on staff to check. Nothing. He didn't have time for this.

He returned to his car and called Estevez. "Harv, we need to talk."

"Damn straight we do. Rachel just called me. You'll never guess who was once a foster kid at the McAllisters'."

"Forget McAllister for now, I need—"

"Jimmy Ray Monteplier."

Short.

Skinny.

Walks with a limp.

Jimmy Ray Monteplier.

He was officially batted over the head. Gina would have a heyday with this news.

He slipped behind the wheel of his SUV and sank against the seat. "Jesus Christ on the dashboard."

"I thought that would get your attention," Estevez went on. "Rachel stumbled on the records in the Aiden McAllister disappearance files. It looks like they took in a string of foster kids for a while; Mason's wife couldn't have kids, and they wanted to do something for the community. Jimmy Ray had already been through a string of fosters when he landed there at fourteen. He stayed out of trouble for the first year. Then, surprise! Ina gets pregnant and everything changes. When Aiden is born, Monteplier acts out; the details are locked, but whatever he did sends him up to adult detention instead of back in the system. You know most of his history from there."

Luke's shoulders tightened. "If the guy wasn't in prison, I'd say he was a good candidate for Gina's mystery man. The description fits." And, now that he thought of it, it fit Fiona's mystery man, too. "He's a major slime ball."

Estevez cleared his throat. "You sitting down?"

Luke set his jaw, the bottom dropping out of his stomach. "Holy fuck, he's out."

"Yeah. About a month ago. Ratted credible information about another inmate. There's been no sign of him since."

The facts twirled through Luke's brain and lined up on the only thing that made sense. Jimmy Ray and his father were connected to Aiden McAllister's disappearance and had kept it a secret all these years. The thought turned his heart to a cold stone in his chest. Ina McAllister had been smothered with a pillow and a picture of Aiden McAllister. He'd bet his left nut that the prints found at the McAllister residence belonged to Jimmy Ray.

He filled Estevez in on the situation with Fiona Blanchard. "Get a BOLO out for him, and a light gray, older model small pickup, last seen between Montecito Village and the Four Seasons."

"Send a couple of units over to the Inn to check out her car. If she shows up, they need to let me know. What's the status on your end?"

"The Coroner called in a special team because of the deteriorated state. He says they could be here until after midnight. I sent Nick off to meet Maddie in Santa Barbara. Suggested they stay there in a hotel."

"That was some creative police work, my friend."

"Least I could do. He wanted to keep her away so it made sense."

"Good idea. I'm still playing phone tag with Gina. Hopefully I can hold her off a while longer. I want to go back to the office and have a look at those files. I'd like to get a look at those juvenile records. Call Rachel and let her know I'm on my way."

Chapter 35

Jimmy Ray glances at the woman slumped on the floorboard of his truck, her shoulders pressed against the firewall at an awkward angle, her legs propped on the passenger seat. She's pale as a con fresh out of solitary. He'd hit her hard. Maybe too hard. He just wanted to talk to her, dammit. That was all. Now she was one of those cats you wish you could shove back into the bag. A mistake he couldn't unmake.

A *fuck-ing* big one.

He pulls onto the 101, jamming his foot on the gas to get his pitiful excuse for a truck ahead of a tanker hogging the right lane. When this is over, he's getting himself one of those big, honkin' diesel dualies with a six hundred horsepower engine.

He rubs at the ache in his calf, the teeth marks permanently tattooed there a constant reminder of the job of a lifetime he'd royally screwed up. He's lucky the sheik didn't send a hitman instead of his son. He could be laying somewhere in the Ventura river bottom instead of getting a second chance.

He wasn't sure exactly what the handsome Arab had in mind, but so far, he'd made five hundred bucks on a promise of information. It was a start. The last thing he needed was a bunch of cops snooping into that damn body at the Berlin's. He needed to call Fiona off before she published that stupid story.

All he'd wanted was to tell her to forget it. When he'd caught up with her in front of that fancy hotel, she'd took one look at him and started to scream. He'd had no choice but to shut her up.

She's still out when he parks his car in front of his ground floor room at the Motel Six in Carpinteria. It's a far cry from the Fess Parker, but he's got to admit, last night had been the best sleep he'd had in years and well worth the dent it had put in the advance payment he'd gotten from Maserati man. Clean sheets. Soft bed, private bath. He could get used to all that.

He shuts down his engine and scans the parking lot. Only a couple of cars remain after the Sunday afternoon checkout. Good. If he's lucky, he'll never sleep in a room with a dozen snoring men again.

Hell. Who is he kidding? He's never been lucky in his life. This thing could go wrong every which way.

Grabbing Fiona was the sort of spur-of-the-moment thing his con mentors in state prison had warned him against. "Don't let getting revenge get in the way of what you really want."

What he really wants is what should have been his all along. And he is damn well going to get it.

He fishes his room key out of his pants pocket, steps across the sidewalk, and opens the door, leaving it ajar.

One more glance around the lot.

Clear.

Back at his truck, he opens the passenger door, grabs a roll of duct tape from the glove box, and threads it over his wrist. The woman is rag-doll limp and dead-weight heavy, but he manages to lug her out of the car. His arm around her waist, he drapes her arm around his neck and holds her tight against him, kicking the car door shut behind him with his good leg. Anyone watching will think he's helping his girlfriend into the room after too many margaritas with the hope of getting lucky.

"This is all your fault, you know," he says to her inert form as he lays her noodle-limp body on the bed. There's a raised red mark just above her ear where the blood has caked, and it leaves a rusty, red smudge on the duvet. Her color is still cadaver white, but at least she's breathing.

He yanks a strip of duct tape from the roll on his wrist, gathers her arms behind her back and wraps her hands together; does the same with her ankles. Next, he stretches a long piece tight over her mouth from ear to ear.

She groans and her eyelids flutter, then round with fear when they focus on him. She rolls away, shaking her head side-to-side; a muffled shriek escapes her throat.

He wags a finger at her. "Now, Fiona. If you hadn't fought me, we could be having a rational conversation right now."

She shakes her head violently, slams her feet into the bed, arching her back and flopping like a fish gaffed into a rowboat.

He jumps out of her way.

"Come on, Fiona. I just want to talk. I got a proposition for you. If you settle down, promise not to scream, I'll take the tape off your mouth."

She glares at him, shakes her head, squeezes her eyes shut, and tries to kick the wall behind her.

"Broads," he mumbles. "I never met one that wasn't a major pain in my skinny ass."

He rips off another long piece of duct tape, grapples her legs to contain her fury, and circles her ankles twice with the tape, then loops the ends around the slats in the footboard.

She growls unintelligibly from behind the tape, her pupils dilated to the max. Her shiny black eyes, sharp features, and narrow face reminds him of a rat he once caught in a trap by its tail—beaten and angry, but definitely not dead. It's probably a good thing. He isn't into rat-faced women and he doesn't have time for distractions.

Maddie had been a problem that night in Long Beach. The sight of her elegant features, soft breasts peaked with cold, and her pale blue eyes had him vacillating between getting the job done and fucking her brains out. Toying with her had cost him time and eventually cost him the job. Instead of walking away with a million bucks for delivering the sheik a container load of classic American cars, he'd had to slink away with nothing. Just the thought of it sends a stabbing pain through his leg.

He's messed this up good, but he can fix it. He's got to. His stomach growls, reminding him he hasn't eaten anything since the stale bear claw wrapped in cellophane they put out at the so-called continental breakfast this morning.

He retrieves one of the Baby Ruth bars he'd gotten from a machine outside his room, unwraps it, takes a big bite, relishing the way the chocolate, nougat and peanuts create a rush of pleasure in his mouth. He takes a deep breath and exhales through his nose while he chews. The milk chocolate is like a salve to a deep longing in his soul, but there's not enough candy in the world to satisfy the burning need in his gut.

Maybe. Just maybe, he can turn this dumbass idea to his favor.

He paces back and forth from the bed to the door, finishing off the candy bar. He can almost feel the woman's eyes drilling into his skull each time he turns his back on her.

She grunts again, this time more of a whimper. When he turns, her eyes have softened to a pitiful appeal.

He throws up his hands. "Okay. I'm going to uncover your mouth. But I swear, if you start to scream I'll squash that pillow over your face and you'll never scream again."

She nods in earnest now, panting through her nose.

He returns to the bed and carefully peels the tape away from her cheek then hovers there before removing the section over her lips. "I mean it, woman. I got nothing to lose here. If you so much as sneeze too loud, it will be your last."

She nods.

He pulls off the tape.

"Water," she rasps on a whimper. "Please. I won't make a sound."

"Okay. Don't move."

He goes to the bathroom, pulls the paper cover off a plastic cup and fills it at the sink.

When he returns, she has done a sit-up, her knees in front of her near the foot of the bed. He tips the glass to her lips.

"Who are you?" she asks, some of the fear gone out of her.

He considers her for a moment, a plan taking vague shape in his head. Judging by the shabby car she drove and the worn soles of her shoes, and the crow's feet spreading at eyes that might at one time have been beautiful, here was a broad who might appreciate a little cash she wasn't planning on.

"Let's just say I'm a guy on a mission."

"You were going to tell me about a body."

"Forget the body. I got a new plan."

She eyes him suspiciously. "Let me get this straight in my head. You call me, tell me some juicy story about a body buried at the Berlins, want me to break it in *The Bomb*, threaten me when I don't do it right away, stalk me, bash me over the head and kidnap me, and now you want me to just forget about it?"

Her words start a slow burn in his gut. "I wasn't stalking you and I didn't kidnap you."

"Really? Then why am I trussed up here in a motel room? Have you really thought this plan through?"

The burn spikes hot, all the way to his ears. He grabs a pillow and mashes it between his closed fists. "I. Just. Want. To. Talk. To. You," he says through clenched teeth.

She recoils, scooting as far away from him as her tied ankles will allow. "Okay, okay. It … seems like you've gotten a bit carried away, is all."

He glares at her. Goddammit, he hates when women are right. "I have a new plan. A better one. And you're part of it. There's a big, fat paycheck in it for you, too, if you cooperate." He tosses her a challenging look. "And … if you don't …"

The possibility of what he might do if she doesn't agree to go along with him rears its ugly head. She has already questioned his ability. Why is it everyone assumes the worst about him? It isn't like he goes around killing people for sport. It just … happens.

He throws his head back and glares at the ceiling, thinking about the day his brother dragged him away from his mother's lifeless body in the bathroom of the home where he grew up.

Runs in the family, maybe.

"Shit gets out of hand, you do things you don't intend."

He'd never intended to leave a string of bodies in his wake. None of them were his fault. Like now. She could have just listened to him, agreed not to print the story. Done deal. But she fought him. He'd hit her and then it was too late. Not his fault. And now he's stuck with her.

Unless …

He fingers the scrawny goat beard at his chin. Unless he ends it right now. Does her and leaves and turns his back on the whole fuckin' mess. He still has a couple hundred bucks. He can fill up his gas tank and drive. Drive somewhere nobody knows him. Lay low. Stay out of trouble. Let things cool down.

And never lay eyes on your Corvette again.

Fuck that.

Twenty years is long enough to wait for what's his. And, when he thinks about it, something about Fiona gives him pause. She's hungry. He can see it in her eyes, in her gaunt, hollow cheeks, in the predatory grin she is giving him right now. She's been in the game somewhere. He knows it in his bones.

Can he trust her?

He lowers his head to find her shiny black eyes staring fearlessly into his.

No. Probably not.

But for the first time since this whole thing went off the rails, he has an exit plan. And that is a good thing.

He unwraps the other Baby Ruth bar and tosses it on the bed next to her.

Fiona snorts. "What am I supposed to do with that?"

"Use your mouth. And do it quick because I need to put that tape back on before I leave."

"Leave?" Her voice is a desperate squeal.

"Sh-h-h-h-h-h! I'll be back soon. And if you're lucky, I'll make all your dreams come true."

"And if I'm not lucky?"

Jimmy's hands twitch, adrenaline shoots to his fingertips in a scintillating rush. He strips another piece of duct tape off the roll and stretches it wide. "You got just one minute to eat that candy bar before I put this back on."

She glares at him with those obsidian eyes and noshes a mouthful of candy. Before she can finish chewing, he plasters the tape across her mouth.

Chapter 36

Gina plowed out of Mason's driveway, waving at the security unit as she cleared the iron gate. All the while, an unsettling fear gripped the back of her neck with an icy hand.

As she pulled onto Highway 101, images battled for her mind's attention. The wrecked Corvette in Maddie's garage, the broken windshield, the rusty brown stains on the leather seats.

Toni's theory.

It had only been a few weeks ago when they'd laughed and talked in the garage while Maddie removed the steering wheel from the old car and reinstalled it on her own.

They'd spent the day together, Maddie working her way through a pile of sandwiches while Toni chattered about her new school, clothes, and how she wished she was a blonde because she wanted to be like Katniss of Hunger Games fame.

"Please, don't do anything like try to bleach it out on your own," Maddie protested behind the wheel of the wrecked Corvette. "I promise you, you'll hate the results." She let out a frustrated groan.

"You okay?" Gina asked.

"Yes. No. I need to get some muscle here. This wheel puller is a tricky SOB and I'm in no shape to power through it right now. Is your dad home?" she asked Toni.

"Yeah. I think so."

"See if he'll come down and help me with this, will you?"

Toni punched his number into her cell.

"And how about ordering us some pizza, while you're at it."

Two hours and a large pepperoni pizza later, the classic Corvette steering wheel had gleamed as the showpiece of Gina's dashboard. Toni glowered at Gina as she chewed on a last piece of pizza crust.

"What?" She elbowed the girl in the ribs, rocking her off her seat.

"James Dean?"

Gina held up her hand. "I don't want to hear any more about it."

"But—"

"It's a Hollywood myth, honey. Steven King stuff," Maddie chimed in.

"What if it's not though? Look at that old car. Looks like someone went through the windshield to me. Lionel had some badges, and Roland had some trim. Now you have the steering wheel. What if something happens to you like Lionel and Roland?"

"Nothing's going to happen to me," Gina told her.

Toni crossed her arms over her chest, going into a pout like the teenager she was. "I just don't like it. What's that old wreck doing in here, anyway?"

Maddie eyeballed the two of them, then got up and dusted her hands off on her pants. "Will it make you any happier if I put Gina's car up on the rack and give it a good once over?"

"You sure you're up to it?" Gina asked.

Maddie patted her stomach. "Did you just see me plough through two tuna sandwiches and three quarters of that pizza? We feel just fine, don't we, baby?"

The next day, Maddie had flash lighted every square inch of the car's undercarriage, the wheels, the tires and brakes, and given Little Red a glowing report. Gina had no doubts about Maddie's ability to judge the soundness of a car, especially an old classic. And it had run beautifully on the drive home. Still, except for the day she and Luke drove it to the memorial, it sat idle, under its blanket in her garage.

She told herself she was saving it for something special. But, if she were honest, it made her nervous. What if some element of Toni's story was true? Her brain said the notion was ridiculous, but every bone in her body said otherwise. She couldn't shake the nagging sense that Toni had asked a damn good question. How *had* the wrecked Corvette gotten into Berlin's garage?

Gawd, could she just leave it alone? She punched a random station on the radio; Prince's "Little Red Corvette" blasted out of her speakers. Once she recovered from the shock, she began belting out the lyrics at the top of her lungs.

By the time she turned onto Stearns Wharf and bumped over the rough-hewn planks to a parking spot in front of Longboard's Grill, she'd convinced herself she'd been seriously overreacting. She made one more attempt to get a hold of Luke. The call went straight to voicemail. Leaving her phone in its charger in the Jetta's hot socket, she gathered her purse and headed into the restaurant.

Maddie and Toni had their heads together paging through photos on Toni's iPad when Gina joined them at their outside table. Maddie's face glowed, just glowed.

"Gina, look at this!" Toni turned the iPad so Gina could see the surface. There was Toni's face, feathered all around in a short blonde bob.

"Mmmmmm, I don't think your father would appreciate that one," Gina told her and sat down next to a wall of glass windows that offered a view of the bay and marina. Just being in the presence of her two favorite women took away some of her earlier anxiety. She scooted her chair in and helped herself to a handful of roasted peanuts. "So what can I do for you ladies?"

Maddie leaned in for a hug. "Well, I had planned to meet Nick to look at some baby furniture, but now he wants to spend the night here in Santa Barbara. I guess he misses me."

Toni rolled her eyes.

"Thing is, Toni has a sleepover tonight and I'd promised to take her there."

Toni scooted to the edge of her seat. "It's at Nadine's. From Cate School?" Being new at the school, it had taken her a bit to be accepted, especially by the girls who saw every new face as competition. To be invited to a sleepover on the first weekend of summer meant she'd been accepted as one of the group. Gina could hear the excitement in her voice. "She lives in Ojai, and it starts at 3:00."

Gina checked her watch, raised a brow. "That's only two hours from now."

"It's not that far—"

"Of course I'll take you," Gina said on a laugh. "And pick you up in the morning."

"Thanks, Geen," Maddie crooned. "I'm ordering desert. Want some?" She signaled the server.

Gina grabbed her arm and lowered it to the table. "No thanks. I'm only eating for one right now, and I had lunch at Mason's." And then to Toni, she said, "I just need to run home and feed the cats, then we'll stop by the compound on the way and pick up your stuff." And hopefully catch Luke there to find out what the heck is going on.

Toni laughed and yanked her backpack off the floor. "Don't need to, I have everything right here, ready to go."

Gina cracked open another peanut, unable to stop herself. "Boy, you two really had this thing planned out."

Toni folded her arms over her bag. "*Sí.*"

Gina watched Maddie and Toni devour the banana split between them and managed to keep her fingers out of all but a tiny taste of crushed pineapple she couldn't resist.

By the time she and Toni slipped into her car, they had just enough time to make it to the East end of Ojai by three. The cats would live for another hour.

Like any parent, Gina escorted Toni to the door, met Nadine's mother, and extracted her promise that at least one parent was going to be there all night. She issued private instructions to Toni to be on her best behavior and be safe. In the driveway, she started her car and checked her messages with one hand while buckling her seatbelt with the other. Damn. She had missed a call from Luke while the cell had been in the charger.

Sorry I missed you, babe. We picked up the case from Hell today. I'll be working this one late tonight and hopefully have the team set up to take over by morning. I'll call you first thing. Breakfast at the Boat House, on me.

Gina sighed, tossed the phone back in her purse. Typical. Trying to bribe her with food. What the hell was he up to? *Dammit.* The old pattern set up like a storm on the horizon, threatening rain. Reality sank in. This is what she had signed up for. The Significant Other of a lawman had mixed priorities. Take it or leave it. Her part of the bargain she'd made with herself while she watched her friend's coffin sink into the earth was to give Luke the time and space he needed to follow his calling. She had promised herself she wouldn't be a pain in the ass. If this was going to be their life, then so be it.

But her new resolve didn't keep her from worrying all the way back to Santa Barbara. Her mind just couldn't stop spinning pieces of the puzzle. Like clothes endlessly tossed in a dryer, the pieces twisted and turned. Lionel and Roland had parts of that damned Corvette. They were both dead. Mason's wife had been killed. Mason's son had disappeared twenty years earlier. If she wasn't mistaken, in the photo on the mantel, he was leaning against the hood of an old Corvette. What if the photo was the missing piece they needed to link the three deaths together? A white 1953 Corvette just like the wrecked one in Maddie's garage. Just like the one in her own, for that matter.

When a polite "ding" sounded, she reflexively glanced at her phone before she realized the ding was her first warning that the Jetta was almost out of gas.

She exhaled her frustration, and the fatigue that had been creeping up on her all day finally smacked her down. She was near her regular gas station, but there would be plenty to get home on and she could gas up in the morning.

She pulled into her driveway, let out a deep yawn as the garage door opened, and parked next to Little Red in a sleepy haze.

Peetie and Milo were circling their bowls on top of the dryer when she opened the back door, and Jabba, who had never missed a meal in his life, lay like a fat, black velvet pillow next to his dish on the floor. She fed the trio and sloughed off her shoes in the kitchen. She would rather be curling up with Luke tonight, but she was just tired enough to be happy, just for tonight, to curl up with her cats, a cup `of hot tea, and binge watch whatever she had on the recorder until she fell asleep. Considering her sleep deficit from last night, it wouldn't take long.

Chapter 37

Jimmy Ray sits in the gloaming, overlooking the Carpinteria Bluffs, the heft of his old Ruger pistol unfamiliar in his grasp. He's never been much for guns. Never shot anyone on purpose. Never needed to. This one had been shoved under the passenger seat of his truck for so long it was stuck to the floor by bits of candy, French fries, and other unidentified crap. He'd had to pry it loose with his tire iron.

He'd driven from Santa Barbara to Ventura, parking first under the bridge near the railroad tracks, then at the fairgrounds, killing time. Any real sense of a plan escaped him. When he got hungry, he'd driven back up the coast toward Santa Barbara again. He had a ridiculously expensive meal at Sly's in Carp, which put another huge dent in his finances. *Is he losing his grip? Who spends half his money on one meal?* With a belly full of a ten-ounce steak and a hollow soul, he had driven to the bluffs with no more idea what to do than he had when he stuffed that woman in the cab of his truck. Until then, he'd done nothing more than trespass on private property. Hardly a parole breaker. Well, okay, there was the firearm, but he hadn't planned to use it. At least, not then. But now that, as

Fiona pointed out, he was a kidnapper, the stakes were a little higher. And she was no dummy. No way could let her go.

He aims the gun at a seagull soaring in the updraft, flinches at the impotent click when he pulls the trigger.

Thing about shooting an unloaded gun, you can shoot it as many times as you want and you never run out of bullets. The other thing about it is, it's about as useless as a con without a plan.

Jimmy isn't used to freedom. It's foreign to him, like a kite without wind.

He sighs, puts the gun to his head, snaps the trigger and is surprised at the sharp jolt it delivers. *Won't do that again.*

He slumps, the smell of oil wafting up from the natural seeps on the beach below. He'd felt such energy when he woke this morning in a comfortable bed; the prospect of shaping his own destiny within his reach. Ready to right a wrong.

But the moment he looked into Fiona's eyes, tied up like a pig on his hotel room bed, something inside him cringed and shrank back. The answer to the question that had plagued him his whole shitty life was written right there in her eyes. *What the fuck are you thinking?*

Why was it every time he had some kind of grasp on a future—a shot at a new beginning, something to believe in— some asshole up and got in his way?

"That asshole is you," he said aloud. "Always has been." He thought about chucking the gun over the cliff and turning himself in.

Trespassing.

Parole violation.

Murder.

They'd throw the proverbial book at him, and they'd be right.

What pisses him off the most is he can't decide if going back to prison would be a bad thing.

He pulls his pea coat around his shoulders and lays back against the rocks, picking out constellations as they appear. The old man had taught him how to find them, how they moved around Polaris. A cold knot twists in his chest. That was before the betrayal. The best thing he ever had. Gone. And it wasn't his fault. Really.

He closes his eyes, unable to stop tears from flowing down his cheeks.

He startles awake at a rustling near his head. His coat has fallen away and he's freezing cold, but the thought comes to him anyway.

He knows what he's got to do, and he knows how he's going to do it, to hell with an exit plan. It's a longshot, but he's got to take it, or none of his life makes any sense at all.

He stuffs his gun into his pants, drags himself back to his truck. He is going to damn well get all the parts back that belong on his car. Might be difficult, considering two of the Corvettes were likely in the police yard. But there was one more out there. The one with the goddamned steering wheel. And he knew exactly where that one was.

Kat Drennan

Chapter 38

"Why, Mr. Berlin. We haven't seen you here in a long time."

The woman behind the desk at the senior care home greeted him warmly, as if he visited every day. There was no hint of reprimand in her tone, and Luke was relieved. The truth was, he hadn't been to see his father since they'd put him away six months ago. He didn't owe the old man a damned thing, but he didn't want to be viewed as heartless either, even though in his father's case, that was probably an accurate description of their relationship.

"Ms. Morrison," he said politely, thankful there was a nameplate on her desk. "I know it's late, but it's important that I see my father immediately."

"Of course. Have a seat." She gestured at a chair opposite her desk.

Luke remained standing. "No thanks, I'm in a bit of a hurry."

She sent him a confused look. "No, problem." Her tone changed from politeness to concern. The establishment prided itself on providing access to its residents' families, day or night, and he was relieved to find the pride was not unfounded. He'd spent the last few hours in his office, pouring over the old McAllister files and time had gotten away from him. Convinced there was a reason the missing kid's body ended up on their estate, he'd headed out on his mission to confront Nicholas Berlin before he realized how late it was.

"Let me call one of the night staff to take you in." She buzzed an intercom and a male voice answered. "Paco? Will you check on Mr. Berlin and see if he's awake? His son is here to see him."

She settled into her wing-backed chair and returned her attention to Luke. "He might be a little groggy if we wake him. He's been a bit agitated lately. The psychiatrist recommended some extra meds to help him sleep."

Luke frowned, shoved his hands in his pockets. "Agitated? In what way?"

"Well, it's hard to say why. Our residents are often prone to mood swings; it comes with the territory. Although, it seems to have started after his visit with his friend the other day. He's been particularly … irritable."

"His friend?"

"I'm sorry. I don't have a name for you. The gentleman seems to have gotten in without signing our register. But we talked to him in the hallway. We make sure we always know when visitors are here. Security isn't usually an issue, but our staff are trained to determine who is on the property at any given time."

"What did this friend look like?"

Morrison shrugged. "I didn't see him, personally, but—" The door to the interior opened and a large Hispanic man stuck his head in. "He's up, Ms. Morrison," he said, and turning to Luke he went on, "Ready to go in?"

"Hold on, Paco," Morrison said. "Come in a moment, will you?"

Morrison introduced the two of them. "Paco was the attendant on duty the day your father's friend visited." She turned to her employee. "Mr. Berlin wants to know what the gentleman looked like."

Luke rubbed the back of his neck, fatigue wearing him down. "Wait. Let me guess. A slight man, walks with a limp?"

Paco looked bewildered. "How'd you know?"

"Just a hunch."

The woman pulled a file from the cabinet behind her and opened it on her desk, her face contorting into concern. "Is there a problem?" she asked, running her finger down the page. "We don't have any instructions about restricting visitors for him."

"No. No problem. Just, take me to him, please."

His father's room was one of only four private suites at the facility. With a private entrance and bath, and room service as part of his contract, he had no reason to mingle with the other residents, which was probably fine with him.

Paco knocked first, per protocol, then pushed open the door.

He showed Luke a button high on the inside door panel. "If you need anything, just press this and I'll come back."

Luke nodded. "Thanks, man. I won't be long."

The only light in the room came from the hallway outside the door. When it closed, Luke turned to see a figure in a wheelchair silhouetted against the soft glow of perimeter lights on the fence outside the private patio.

"Well, if it isn't the esteemed Executive Prosecutor. What do you want?" The voice was low and ragged, like it had been dragged through a cheese grater; the words slow, deliberate, and slightly slurred, each pushed out with some effort. Luke couldn't decide if it was because of the sleep aid he'd been given or something else.

No point in beating around the bush. Luke had no time or inclinations for civility. "Tell me about the body."

"Body?"

"Is it the only one?"

The older man exhaled a ragged breath, then groaned as he readjusted in his chair. "What do you take me for?"

A murderous, spiteful animal. "Don't fuck with me, *Dad.*" No point in hiding his contempt for the bastard. They had long since dispensed with any civility between them.

His father's guttural laugh assaulted the quiet, triggering a wave of nausea in Luke's stomach. The boy inside him cringed and wanted to run. But the man in him stood his ground. "I know Jimmy Ray was here."

A claw-like hand gripped the armrest of the wheelchair. The old man's shoulders hunched around his ears each time he dragged in a breath. "He turned out to be worthless just like his slut of a mother." He ground out the words as though they tasted like bile.

"You knew his mother?"

There was a low whir of an electric motor, the chair rotated, and the outdoor lights lit his father's face. It was all Luke could do not to back away. The source of the slurred words was evident in the slack features on the left side of the old man's face; his left arm lay like a useless insect claw across his lap. "A filthy, blackmailing whore," Nicholas ground out. "Ruined herself with drugs. Tried to push her whelps off on me. Tried to make me promise I'd take care of her bastard kids."

Luke shook his head. Maybe his father was delusional. "What are you talking about?"

"What? The big important detective doesn't know?" He threw his head back and let out another garbled laugh. "Jimmy Ray and his brother, Ron, rest his deplorable soul, are your cousins."

Luke's knees wavered a moment, the words gut punching him hard. "Cousins?"

"Quarter cousins, if people keep track of such things. When my half-sister found out I was living the life up in Montecito, she started in. *Jimmy needs shoes, and Ronnie has bad teeth.* She left her two boys in Blythe, drove to Vegas, and died in some fancy hotel room. I had your brother to raise, plus an ungrateful wife who bitched all the time; no way was I going to get strapped with her spawn."

That *ungrateful* wife had been Luke's mother whose bitching Luke knew was more accurately begging for a little peace and quiet at home. Luke slumped into a straight-backed chair next to the door, raked fingers through his hair. His heart went cold in his chest. He had never heard anything about his father having a sister, let alone that he and Nick had cousins. Now he learns the surviving cousin is Jimmy Ray Monteplier?

The room felt suddenly stale; the air soured with the odor of a cigar stub in the ashtray. The sharp tinge of Lysol stung his nose.

"Don't worry, son. It's likely she lied to their dad they were his, so there's probably no blood in it."

Luke sucked in a breath. It was all he could do not to drag the old man up by his nightshirt and choke him. But he needed to know the truth. Get it all out like the last retch of bile spewed from a sick stomach. This talk with daddy was long overdue.

"Go on," he said, holding himself in check.

"Ronnie was dead before he was seventeen. San Bernardino County Child Protective Services contacted me about the kid, Jimmy Ray. I told them to go fuck themselves and Jimmy went into the system. I didn't hear any more out of him until years later. Came to me for a job. I was setting up a … deal … in Vegas. Decided to cut him in. Kid has shit for brains. Got himself arrested."

Luke was losing patience. It was far from the end of that story, but that wasn't what he'd come for. He'd already been here longer than he intended.

"Like I said. I need to know about that body in the yard. Don't try to tell me you don't know what happened."

His father's face contorted into a lopsided sneer. "Still think you can put me behind bars? Big shot DA?" He cleared his throat. "I hear you're good at putting innocent old men in jail."

"You're no innocent," Luke growled, then checked himself. The uncanny resemblance to his father's tone set him back. He deliberately relaxed the hands that had involuntarily clenched at his sides. "You pushed Nick's mother down those stairs and we all know it."

Gnarled fingers pushed the joystick on the wheelchair arm, propelling his father nearly to meet Luke's knees.

"Prove it," he snarled. Flecks of spittle collected on the slack side of his mouth. "But know this. You'll drag your brother and his new wife along with Nurse Redhead into a battle you'll wish you never started, and nothing—*abso-fucking-lutely* nothing—will come of it."

Luke stood, bending to take the arms of the wheelchair in a steely grip. He pushed his face into his father's until he could smell the stale cigar on the old man's breath.

"That's where you're wrong, Dad. Looks to me like you landed yourself in prison already, and since your psychiatrist has declared you incompetent, there's not a goddamned thing you can do about it."

He shoved the chair out of his way and stood, arms folded over his chest. Berlin senior let out a shocked yelp that did Luke's aching heart good. Let the old man live in fear for a moment.

"There may be nothing I can prove about your crimes over the years. But I can damn well charge you with accessory to murder of the young man buried on your property. That is, unless you want to tell me what Jimmy Ray has to do with it."

Nicholas wiped at his mouth with his good hand, then cut his eyes away. "I told him that car would be the death of him." The elder Berlin's good hand trembled on the joystick.

The hairs went up at the back on Luke's neck, Gina's words echoing in his mind. "What car?"

Nicholas drew himself up, reclaiming what command he had left in him. "That piece of shit Corvette in my old garage. That sniveling little shit lived his whole life in fear I'd tell someone what happened the night that McAllister kid went missing. Shithead would do anything I told him to do to keep me from telling what I saw." He slumped again, gasping as though he were short of breath. "Ungrateful son of a bitch came in here demanding the car or he'd tell—" He cut himself off, pinching his mouth in a tight frown.

Luke took a step closer to the man cowering in the chair in front of him. For the first time in his life, he saw the pathetic bully for the frightened husk of a man that he was. He'd built himself a real estate empire—albeit founded on ill-gotten means—had two sons who might have loved and emulated him, a wife that wanted nothing more than to be loved, and he'd trampled all of it under his insatiable hatred for anything good. For a moment, Luke wondered now what monstrous event in his father's life had created such dysfunction, but the moment passed. The look on his father's face said it all. The person he hated most in the world was himself.

Suddenly all the bitterness Luke had held against his father seemed pointless and empty. There wasn't anything the system could do to the old man worse than the nightmare he was living now. He was stuck in a prison of his own making, with no one to blame but himself.

Still, there was the body. Luke needed answers. "What would he tell?"

The older man lifted his chin defiantly. "I got *nuthin'* more to say except hit that buzzer on your way out. I've got to piss like a goddamn racehorse."

Luke stared at his father, suddenly realizing Gina was right. Nothing in the contorted face bore any resemblance to himself or his brother. The gripping cold he'd felt when he'd entered the room melted away. An unexpected smile spread over his face. There were better ways to get even with Nicholas Berlin than dragging his family back through the pain. He'd take the first step the moment Macy's opened in the morning.

He rested his hand on the door jamb, exhaled slowly. "Have a nice evening, *Dad,*" he said without malice, and he pushed through the doorway.

Chapter 39

The alarm went off at midnight. Gina shot up out of a troubled sleep. A shadowy man stalked her dreams, watching her from behind lamp posts, perched on park benches. Relieved to discover she was safe in her own bed with Peetie curled up against her tummy and Milo at her feet, she was almost grateful for the disturbance. Now that she was half awake, she realized it wasn't her alarm. It was her cell phone.

Luke said he'd call first thing, but even he wouldn't consider twelve oh one *morning*.

She blinked at the number. It didn't register. It wasn't Luke, that was for sure. In fact, it wasn't any number she recognized. Damn robo callers. Used to be you could tell by the area code, but this one was in the local 805. She swiped the screen to answer the call. Someone was about to get an earful.

"Gina?"

The voice jolted her to full consciousness. "Toni?" What on earth?"

"I'm sorry," Toni said, her voice muffled like she was covering the phone. "Can …" Sobs. "… you come and get me?" Her voice quavered, making Gina's stomach clench.

She slurped water from a bottle on the nightstand, her senses wide awake. There was just enough fear in the girl's voice to have Gina jumping out of bed. "Where are you?"

More sobs. "In … Ojai … Just down the hill from Nadine's. Just … please … can you come? I can't stay here."

"Honey, why not?"

"I just can't, that's all. I'll be by the mailboxes, just before the big dip in the road."

Gina grabbed her jeans off the hook on the back of the bathroom door. "Are you safe?"

"I … just … want to come home." Gina had never heard Toni sound so miserable. "I'll text you the mailbox number here."

Gina shrugged into a sweater, shoved her feet into a pair of mules. "Okay. Okay. I'm on my way."

Why on earth had Toni called her and not her father? But Gina knew the answer. Her dad was a quiet, gentle soul and his daughter saw that as weak. Toni felt closer to Maddie and Gina.

Gina grabbed her purse, and raced to the garage, nabbing her Krewe jacket as she passed the closet.

Jetta keys in her hand, she made it all the way to the driver side door before she realized her mistake. The Jetta was out of gas. She'd burn an extra ten minutes getting down to the station. She eyeballed the Corvette. Its tank was practically full. It hadn't moved since the memorial. She had a hard time looking at it, let alone driving it.

She opened the Jetta door, then groaned. She could waste fifteen minutes getting gas. That fifteen minutes could mean a lifetime where a teenage girl was concerned. The possibilities shredded Gina's resolve.

She swung back into the house, grabbed her Vette keys off the rack, then backed the little sports car down the driveway without taking time to put up the convertible top.

Stars shone clear and bright overhead. Crisp, clean air helped to clear the sleep out of her brain. With a heavy hand, she pushed irrational fears as far down inside as she could. She was still terrified, but not because of any ridiculous stories about ghostly car parts causing accidents on the road.

She was afraid for Toni.

What had she let the young girl get herself into? Gina had been the one to convince Salazar to let his daughter go to the party. Now, she felt guilty as hell. Not only would he come down harder on Toni, but he would never trust Gina again. She could hear Toni begging her not to tell her father. Something she could be tempted to do. It would depend on the circumstances, wouldn't it?

Gina yawned, then pulled in another huge gulp of air. Fresh air or not, Gina tended to turn into a pumpkin at midnight. It wasn't her best driving hour. Was it anyone's? In nearby Los Angeles, some people were just going out for the evening; but in Santa Barbara, most people were settled down for the night. She wasn't the only one on the road, but there weren't many other cars to worry about. She rolled her shoulders and concentrated on the highway.

At the top of the turnoff leading to the road behind the lake, she pawed through her purse, looking for her phone. A car ambled up the ramp behind her. "Sorry," she groaned out loud, glancing in the rearview mirror. She dumped the contents out on the seat. Not there. Had she really left it on her nightstand? *Dammit.*

The car behind flashed its brights. "Okay, okay." She abandoned her purse and turned onto the back road.

<h1 style="text-align:center">Chapter 40</h1>

Gina took the back road often as she had a couple of clients in the Ojai Valley. Winding over the pass behind Lake Casitas, the road was nicely cambered. Her new Jetta cruised it easily, taking the turns in stride. By modern standards, the Vette was a bit of a challenge. Maybe it was the steering wheel Maddie had installed. Or simply Gina's own fatigue, but it seemed she had to tug harder to get cooperation from the old wheel.

It suddenly felt like a dumb idea to be out here after midnight without anyone knowing where she was. If anything happened, anything at all, a flat tire, or, heaven forbid, a deer like before—she would be out here all alone. No one would happen upon her much before five or six in the morning when people began heading over the pass on their Monday commute.

She took the first curve slow and deliberate, careful to brake into it, then accelerate out, like Lionel had coached her.

Once over the first pass, the road narrowed and was edged with tall eucalyptus, avocado, and orange trees, interrupted by a few remote driveways coming in from the side.

At one turn, a dark, furry smudge on the road and an overwhelming odor said a skunk hadn't made it home for dinner. She'd narrowly missed deer on this road before, and twice that she remembered, she'd topped the summit and come upon some unfortunate soul who had probably been speeding and flipped his car.

The thought had her gripping the wheel a little tighter, worry settling in. Maybe she wasn't doing Toni any favors, stepping in on her father's authority. But it was too late now. She was committed. And, she was going to give the young lady a piece of her mind, when she got her in the car. A big piece.

She breathed a little sigh of relief after passing the summit, and began to slow for the narrow curves leading down the other side. There was no wiggle room if someone crossed the yellow line and it was wise to take it below the posted speed.

She downshifted, using engine compression to slow into the curve before she tapped the brake.

Her foot went halfway to the floor before taking hold.

Well now, isn't that special. She didn't like it one bit. It was probably just the difference between her brand-new Jetta, and sixty-something years of automotive progress, but it was disturbing just the same. She glanced in the mirror, relieved to see that there was at least one other driver on the road if something happened.

She was grateful when the road flattened and the signal ahead meant she was nearing town. She should have no problem finding Toni. Every high school kid in Ojai knew the road on the East end with the big dip in it. Gina had taken care of a woman after heart surgery out that road. If Toni was where she said she was, she couldn't be missed.

A few minutes later Gina saw her sitting hunched against the row of mailboxes. She stood as Gina pulled onto the gravel shoulder and shut down the engine.

"Thanks for coming." Toni's voice was contrite. She scooped up her backpack, slung it over her shoulder, and slumped into the passenger seat. "I … I'm … sorry."

Gina stared at her a moment, willing herself to be calm. "Does Nadine's mother know you left?"

Toni shook her head. "It's after midnight. I didn't want to wake her," she said, sliding her eyes away.

"She told me she would be there all night."

"She was … at the *main* house. But the party was in the *guest* house."

Swell. On these properties, that could mean a block away on the other side of a citrus grove. At best, Nadine's mother had been less than truthful.

"What happened that made you want to leave?"

"Nothing," Toni squeaked.

"So, you left the party, hiked this far down the road and got me out of bed for *nothing*?" She mimicked Toni's tone.

Toni gripped the straps of her backpack in both hands. "I—didn't want to get Nadine in trouble. It wasn't her fault." Tears began to flow. "Her older sister came home and brought alcohol, and some older kids, and next thing I know this guy is coming on to me. He was friendly, sort of. Put his arm around me and walked me out to the pool. It was dark and no one else was out there. I didn't want to go."

Alarm sent a white-hot spike up Gina's back. "Did he hurt you?"

"No! No. Nothing like that." She wiped at a tear. "I just, I didn't want to—do anything—and he laughed at me. Called me a crybaby, pushed me away. I ran back to the guesthouse. I couldn't find Nadine and I panicked. I just grabbed my stuff and ran."

Gina's heart thudded. She checked her watch. It was after one a.m. She was seriously considering waking Nadine's mother herself, but held off because of the pleading expression on Toni's face. She let out a breath. The girl had been humiliated. But it could have been worse.

"Well, at least you're okay. Let's get you home. I'll take you to my house and your dad will be none the wiser, but I will be making a call to Nadine's mother in the morning."

"I'm sorry I made you get out of bed and drive all the way here. I should have just stayed and gone to bed."

Gina reached over and took Toni's hand. "You did the right thing, honey. I'm proud of you."

Toni rolled her head on the seat to look at Gina. "Thank you."

She squeezed the girl's knee and started the engine. "Put on your seatbelt."

Gina hung a U-turn in the street and headed back through town toward the Casitas pass. They were nearly to the summit when she noticed headlights in her rearview mirror. Now that was odd. She had had company on the way over the pass, and now someone was on the road with her again? The only other car she'd seen on the way back and it was right on her tail. At almost two in the morning?

The headlights grew larger in her rearview mirror with each turn. She checked her speed, thinking maybe she was driving too slow. But she was doing the maximum.

The headlights gained on them, only four or five car lengths away, now.

Gina upped her speed.

The headlights gained.

She divided her gaze between the road ahead and the rearview mirror. The idiot was closing the space between them, so close, she could see that it was man in a small truck. He was pushing her, making her drive faster than she knew was safe.

Toni turned to look over her shoulder. "What is that guy doing, trying to run us off the road?"

He was almost on her bumper. Gina's heartbeat nearly choked her. "I don't know, but I've had enough."

There was a pullout ahead. Without a signal or brake tap to show her intent, she swerved onto the shoulder and skidded to a stop, dust billowing around them.

The small pickup roared by.

"Asshole. Sorry." Gina dropped her head to the steering wheel a moment, catching her breath.

Toni touched her arm. "It's okay. You did good. Let's just go. He's probably way ahead of us by now."

Gina took a deep breath, spewed it out hard. Their headlights were bright beacons shining into the avocado grove. Everything else around them was black as pitch. Gina had to work to slow her breathing. Toni was right. The brakes had worked, she'd managed the skid, and they were okay. "Okay. Right."

Gripping the wheel with shaky fingers, Gina eased back onto the road and started over the pass.

Chapter 41

It was after midnight when Luke slipped behind the wheel of his SUV. He'd felt disgusted and angry when the attendant let him out of the security gate at the senior facility. But by the time he hit the parking lot, he felt energized. Despite the circus going on at the Berlin estate, and the pressure building around the pending election run, he felt like he'd dumped a shitload of weight off his shoulders. He wanted to talk to Gina. Tell her she'd been right. All right, and he wanted to sink himself into her sweet, lush body and never come up for air.

He punched her number. Still no answer. There was no way she shouldn't be home in bed at this hour. Tomorrow was Monday, and Gina was nothing if not conscientious about showing up at her clients' homes on time and ready to give her all.

He cranked the wheel hard out of the parking lot, activated voice control on his console, and ordered the system to call Estevez.

"You still on site?"

"Yeah. The team is cleaning up."

"Any word on the BOLO?"

"Not yet."

"It's been a long day. Why don't you post someone at the site and head home for some rest?"

"We'll be done here in an hour. I'll stick around until then."

"Tell your boss he doesn't pay you enough," Luke said, releasing more of the tension he'd been holding in his shoulders.

"I'll put that in my report," Estevez said, and ended the call.

Next, Luke ordered a call to Nick. "Hey. Sorry for calling so late. I didn't get to talk to you before I left. Everything good?"

"No problem. We're up watching the late nights." Nick said something to Maddie before he continued. "So far, so good. We have an entire nursery full of furniture being delivered in the morning. I had no idea a kid the size of a basketball right now would need so much stuff." The phone sounded muffled. "The *potholes* in the driveway be cleared up by then, I hope."

"Yeah. Should be fine." Luke tried to keep his voice even while his heart jackhammered in his chest. "So, Maddie still up then, right?"

"Sure."

"Can I talk to her a minute?"

Luke heard Nick tell her. "You sure you're okay, you sound a little … manic."

Manic? Luke's stomach felt like it had been put through a blender, but his spirit was flying a bit high.

"Actually, I've got some information that will blow your socks off, but it can wait till the morning."

"Wait, you can't just—"

"Put your wife on the phone and go to sleep. I need you fresh and rested tomorrow."

Luke heard a rustling sound, then "Hey, little brother," Maddie crooned. "What's keeping you up so late on a Sunday night?"

It was a relief to hear the voice of calm after a day of utter chaos and disruption.

"I thought by the look of things at the rehearsal dinner you'd be snuggled back in Gina's arms by now. Where is she, anyway?"

He laughed. Maddie was always a welcome conspirator in his quest to end the impasse with her best friend. "I was hoping you could tell me. We've been playing phone tag all day and I called her just now and, nothing."

She giggled a moment, sighed, and mumbled something unintelligible, obviously intended for Nick, who Luke imagined was coaxing her to end the call and get off to bed. "I assumed she'd be home in bed by now, knowing her."

"When did you last see her?"

"She had a late lunch with us. Toni and me." He could hear the concern in her voice now. "She was going to take Toni to Ojai for a sleepover and then head home."

The bottom dropped out of Luke's stomach. First Fiona, now Gina. With Jimmy Ray out there somewhere, his imagination spun out of control.

"Shit," he grunted, before he could stop himself. He didn't want to alarm Maddie.

"Luke? What is it? What's happened."

"Nothing. Everything's fine. I've got to go. Tell Nick I want to meet him first thing, all right?"

"Sure, but—"

Luke clicked off the phone and headed for Gina's condo. Twenty minutes later, he laid on the front door bell without getting a response.

"Dammit." He charged around the side of the building to her back porch, feeling for the spare key she'd always kept under a rock. No luck. He tried the slider. It didn't budge.

Not to be deterred, he headed for the high windows of her bedroom, where he could see the light was on. Stepping on the gas meter, he raised himself up enough to see inside. The bed was unmade, but empty. Cupping his eyes against the screened window, he could see her phone on the nightstand. The bathroom light was off.

He scratched the back of his head. Something was seriously wrong. He could feel it in his bones. He considered smashing the spare room window with a rock when he had a better idea.

The back door to the garage. It was flimsy veneer over a light frame; he could easily kick it down if he had to, and if this all proved to be silly, it could be easily replaced. He rounded the side of the house to the path leading to the door, and his heart stopped. Someone had beaten him to it. The door frame was splintered and the door slightly ajar.

Blood rushed through his veins. Suddenly, he felt naked without the weight of his Glock in a shoulder holster. Since he'd moved into the DA's office he'd had no reason to carry. He thought about retrieving it from the glovebox in his vehicle, but decided against. Anyone still in the garage would already have heard him storming around the place like a crazy person. In fact, he was surprised a neighbor hadn't already called the police.

Heart pounding, he flattened himself against the outside wall and used two fingers to push open the door.

His pupils flared to draw in what little light was available.

Gina's Jetta was parked in its usual place.

The Corvette was gone.

<h1 style="text-align:center">Chapter 42</h1>

Gina didn't see the truck skewed across the curve until they were almost on top of it. She hit the brakes hard. They mushed nearly to the floorboard, then grabbed and stopped them less than ten feet away.

The truck's driver-side door was open. There was no one behind the wheel.

Toni lurched forward as much as the lap belt would allow. "That's the truck that tried to run us off the road!"

"Yup." The Corvette's headlights speared into the grove ahead. Gina craned her neck to see around the truck. If she passed on the left, she'd be on the wrong side of the road. If someone was coming around the narrow curve they'd have no place to go. She eased her foot off the clutch and teased the accelerator to creep forward toward the shoulder. There was barely enough room for a bicycle to get by on that side, let alone a car.

"Dammit."

She stopped, letting the car idle, and caught her breath. A man strolled toward them out of the shadows, waving them down as if it were broad daylight.

His other hand was hidden behind his back.

"Toni," she said low. "911."

Toni nodded, and reached for her backpack as the man came nearer.

"Nice car," he drawled, his eyes roaming over the dashboard. "I used to have one just like it, except mine was white."

His lips pulled back from his teeth, splitting the lower half of his face. He was smallish, a raggedy goatee clung to his chin.

Toni pulled at the zipper on her bag.

Gina's eyes flicked to his. The sight of him standing next to the passenger door made her skin crawl. And then she knew. Knew it like her own name. It was him. The man she'd seen at the memorial; and at the bus stop outside the coffee shop.

"Don't come any closer," she warned, shoving the car into reverse. But she was too late. His left arm shot out and caught Toni's neck; his right hand whipped from behind his back and held a gun to her temple.

Toni screamed and squirmed against his grip, her hand still inside the pack.

"Nice of your girls to drop by. Now shut down that engine and get out of the car."

"Let her go!" Gina demanded.

The man pushed the gun barrel hard against Toni's head. "I said shut it down!"

Gina switched off the key, and everything went silent, except for the sound of her own blood slamming in her ears.

Toni yanked out her phone. He tightened his grip on her neck. "Throw it out."

"No," she cried in her signature rebellious spirit, clutching the phone between her knees.

"Toni," Gina hissed. Her chest heaved like a rickety rollercoaster tipping off the rails. She fought back the urge to scream, pushing down her fear. No way was this asshole going to do this to them. No way in *hell*.

He shook Toni's neck hard. "I said get rid of it."

"No-wah!" she shouted.

He lifted the muzzle of the gun and pointed it right between Gina's eyes. "Throw it out. Now. Or Red gets it."

Her heart pounded like fists in her chest as she stared down the barrel only inches from her face. Even in the dim accessory light from the dash, she could see that the chambers were empty. Everything she knew about guns she learned from the old Ruger her mother had kept loaded in her nightstand. When that gun was pointed at you like he pointed his at her right now, you could see if there were bullets in the cylinder. There weren't. There might still be a bullet in the chamber, or in the one other hole she couldn't see, but, the gun also had a safety, and you had to release that safety before you could cock the gun and shoot. At this close range, she could see that the safety was engaged. And, his hand was shaking just a little bit.

She gripped the steering wheel tighter to stop her own hands shaking. "Toni, do what he says," she said, keeping her voice as calm as possible under the circumstances.

He jerked the gun back to Toni. "*Now!*"

A bevy of doves fluttered off the electrical lines overhead. Toni shrieked and tossed the phone into the bushes.

"Yours too," he ordered Gina, gesturing with the gun.

"I don't have it," she said. She swallowed on a dry mouth. If she was right about the bullets, she could stall. It wasn't too late for people to be heading over the pass from a Sunday concert in Santa Barbara. Someone could come by, derail this whole thing. Or not.

The man flicked his gaze up the road, as if reading her mind. "Like hell," he said, leveling the pistol at her face.

She lifted her chin. "I left it on my nightstand. Here, you can look in my purse." She started to reach for her bag near Toni's feet. He shifted the barrel of the gun back to the girl.

Gina's heart felt like it would leap out of her chest. *Keep talking.*

"Look, I … I know you've been following me. What do you want? Surely you don't have to shoot us over it."

"I want what's *mine*." His nostrils flared with each word. There was desperation in his voice, and something else. He hesitated, like he had no idea what to do next. That could work in their favor.

"There's cash in my purse. Just get it, and let us go."

He laughed low and mean. "Cash? You think I want *cash*?" The concept set him off. He rolled his eyes up like a petulant child. "No one in his right mind would follow you all over town, all the way out here, and run you off the road just for a little cash."

She'd give him that. "I don't know, I just thought—"

"You think I'm stupid, like everyone else. That I don't have a plan."

There was a tremor in is voice now. His chin puckered under that scraggly goatee and his expression slipped from threatening to something else. This man was *not* in his right mind, and he *had* followed them and run them off the road. Now he looked desperate. Or was he hurting? She couldn't be sure. He was definitely on the edge. She could use that. Maybe talk him down.

Swallowing hard, she took a chance. "So, why did you follow me?" she asked, adding an even, reasonable tone.

"Fuck me, why is it women never get anything?" His chin hardened, the focused anger was back.

So much for Psychology 101.

"You got your hands right on it."

"It's the steering wheel!" Toni yelped. "It's from that Corvette. In the garage!"

"Bingo," the man said with a self-satisfied grin. He puffed out his chest like he'd just won a prize in a shooting gallery. "No one gets away with parts from my car, not even a do goody like you." Then his grey eyes narrowed on her. "And I plan on getting all her parts back before I'm done."

"I told you," Toni said out the corner of her mouth. She grabbed his arm with both hands and tried to get out of his grip.

"Toni." Gina sent the girl a warning look, then leveled her gaze back on him. "I ... don't know what you're talking about."

She knew exactly what, but she wanted to hear it from him. Keep him talking. Anything to stretch out the time until maybe someone would come along and end this nightmare.

"The hell you don't. I watched your friend take the badges off my Corvette and put 'em on those faggots' cars. You saw what happened to them."

She could no longer hide her contempt. "What did you do?"

"I prefer to keep my methods to myself. Let's just say I learned my craft from the experts at State Prison U."

Toni's eyes nearly popped out of her head. "You killed Lionel and Roland?"

His gaze softened, drifted to the side of the road. "They had no right to parts from my car."

Toni kicked her feet, tried to pull his arm off her neck. "*¡Cabrón bastardo! ¡Déjame ir pendejo!*"

Gina's Spanish wasn't perfect, but she was pretty sure the fifteen-year-old had called the guy a stupid bastard, and ordered the asshole to let her go. What she didn't understand could be gleaned from the attitude. She was proud of Toni, except that attitude could get them killed. Gina sent her a shut-your-mouth look.

What did he mean the Corvette in the garage was his? Unless … Oh my god!

When he leveled his gaze on her, there was no doubt in her mind she was looking into the eyes of a killer. "You killed Ina McAllister," she said.

And then, like switching off a light, the fight went out of him. His jaw slackened and he took a half step back; his gun arm dropped to his side. His eyes fluttered as if he were about to faint.

She held her breath. What the hell was happening?

A siren moaned somewhere in the distance. Toni's eyes flashed to Gina. She put a finger to her lips and a calming hand on the girl's arm. Something had drawn his focus away from them, if only for the moment.

He stared into the dark beyond her headlights, his eyes stricken with … what? Grief? Remorse?

She had to do something, but what? Her mind spun through a list of possibilities, each one leading to a bad end. He'd killed three people they knew of. There was nothing stopping him from adding two more to his list.

Tension built at the back of her neck, fight or flight kicking in. But then, without a word, he relaxed his grip around Toni's neck, his brow furrowed deeper as he stared into the shadows in the avocado grove.

Gina cut her eyes to Toni. If she had any chance at all to get away, this was it.

She nodded and the girl began to slip sideways toward the driver's seat.

She froze when he dragged in a watery breath. "It was her own fault," he whined, like a child hoping to escape blame.

Gina held her breath, motioned with a nod for Toni to keep moving toward her.

"I wanted to know why she sent me away, but she wouldn't talk to me."

Gina pressed back against the seat to let Toni by. Now she was wedged against the driver's side door. It wasn't much safer, but it was better than having his arm around her neck.

"Ina sent you away?"

His shoulders tensed.

Crap. She shouldn't have said it, but it was too late.

His eyes shot back to Gina's. "She wouldn't talk to me," he cried, more anguish than anger in his voice, his eyes brimmed wet and red.

Gina turned her body to shield Toni as much as possible, though he seemed not to be fully in the moment. Was he describing that morning when Ina was killed?

"She couldn't have answered you," Gina offered, keeping her voice as calm and even as the terror in her heart would allow. *Play on his guilt.* "She had Alzheimer's."

"Alzheimer's?"

"It robs people of their memories, old and new. She probably didn't recognize you."

He let out a low moan. "I just wanted …" He squeezed his eyes shut, gritting his teeth, and breathed heavily.

The angry, gun-wielding man seemed to have disappeared. This man was headed for a breakdown.

She had to act now, before Angry Bastard showed up again.

"What did you want?" Gina said, her voice a practiced reassurance. She pushed down the door handle, felt it give.

Anguish twisted his trembling lips. He looked away.

Toni saw her chance, leaned against the door and slid down, flattening on the ground. Gina let out the breath she'd been holding, keeping her eyes on him.

His shoulders heaved; the hand still held the gun but it was limp at his side. "They promised me. I wanted them to love me and they promised." The words came out a tortured whisper.

If Gina could keep his attention a little longer, Toni could reach the berm a few feet away and slip down and out of sight. From there it would be only a couple of yards to the bushes where she had tossed her phone.

"What did they promise?" Gina prompted.

"That Corvette was mine," he declared possessively. "A reward for getting myself under control. Staying out of trouble. Then she got pregnant with *him*, and it was, 'so long, Jimmy Ray'."

Jimmy Ray?

She covered her mouth with her hand to hold back a gasp. *Of course it was Jimmy Ray.*

"You mean Ina's son. The one who went missing?"

His fingers tightened around the gun. *Shit. Shit. Shit.* "They acted like the kid was some kind of miracle."

He was coming back to himself, his voice swinging from grief back to contempt. "No more camping in the Sespe. No more talk of restoring the Corvette. It was all, 'Isn't he just the cutest thing,' and 'Jimmy, see how he took a first step.' They were a tight little family, all cozied up together like peas in a pod. I couldn't take it anymore. I ditched school and took the car for a little spin. That's all."

"And Mason took it away from you."

"Took it away?" He threw back his head and hooted a laugh.

She risked a glance toward the brush line to see that Toni had made it. *Please, please, let her find her phone.*

"He called the cops. Had me arrested. They put me in jail with the adults. Said I knew what I was doing." He laughed again, this time drilling a contemptuous look directly into her eyes. "They got out of the foster parent business, and me?" he said, pointing at his chest with the gun, "I started my liberal education."

Chapter 43

Gina barely breathed. Jimmy Ray was so absorbed in his own story he hadn't noticed Toni was gone. With Toni out of danger, Gina could bail out of the car and run like hell. His gun wasn't even loaded. Maybe. Except for the one that could be in that chamber.

Calm down.

Breathe.

Keep talking.

"I … don't understand how your car got into the Berlin's garage."

His laugh was so evil, she reconsidered running. His eyes narrowed and for a moment, she thought he'd finally missed Toni. Instead, he raised his gaze to the stars and spread his arms as if his next revelation would be his most cherished *coup d'etat.*

"That was my dream come true." He scratched the side of his chin with the gun barrel. "I was visiting my favorite uncle one night during a heavy rainstorm, and damned if miracle boy, nearly grown up, didn't run himself into a light pole down at the end of Berlin's driveway."

Uncle? Berlin?

"I backed the car right up the driveway and into the old garage. Covered her with a tarp," he went on, searching the sky.

And miracle boy was never seen again.

Gina glanced over her shoulder, straining to hear any sound on the road, her heart beating faster by the second. No one was coming to save her. She had to get out of this on her own.

"She's been there ever since, waiting for me," Jimmy crooned like he was talking about a long-lost lover. He swayed on his feet, almost trancelike, caught up in his own mini-drama.

Now or never. Gina pushed open the door enough to get a foot out, scooted to the edge of the seat, and leaned her weight on it.

"Then Nick's bitch started stripping parts off her."

His eyes flashed back to the car, strayed possessively to the steering wheel for an agonizing moment, then slowly rose back to hers. She froze, half out of the driver's seat. The pale, wretched pain she'd seen in those eyes earlier now burned wicked and dark. He trained the gun back on her chest. "Where is she," he growled.

Gina caught her breath, and then a loud snap in the bushes made them both jump.

Jimmy Ray spun his gun arm in the direction of the noise. He cocked his head like a cyborg, took a step toward the chaparral edging the turnout.

"Wait," Gina shouted.

He swung the gun back to her. "Tell her to get her ass out here, *now!*"

Gina shot out of the car. "Toni, run!" At least one of them might get away.

"No!" His eyes went wide, desperate, as he pointed the gun into the bushes. "Get out here you little shit, or Red's going down."

Gina grit her teeth. She searched the ground at her feet for a rock, a branch, anything she could throw to distract him. Let him shoot her if that's what he wanted, but, not Toni.

Wait.

He *wanted* the goddamned steering wheel? She could give that to him.

Every bone in her body wanted to run; instead, she drew herself up and cocked her fists at her hips.

"You want the steering wheel back? Take the whole damn car!" Her words came out stronger than she felt. "Leave us here and *take* it."

He turned slowly back to her, raised the gun. "It's red."

Crap. Her mother's words echoed in her head. *You can't reason with a madman.* But she had to try.

She raised her hand, palm out in resignation. "I … I know it's not *your* car, but it's …" She started to say *better*, but that might piss him off. "It's … one of a kind. A genuine Blue Flame Six. Rare. Worth a lot of money, especially with your steering wheel in it. You can just get in it and drive away. Right now." She gulped down a breath.

He lowered the gun an inch, his eyes glittered in hesitation, then returned to the steering wheel and the gun lowered again.

Time to go. She sprinted in a low crouch across the space between her car and his truck and ducked behind it, her breath coming in panicked gasps.

"Gina?" Toni hissed from the brushes behind her.

"Shhhhh, stay down."

"I got Luke. He's on his way."

Gina's heart leapt into her throat, but it was too late. Boots crunched on the gravel. Jimmy Ray was on the move.

"How long?" she said, her voice quivering.

"Long enough." Toni's voice was closer now, just near her shoulder. "He should be here any minute."

From her vantage point behind the truck, she could see down the other side of the pass. A set of headlights were winding their way up the curving road toward them.

"Someone's coming," she announced, hoping to goad him to action. "You'd better hurry if you want to get away," she prompted.

"No," Toni complained. "He'll leave us here alone."

"That's the idea," Gina hissed.

"But—"

"Sh-h-h-h-h."

"Son of a bitch," Jimmy growled.

Gina crouched and peered underneath the truck. He'd come around to the Corvette's driver side. One by one, his boots lifted out of sight, and the car's chassis sank under his weight, then the engine thrummed to life.

Toni scurried up behind her. "He's taking your car!" She stood, raised her fist. "Hey!"

Gina grabbed Toni's arm and yanked her down. "Stay put."

They huddled together behind the truck as Jimmy Ray revved the Corvette engine, hit the gas, and fishtailed out of the turnout. He careened around the old truck on the blind side of the curve over the summit, tires squealing.

Toni shot up again and shouted, "*¡Pendejo!*"

Gina breathed out the breath she'd been holding and threw her arms around the indignant teenager. "Let it go," she said on a laugh that was closer to hysteria than she wanted to admit. They were safe, for the moment. And that's all that mattered. "I was done with that car anyway."

Chapter 44

Luke pulled off the road into the driveway of a large avocado ranch right before the Casitas pass summit. From the location Toni had given, the girls had to be just on the other side. He backed his truck behind the resident's roadside fruit stand, shut down the lights and engine, and listened. Except for coyotes whooping somewhere down nearer the lake, all was quiet.

He slipped from behind the wheel and held his Glock out in front of him, his finger resting alongside the trigger, then inched forward to get a view of the approach to the summit.

The road cut sharply through a layered, crumbling wall of roots and stone. There was no shoulder and no cover for the hundred feet he could see. He was debating how far he could get up the curve on foot before he would be made, when he heard an engine start up and tires squeal. He dove behind the fruit stand as the red Corvette careened wildly through the turn and hurtled past him, the driver howling like a madman.

Chapter 45

A white-hot shot of adrenaline snaps from the back of his neck to his fingertips. To hell with the old wreck in the garage. This is a hundred times better.

He shifts into gear, slips the clutch and throttles over the summit, then careens down the other side, his head back, a howl gushing out of him like a water from a fire hydrant.

"This is better than sex," he growls, downshifting the turn. He's fifteen again. Alive! Free! Off the fucking hook!

The road straightens, he floors the accelerator, picks up speed.

Nobody! Nobody stops Jimmy Ray. Not Berlin, not McAllister or his old lady, not even the effing DA's red-assed girlfriend.

Blood rushes through his veins hard, fast, pumping like it hasn't in years.

The squiggly arrow on the road sign shows curves ahead.

Better slow down. The first one, a right, is posted twenty miles per hour.

He taps the brake.

It's mushy. He pumps. It grabs at the last second.

The next curve is tighter, steeper. He hits the brake again, barely making the second turn. And then, he sees a movie playing on the inside of his skull: he crawls under a car, he pokes an icepick into the brake line, then he melts blue birthday candle wax into each little hole.

Hap-py birth-day to you. Lionel's car goes off the cliff.

Hap-py birth-day to you. Roland's …

Hap-py birth-day dear—

The next curve is on him when he realizes what he's done. The brake pedal goes straight to the floor. *Holy shit.*

He jams his foot on a nonexistent emergency brake. Nothing.

He looks to his side, to the console. Nothing. The car is hurtling out of control, and then the world around him segues into an eerie slow motion, centrifugal force pinning his cheek to his shoulder.

Fighting to straighten the wheel, he forces his head up in time to see the pink smooth trunk of a eucalyptus tree in the headlights.

"Fuck me."

Chapter 46

Luke took off running, dodging fallen rock and debris along the road. The moment he rounded the turn, he saw the women standing behind the small, gray truck, their arms wrapped around each other.

"Oh my God, Luke." Gina ran at him, her fingers digging into her mass of red hair. He scooped her into his arms and held on tight, then planted a desperate kiss on her mouth. "God, I was afraid I'd lost you."

Toni brushed dirt and dried leaves off her clothes. "Sure. I'm Okay. In case you're wondering."

Luke extended his arm to include her in his embrace. He had a hundred questions, but right then, all that mattered was they were safe. A siren whined in the distance. Estevez was on his way. "Let's get you ladies out of the road."

At his SUV, he held Gina against his body while he opened the passenger door. Her face was ashen, her skin cold. She noodled into the seat. "Stay with me, baby. Can you do that?"

"I think so," she whispered, but her pupils had nearly erased the gold in her eyes, and that worried him. He stripped off his jacket and tucked it around her shoulders, then buckled her in.

Toni sprang into the backseat as if they were leaving a night at the county fair. "Let's go," she cried impatiently. "He stole Little Red!"

Luke turned his attention to Toni. She was excited, but showed no other signs of shock. "Estevez and his partner are on their way," he said, keeping his voice even. "We're going to sit tight until they get here." He hurried around the front of his SUV and slipped behind the wheel.

Toni harrumphed. "But we're right *here*. Don't you have one of those lights you can stick on the roof?"

Gina slumped further in the seat. Luke reached across the console and took her hand. She was trembling. There were no outward signs of injury, but it was clear whatever they'd been through, Gina had taken the brunt of it to protect her charge. From the looks of it, she'd been successful, to her own detriment.

He leveled his most serious scowl into the rearview mirror. "Toni. Gina needs you to be calm."

"Okay," she whined, and sat.

"Put on your seatbelt."

He started the engine and inched to the edge of the highway, the image of the Corvette barreling over the pass fresh on his mind.

Gina's head lay back on the headrest. The incident that had wound Toni up like a Mexican top had Gina fading fast. He deliberately took his time, giving her the smoothest ride he could.

They had just covered the last stretch of straight road before it wound sharply toward Carpinteria when a booming explosion shattered the night. A scant second later a ball of orange flame unfurled around the next bend, then disappeared into a mushroom cloud of black smoke.

Gina bolted upright, grabbed the handhold near the window. "Oh my God! What was that?"

Luke hit VOICE COMMAND on his steering wheel. "Call Lieutenant Estevez."

Estevez answered before the first ring ended. "I saw it. Good to know it wasn't you. I'm coming up on it now." Luke heard Estevez's big sedan come to a skidding stop. "Luke. It's … This isn't good."

"I've got the girls with me. It's Monteplier."

"Right." Estevez breathed relief into his words.

"Coming at you from the other side. Hold that bastard till I get there."

"Uh, that … won't be necessary."

Kat Drennan

Chapter 47

Gina pressed her hand against the passenger window; the glass was cool against her fingertips. She couldn't stop her teeth chattering. The rest of her was numb.

It could have been us.

Her eyes felt too big for their sockets as they took in the twisted metal, the body sprawled against the tree, a bloody boot upended against a flattened tire, flames claiming the hillside.

A knock on the window made her jump. She dragged her eyes away from the crash. Estevez's partner, Rachel, her thumbs hooked into her service belt, gave her a tentative smile as she opened the SUV door. "You okay Ms. McBain?"

Gina blinked.

Okay? Considering Jimmy Ray Monteplier had driven her one-of-a-kind, classic, get-on-with-her-life Corvette into a massive eucalyptus tree and splattered himself all over it without so much as a skid mark; the same car she and Gina had been driving only moments before?

No.

She was not okay.

She wasn't going to be okay for a long time.

"I've been better, and, we're alive, so …" It was as close to the truth as she could get for now. The twisted metal recaptured her gaze. Rachel stepped to the side, deliberately blocking her view.

"Ewe, is that brains all over the tree?" Toni's nose was plastered against the passenger window.

Luke put himself between her and a clear view of the carnage. "The paramedics are on their way," he said to Rachel. "How about you transfer Toni to your vehicle and wait for them there? I need to talk to Gina."

"I'm okay! I want to stay," Toni protested.

Luke kept his eyes on Gina and continued, unfazed. "And take her back to your house after."

"Got it." Rachel nodded and opened the back door.

"No-wah!" Toni complained. "I want to—"

Luke shoved his hands in his pockets and used his lawyer voice. "If you prefer, she could take you home to your father right now and you could explain to him what you were doing out on the road at midnight when you were supposed to be at a sleepover."

She hesitated, slumping in the seat. "No. I'll go with Rachel." Gina heard fatigue in the girl's voice along with defeat. They'd both been through hell tonight.

Gina was tired. No. Make that exhausted. But she convinced the paramedics she didn't need hospitalization.

What she needed was her own bed with Luke curled beside her. She wasn't moving until she had his assurance that's exactly how this horrific night would end.

The adrenaline rush that had fueled her courage on the road had abandoned her completely, leaving her raw and empty. With the sound of Luke's voice in her ears as he consulted with Estevez a few yards away, she succumbed to the lethargy, closed her eyes and let herself drift into oblivion.

When next she opened her eyes, emergency lights strobed through the orchards, fire hoses stiff with water pressure snaked across the road, manned by firefighters in turnout gear ensuring every ember was out.

A portable canopy had been setup over the crash area, which was cordoned off by hazard tape. Luke and Estevez consulted with the coroner, whose van was parked in front of the SUV.

As if feeling her eyes on him, he excused himself and trotted to her door.

He offered his hand and she wrapped her fingers around his. She stood, turned her face into his chest, letting his warmth radiate into her flesh. His hands ran over her back, her shoulders, pulling her to him in a fierce embrace.

"What the fuck, Gina. I've been trying to find you all night. Then Toni calls, and—"

Anger fueled his curse. They could share the blame for not communicating this week. But he held her tight. And he wasn't letting go. He needed to know the truth.

"It could have been us, Luke." She pressed her palms into his chest and caught hint of fear in his eyes.

"What do you mean, it could have been us?"

"Me and Toni. My car was going to crash; it was only a matter of time—"

"Back to the myth? Gina, I know you're upset, but—"

She pushed back. "No. You don't get to blow this off. He rigged the cars. Bragged about it. He killed Lionel and Roland. And ..." she fought to speak around a lump in her throat. "It may not have been a Hollywood myth, but whoever got a piece of that Corvette in the garage was going to die."

Estevez cleared his throat behind them. Luke kept his arm around Gina's shoulders and sent him a troubled glance.

Estevez held up his phone. "We, uh, we got Fiona."

Gina jerked her head up. "Fiona?"

Luke's body stiffened in her arms. What the hell? "Is she—"

"She's fine. Jimmy Ray tied her up in in a hotel room in Carp, but she Houdinied out of it and kicked the walls until someone called the front desk. She's mad as hell, but she's okay. Just thought you'd want to know."

Gina glared at the two of them. No way were they keeping this little tidbit away from her. "Want to know what?"

He curled a finger under her chin and lifted, his eyes the dark cobalt she loved to get lost in. Despite her annoyance, she could see another layer of relief. "Later, baby."

She shook her head. "Not later. Now." The new information had her blood pumping again and not in a good way. "You need to tell me now."

Estevez raised a brow. "I got this, counselor," he said, indicating the crash site. "Take your girl home. Give her the story on the way."

Chapter 48

Luke stood in the doorway, his blue silk tie hung loose at this neck. Their eyes locked on one another as she dumped her purse on the kitchen table and stripped of her Krewe jacket. They'd hardly said a word on the drive home. She'd shed a few tears. It would have been impossible not to under the circumstances. But overall, what she felt at this moment was overwhelming relief and a crushing need to have Luke Berlin all over her.

"I'm sorry about your car, babe," he told her. "We can…"

Words failed him as she knew they would when she dragged her sweater over her head, trailed it in her fingers, and stalked toward him. "To hell with the car."

She dropped the sweater at her feet and stooped to strip off her jeans, then rose slowly and took the last step between them. She enjoyed his slow grin as he recognized she was wearing the pink bra and panties he loved to take off her.

He swallowed hard, cleared his throat. "You sure you're up to this? It's been a pretty scary night. I wouldn't blame you if you didn't—"

She circled his waist and pulled herself against him, cutting him off. He was already rock hard against her stomach. Her knees went a little liquid and she took this in. She tipped her head back and stared up into the deep blue eyes that never failed to make her ache inside.

"You want to know the most terrifying thing about tonight?" she asked, her voice husky with desire.

He cupped her face in his hands, ran his thumbs over her eyebrows, then trailed his fingers through the loose tangles of her hair.

She pressed two fingers against his lips. "It was standing out there alone in that pass thinking I'd spent the last days of my life denying the only thing I've ever wanted."

"Gina, you don't have to—"

She lifted on tiptoe and covered his words with a deep promise of a kiss. "I'm done with that, counselor. So help me god, that's the whole truth and nothing but the truth."

She melded her body against his, the heat of him had her nipples drawing up tight.

She felt the low growl roll through his chest. He was fighting to keep the grin off his face. "I could come back in the morning," he teased, growing harder by the second.

Her hand slipped between them, loosened his belt, undid the clasp on his pants. "Sure," she crooned, easing his zipper down. "If that's what you want."

He ran his hands over her shoulders, slid her bra straps down, touching his lips to hers. "I want *you*. Today. Tomorrow. Forever."

The smile vanished, replaced by a look so intense, she nearly lost her breath. He slipped a hand behind her back and released the clasp on her bra. Her breast tumbled free, he dipped his head and lifted it to his lips, then sucked her nipple into his mouth, circling it with his tongue. She could feel the heat all the way to her toes.

"Luke," she moaned. One hand moved to cup her backside as the other sloughed off his pants. He walked her backward toward the hallway, sliding his hand along her thigh. She circled her arms around his neck and he lifted her, the muscles of his shoulders tensing as he took her weight, a move they'd practiced more times than she could remember. Had down to a science. Her legs came around his waist and she captured his mouth in hers and kissed him greedily as she unbuttoned his shirt and slipped it off his shoulders.

By the time they reached her bed, their underwear was history, too.

Luke bent to set her on the bed, straddled her, then speared one arm behind her shoulders and dragged her up to the headboard. Peetie and Milo saw the writing on the wall and scattered.

She ran her hands over his chest, her fingers teasing the swirl of soft hair over his pecs as her eyes scanned down. The sight of him hard and thick and ready for her made her insides curl with expectation.

She reached for the nightstand. He caught her wrist and pinned it to the bed. "We don't need those anymore, baby. Remember?"

She laughed. "The other night, when we … you know … lost our heads? The timing was right. It wasn't likely I'd conceive, or I would have insisted. But now," she cupped her breasts in a move that made his eyes go round. "I'd say, I'm about as ripe as it gets. So, you better be sure."

He pinned her other wrist to the bed next to her ears, settled himself between her legs and kissed her until they were both breathless. "I'm done with all that, too," he whispered, and his words came with a conviction she hadn't heard before. His gaze took on a hardness unfamiliar to her, the cleft between his brows deepened. "You were right, Gina."

By the tortured look on his face she wasn't sure she wanted to be. Then he let go of her wrists and rolled, bringing her on top of him. His hands moved over her shoulders and down her sides, while his eyes caressed every inch of her. She melted against him. How could she have ever said no to this man? "Right about what?"

At that, he smiled. It was one of those lazy half-smiles that made her want to cover his mouth with hers. And then, like closing the door on a Santa Ana wind, the tension left his brows.

"I'm not anything like *him*," he said, the words rushing out on a sigh. He framed her face in his hands, sitting up and kissing her gently, tenderly, almost reverently.

She returned the kiss, wrapping her legs around him to sit facing him in his lap. His arms came around her shoulders and hers went under his and they rocked in the closeness, the surrender of self to other. They were meant to be together. Always had been. She could have stayed that way all night, basking in the magical reality of what was now, and always had been, them.

Except that, they were Luke and Gina; and because they were Luke and Gina …

Luke's hard on went from heavy to painful. He slid his hands down her sides, feathered them across her belly, and slipped two fingers inside her, testing her wetness.

"Luke, I need *you* inside me," she cried, arching against his hand. The way she did it sent him nearly over the edge.

"Oh hell yes," he moaned, and lifted her, while she guided him into her heat. He sank into her and gasped like a swimmer coming up for air.

He cupped her breasts as she rode him, slowly at first, her eyes glittering, telling him everything he wanted to know; then faster, harder, lost in her passion. God how he loved to watch her. Needed to. He rose to match her rhythm as she ground against him until she froze, threw her head back, and her slick, hot insides clamped around him. His chest expanded beyond anything he'd ever experienced before.

"Gina," he growled, rolled her beneath him. Silky red waves of her hair spilled over her pillow, her eyes still on his, he buried himself deep, and let go of everything but their wet, pulsing union.

Chapter 49

Gina led the florist's entourage to the gazebo Luke and Nick were so proud of, directing them to place large potted vines next to each column. They were late, forcing her to remain at the site while the rest of the wedding party headed for the guesthouse to get dressed for the ceremony. She'd had her hair and makeup done with the girls earlier, but still wore a pair of black leggings and one of Luke's tailored shirts when the florist called with his apologies. Next time a friend asked her to plan a wedding she would respectfully decline, especially if that friend also wanted her to be the maid of honor. Still, as she gazed over the site, she couldn't help feeling a bit giddy at seeing her vision for the event playing out the way she'd planned. Maddie was going to be thrilled.

Garlands of ivy and satin ribbon had replaced Luke's crime scene tape to delineate the guest seating area; a potted gardenia at each row sent its distinctive fragrance over the scene, a nod to Maddie's grandfather's favorite flower, whom she had insisted would be watching over the affair with great pleasure.

After the ceremony, the guests would follow a winding path lit with fairy lights through the landscaped yard to a large patio area behind the main mansion, where dinner and cake would be served with a sunset view of the Pacific Ocean, if the weather held. So far, the prospects were good for a glorious display.

A diamond-studded cabochon ruby the size of a cherry glinted on her finger in the late afternoon sun as she made last minute adjustments to the mandevilla vines.

In the few days since her ordeal with Jimmy Ray, Luke had redeemed himself in every way possible, surprising her with the ring at a last-minute rendezvous at Joe's.

When a mariachi band wandered in playing a lively version of *Cielito Lindo*, Gina had craned her neck to see who might have put in the request. But when the players stopped at *their* table and switched to a slow rendition of *Te Amaré Todo La Vida*, Luke had slipped to his knee, and opened the black velvet box in front of her.

"For the rest of my days," he'd said, echoing the words of the song. "The ruby reminded me of the beach glass in your *Luke-is-never-here* collection. I promise you, you'll never collect beach glass alone again."

She'd been speechless, taken completely off guard. She'd all but resigned herself never to walk down the aisle, and that would be okay with her. After staring down the barrel of Jimmy Ray's gun, little else bothered her, including the missing piece of paper between her and Luke.

"You don't like it?" His eyes darkened when her eyes brimmed with tears. "We can change it if you want."

"No, silly. I love it," she'd told him, and "Of course we're not going to change it."

That night, they'd celebrated make-up sex in every room of her condo, and once in the guest room of the mansion she'd helped him prepare for Maddie's beloved old housekeepers, Walt and Flo,. The ring on her finger said all she'd ever wanted was coming. The when didn't seem to matter anymore. "The rest would take care of itself," they'd promised each other, and the peace in her heart at this moment said she had truly let it go.

Right now, it was all about Nick and Maddie and the little girl she'd carry down the aisle under her bride's bouquet today.

By the time Gina signed for the floral delivery and escorted the workers off the property, the first of the guests were being ushered in. Gina was surprised to see so many of Luke's friends among them, but then, the brothers were close and their lives overlapped in many venues; especially now that Luke was about to enter the local political arena.

Now Gina rushed into the guesthouse, nearly out of breath, to find Maddie already in her gown, posing for her photographer along with Toni and Flo.

"Oh, gosh, I'm so sorry," Gina blurted as she hurried past them down to the bedroom where she'd left her dress. "The florist was late, can you believe it? To a wedding?"

"Imagine that," Maddie teased, and beamed her an unruffled smile. "Take your time, sweetie. It's our wedding. We can be as late as we want."

Gina puzzled a moment.

We?

Our?

Of course.

Maddie carried a baby along with her bride's bouquet. It was true, the two of them were getting married today.

Gina swung into the bedroom and shot her gaze around the room. Oh my god, where was her dress? She'd left it hanging in the doorway of this room, she was sure of it.

"Maddie? Toni? Did someone move my dress?" she called.

Giggling. Coming from the other room.

She stuck her head out into the hallway. "Maddie?"

"Try the office, Geen. We may have moved it in there earlier." Her voice was uncharacteristically sing-songy.

Gina shot out of the bedroom to the office across the hall. She was already pressed for time. There was no sign of the aqua blue dress. "Sorry, I don't see—"

Then she caught her breath. There was a dress all right, but it wasn't the fluffy aquamarine maid of honor's dress she'd had fitted at the bridal shop. Standing in the center of the room was a dress form draped in the most beautiful ball gown she had ever seen: strapless, dropped waist bodice, plunging neckline, pearl-beaded, and soft champagne tulle. An elaborate bride's bouquet that matched Maddie's was fastened at the neck of the form.

Oh my god. She traced a finger along the seed pearls that circled the hipline of the gown, her breath coming in gasps.

"Maddie?" She turned to find all three women smiling at her from the hallway.

"What is this?" she asked, her heart in her throat.

"What does it look like?" Toni brought her hands from behind her back and handed her a delicate veil sewn to a band of red satin and seed pearls that matched her dress.

Gina shook her head, her knees nearly buckled. Tears welled in her eyes, threatened to spill. She covered her lips with quivering fingers.

Maddie moved in for a hug. "Oh, honey. It was my idea. I wanted to tell you. But Luke wanted it to be a surprise. I tried to tell him it would be too much, but—"

"Too much? What? Oh my god. You mean *We, we, our.* You and me—*our* wedding?"

"Um hum. It couldn't be better, right? Marrying brothers?"

Gina's phone buzzed a text in her back pocket, making her jump.

She pulled it out, her hand still shaking. "Luke's sending one of the boys up with the golf cart to get us in ten minutes."

Maddie turned her around to face the office door. "Then I guess you'd better hurry, after all."

Toni bubbled into the room, began unzipping the dress.

Gina was still baffled. "But I don't get it. That dress cost a fortune. I could never have—"

Maddie pushed her forward. "It's a gift, Gina. From Nick and me. Because there's no one else on this planet we want married to Luke Berlin. Call it your 'something new'."

"I … don't know what to say."

"No one else would marry him," Toni put in, breaking the tension.

Gina took a step forward, dared to touch the dress again. "When did you—?"

"You mean how long have we been at this?" Maddie laughed, rested her hand on the rise of her baby bump. "Let's just say, you've been planning your own wedding for a couple of weeks now."

Gina's tears gave way to laughter. "It's a damn good thing I said yes, then isn't it."

Maddie leaned in and kissed her cheek. "I was never worried."

Kat Drennan

Chapter 50

Gina's heart fluttered in her chest like it had wings. The wedding party had taken their places under the gazebo, Nick on the left and Luke on the right, like handsome bookends, one blonde and one dark.

The events of the past few weeks—losing Lionel, Roland, and Ina; the crash and all the last-minute planning to make this moment possible—faded under the brilliant light of Luke's smile. They had locked eyes the moment he stepped into line and everything else disappeared.

At the first notes of the "Bridal Chorus," Walt stepped in to take Maddie by the arm. Gina's heart swelled at the glow on Maddie's face when she looked at him.

A moment later, Angie led Mason to Gina's side. When he offered his arm, Gina nearly lost it. They had thought of everything.

Gina floated down the aisle in a disbelieving trance. That woodpecker was going to start pounding her skull any minute and she'd wake up and find this was all a dream. But when Mason offered her arm to Luke and she felt the heat of his body standing next to hers, the worry fell away.

His kiss was all the promise she'd ever need. The chaplain cleared his throat to remind them where they were. "May I present to you Luke and Gina Berlin."

⌘

Luke awoke to a deliciously warm heat between his legs and a morning woodie that surprised the hell out of him since he figured he'd worn it out the night before. He spread his arms wide; the bed was empty. He sat up, coming fully awake to find that the luxuriant heat was Peetie curled up against his balls.

"Jesus, cat," he said, urging her to move away without provoking her claws. The aroma of chorizo and fresh brewed coffee wafted into the bedroom.

"Gina?"

"Coming," she called from the kitchen. She appeared in the doorway wearing a pale pink cami and panties he couldn't wait to remove, sending a new surge of heat to his groin.

He relaxed against the headboard.

"Hungry?" She brushed her fingers through cherry coke hair he loved to touch.

"Um hum," he said, crooking a finger at her. "But at the moment, not for chorizo."

Gina grinned and knee-walked across the bed to straddle him. "Yeah, so, what do you want, then?" she teased.

He rested his palms on her hips. "Did I tell you I love you?"

She dipped her head, kissed him softly. "About a thousand times."

"I love you, Gina," he whispered, slipping a tendril of her hair between his fingers. "A thousand and one, and counting."

She cocked her hips against him. "You sure you're up to this?"

She raised up, he caught her wrists, and pulled her back to him. All the worry and doubt he'd allowed to compromise his future had vanished like the fog when the sun breaks through. She was his sun. He would never hurt her, never doubt. He would just love her the way she wanted to be loved, now, and as long as he lived.

"Of course. I may not be twenty-one anymore, but I got what it takes, baby. Besides, you want to be visibly pregnant before election day, don't you?"

Gina's laugh lit a fire inside him. "Oh, I think we got a pretty good head start on that, already."

He cupped her cheek, ran his thumb along her jaw. "I think we'd better make sure. Can't be too cavalier about these things."

"The chorizo—"

"Can wait."

She cocked her hips, gave him a smile that lit up the room. "You really sure about this, Luke? Because I can——"

He was so goddamn sure he was ready to explode. "He's gone, Gina. Completely out of my head. You did that."

She lowered her lips to his, kissed him gently at first then sucked his tongue into her sweet mouth. His erection hardened to near pain.

He seized her hips, lifted, and lowered her to sheath him in her silky, wet heat. She took him all the way in.

"God, Gina," was all he could say. She felt so good, there simply weren't any words. He pulled the big pin out of her messy bun and her hair fell around her shoulders, curled over the peaks of her breasts. He savored the creamy white skin under his fingertips as brushed his hands over her breasts, cupped them, ran his thumbs over the hard nubs of her nipples the way she liked.

"Luke." Her voice was husky, hungry. If he never heard another sound, it would be enough to last him the rest of his life.

He'd never dreamed he'd come as close to losing her, first the result of his own stubbornness, then at the hands of Jimmy Ray. Never mind their recent separation. That wouldn't have lasted. It never had.

But the other night when he'd found her house empty, broken into, he thought he'd go crazy until he saw her running toward him up on the pass.

Now, he ran his hands over her shoulders and eased her against him, the wave of emotion overtaking even his desire. His chest tightened and the words came in near sobs. "Gina. I thought I'd lost you."

She pulled back and caught his eyes with hers. "I thought for a while there I'd lost me, too."

He pushed her hair away from her face and cradled her cheeks between his hands. "What I mean is, I thought I'd lost you. Forever. For being an ass. For not being what you needed me to be. I was lost without you and you knew it. Knew it all along."

"Sh-h-h-h-h-h." She kissed him, touched the tip of her tongue to his. "Some things are worth waiting for."

<h1 align="center">*Epilogue*</h1>

The night was crystal clear. Indian Summer was the Central Coast's best-kept secret. Long after the tourists had packed up their bags and headed home, the sun bathed the afternoons in golden light. Dinner under the stars was still possible wearing only a light pashmina.

Gina hosted the evening in the gazebo, which had turned out to be their go to place. She and Luke would live in the downstairs sitting room in the mansion until March, when the remodel would be complete, a date which coincided with the date their baby was due.

Luke and Nick had taken part in the complete demolition of the infamous foyer and stairway. The new design would restore the Spanish revival home to its original glory, the marble monstrosity of a stairway replaced by a graceful winding stair with hand-painted ceramic tiles on the risers. The cold glass-walled foyer was now plastered and stuccoed, surrounded by a wooden balcony with arched doorways leading to four upstairs bedrooms and a master suite that had been completely reconfigured from the original floorplan.

Luke reached under the table, rested his hand on her thigh, squeezed lightly. She covered it with her own and threaded her fingers in his. They had watched the wedding video for the umpteenth time. Maddie and Gina never tired of seeing the surprised and delighted faces of their guests come into view as Butch defied Gina's orders and flew his drone over the wedding before, after, and during the ceremony.

One of her favorite faces was Mason, who'd made major strides over the last four months. His daughter had made time to visit over the summer, bringing his grandchildren to visit. He'd never again spoken about the night his wife was killed. His recovery got a major boost when Gina had told him about Jimmy Ray, and had improved exponentially since.

Estevez and Angela had been caught more than once on camera with stars in their eyes for each other. Even Fiona Blanchard looked happy as she gossiped with the Sheik's son, Kamal.

Since the wedding, Maddie had agreed to sell three of her rusty zombie cars to Kamal's father. He'd apologized profusely for not telling them about Jimmy Ray's trespassing sooner, something he feared could have led to disaster. Since then, he'd become a regular at their social gatherings.

Now, he scooted away from the table.

"You're not leaving us," Gina said. "I've got a brandied cherry cheesecake for dessert."

He gave her an apologetic smile. "That was a lovely dinner, Gina. The salmon was magnificent, and I'm grateful for the invitation but I'm afraid I must forego dessert. I've already taken advantage of your hospitality too much."

Read, he had a date lined up for the evening. "Oh, you can't go yet, you're our guest of honor tonight," Gina said. She lifted a newspaper from her lap and waved it in the air, then opened it up to show a picture of Kamal grinning from the back of his polo pony, with the headline: SANTA BARBARA'S MOST ELIGIBLE BACHELOR.

Luke suppressed a laugh. "It seems we have a celebrity in our midst."

Estevez faked relief. "Better you than me," he said, laughing. But the look in his eyes when he smiled at Angela said he'd never been in the running.

Kamal's face turned crimson. He snatched the paper out of Gina's hands. "She said the photo was for her private collection."

Luke busted out laughing. "No one tells Fiona Blanchard no. Where is she, anyway? I thought you said you'd invited her?"

Gina shrugged. "I did. She said she'd be here. She was anxious to make an announcement."

Luke cringed. An announcement from Fiona was the last thing he wanted. Just then, they heard the growl of a motorcycle on the other side of the house.

"Could we be speaking of the devil herself?" Estevez asked.

A moment later, a hot pink and silver crotch rocket rounded the corner of the house, threading its way through piles of construction debris toward the gazebo. When it reached the steps, a tallish, thin figure dressed all in black dismounted and removed a cock's combed helmet.

Fiona Blanchard pinched Luke's shoulder as she sat down at the place setting next to him and smiled at Kamal, ignoring the copy of *The Bomb* spread out in the middle of the table.

"Hey, we were just admiring your work," Gina said, smiling.

Fiona grabbed the newspaper off the table and crumpled it up. "That rag?" She reached behind her and pulled out a paper that had apparently been stuffed down the back of her leather pants. Her face beamed brighter than Gina thought possible.

Gina picked up the newspaper. "The *LA Times?*"

Fiona snatched it out of her hands, pointed to one of the titles on the front page. "PAGE 3: JOURNALIST, FIONA BLANCHARD," she read, "…HELPS SOLVE A TWENTY-YEAR-OLD SANTA BARBARA COLD CASE."

She flipped the paper to the Post-it she'd stuck inside and held up the page showing a selfie of her in the police wrecking yard with her arm around Estevez, the three Corvettes lined up in the background.

Luke burst out laughing and ended by putting his arm around her. "Hell, we've got two celebrities here tonight."

Fiona whipped up her cellphone and snapped the shot.

"Not me, Fi. You and Estevez."

"Nope. That's my original shot. Me and the new District Attorney of Santa Barbara County. It's going on the cover of the *Santa Barbara News Press* the morning after the election."

Nick stood and helped Maddie out of her chair. "Let's hope you're right about that. But for now, I need to get my little mama to bed."

Fiona beamed. "Darn. I didn't miss dinner, did I?"

Gina uncovered the platter of salmon and vegetables and passed it to her. "Not at all."

⌒

Luke turned out the lights, slipped into bed with his wife, and pulled her against him, his hand resting gently over the small rise in her belly. "I told the guys in the office you didn't want to know the baby's sex. They started a pool. Girl or boy."

"What do you say?"

He shrugged. "Doesn't matter to me."

Gina shrugged. "I don't want to know, but I do secretly wish it's a boy. If I had a girl, I'm afraid she would steal your heart away from me."

He kissed the back of her neck, behind her ear, then rose on an elbow and bent to kiss her on the lush lips he loved. "Not gonna happen, baby." He kissed her again, this time more intensely, savoring the taste of the woman he had always known he would spend his life with. Then he lay down, pulled her into his body, and snuggled his face into her hair. A peace settled over him like he'd never experienced in his life. She'd given that to him by showing him it was all he'd ever really wanted. "You are my one of a kind, Gina Berlin."

Thank you so much for reading Luke and Gina's story in **One of a Kind.** For more "Found Family" fun, games, and intrigue, continue the Mad Monkey Motors adventure with Griffin and Nadine's story in **A Classic Car Romance Series, Book 3:** <u>Hotrod Lincoln</u>

Want to see One of a Kind and the rest of the Classic Car Romance Series move up in the ranks so other readers will see them? Leave a brief review on Goodreads or Amazon books!

To join my Super Fans team and get the inside scoop on books in progress, promos, and the Writer's Life go to Katdrennanbooks.com, or scan the QR code to sign up for my newsletter now.

More Books by Kat Drennan

The Love on the Faultline Romantic Mystery series
Borrego Moon

Love on the Faultline Historical Novella
Lies In White Satin

Love on the Faultline Standalone Romance
High Tide

Serpent's Coil Historical Time-Travel
The Cloisonné Brooch
Lesidi's Coin
The Serpent's Coil

A Classic Car Romance - Romantic Suspense
Book One - Mint Condition
Book Two - One of a Kind
Book Three – Hotrod Lincoln
Book Four – Five Window Pickup Coming Soon

Award-Winning Women's Fiction
The Goddess of Undo

About the Author

Sign up to receive Kat's newsletter for new book announcements and great promos and giveaways at www.katdrennanbooks.com.

Kat Drennan writes sensual stories from the heart of the Golden State.

From the curling surf at the edge of the continent, to the granite sculptures of the Sierra Nevada; from San Francisco to Death Valley and all the way to the Mexican border, California's unique landscape and history step forward as characters in each of her novels.

She is an alumna of the Squaw Valley Community of Writers, as well as a member of Romance Writers of America.

Based in Ojai, California, Kat loves the beach, a challenging bike ride, cooking for a crowd, and making riding shirts for her granddaughters' equestrian team.

Kat loves to hear from her readers. You can follow her at www.katdrennanbooks.com, sign up for her newsletter to find out about new releases, or follow her Facebook page at www.facebook.com/KatDrennan.

9 798999 452764